CHORD OF EVIL

Recent Titles by Sarah Rayne from Severn House

The Phineas Fox Mysteries

DEATH NOTES
CHORD OF EVIL

The Nell West and Michael Flint Series

PROPERTY OF A LADY
THE SIN EATER
THE SILENCE
THE WHISPERING
DEADLIGHT HALL
THE BELL TOWER

CHORD OF EVIL

A Phineas Fox Mystery

Sarah Rayne

This first world edition published 2017
in Great Britain and the USA by
SEVERN HOUSE PUBLISHERS LTD of
19 Cedar Road, Sutton, Surrey, England, SM2 5DA.
Trade paperback edition first published
in Great Britain and the USA 2018 by
SEVERN HOUSE PUBLISHERS LTD

British Library Cataloguing in Publication Data
A CIP catalogue record for this title is available from the British Library.

ISBN-13: 978-0-7278-8741-2 (cased)
ISBN-13: 978-1-84751-856-9 (trade paper)
ISBN-13: 978-1-78010-916-9 (e-book)

All Severn House titles are printed on acid-free paper.

Severn House Publishers support the Forest Stewardship Council™ [FSC™],
the leading international forest certification organisation.
All our titles that are printed on FSC certified paper carry the FSC logo.

MIX
Paper from
responsible sources
FSC
www.fsc.org   FSC® C013056

Typeset by Palimpsest Book Production Ltd.,
Falkirk, Stirlingshire, Scotland.
Printed and bound in Great Britain by
TJ International, Padstow, Cornwall.

ONE

It was halfway through the party when Toby Tallis said, anxiously, 'Phin, I'm worried about my cousin Arabella.'

Phineas Fox had not actually wanted to attend this party, but it was being given by his ebullient, rugby-playing neighbour, whose flat occupied part of the big North London house where Phineas lived. Since the party would certainly be loud and long, and would probably spill cheerfully out of Toby's flat into everybody else's, Phin had thought he might as well go to the centre of the storm and be part of it, rather than fume crossly on the outskirts or bang angrily on the walls.

He had in fact started to enjoy himself. He was on his third glass of wine, somebody had handed him a plate of smoked-salmon sandwiches, and he had become involved in a lively argument with four complete strangers about the rival bawdiness of Elizabethan round songs as opposed to Victorian street ballads. A suggestion had just been made that Phin and Toby collaborate on a book about bawdy ballads, and Phin was trying to decide how seriously to view this. But Toby's cherubic face was uncharacteristically anxious, so Phin said, 'What's wrong with Arabella?'

'She hasn't turned up. And,' said Toby, 'she definitely intended to come tonight, because – wait a minute, the email's still on the phone . . .'

He fished in a pocket, flipped his phone to email, and passed it to Phin.

Arabella's email said:

> Toby, I'm looking forward to your party, because I want to meet your intriguing new neighbour, the one I saw from the window of your flat that day – the one with the silver eyes and the look of remote and intellectual sexiness. Is he sufficiently remote that I'll have to call him Mr Fox, do you know? I hope not, because it sounds like something out of *Aesop's Fables*. Anyway, short of Armageddon or the bailiffs

arriving, I'll be there. I'm disastrously broke again, in fact
my entire wardrobe is currently on eBay, so don't be surprised
if I turn up at the party wearing the drawing room curtains
like Scarlett O'Hara.
Lots of love.

'It's not like her not to turn up without letting me know,' said Toby.
'And her phone goes straight to voicemail. I know she's a bit
scatty, but it's almost midnight and I'm really concerned.'

'What exactly were you thinking of doing?'

'I think I should just dash along to her flat,' said Toby.

'Now, d'you mean?'

'I can pick up a taxi and be there and back before anyone notices
I've gone.'

He waited, and Phin said, 'Did you want me to – to keep an
eye on things while you're gone?'

'Actually,' said Toby, 'I wondered if you'd come with me.'

'Where does your cousin live?' asked Phin as they bucketed across
London ten minutes later.

Toby had summoned a taxi with remarkable efficiency and
speed, considering he had been drinking alcohol with some gusto
for the last three hours. Phin, for whom the cold night air had felt
like a wall rearing up to smack him in the face, was not sure if
he could have flagged down so much as a pushbike.

'She's got a flat in Pimlico.'

Phin thought that of course Arabella would live somewhere like
Pimlico.

'She likes the echoes of painters and writers and whatnot who've
lived in the area,' said Toby, indulgently. 'She says she can hear them
like footsteps just out of hearing or something. She's perfectly capable
of managing her own life,' he added, firmly. 'But she's apt to be a
bit unpredictable. She darts around after half a dozen things at the
same time, like that winged creature with blue and green wings.'

'Dragonfly?'

'That's the one. Her parents died when she was very young, so
apart from me, she hasn't got any family to speak of.'

The house in which Arabella Tallis pursued her dragonfly existence was a tall redbrick building, overlooking a small park.

'I've got a key and the code for the front door,' said Toby, as they got out of the taxi. 'And I'm very glad you've come with me, Phin, because between ourselves you never know quite what you might find in Arabella's flat.'

By this time, Phin was prepared for anything, from abandoned lovers languishing on the doorstep, bodies littering the carpets, and décor ranging from suggestive French boudoir to floral chintz. The reality was completely normal and pleasingly tasteful. There were comfortable sofas with extravagant cushions, and walls the colour of amber with light behind it. Floor-to-ceiling bookshelves filled two fireplace alcoves – the contents included Chekhov and Charles Dickens, chick-lit, crime fiction, the C. S. Lewis *Narnia* books, and assorted biographies. Phin was relieved to see all the curtains seemed to be in place.

'Everything looks all right,' said Toby, having switched on the lights. 'I'll make a quick tour, though.' He left Phin in the sitting room, and came cheerfully back several moments later. 'All good. So I'm probably being totally neurotic, and . . . Jesus God Almighty, what's that doing here?'

He was staring at a small portrait resting on a low table, propped against the wall.

'It's a portrait,' said Phin, having turned to look.

'I know it's a bloody portrait, the question is how it got here.'

'Isn't it Arabella's?' The possibility that Arabella might have added art theft to her dragonfly activities flickered alarmingly across Phin's mind.

'It certainly is not,' said Toby, very forcefully. 'It belongs to the godfather.' Then, as Phin looked startled, he said, 'Sorry – I know that sounds Marlon Brando or Al Pacino and a horse's head on the pillow. I mean a real godfather. Arabella's and mine. Nice old boy. Stefan Cain. Came to England from Germany in the late 1940s, I think. Refugee after World War Two – he was very young of course, barely in his teens. And that,' said Toby, jabbing a finger at the portrait, 'has been on his wall since anyone can remember. It's a painting of his sister and it's practically a holy relic.'

The portrait that had apparently transported itself to the Pimlico flat was not very large – probably about 25 by 20 inches – and set in a narrow frame. The subject was a dark-eyed lady in her mid-twenties or early thirties. She was holding what looked like a letter, but she was looking out of the canvas as if pleased to see someone. Phin thought her gown, which was green silk, was from the 1940s, and she had dark hair, looped smoothly back from her brow.

'Did you say it's your godfather's sister?' said Phin.

'Yes. Her name was Christa. I'd forgotten how striking the portrait is,' said Toby. 'I can't believe Stefan's given it away, not even to Arabella.'

Phin, who had been examining the back of the portrait in case there might be a date, said, 'I don't think he did give it away. Not in that sense, anyway. Look.'

Taped lightly to the back of the painting was a handwritten note, folded untidily, the writing careless, as if an emotion so strong had driven the writer he had not bothered about legibility. It said:

> Arabella, my dear – I would much rather have destroyed this painting, but since you insisted, here it is. I don't care what you do with it – you can burn it and scatter the ashes to the four winds for all I care. I never want to see it again.
>
> Best love to you and Toby, as always. Both of you come to Greymarsh soon, please.
>
> Stefan

'That's the most extraordinary thing I've ever come across,' said Toby, taking the note from Phin and re-reading it. 'Christa died years ago – I never knew her, of course, and neither did Arabella. But Stefan adored her, and I'm sure this is the only likeness of her that he's got. And yet he's flung this out so – so *theatrically*.'

'It sounds as if he was going to destroy it, but Arabella persuaded him to let her have it instead. What's Greymarsh?'

'It's the godfather's house in Romney Marsh – beautifully Bronte-esque sounding, isn't it? Straggling old place, all twisty stairs and windows looking across marshlands. Arabella loves it; she goes there more often than I do – she says the place is in tune with her inner gothic soul, or something.'

Phin hesitated, then asked a careful question as to Stefan Cain's mental state. 'Elderly people sometimes start giving their possessions away – I mean, they can become a bit eccentric—'

'Tactfully put. But Stefan's as sharp as a pin,' said Toby. 'All the mental connections are still absolutely in the right places. I saw him at Christmas, and Arabella clearly saw him more recently. She'd have said if he'd succumbed to sudden madness like Lear or George the Third, and been babbling of green fields or addressing his pillow as Prince Octavius. Do I mean Prince Octavius?'

'No idea. What's the date on that note?'

'Um – two days ago.'

'And,' said Phin, thoughtfully, 'within forty-eight hours of your cousin having this painting in her flat—'

'She's apparently disappeared? Well,' said Toby, on a note of decision, 'that settles one thing. I've got no idea where Arabella is, but I'm not leaving that painting here.'

He wrote a careful note for his cousin, explaining that he had kidnapped the portrait for safety, and Sellotaped it to the sitting-room door, where, as he said, it could not be missed.

When they reached Toby's flat, the party was still going happily on.

'I told you they wouldn't miss me,' said Toby. 'And now I come to think about it, I don't think it'll be a good idea to keep Christa in my flat tonight, do you? I'd hate something to be spilled on it or find it's been used as a dartboard – you know how these things happen – and Arabella would never forgive me.' He eyed Phin hopefully.

With a feeling of inevitability, Phin said, 'We could put it in my flat for the night.'

'Good man. Knew you'd understand.'

The painting was duly deposited in Phin's bedroom.

'Very nice,' said Toby, approvingly. 'You'll wake up to see her at the foot of your bed. I can think of worse sights, can't you?'

Phin was sitting on the edge of the bed, looking at the painted figure. 'She had beautiful hands, didn't she?' he said, thoughtfully.

'Careful, Phin, she's been dead for years. Next thing you know, you'll be getting ideas like that bloke in the old film – Laura, was it?'

'Dana Andrews and Gene Tierney,' said Phin absently, his eyes still on the painting. 'And some marvellous backing music. But I'm not getting any ideas.'

'Well, I'm getting ideas about another drink. Let's get back to the party. We might even find that Arabella's turned up.'

By this time Phin did not really want to return to the party, but he said that a quick drink was a good idea, only after that, if Toby did not mind, he would call it a night.

There was not, in fact, a great deal of the night left, and although there was no sign of Arabella, the guests appeared to have recognized the lateness of the hour, because there had been a move to fry bacon and eggs. Toby was greeted with the news that there had been a bit of a crisis while he was out, absolutely nothing to worry about though, and it had been the purest oversight that had caused the frying pan to burst into flames. But hardly any damage had been done, and probably the kitchen ceiling had needed re-painting anyway.

Several pyjama'd people had come crossly along landings to ask whether Mr Tallis *realized* it was three a.m., and Miss Pringle from the garden flat, who usually went to bed with ear plugs and Inspector Barnaby when Toby had a party, had panicked at the shouts of Fire, and had ventured timidly up the stairs. She had been taken into the sitting room and given a large glass of whisky on the grounds that whisky was great for a shock, together with a bacon sandwich.

Phin finally escaped to his own flat around five. He sat down on the edge of the bed, and studied Christa Cain's enigmatic regard.

The eyes drew him, but so, too, did the hands. They were expressive hands with slender wrists, and they might even be the hands of a musician – a pianist, perhaps. Phin thought he would ask Toby about that. He liked the idea of Christa having been a pianist.

It was not until he got up to examine the portrait more closely, that he saw something that had probably planted the thought that she might have been a musician. The sheaf of papers in her hands were not letters after all, but music scores. There were two – or was it three? – sheets of music. Only the first page and the edges of the lower ones were visible, and although they did not look particularly faded or foxed, there was somehow a secretive air to them – almost as if the painter had wanted to convey the impression that the music might have been locked away for a very long time. This was so intriguing that Phin carried the portrait into his study, propping it up on his desk, and tilting the desk lamp so that the light fell fully across the music. At once the details came into sharper focus. The music was handwritten, and the title was clear – it was *'Giselle's Music'*.

And then he saw something else, and he stopped wondering who Giselle might have been, and he forget about going to bed, and began to tumble reference books from the shelves.

TWO

I t was not really a surprise when Toby appeared later in the day. Phin let him in, and expressed suitable thanks for the party.

'Bit of an unexpected night at times, wasn't it?' said Toby, grinning. 'I'm glad I'm not disturbing you. I wanted to make sure that Christa's still here.'

'She is.' Phin indicated the painting propped up on his desk. 'D'you want some coffee? I only made it half an hour ago, so it's still hot. Have you managed to reach your cousin?'

Toby, accepting the coffee, said there was still no reply from Arabella's phone. 'But I can't report her as a missing person yet, can I? You have to allow forty-eight hours for an adult, don't you? She'll have turned up by then,' he said, firmly. 'Have you found out why the godfather suddenly flung Christa out of the house like a Victorian zealot faced with a sinning housemaid?'

'Not exactly a reason,' said Phin, slowly. 'But there's something that is a bit unexpected.' He tilted the portrait so that the light fell across it again, and indicated the music. 'That chord there – d'you see? – is a tritone.'

'What on earth—?'

'It's what's called an interval of three tones, with an augmented fourth.'

'Oh, well, of course I knew that,' said Toby at once, and Phin grinned.

'It's not used very often,' he said. 'It's quite discordant, and it was once called the *diabolus in musica* – the devil in music. It was banned in Renaissance church music, in fact. Church music was supposed to be a paean of praise to God, and the tritone was considered so ugly that it wasn't thought suitable. Medieval arrangements even used it to represent the devil, and Roman Catholic composers sometimes used it for referencing the crucifixion. Its dissonance can work to advantage in some cases, though. In emergency sirens, for instance.'

'Seriously?'

'Yes, certainly.'

'I'll never hear a police car again without thinking about that.'

'But assuming Giselle was a composer of the era – possibly an amateur, because the music's handwritten – that isn't a chord you'd expect to find,' said Phin. 'Who was Giselle, do you know? Someone in Stefan Cain's family?'

'No idea. I've never heard of her. I don't know anything about his family – I think he lost his parents in the war. They were a Jewish family, so it would have been a bad time.' Toby set down his coffee mug and stood up. 'You carry on chasing evil chords and mysterious ladies,' he said. 'But be careful you don't end up too intrigued by Christa and Giselle.'

'I'm not so susceptible.'

'That's not what I heard,' said Toby. 'Weren't you seen with a rather good-looking redhead a week or so back? Wining and dining in a Covent Garden bistro, and probably indulging in a few other activities we needn't specify.'

'She's an editor I worked with on a biography about Oscar Peterson,' said Phin. 'She's gone back to Canada. Nothing much in it.'

'It apparently warrants a reminiscent smile, though,' said Toby, grinning. 'But a gentleman never tells; well, not unless he's a D-list celeb and being paid by the tabloids. I hope she was nice, your redhead.'

'She was,' said Phin, remembering how they had eaten grilled sea bass and drunk white Bordeaux at the bistro. She had said something about him having silver eyes. He had countered this by saying she had copper hair, and she had said, 'Shall we see if silver and copper can be satisfactorily blended.'

He then realized he really was smiling reminiscently, so he got up to examine the painting again.

'It's definitely a tritone,' he said, and with the words he again had the feeling that he was twining his hand around something that had lain hunched into a dark corner for a very long time – something that would resist being forced back into the world. He glanced at Toby, but he was not sure if Toby would understand this feeling; in fact he was not sure if anyone would understand. He thought with a pang of regret that his copper-haired dinner companion of last week, intelligent and intuitive and musically knowledgeable though she was, certainly would not. And then he had the absurd thought that Arabella Tallis might understand.

'I'll leave you to it,' said Toby, getting up. 'I'm off to my bed for a couple of hours – it was a very long night, wasn't it? If the phone rings while I'm asleep, I'll curse the caller from here to the next millennium.'

'Well, don't curse too loudly, because I'll be working.'

Phin's current commission was to trace the erratic journeys and various fates of several eminent composers and conductors sent into exile by the Nazis in the 1930s and 1940s, and to provide factual evidence for a textbook intended to grace the shelves of a music faculty at a northern university. It was a serious and scholarly commission which Phin was quite enjoying. It brought back childhood memories of his grandfather, who had fought in World War II as an idealistic young nineteen-year-old, and who later in his life had led the small Phineas into the world of music.

But this morning, Christa Cain and the unknown Giselle were getting in the way of work, so he put the exiled musicians aside and considered *Giselle's Music*. The music might simply once have belonged to someone called Giselle who had wanted to stamp it with her ownership. It might be a title, though – it was certainly common for music to be named for a person or, of course, a place. But it might be the composer's name.

Phin wondered how far Toby's story about his godfather and the portrait could be believed. He did not know Toby very well, and he did not know Toby's cousin, Arabella, at all. Was it only coincidence that she seemed to have vanished immediately after acquiring Christa's portrait? Phin toyed with the idea of the painting being a lost or stolen art treasure, but this seemed so fantastic that he dismissed it.

Presumably Stefan Cain existed, though. Phin called up an online directory enquiry service, and entered Stefan Cain's name and as much of the address as he had. The name and address came up without hesitation. Stefan Cain, address, Greymarsh, Thornchurch, Kent. The phone number was ex-directory, but there was a postcode. So it seemed safe to accept that, if nothing else, Toby and Arabella Tallis's godfather was real.

But he could find no glimmering of Giselle.

* * *

'The phone rang while I was asleep,' said Toby, reappearing towards the end of the afternoon. 'I knew it would, but I'm very glad I didn't utter any curses, because it turns out that somebody broke into Greymarsh, and clumped Stefan on the head. The poor old boy has been carted off to the local hospital.'

'That's dreadful.' Phin was horrified. 'Will he be all right?'

'Bit groggy, but no signs of concussion, and all the scans are clear. The medics will keep him in hospital for another day or so to be sure, but he's as tough as shoe leather. They tried Arabella's number, and when they got no reply, Stefan was sufficiently *compos mentis* to give them mine. I managed to reach the police in Thornchurch, and it seems it all happened in the small hours of the morning. Stefan heard someone prowling around, and went down to investigate. He didn't see who it was, but he was knocked out.'

'Was anything stolen?'

'There's a bit of a mess in the study, but the police don't know if anything's actually been taken, not until Stefan's well enough to be let home and check. They think he probably disturbed the burglar before he actually got his hands on anything, though.' Toby looked at Phin. 'But you know what I'm thinking, don't you?'

'You're wondering if there's a connection between your god-father throwing out the portrait, your cousin disappearing from the scene and this break-in,' said Phin.

'Yes. So I think what I'd better do, I'd better go down to Romney Marsh myself. It's a bit of a trek, but I can't leave the dear old boy in hospital all on his own. He'll be worrying about the break-in as well, and if I'm on the spot I can organize new locks and things.'

'Also,' said Phin, 'he and Arabella were obviously in touch recently, because of the painting and that note, so he might know what she's been up to.'

Toby looked at him gratefully. 'He might, mightn't he? I really think it'll be a good idea to go to Greymarsh.'

His tone was elaborately casual and Phin discovered he was wrestling with his conscience. It was not necessary to suggest he accompany Toby. There were probably any number of people who would want – and be entitled – to be involved in Stefan Cain's burglary and attack. And Phin himself had a deadline to meet.

On the other hand, if Arabella had got herself into some kind of scrape and was not just dragon-flying somewhere, both she and Toby might prefer it kept as quiet as possible.

Also, there was Christa, and there was Giselle, and there was the devil's tritone in Giselle's music. And Phin's present commission could be worked on more or less anywhere.

He said, 'Would you like me to come with you?'

Toby turned his head to look at Phin directly. 'Yes,' he said on a note of unmistakable relief. 'Yes, I would. It's not a very long journey – couple of hours, traffic permitting. Straight down the M20 and into Kent. You'll like Thornchurch; it's a market town – quite lively and prosperous. We can go in my car – it's coming up to its MOT, but it'll be absolutely fine, and as long as you remember to pump the accelerator before turning the ignition, it starts practically every time. Would tomorrow be all right for you?'

'Well—'

'You did say your redhead's gone back to Canada, didn't you? And I know one of the girls last night gave you her phone number, so if you were planning on—'

Phin hastily disclaimed any immediate plans to phone any girl whose number he might have acquired, particularly as he could not remember having done so. 'I'll have to bring the laptop to do some work, but that isn't a problem for me, as long as it isn't for you.'

'Of course not. We might as well stay at Greymarsh itself – there's plenty of room, as long as you don't mind making up your own bed. I'll phone some neighbours of the godfather before we go, to suss out the situation a bit more. I'm trying to remember their names, but . . . oh, wait, it's Mander. Brother and sister. Marcus and Margot Mander,' he said. 'It sounds like a variety double act from the Fifties, doesn't it? Trapeze artists or illusionists, and sequinned tights and top hats. They aren't in the least like that, though. He's a translator for some highly respectable firm – trade conventions and even political conferences. I'll track down their number and give them a call.'

'What had we better do about Christa?' said Phin, glancing across at the portrait.

'Take her with us,' said Toby, cheerfully.

'At this rate,' said Phin, 'she'll be able to write a travel memoir.'

* * *

As he put a few things into a small suitcase, and looked out a couple of bath towels in which to wrap the portrait for its journey, Phin found himself constantly meeting the level gaze of the painted eyes. He had a strong feeling that – whatever the truth about her – he might rather have liked Christa Cain.

THREE

Margot Mander supposed it would have been impossible to be born into her family and escape the hatred that had been generated by Christa Klein.

'She lived and died before we were born,' Margot's brother, Marcus, once said, 'but we've grown up surrounded by that hatred.'

The hatred came mostly from their aunt – great-aunt, actually, Marcus said, or even a cousin – who was called Lina and with whom they lived. But Margot and Marcus's mother usually added her contribution to the invective.

'That's because she's so grateful to Lina for taking her in when our father left,' Marcus said.

Marcus was going to get away from the hatred, because he was going to university. When he had the letter offering him a place, he told their mother and Lina that he was glad he would no longer have to listen to their constant droning about the past.

'It's like a . . . a legacy of bitterness, all that stuff about Christa,' he said. 'And neither of you will let it go.'

Lina was furious. She said Marcus was trying to pretend that the wickedness of the past had never happened. 'You're dressing up evil, Marcus. Hiding it behind clever words.'

'Like,' said his mother, darting in, 'a murderess putting on silk gloves to hide the blood on her hands.'

A murderess. Christa had probably not worn silk gloves, but she had committed a vicious murder.

'It was seventy-odd years ago,' said Marcus. 'For God's sake, let it die.'

But Lina would not. She said it was all very well for Marcus to talk like that; a dreadful, tragic injustice had been dealt to their family, and it should never be forgotten. One day the balance must be redressed.

'I relied on you to do that, Marcus.'

'Lina depended on you; well, on both of you.' Mother accorded Margot a grudging nod.

'But now it seems all we've done is bore you.'

In the end, Marcus relented. He apologized and said he had got a bit carried away, and they clung to him gratefully.

'My father was a wonderful man,' said Lina. 'He died a terrible death in a great cause.' There was a pause, as there generally was at this point. 'He was butchered by that harlot, Christa Klein – the family changed its name later, but it's how I still think of her. Christa Klein. A murderer and a traitor to her own people.'

Margot said, daringly, 'Was she really a traitor?' They had learned about traitors at school. People who were traitors got beheaded or burned.

'She was a black traitor and a vicious murderess. There was a clumsy attempt to cover it up afterwards, but there were people who knew the truth.'

'Lina was one of those people,' put in Margot's mother, proudly.

'Nothing was ever proved but, at the time, everyone knew that Christa Klein committed a terrible crime inside Wewelsburg Castle.'

Wewelsburg Castle. The name always had the power to thrill Margot. It conjured up all the dark fairy tales of fiction – all the brooding castles on hillsides where ogres and enchanters dwelled, and to which courageous and handsome princes travelled to rescue beautiful maidens. Lina had never actually said she had been at Wewelsburg, but she had been born in 1940 or perhaps 1941, so she could have been. It was quite difficult to see her as a child. She had a severe face and bushy eyebrows and a skin that looked as if it had been sandpapered, but when she was young she had probably been nice-looking and her figure would not have been like a cushion.

Occasionally, Lina went into the small, sunless sitting room at the back of the house, which was rather grandly referred to as the music room, and played the tinny, out-of-tune piano. Nobody was supposed to interrupt her at those times, but Margot sometimes stole along to the door and peeped through the badly fitting frame. Like that, lost in whatever music she was playing, Lina looked different – she looked softer, as if the music had brought back the ghost of the young girl she had once been, the child who had adored her father and never been able to forget him. Margot thought he must have been dazzling and marvellous for her to remember him so intensely for all these years, but Marcus disagreed.

'He was probably a horrid old lecher, romping through the 1930s,' he said. 'And Lina's brooded over it all her life, and now she and Ma believe their own version of the truth.'

'Don't say Ma, she hates it.'

'Well, whatever the truth is,' said Marcus, 'the whole thing's morbid, and whatever did happen to the old boy, I'm not interested.'

Marcus was at Warwick University, at the School of Modern Languages and Cultures, studying German, and German culture, and Margot was intensely proud of him. Their mother said it was all very clever, and she did not understand a tenth of it. Lina said it was only what she would expect, and she was very glad that Marcus was being true to the memory of her father, and to his own ancestry.

Margot was determined not to mind that Marcus was going away. She was determined not to feel jealous of the friends he would make, the people she would probably never know. There would probably be girlfriends, but they would not really mean anything, Margot knew that.

When he came home in the holidays he did not talk about girlfriends and he did not bring any home, although that did not surprise Margot, because it was not a house you would want to bring a friend to. It was not a house that had any sense of welcome.

And one day Margot and Marcus would go out into the world together, just the two of them. One day they would have a marvellous life together.

She kept a private calendar to cross off the days until Marcus would finish his student years.

There had never been any thought of Margot trying for university. She learned shorthand and typing and word-processing in her last year at school, although the teachers said shorthand was something of a dying art. Everyone was beginning to type their own letters and reports – still, it did not hurt to have the extra skill, and shorthand could be useful for professions like the police and journalism.

Armed with these skills, which were modest in comparison to what Marcus would eventually have, Margot got a job in a small local office. The company sold or imported things, and the work was not very interesting, but there was a small salary and it got her away from the stifling atmosphere of home each day.

'In any case, the salary doesn't matter,' Margot's mother said. 'You and Marcus will have my money one day.'

'And mine,' said Lina. 'And this house, of course.'

Margot did not like to ask how much money there might be, but she thought it might be quite substantial. Houses in this street sometimes had 'For Sale' boards outside them, and Margot thought they were quite expensive to buy. It was useful to know all this because of the real life that was waiting – the life in which she and Marcus would buy their own house. Quite often she visualized the house, and occasionally in her lunch hour she went into furniture stores to look at sofas and tables.

Sometimes the girls in the office invited her to go out with them – they were going clubbing, or to the cinema and a meal afterwards. Margot went a couple of times, but she did not much enjoy it, and she knew Marcus would not like to think of her with a crowd of slightly tipsy girls, giggling and vying with each other for the attention of various men. When the girls asked her if she had a boyfriend, she smiled, and said, Oh, yes, there was someone, but he was away at university. Studying hard. It would be almost two years until he came home. She saw them glance pityingly at her and exchange sly glances, and she understood they thought she was spinning a story, and that there was no boyfriend, except in her imagination. After that, they did not ask her out again. It did not matter.

It was after one of Marcus's weekend visits home – one of his all-too-rare visits – that Margot woke to hear the faint sounds of the piano from below. She listened for a moment, then got out of bed, reached for a dressing gown and slippers, and stole down the stairs.

It was a cold, rainy night and the house was in darkness. The window on the half-landing had no curtains; it was an oblong of blackness, misty with condensation and the lashing rain. The piano music had stopped, and the only sound was the ticking of the long-case clock in the hall.

Margot sank down on the stairs, peering through the banisters towards the music room. The door was slightly open and the room was in shadow, but Lina did not seem aware of the darkness. Margot wondered if she might be sleepwalking, or whether she was simply pulling her memories around her with the music. Her eyes were open, but Margot did not think that meant anything.

There was a movement from the room, and a rustle of papers, and Margot, her heart pounding, crept down the remaining stairs, to get nearer. Lina had opened the old tapestry piano stool and taken a piece of music from it. She placed it on the stand and sat down again, staring at it. This was unusual, because she generally played from memory, and what was even more unusual was that, even from here, Margot could see that the music was not printed, but handwritten. She waited, expecting Lina to start playing again, but she did not. After a while she replaced the music in the stool, and closed the lid.

Margot, not daring to run back upstairs in case she was seen, pressed back into the deep shadow cast by the old clock. The faint vibration of the mechanism tapped against her, like a ticking heart.

Lina came out of the music room, and Margot waited until she heard the bedroom door open and close, then went into the music room.

There was a scent of age and dust, and when she bent down to open the lid of the tapestry stool, there was the feeling of memories, stored away and almost forgotten. There was the music just inside. Across the top were the words, *Giselle's Music.*

There were only four pages, and there was nothing else written anywhere. Margot went back to bed. She did not think she had ever heard the name Giselle mentioned, but perhaps the music had belonged to some long-ago friend of Lina's who had been called Giselle, and Lina kept the music in her memory.

FOUR

Marcus usually came home at half-term; Margot looked forward to this for weeks ahead, and planned the meals she would cook.

The first night, over supper, he told them about his studies. The modern languages school was very lively, he said, very interesting. There was a great mixture of students, but there was seldom any culture clash, although the French could get a bit excitable, and you could not always tell what the Russians were thinking.

It was a good evening; Marcus looked marvellous, and he made them all laugh. It was rare to hear laughter in that house.

But when their mother and Lina had gone up to bed, he said, 'The old girl's still stuck in her time warp, isn't she? Bloody Christa and all the rest of it.'

'Yes. And she goes down to the music room in the middle of the night, sometimes.'

'Oh, God, does she? D'you know, I have to really psych myself up to come back to this house. All that crap about avenging people's memories, and getting justice for ancient murders. Lina's living in some slushy old-fashioned novel. Like that Rider Haggard book, where each generation's taxed with hunting down the killer of some long-ago Egyptian Queen, but they all just write on an old document things like, "I could not go." And, "To my son, who may have better fortune in the task." And it goes on for centuries. You know the book I mean, don't you?'

Margot did not know the book, and she had never heard of Rider Haggard, but she loved it when Marcus talked to her like this, so she instantly said, 'Oh, yes, I know the one. Yes, you're right.'

'And Ma's almost as bad. She's been dragged into the same time warp. No wonder father left. Probably he was relieved to let Ma go to live with Lina and the memories of her sainted father.'

'You're exaggerating.'

'I'm not. I'm even starting to think we need to talk to a doctor about Lina.'

'I don't think it's as bad that—'

Marcus stood up, and grabbed her hand. 'Come with me,' he said, and pulled her from the room into the dim hall beyond.

'Where are we—'

'Ssh. The old girl's music room. Something I found ages ago.'

The music, thought Margot. *Giselle's Music*. I know about that, though.

But it was not *Giselle's Music* at all.

Marcus shut the music-room door, switched on a table lamp, and opened up the tapestry stool. There were the yellowing sheets of old music and the faded covers of song sheets. And *Giselle's Music*. That was there, too, of course. But Marcus did not seem particularly to notice it; he lifted the stack of music out and put it on the floor, then reached down to the bottom of the stool's interior for a large envelope.

'I found this years ago,' he said. 'Lina moves it around to different hiding places. She puts it under those books, or she hides it in between music scores, or wedges it behind a picture.'

'Because she doesn't want us to find it?'

'Yes. But I think she takes it out and broods over it when she's on her own,' said Marcus. 'I bet she's squirrelled other, similar things away as well, only I've never found them; well, I've never looked, because this house is so stuffed with junk it would take seven men seven years . . .'

He opened the envelope carefully, and put a dog-eared photograph and a faded newspaper cutting on the side table, where the lamp's light fell on them.

The photo was of a man who looked to be in his late thirties or early forties – although it was difficult to judge from such an old black-and-white image. He was narrowing his eyes at the camera, as if strong sunlight might be shining on to his face. His hair might have been any colour, but he had dark, strongly marked brows, and a wide mouth that might be either very sensitive or that might be cold and even cruel. Margot was not sure if she would have liked him very much – she thought she might have been a bit frightened of him – but she could not stop looking at him.

'Who is he? And where—'

'If you look here, and here—' Marcus indicated on the photograph.

'The outline of a turret?'

'Yes. See what it says on the back.'

On the back of the photograph, in Lina's writing, familiar from Christmas and birthday cards, were the words, 'My dear and beloved father at Wewelsburg Castle in 1939.'

'Wewelsburg,' said Margot, softly.

'Yes. And that's the murdered martyr himself.'

'He looks quite young,' said Margot.

The other thing in the envelope was a newspaper cutting, brown-spotted with age, the paper brittle, but the print still readable. The date at the top was March 1976, and the heading said: THE WILDCARDS OF MURDER. A subheading said, 'Vanished Killers'.

Margot looked questioningly at Marcus, but he only said, 'Read it.'

The article was about people who had been suspected of murder – suspected so strongly it would have been difficult for those people to prove their innocence if they had not vanished. There were three or four pictures of these people, with brief descriptions of what they were thought to have done. They all looked perfectly normal, and the details given were carefully phrased – Margot supposed the newspaper had to be careful about printing anything that might be wrong. It was libel or slander or something.

'Why would Lina keep this?' she began, then saw that one of the photos was of a girl, who looked to be about twelve or thirteen. She had smooth dark hair and narrow eyes and a shy smile, as if she was not sure if she entirely liked having her photo taken. At her side was a small boy, who strongly resembled her, even in the grainy newsprint. He was hunching his shoulders and looking slightly anxious.

The caption said, 'An early photograph of Christa Klein with her younger brother, possibly at their childhood home just outside Berlin in the late 1930s. The fate of Klein's family was never established, but Klein was believed to have played a key role in an horrific slaughter during the early years of World War II at Wewelsburg. A number of rumours circulated after the war, and Klein's extreme youth at the time of the killing has always been stressed.

'Christa Klein was never brought to justice – and her age at the time of the deaths would severely have restricted any actual sentencing. It was never known what happened to her.'

Margot, reading this, had the curious sensation that for a few moments she and Marcus had stepped into a grisly, lamplit fragment of history that had its place seven decades earlier in Nazi Germany.

'So now you see,' said Marcus, replacing the photo and the article in the envelope, 'how obsessed Lina is. She'll bang on for ever about justice for the woman who murdered her father, and she'll never let go of it – neither will Mother.' He put the envelope back in the music stool, careful to replace it in the exact same place, and laying the old music scores on the top again before closing the lid. *Giselle's Music* was still on the top.

'Marg, I've more or less left home, but you're still here. If you aren't careful they'll drag you into that time warp with them.'

Margot knew he was right. She had a moment of panic, because she could see the years of dreariness stretching out in front of her, and she could see herself repeating the pattern, sinking into the same dreary, whining life as her mother had.

'But one day we'll be out of this, won't we? And then we'll be together. Won't we?'

'That'd be nice. Pity there's no dosh. Unless—'

'Yes?'

Marcus paused, then said, very softly, 'You know what I'm thinking, don't you? You know what would have to happen to make us – especially you – really free? And give us a bit of money into the bargain?'

A sudden silence came down between them. Margot stared at him, and had the eerie impression that a light had kindled behind his eyes.

Then he smiled, and said, 'Bad thoughts to have. Not to be put into words. I'm for my bed. Night, Marg.'

Sleep was impossible. Margot lay awake, unable to stop Marcus's words playing and replaying in her mind. He would be asleep by now, of course. She liked to think of him just along the landing. His hair would be tousled on the pillow, and his lashes would lie like dark half-moons on his cheeks.

She turned over, trying to find a comfortable place on the pillow, but her thoughts were scurrying back and forth. Was this to be one of the nights when Lina stole down to the music room, and looked at *Giselle's Music*, and at the photograph Marcus had found? 'My dear and beloved father at Wewelsburg Castle . . .'

The bedside clock was showing twenty minutes past midnight when Margot got out of bed and went downstairs. It was very quiet, save for the ticking of the long-case clock. One day Margot was going to silence it, so that it could no longer tick and chime away the hours and the days and the years of her life.

She went cautiously into the music room, and reached into the tapestry stool. Here was the music, and right at the bottom the photograph and the newspaper cutting. Margot propped them all up on the music stand, and sat down, staring at them. Giselle and Christa. And Lina's father, murdered all those years ago. Marcus's words earlier were still running through her mind. *You know what would have to happen to make us really free?* he had said. *And give us a bit of money into the bargain . . .?*

The curtains were open to the rain-drenched night and Margot could see her reflection in the blurred glass. When she moved, her reflection moved with her. It was an indistinct reflection, though, and she had a brief impression of a figure sitting next to her on the piano stool. She turned her head sharply, but of course there was no one there. But when she looked back at the window, there again was the impression of a small wavering shape like a phantom image within the darkness. Almost like a child pressing up against the glass, trying to get in . . .

There was a faint sound within the room, and Margot spun round. Her heart leapt. Walking towards her was a figure with a pale face and dark pits where the eyes were. A voice hissed, 'So you're back, you evil bitch.'

It was several panic-filled seconds before Margot realized it was Lina, and several more before she managed to say, in a shaky voice, 'Lina – it's me. Margot.'

A dreadful look of sly cunning came into the pallid face. 'No you're not,' said Lina. 'I know who you really are. You're Christa. I can see her looking out of your eyes.'

Margot said, 'Christa isn't here, Lina. And I really am Margot. Let's go back upstairs. It's cold down here, isn't it?'

'You don't fool me, you murderous bitch,' said Lina, in the

same eerie, blurred voice. 'I always knew you'd come back one day. I've listened for you and watched for you all my life.'

Marcus was right, thought Margot, trying not to panic. She needs help – proper professional help. I'll shout to him – he'll know what to do. But she did not move and she did not call out to Marcus. The room was very quiet, except for the clock's ticking, and a soft creak from the old window frame. And there's something here that isn't usually here, Margot thought. And then – no, not something, *someone* . . . Something that had pressed up against the window, wanting to be let in . . .? Something that was reaching out to her with dead, juiceless fingers, brushing against her skin like icy spider strands . . .?

Then she heard herself say, very softly, 'So you recognized me. Yes, I'm here, Lina. I'm here with you.'

The words sounded thin and spiteful, and hearing them shocked Margot.

Lina was backing away, knocking over the piano stool, one hand going to her heart in the classic gesture of fear or defence or both.

'I'm dreaming this,' she said in a strangled voice. 'You're a nightmare, that's all you are.'

The voice that did not seem to belong to Margot said, 'All those years of hating me, Lina . . . All those years of telling your family I'm a murderess – didn't it ever occur to you that one day the hatred would be so strong I'd hear it . . .? That I'd come to find you . . .'

'No,' said Lina, in a strangled voice. Her face was no longer just pale, it was taking a bluish tinge, especially around the lips. She was gasping for breath. 'You're not real . . .'

'Aren't I? *Aren't I . . .?*'

Lina gave a strangled cry, clutched at the edges of the piano as if trying to stand, then fell forward across the edge of the piano frame. A faint resonance came from inside it, like the struggling moan of something dying.

Something dying . . . Lina was sprawled on the floor. She looked dead, but she might not be. She might be unconscious – from a stroke or a heart attack. If Margot summoned help, dialled 999 for an ambulance, Lina might be saved. But if she did nothing . . .

We need to be free, Marcus had said. And then, *You know what would have to happen first . . .*

Margot stood very still, staring down at the prone figure. The only emotion she felt was relief that the focus of the smothering hatred had gone. At last, moving very quietly, she went back upstairs to bed.

The following morning, her mother came running into her bedroom, crying, and saying she had found Lina – dear Lina, who had so generously given them a home for all these years – lying in the music room. She was cold and still, and certainly dead; what a shocking way to go, and whatever were they to do?

What they did – what Marcus and Margot did between them – was to call the paramedics, who came quickly. They were very kind; they said it looked like a heart attack, which would have been quick and quite merciful in its way. Well, yes, it was certainly a bit unusual that she had apparently gone down to play the piano after having gone to bed, but elderly people sometimes did reach out for their earlier years. Possibly she had been doing that. If so, it might be a comfort to them all to think she had met her death surrounded by happy memories of her past.

Margot did not say that the memories of Lina's past would not be particularly happy, and her mother refused to be comforted anyway. She said Lina's life had been very unhappy; it had been filled with sadness and violence and betrayal. She sat crying in a chair for the entire day, with the curtains all closed, wearing a dressing gown and refusing to eat. The GP, appealed to for help over the phone, said he would leave a prescription for a mild sedative at reception. Margot had to collect this and take it to the nearest pharmacy, because their mother refused to let Marcus out of her sight. It took her nearly two hours because she had to wait for buses that were late, and by the time she got back, Marcus was on the phone to the infirmary. He sounded angry. He said the family did not want a post mortem to be performed; his mother's aunt had surely been so old that there was no question of anything other than death from – well, from old age, and no, he did not mean to be disrespectful, he was simply stating a fact. It was unkind to put his mother through such a trauma, said Marcus. He avoided looking at Margot when he said this.

But it seemed a post mortem was necessary, because the cause of death was not immediately clear, and as no physician had been in attendance for the preceding three weeks, the law required this investigation. The hospital said it would be done quickly and it would be very respectful, and in the end Marcus had to give in. The following day somebody from the coroner's office phoned to say the cause had been myocardial infarction. A simple heart attack, exactly as the paramedics had thought. It was a pity there had been no warning, but that was how it happened sometimes. A good age, though. And a quick and painless death, which was surely what everybody wanted for their loved ones.

Marcus stayed until after the funeral, of course. He had to make some phone calls explaining what had happened, and later, as she was going along to her own bedroom, Margot heard him make another call. She paused outside his door. His voice had slid down into a soft purr – Margot had never heard him use that voice before, and she clenched her fists. Marcus was saying, 'Of course I'll soon be back with you. Girl, dear, why do you think I want to be back with you?'

There was a pause, then he said, 'Listen, though, it's probably as well you aren't here, because I'm bloody drunk tonight – it's like a gothic novel in this house at the moment, and I had to get pissed to get through the evening. So you might find I was from suffering brewers' droop – although it'd be a first if so, wouldn't it—'

The girl must have said something at this point, because Marcus laughed, very quietly, in a way Margot had never heard him laugh before. He said, 'Oh, that's more than worth coming back for. I'll be with you as soon as I can.'

It would not mean anything, of course. That girl, whoever she was, would not be important.

When, the next morning, Marcus said, 'Margot, have you realized we're one step nearer to freedom,' Margot's heart leapt and she stopped thinking about the unknown girl she had heard him phone, (and *hating* that girl), and knew that when it came to the really important things, she and Marcus were still of one mind. A life together, that was what they both wanted, and that was what would eventually happen. One day they would be free to sell this house.

One half of the stifling hatred had vanished. What of the other half? How long was their mother likely to live?

The funeral was very plain, because Margot's mother said they did not need to be extravagant.

There was no get-together with friends or family afterwards, mostly because there was no family except themselves, and neither Lina nor Margot's mother had any friends. Two of their neighbours came to the crematorium, but that was all.

When they got back to the house, Margot's mother said she could not face eating the lunch Margot had got up early to make, in readiness for their return. In the end Marcus and Margot ate it between them, feeling rather guilty. 'But I was ravenously hungry,' said Marcus, a bit defiantly. 'And it was bloody cold in that crematorium.'

After Margot had washed up, her mother thought that after all she might fancy something light. Soup and some toast, perhaps. And if Margot happened to have baked some of those nice fruit scones . . . She did not want to be any trouble, but it had all been such a terrible ordeal, and at her age . . .

It annoyed Margot when her mother represented herself as old, because she was only a bit over fifty, which was not very old at all. You saw lovely people of Mother's age, and older, on television, and there were two women who worked in Margot's office who were in their fifties, and who were modern and smart and lively. But Margot's mother had let her hair turn pepper-and-salt grey and never had it properly styled, and she wore shapeless, porridge-coloured cardigans and skirts. She had embraced old age a good twenty years too early, although Margot supposed that living with Lina and the past would make anybody do that.

The following day, Marcus said thoughtfully to Margot, 'You know, I didn't expect the old girl to die so suddenly. She went downstairs to look at the photo and the newspaper cutting again, I suppose.'

'I suppose so. Marcus – couldn't we go away now? Be free of this house and all the past immediately? Mum would be all right on her own, wouldn't she? We'd come to visit and make sure she was all right. But—'

He spread his hands ruefully. 'Can't be done. I told you – there's no money. Even if I get a half-decent job after my degree, there won't be much spare cash for ages. If we're going to live in any reasonable comfort, we need to be able to sell this house. We need Ma's savings, and whatever Lina left her, as well. Don't look so shocked, you know it's true. And I'm not going to live in poverty, even for you.' He touched her cheek with a fingertip and leaned forward to drop a kiss on her cheek. His hair fell forward and brushed Margot's face, and she wanted to touch it so much it almost hurt.

Tomorrow would be Marcus's last day, which meant Margot would have a perfectly good reason for suggesting the two of them go out for a farewell meal in the evening. Her treat, she would say, speaking casually, as if it did not matter very much either way. She thought Marcus would be glad to go out for a couple of hours, away from the dismal atmosphere of this house, away from their mother who was having to be given cups of tea and bowls of soup at regular intervals, together with an assortment of pills. She would certainly refuse to go out to a restaurant. She was currently reminiscing about Lina's life, and she had already disinterred the ghost of Lina's father, whom she had never known, and had picked over the details of Christa Klein's murderous villainy. Marcus said most of the details were from their mother's imagination, because nobody knew the truth about Christa.

Margot thought she would take Marcus to the bar where the office people went – it had recently opened a small restaurant, and she would book a table. Perhaps those suspicious girls would be there and they would see Marcus and think he was her boyfriend, and be jealous.

She began to imagine little pieces of dialogue between them at the table – what she would say to Marcus, and what he would reply. There would be soft lights, maybe even candlelight, and attentive waiters.

Marcus might not want to drink very much because of driving, but there was no reason why he could not get a bit drunk when they got home. There was a bottle of wine in the sideboard – it had been there for years, and Margot could put it out without him seeing before they left. Somewhere, she knew, there were some nice wine glasses that had never been used – she would look them out and wash them – and there was bound to be a corkscrew somewhere.

How about background music? Mood music, people called it. Margot spent a long time turning the radio dial to find a suitable station. It was important not to choose one that had loud, bouncy adverts; she did not want a jingly ad for home insurance or cut-rate holidays spoiling the atmosphere.

They would be relaxed and happy from their evening out. Marcus would open the wine and pour a glass each for them, and they would drink it seated together on the settee. It was a pity there was no firelight, but Mother could not be doing with coal and ashes and scraping out cinders. But the gas fire was pretty good and, with the radio on, the belching sound it made when the room got warm would be scarcely noticeable.

Beyond this, Margot was trying not to think. It was important to remember that what she was imagining was forbidden. She clung to the word obstinately. Forbidden.

She had no experience of what it felt like to make love or to be made love to. It was ridiculous and shameful to have reached this age and still be a virgin, but at least there was the consolation that no one knew. And there had been biology lessons at school, and occasionally the girls in her office would gigglingly describe a raunchy night with a boyfriend, or tell how one of their husbands had come randily home from the pub and embarked on a marathon bedroom session. So Margot knew what the mechanics were.

When she thought about them in connection with Marcus, she was alternately terrified and excited.

Margot experienced a mixture of disappointment and relief when Marcus said he could not afford the time to go out that evening. He had an essay which had to be handed in on Monday, and he had to work on that. Also, he would need to make a very early start in the morning, to be in time for a lecture. French conversation, he said. He was doing quite well with French, which he was taking as his second language and which could be very useful later on. They could just have something here, couldn't they? Margot could cook something, couldn't she?

Margot said at once that of course she could, and going out had only been an idea. There would be another opportunity. Marcus smiled and said, Yes, there would, and perhaps he ought to spend this last evening with Ma, anyway.

'You understand, don't you? Well, you always do.'

Margot did understand. She knew that she and Marcus understood one another perfectly.

After he left next morning, she sat in her bedroom for a long time, staring through the window at the garden with the thick old shrubbery that blocked so much light.

With Lina's death, half – perhaps more than half – of the hatred that tainted this house had been removed. But what about the other half? Would that one day be removed? If so, it would mean she could leave this house, and she and Marcus would be together. It would mean that finally they had shaken off the ghosts.

But it seemed that the ghosts were closer and more substantial than either Margot or Marcus had known. And they were in this very house, waiting to be brought into the light.

FIVE

I t was a good three months after Lina's death that Margot's mother said, with an air of brave resignation, that somebody should sort through the things in her room. There were probably papers in the desk in there – well, no, not a will, of course, because no will had ever been made. Lina had made this house over to her years ago, said Margot's mother.

'And there's her piano. I don't know what we ought to do about that. Neither of you were ever interested in learning, and in any case I couldn't have afforded music lessons. I always disliked that room – dreadfully gloomy, I thought it – although Lina sometimes went in there. And now the piano will be gathering dust, and I daresay the wires will start rotting. I hate to think of it.'

'I expect there are people who buy pianos,' said Margot, who hated the piano with its macabre links to Lina. 'And I can go through the desk and throw things away.'

'Oh, you couldn't do that on your own,' said her mother at once. 'You wouldn't know what to keep and what not to. We'd better ask Marcus to come for a weekend. You can call him, can't you? Using the phone gives me a headache nowadays.'

The prospect of having Marcus home brought the familiar surge of delight. Margot's mind flew ahead, seeing the two of them shut away in Lina's bedroom, sorting through the contents of her desk. There was no knowing what they might find, and it would be an intimate thing to do. He would be here for two whole days, so there might be a Sunday afternoon walk on the heath, and Margot might even try to set up that candlelit dinner again – Mother could easily be persuaded to go up to bed early.

Mother said they must make the house particularly welcoming and comfortable for Marcus, because he did not come home very often, and his last visit had been such a sad one. And she was not one to complain, but she did think Margot had let things go a bit. The paintwork could do with washing down for one thing, and the sitting-room curtains would benefit from being washed.

The dining-room ones might as well be done at the same time. And it would do Marcus good to have some specially nice, home-cooked food, as well; everyone knew students lived on junk food.

All of this effectively meant that Margot would wash paintwork and get curtains cleaned and cook the specially nice meals, because her mother would not do a hand's turn for the entire weekend.

But it was worth it. Marcus enjoyed the food Margot had cooked, and he had brought some wine. Margot had one glass, and Mother took a small sip of hers, screwing up her face with distaste, saying she could not understand why people liked the stuff. In the end, Marcus drank the remainder of the first bottle, and nearly all of the second one. It did not make him drunk or slurry or embarrassing; it made his eyes brilliant and his hair flopped forward over his forehead.

By the time Margot had washed up and their mother had told Marcus about her health, it was after ten o'clock before they finally went up to Lina's bedroom.

'I'm not going to be much good at sorting through old papers now,' said Marcus. 'I've had far too much to drink. In fact I'm seeing everything through a fuzz, and you'll have to help me up the stairs.' He laughed, and put his hand out, pulling Margot against him to support him. He smelled of clean skin and clean hair and masculinity.

Lina's room was in darkness, but Margot closed the curtains and switched on the bedside light before opening the old-fashioned roll-top desk.

'There won't be anything much,' Marcus said, sitting on the bed and watching her. 'Even if the old girl did have anything of interest, she'd have hidden it, like she hid that photograph and the newspaper article in the music room.'

The music room. To smother the memories, Margot said, 'Mother wants to get rid of the piano. She says it's never going to be played.'

'Shouldn't think it is.' He lay back on the pillows, his hands linked behind his head

Margot began sifting the desk's contents, but it was almost immediately clear that Marcus was right; there was nothing of any interest in the desk, and certainly nothing of any value. Some old calendars – goodness knew why Lina had kept those – and one or two mail-order catalogues from which she used to order all her clothes.

'I told you there wouldn't be anything,' said Marcus, when Margot finally closed the desk. 'Let's go to bed.' He put out a hand to her.

Margot felt as if something had squeezed all the breath from her body.

Let's go to bed . . .

He meant that they should both go to their separate beds in their own bedrooms, but there was a moment when his reaching hand closed around hers very firmly indeed. But of course he was simply wanting her to help him up off the bed, and this was nothing more than a brother wanting his sister's help, because he had had too much to drink.

He got off the bed a bit awkwardly, and put an arm round her waist, leaning heavily against her. 'You'll have to help me to bed, I think,' he said, laughing.

Out on the landing, a faint smell of the roast lamb from their meal earlier lay greasily on the air. Mother had said lamb was a fatty meat; she wondered at Margot choosing it and it was to be hoped Marcus had not become a vegetarian.

Margot, with Marcus's arm still around her waist, the two of them making a somewhat uncertain progress along the landing, had the bizarre thought that if tonight was to be the night when she was finally going to Marcus's bed, it was a pity if it was to an oily background of cooling roast lamb. It was an even greater pity that she was wearing run-down house shoes and an old sweater which had bobbled a bit in the wash.

But at least the clock was chiming midnight, and midnight somehow held its own romantic aura. It went hand-in-hand with moonlight and soft music from an invisible orchestra playing one of the old romantic songs. Fred Astaire and Ginger Rogers dancing to the strains of 'The Way You Look Tonight'.

This was a ridiculous way to think – it was starry-eyed pre-teen thinking, and none of it bore any resemblance to the reality. Not that there was actually going to be any reality, not tonight, not ever. But being so close to Marcus sent the familiar shiver through her.

And then a light went on in the bedroom at the far end, and

their mother's voice called querulously out to them not to stay up all night poring over Lina's papers; didn't they realize it was midnight and people wanted to sleep.

Marcus grinned, and removed his hand from around Margot's waist. 'I think I'm all right from here,' he said. 'Shocking to get pissed in your own home, isn't it? First night back, as well. Night, Margot.'

'Goodnight.'

When Margot finally fell asleep, her dreams were confused. They were mixed up with old photographs of brooding German castles, and with the image of the man who had been the dear and beloved father of Lina . . . Margot could almost believe she was hearing Lina now, stealing downstairs to brood over the photographs while the house slept. She could hear the soft footsteps on the stairs . . .

Footsteps.

She came up out of sleep to the realization that someone really was going down the stairs. There was nothing remarkable about that, though, and if Marcus or Mother had gone downstairs for something – a drink, a book – they would move quietly so as not to wake anyone. Margot prepared to go back to sleep, but then she heard the familiar slow creak of the music-room door being opened.

At this, she got out of bed, slid her feet into slippers and went softly down to the hall. Shadows lay across the hall floor like questing fingers – were they the same shadows that had oozed forward on the night Lina died? The music-room door was slightly ajar. Marcus had switched on the small lamp, and he was kneeling by the piano. The lid of the tapestry-covered piano stool was open, and he was going through its contents.

He heard her at once; he turned sharply round, then, sounding relieved, he said, 'Oh, it's only you. I thought it might be Ma. Come in and shut the door, but be quiet about it. It doesn't really matter, but I'd rather she didn't know what I'm doing.'

'What are you doing?'

'I'm not quite sure.' He still looked a bit drunk, but he was no longer unfocused or unsteady. 'There was something we said earlier – about the old girl not leaving anything for us to find in the desk. It stuck in my mind, and I couldn't sleep for thinking about it.'

Margot said in a whisper, 'We said if there was anything she wanted to keep secret, she'd have hidden it somewhere no one ever looked—'

'—like she hid the photograph and the newspaper cutting. Exactly. So I thought it was worth checking this room. She was the only one who ever came in here, wasn't she? The tapestry stool's the obvious hiding place, but there doesn't seem to be anything apart from old music.'

Margot said slowly, 'What about the piano?'

'The piano? How would you hide anything inside a piano? Oh, wait, does the front come off somehow?'

'I'm not sure. Or – does the top lift up?' said Margot. 'Like a lid?'

'Does it? Yes, you're right – it's hinged.'

He grasped the piano's top, and began to ease it upwards. It was a small piano – Margot thought it was what had once been called a cottage piano – and the top was reluctant to give way at first, as if it did not want to yield any secrets. But Marcus persisted, and it suddenly came free. He pushed it back against the wall and peered inside.

'Black as the devil's cave. Can you get a torch? I daren't switch any more lights on in case Mother sees.'

Margot sped out to the kitchen for a torch. When she came back Marcus was peering into the piano's depths. 'I'm afraid to touch anything without seeing what I'm actually touching,' he said. 'I don't want to twang any of the strings.'

'Mother sleeps through most things.'

'She wouldn't sleep through a cacophony of piano-string twanging,' said Marcus, then grinned. 'I must be sobering up. I couldn't have said cacophony if I was still pissed, could I? Did you close the door? Oh, yes, you did. OK, shine the torch downwards into the piano's guts. Can you see anything?'

'Only wires and strings.'

'That's all I can see, too. And I don't really think . . .'

It was then that he drew in his breath sharply, and it was then that Margot saw the paper that was stuck to the inner side of the piano – immediately behind the music stand.

'Christ al-bloody-mighty,' said Marcus. 'Have we fallen into a gothic romance, and not noticed it?' He looked up at her, and his eyes were no longer liquid from the wine, they were blazing like sapphires with excitement. 'Is this going to be the ancient document that tells the truth about all that crap from the past – Lina's murdered father, and Wewelsburg and Christa the killer?'

Margot said, 'You're getting carried away. It's probably the receipt for the original purchase of the piano, or the address of the man who tunes it.'

'Don't be so sodding down-to-earth. This is a cobwebby document that hasn't seen the light of day for years, and it could be anything.' He was reaching for the paper, slowly and cautiously, trying not to disturb the piano's mechanism, but a faint thrum came from the wires – not music exactly, but music that might be struggling to be born. Margot looked nervously towards the door.

'I think,' said Marcus, 'that it's glued to the wood, because I can't get it free . . . Oh, no, wait, there's a drawing pin holding it in place. I hadn't seen that. Tilt the torch there – no, *there* . . .'

There was a faint dry crackle, then the document was out, and Marcus was cautiously unfolding it. It had been typed on an old-fashioned typewriter, and the paper was spotted with brown and partly split where it had been creased.

'It's not in English,' said Margot, staring at the typed lines. 'What—?'

'It's German,' said Marcus. 'Good thing I'm reading languages, isn't it?' He gestured impatiently for the torch, and Margot went to sit on the window ledge, not wanting to disturb his concentration.

After a few moments, Marcus said, 'God, of all the things—'

'What? *What?* Marcus, if you don't tell me what it says—'

Marcus was still staring at the paper. Then he said, 'It's dated March 1945, and it's addressed to the old girl herself.'

'To Lina?'

'Yes. 1945 – she'd only have been about four or five then, wouldn't she?' He frowned at the letter, then began to read.

'"My dear Miss Lina, A few years ago, a house in Lindschoen was ceded to your father by Gift, in recognition for, and appreciation of, his work. This means it was given to him for his own.

'"As your father's only surviving relative, one day that house will pass to you. However, the law will not allow you to own a house until you are twenty-one, so I have created what is called a Trust until then. Documents about that will be kept at these offices, and you can look at them if you wish, or ask a grown-up to do so for you. But please be assured that we shall keep the house for you until your twenty-first birthday.

"'If I can give you any more information or guidance about this, I will be very pleased to do so. It is a very important thing to own a house, but we will help you to understand and to make decisions about it when the time comes.

"'I am yours very truly—" And there's a squiggled signature that might be anything,' said Marcus, screwing up his eyes to try to decipher it.

'A house,' said Margot, trying out the words, distrustfully. 'A house that Lina inherited. At least – was set to inherit when she was twenty-one. Where's Lindschoen?'

'In Germany. I don't know where, but it'll be easy enough to check.'

'What's the address at the head of the letter?'

'It's somewhere in Berlin. It says, "Established in 1920".'

Margot considered, then said, 'Could Lina really own a house in Germany? Somebody might easily have got the wrong information, or the wrong person.'

'Or the – what do they call it? – the ceding of the house might not have happened after all. Or it might have been cancelled. March 1945 – that's just before the Second World War ended. There was a lot of confusion about who owned what at that time – especially in Germany, I should think. And if Lina had inherited anything, I would have thought we'd have known,' said Marcus, getting up to investigate the piano again in case there was anything else to be found.

'Also, the house might not have amounted to much, even if she eventually got it,' pointed out Margot. 'It might have been a hovel. Only worth a tiny amount.'

Marcus had closed the piano lid dismissively. 'Or it might have been bombed and destroyed in the war,' he said, 'I don't think it would have been a hovel, though. I think Lina's father would have turned up his nose at a hovel. He always sounded a greedy old devil.'

'Lina might have sold the house years ago, and stashed the money away.'

'Or got through the money,' said Marcus. 'It's a hell of a long

time ago. But if she did sell it, there'd have to be a record somewhere, wouldn't there? Something like a Land Registry. But to
check that, we'd need the property's address, and we haven't got
it. I want to know more about this, though, don't you?'

'Could we talk to those solicitors?'

'I'll try to find out if they're still going, but 1920 is very
far back.'

'What about documents actually here? In this house? Deeds
or something?'

'Um, that's a possibility. Could you look, after I've gone back?
Without letting Ma know?'

'Yes.' Margot would have taken the house apart, brick by brick,
if Marcus had wanted. 'Aren't we going to tell Mother?'

'No,' said Marcus. 'This is going to be ours.' He was brushing
away the sprinkling of dust that opening the piano had created,
and he came to sit next to her on the window ledge. 'One day,'
he said, putting an arm around her, 'we'll find that house. Because
one day it could be ours.'

'It would have to go to Mother first though, wouldn't it?
She automatically inherited everything of Lina's – she said so.'
It was marvellous to sit here in the semi-dark with Marcus's arm
around her.

He said, in a soft voice, 'But one day Mother won't be here.
And if a house in Lindschoen really was made over to Lina – and
if it's still there – after Ma, it'd belong to us. Lina didn't have any
other relatives. We're next in line. All we need—'

'Are the legal documents proving the house was given to
Lina? And then to Mother?'

'Well, yes, certainly that. But I was going to say that all we
need is for Mother not to be here any longer.'

Margot turned her head to stare at him. Before she could speak,
he said, 'We had this conversation once before, didn't we? About
knowing what has to happen before we're really free.'

In a whisper, Margot said, 'Yes, we did.'

'Good girl. One day we'll get that freedom.' He stood up. 'And
now, I really am going to bed.'

Margot stayed where she was. Marcus's words were still echoing
in her mind. *All we need is for Mother not to be here any longer*,
he had said. *We both know what has to happen . . .*

She knew, of course, what Marcus wanted. And she knew that what she had done once – here, in this room – she could do again. Had Marcus known what she had done? Had he guessed she had somehow caused Lina's death?

Margot already knew she could do what Marcus wanted, and she also knew she would do it. She did not yet know how, but that would come.

She knew, as well, that whatever she did she would be quite safe, because Marcus would protect her. Brothers always protected their sisters.

SIX

Lindschoen, Germany, March 1939

Giselle Klein tried to believe that Christa would always protect Stefan. She had explained it to Christa very carefully, saying that sisters had to protect their younger brothers.

Christa, the dear intelligent child, had understood. She was so bright, so intuitive – a daughter to be proud of. Felix often said so, as well, his face soft with love and pride. People sometimes said Christa resembled Giselle, even down to the flyaway hair and the wayward cheekbones, they said. And Stefan would turn out exactly like Felix. Gentle and unworldly and vulnerable.

Told by her mother that she must always look after Stefan, Christa promised, which was reassuring, because as far as Giselle knew, Christa never told lies. If only . . . No. Don't think like that. Think instead that giving Christa this small responsibility was a very good thing.

Yes, but if only there was not this feeling of a darkness somewhere within Christa. Giselle had tried to find another word to describe it, and she had tried, as well, to find an explanation as to why she should have this sense of something menacing. Something there in Christa that ought not to be? Something missing? Or – this was deeply worrying in a wholly different way – was it the feeling that something might be waiting for Christa somewhere in the future? But that was absurd. Giselle believed in a great many things, some of which were laughable, and others which were fantastical, and a few which were probably illegal, but what she did not believe in was the concept of premonition.

And so, because you could not worry about things that were so vague they defied definition, Giselle gave to Christa this small responsibility of taking care of Stefan. Not that Christa would ever need to shoulder the task, of course, but you never knew what might be lying in wait for you, and Christa's father was just about the

most impractical person you could meet. Dearest Felix. People who
came to the house – neighbours and Felix's pupils and his musician
friends – all said, affectionately, what a dear good man Felix Klein
was. A bit unworldly, of course, but that was part of the charm.

Unworldly was exactly the right word for Felix. It was also the
right word for most of the musicians who came to the shop that
was called The Music House. There was a notice on the door
saying that Klein's closed at six o'clock, but it never closed entirely,
because they lived behind and above the shop, and Felix's friends
were always turning up at all kinds of odd hours, and ensconcing
themselves in the big room with its bow windows and deep old
fireplace – the room that was the shop during the day and their
sitting room on most evenings. Velda, Giselle's cousin, and also
most of Giselle's family, found this custom untidy and undisci-
plined, and wondered at Giselle putting up with it. Surely she
realized those people were nothing but a set of scroungers?

Giselle did not bother to tell any of them that Felix's friends
were not scroungers, they were gifted musicians – at least most
of them were – and all of them were splendid company. When
they came to The Music House, they brought wine, or food –
cheeses or meat, or somebody's wife or daughter had baked a
cake. Often the wives and daughters came along, too. But whoever
came, they all sat around happily, drinking and eating, arguing
about music, and planning concerts. It was remarkable that any
of the concerts ever got on to a platform, but they usually did,
and to very good audiences. Giselle always helped with the
concerts, which meant she went out and about, meeting people,
arranging the printing of programmes and orchestra parts, making
sure there would be flowers in the foyer and people to sell tickets
and usher everyone to their seats, enjoying the liveliness and the
glamour of performance nights. Also, it was perfectly acceptable
– you might even say it was obligatory – to wear an evening frock
on those occasions. Giselle enjoyed that; she did not in the least
mind the jealous mutters that she was overdressed, nor did she
mind people speculating as to how such frocks had been afforded,
and spikily observing that Felix Klein scarcely noticed anything
beyond his music and his work.

Giselle knew quite well that Felix did not always notice what
went on in the world, but he was certainly noticing the turmoil and

the momentous events in Germany – and in the whole of Europe – at the moment.

The children were noticing it, as well, but in a worryingly distorted way. Christa, huge-eyed with fearful fascination, had several times had to be reassured about the danger of men forcing their way into people's houses. People at school talked about it, she said. The men could hide in bedrooms, waiting to snatch up the most beautiful of the children so they could carry them off to terrible places where dreadful things were done. The men had what they called skewer eyes that could see through the dark and find all the hiding places. Terrible, said Christa, her small face pale. Because didn't Mum think Stefan was just the kind of beautiful child the skewer-eyed men would like?

Stefan, so much younger than Christa, knew some of the stories as well. Even at four years old he had the same fears. He had curious nightmares, as well – humpbacked surgeons who could pull the bones from your body to make bead necklaces, and about someone called the scissor man who stitched live babies together in order to watch what happened to them when they grew bigger. It was true, he said, clinging to Giselle after one of his nightmares, pleading with her never to let the scissor man or the humpbacked doctor find them.

He was heartbreakingly small, sitting up in the bed, tear-streaked from the bad dream, but so trusting and vulnerable, and so beautiful with his dark eyes and his hair like thin black shavings from a raven's wing. Giselle could not bear seeing him like this. She hugged him to her, and promised that she would not let any of those things happen. She would always be here to protect him, she said, and so would Father and Christa. As for the things he feared – none of them could happen anywhere in the world. They were nightmare phantoms, that was all. Things to be blown away like thistle heads.

Felix, coming in after one of these nightmares, sat on the edge of the bed, and said Stefan – Christa too, for she had come into the bedroom – should remember that although there were a lot of things going on in Germany at the moment, none of them would affect the lives of unimportant music teachers. They certainly would not affect the lives of children.

Giselle glanced at Christa, and yet again had the impression of a darkness gathering behind her daughter's eyes. But this was absurd; fifteen-year-old girls were notoriously moody and strange. She thrust the feeling away, and joined with Felix in telling the children that they were all perfectly safe in their warm snug house overlooking the square. Life would continue quietly along for a great many years.

There was, though, a slight interruption to the quiet life that spring, when Giselle was invited to a cousin's wedding. It meant a long train journey, and although Felix was included in the invitation, he did not think he could close the shop or ignore his pupils for an entire week. Bills had to be paid, he said, ruefully. Giselle must go, though. She would like to see her family – she had always been so close to her cousin, Silke, and Felix would enjoy hearing all about it when she came back.

Giselle thought, but did not say, that Felix was secretly quite pleased to find a reason to stay at home with his music and his work and his pupils. And he might be impractical, but he was quite able to manage without Giselle for four days. He could give Christa and Stefan their breakfast – in fact Christa was perfectly capable of getting breakfast for them all, and taking herself and Stefan to school. Velda would probably help out, anyway.

Velda, approached on the matter, said that of course she would look after Felix and the children. Giselle managed not to remind Velda that Christa was now at an age where she could hardly be classed as a child.

Velda did, though, express doubts as to the wisdom of Giselle's journey.

'All that way when there's so much disruption, and travelling such a nightmare. But I suppose you were up to your eyebrows in gin when the invitation came, and you didn't think about that.'

Giselle had not been up to her eyebrows in gin when the invitation came, and it was ungenerous of Velda to suggest it.

'And I don't see that travelling's any more difficult now than it's been for ages.'

'Of course it is,' said Velda. 'I hear the Schutzstaffel are starting to board trains to ask about people's journeys—'

'I can't think why the Schutzstaffel would be interested in a perfectly ordinary family wedding—'

'—demanding to see people's papers and poking into innocent folks' backgrounds,' finished Velda.

'Oh, pooh to the Schutzstaffel. My papers are perfectly in order, and you're exaggerating. In any case, I'll only be away for four days, well, five at the most. I daresay I can trust you with Felix for such a short time, can't I?' Giselle said this last a bit slyly, because everyone in the family knew that Velda had fallen helplessly and hopelessly in love with Felix from the moment she saw him.

Still, it had to be acknowledged that Velda had uncomplainingly taken on the role of good friend and loyal cousin, although it had been vaguely annoying when she had moved into an apartment so near the shop. Giselle had sometimes felt a bit smothered, especially in the early days of the marriage, when she liked to lure Felix up to bed for the afternoon. At such times you did not want people knocking on the door because they were worried as to why the shop had the 'Closed' sign at three o'clock in the afternoon, or they had brought over a freshly baked cake. To say the very least, it spoiled the romance if you had to open the bedroom window and shout down some excuse about a headache, especially with Felix urging you to get rid of whoever was interrupting them, and come back to bed.

Giselle sometimes wondered, with a pleased chuckle of satisfaction, whether anyone ever guessed how extremely passionate Felix was under the diffident, scholarly exterior. Once or twice she had even wondered if Velda, who to Giselle's certain knowledge had never had any kind of sexual or romantic relationship whatsoever, had unconsciously sensed it, and if that was the reason for her infatuation. Still, all credit to Velda, she was generous with her time, and the cakes were delicious.

Most of Felix's musician friends came to The Music House to say farewell and safe journey before Giselle set off. Velda, who came in to bring a wedding gift for the cousin and stayed to have a glass of wine, said you would think Giselle was travelling to the farthest reaches of Outer Mongolia or the Russian Steppes.

'It's only Salzkotten,' said Velda, a bit grumpily, probably, Giselle thought, because she had not been invited to the wedding. 'Not far.'

'The best part of a day's journey, though.'

Dear chubby Herr Eisler, who liked to think he was a bit of a father-figure to them all, recited the *Tefilat HaDerech*, which was the Jewish travellers' prayer. It did not matter in the least that he got so carried away with emotion he spilled an entire glass of wine on the carpet, and forgot the last lines. After the wine had been mopped up and Eisler's glass refilled, a lively discussion sprang up about the programme for Felix's next concert. Some of the musicians were all for defying Herr Hitler's disapprovals and his bans on composers, and said firmly that they should play whatever they wanted.

'Because we don't care about bans,' said Giselle, who had been drinking her own share of the wine.

'Nor do we. For heaven's sake, they'll have musicians fleeing the country next.'

'They already are fleeing the country. Hindemith went last year. Where have you been living?'

'It's true that Hindemith went,' said Felix's cellist. 'And only last week Karel Ancerl was sent to . . .' The cellist broke off, and looked uneasily round the room. 'He was sent away,' he said, in a quieter voice.

'I heard that too,' said the first speaker. 'But there's a lot of exaggerated gossip around.'

'We might do one of your own pieces at the concert, Felix,' said a violinist, clearly with the idea of changing the subject, and Felix looked up, and mumbled, embarrassedly, that his music was nothing very special, and he had not known anyone realized he had even composed anything.

It was all friendly and safe. The window shutters were not completely closed, because Felix liked being able to see out to the cobbled square. Giselle liked that, as well. At this time of the evening the lamps had been lit, and their light fell across the old buildings, making it almost possible to believe that you had stepped back into Lindschoen's past. It was comforting and reassuring, and Giselle almost wished she were not going away tomorrow. From her chair, she could see the sign outside that hung over the door, and that told people this was The Music House of: *Felix Klein, Music lessons by appointment, musical instruments and sheet music sold and bought. Hours of business: 10.00 a.m. to 6.00 p.m.*

A little flurry of wind blew on the streetlamps and the sign creaked slightly. The fire in the room flared up as if something outside had huffed its breath down into the chimney. It was ridiculous to suddenly feel that the room and some of the people in it might no longer be safe.

Giselle liked train journeys, and she would like this one. You did not often see ladies travelling alone, so it was possible that people might speculate as to who she was and where she was going. She would be a mysterious lady, keeping a romantic and illicit assignation. Or she might be a foreign aristocrat fleeing from some nameless menace – no, that was not a good image to seek; in fact it was a very tasteless idea altogether, with all those poor souls in Czechoslovakia being dispossessed of their homes on account of Herr Hitler laying his greedy hands on the country. Giselle would stay with the illicit love affair idea.

It would be good to see Silke again, and meet the man she was finally going to marry. Giselle hoped the marriage would turn out well, because Silke had been quite a lively girl over the years. There had been several adventures – some of which Aunt Friede and Uncle Avram had known about, but some which they had never so much as suspected. And there had been one man in particular . . . Giselle knew perfectly well that Silke had never got over that, and that probably she never would, but there was nothing that could be done about it.

The train rattled cheerfully along. Giselle had brought a notebook, because she thought she might keep a journal of the trip, like one of the nineteenth-century ladies who recorded their travels for posterity, confiding all manner of scandalous experiences to the pages. She would not have any scandalous experiences, of course, but if she did, she would not record any of them, because Felix might read the journal, and he was apt to get quite jealous over the most trivial of flirtations. He had got in quite a fluster about dear old Eisler once, because he had seen Eisler give Giselle a kiss on her birthday. Giselle had told him there was nothing to worry about, because the wife of the second violinist in Felix's orchestra had once had a brief affair with Eisler, and had reported to Giselle that Eisler could not achieve a crescendo worth mentioning. This, said the violinist's wife, crossly, was the trouble with dedicated musicians; they were apt to pour their passions into their music, leaving nothing to spare for their wives and lovers.

'I didn't tell her that wasn't a criticism that could be levelled at you,' Giselle had said to Felix, who was laughing. 'I didn't want to sound smug.'

She stopped thinking about Felix, and instead contemplated, with pleasure, her costume for the wedding. It was green shantung, with a clinging waistline and it had cost far more than Giselle could really justify, so there had been no need to tell Felix the exact cost. But there would be a great many smart and prosperous people at Silke's wedding, and Giselle was not going to have the family eyeing her disparagingly, or snarky aunts telling one another that poorest Giselle looked very down-at-heel, but what could you expect, with the silly girl marrying a penniless musician.

The train bumbled cheerfully along, and Giselle made a few notes about the scenery. Here was Brandenburg, considerably more citified than she had expected, but still with glimpses of its medieval past. She recorded this, adding a couple of sentences about how Bach had presented bound manuscripts of his marvellous *Brandenburg Concertos* to the Margrave of Brandenburg – and how the Margrave, miserable old miser, had never paid Bach. Reading this over made her feel pleasantly scholarly. She would make sure Felix saw that part.

It was infuriating when Velda's gloomy prognostications turned out to be right, and six or eight Schutzstaffel men boarded the train at the next station. It was even more infuriating that Velda had also been right when she said they demanded to see papers and identification. They worked their way along the train, and when they reached Giselle's compartment, she assumed her best aristocratic air, and languidly handed over the requisite documents. The SS man looked at them coldly, then handed them back, with a curt word of thanks. He might be regarded as good-looking if it had not been for his eyes, which were frosty. Stefan and Christa had been right to talk about skewer eyes.

But the SS man asked, equably enough, about her journey, and Giselle said she was travelling to Salzkotten to attend a cousin's wedding. There seemed no reason not to give Silke's name, which was information that anyone could easily find, although it was slightly disconcerting to see it written down. Giselle was relieved when the Schutzstaffel left the train at the next station and got into several jeeps that were waiting for them. The jeeps drove away with a lot of engine-revving and unnecessary spinning of tyres, and the train trundled on its way again.

Silke had promised that if she could not be at the station to meet Giselle, someone would be waiting for her, but when the train chugged in, the platform was deserted. Still, Giselle could easily hop on a tram that would take her to the end of Silke's road, within a few steps of the house. A porter wandered up and helped carry her case to the tram stop.

It was nice to be coming here again. Giselle pressed eagerly against the window as the tram rattled along, so as not to miss the familiar landmarks. Here was the park where the Hederauenfest was usually held. She and Silke used to go to that if they could – it was marvellous mix of music and market stalls and specially written one-act plays, and interesting people. They had met two boys there one year, and Aunt Friede had been furious when they were late getting home, and even more furious to see that Giselle's lipstick was smudged, and Silke's blouse was wrongly buttoned up.

Giselle smiled at these memories, which, at a distance of years, seemed almost innocent, then looked across at the other window. The frivolous thoughts vanished at once, because in the distance was the grim outline of Wewelsburg Castle. She and Silke used to make up stories about it: how ogres might live inside it, or prisoners be kept chained in its depths for numberless years. All nonsense, of course . . .

Even so, the castle was a place, in which any number of macabre *Grand Guignol* atrocities might have taken place. Silke had said it was rumoured that Heinrich Himmler had acquired it and was intending to turn it into some kind of cultural centre for SS officers. They were bringing in political prisoners from the nearby Sachsenhausen camp to work on the remodelling, said Silke, which scarcely bore thinking about, because Herr Himmler would be a cruel overmaster. As for the cultural centre, Silke did not believe it would ever materialize. Giselle, who had once seen Herr Himmler at a rally, and who did not think he would know culture if it smacked him in the face, did not think so either.

She reached for her notebook. The tram journey would only be a short one, but there were several stops along the way, so she could scribble a note to Felix to let him know she had arrived.

There were SS men on the train, and the officer who came into my carriage had the coldest eyes I have ever seen. He was wearing one of Herr Himmler's death's head rings – all grinning skull and runic symbols and cold-looking silver. I remembered how it's strictly forbidden for those rings to be bought or sold, and how they must never fall into the hands of anyone not entitled to wear them, so I thought the SS man must be quite a high-ranking officer, and I was polite and very nearly demure.

We've just trundled past Wewelsburg Castle. It's like a crouching nightmare, that place. If anyone were to write music about it, it would be the kind of music that's filled with menace. Sonorous and with a feeling of approaching danger. Mussorgsky's *Night on Bald Mountain,* perhaps, or *Mars* from Holst's *Planet Suite.*

Even from the road you can see the stone walls, and visualize dank underground rooms . . . I think that once, people were left in those rooms and forgotten, and I think more people might be left there in the future and they'll be forgotten, too.

Are you smiling as you read all that? Thinking, 'She is so dramatic always, that Giselle.' But I'm only really dramatic for you, Felix, my love, because you're the only one who understands.

The tram's just approaching Silke's road, so I'll seal this up, and coax an envelope and a stamp from somebody.

Very much love.

She did not sign it; she put their private symbol ≣ which was the mark known in music as the *ghost note.* Felix had once tried to explain this command to her, and Giselle had laughed, and said whatever it meant to musicians, she would always be the ghost note in his life and in the children's, because she would always be around. Even though they might not actually see her, she would be close to them, so they had always better behave. Since then she had used it as a signature, even if it was just a note saying she would be late back from shopping, or to ask Christa to switch on the stove to heat their supper.

SEVEN

The wide, tree-lined avenue where Silke's family lived was in quite a prosperous part of Salzkotten, because Silke's parents were quite prosperous.

'My father buys and sells and loans everything and anything – including money – and he always makes a profit,' Silke once said, and Giselle had never been able to decide if Silke meant this admiringly or even affectionately, or if she was being disparaging.

As Giselle got down from the tram, and set off along the street, she was already imagining the turmoil that would greet her. Family would be calling at the house, rabbis would be discussing last-minute details . . . Caterers and florists and dressmakers would be delivering satin-striped boxes. And Silke would be at the centre, loving the fuss and the attention.

The gates were partly open, but the big double doors at the house's centre were closed. No cars or vans were visible, but across one smooth lawn were tyre tracks – tracks that had gouged such deep ruts in the grass that only a very heavy vehicle could have made them. Giselle felt a stab of unease at this, because the lawns were mowed and practically manicured all year round.

She began to walk slowly towards the house, but the nearer she got, the more her unease deepened. There was something very wrong. It was not just that evidence of a large vehicle – several vehicles? – having been driven across the grass; there was something sinister. She took several deep breaths, forcing herself to calm down. Nothing would be wrong. At any minute Silke or her mother would come running out of the house, laughing, telling some story about a disaster, holding out hands of welcome.

As she approached the house, she kept to the narrow grass edges, so as not to make crunching footsteps on the gravel paths that might be heard. This was absurd, and in another minute her mind would start working again, and she would know what seemed to be so dreadfully wrong.

And then she did know. Across the front door, drawn in thick yellow paint, was a symbol that had been part of Giselle's life for as long as she could remember. A symbol that was in synagogues and houses – a symbol that came down from medieval Arabic literature, from the days when it had been used in talismans and protective amulets, and that once had been known as a Seal of Solomon . . . A familiar and ancient outline that illuminated the marvellous sacred manuscripts of the Jewish faith.

But it was also a symbol that the Nazis had seized on with brutal greed, and that they painted with vicious hatred on the doors of Jewish families and Jewish businesses after they had dragged them away to the labour camps. Then, the mark was as damning as the red cross on a plague house or the brand on a murderer's forehead, and the sight of it was as chilling and as frightening as the chime of a leper's bell in the night.

The Star of David.

The Schutzstaffel had broken into the house.

Fear and horror engulfed Giselle in a sick, smothering wave; then she began to run across the last few yards towards the house, dropping her suitcase, not noticing she had done so. A voice close to her was repeating, 'Please let them be all right – please let them all be safe,' and she realized with a shock that it was her own voice.

But even from here, she could see that beneath the crudely painted hexagram were the words, *Die Juden sind unser Unglück!* 'The Jews Are Our Misfortune!'

It might still be all right. They might still be in there – Silke with her mischievous grin and her warm charm might be perfectly safe. Silke's mother, who was a plumper, softer version of Silke, would surely be unscathed. As for Uncle Avram – it was impossible to think of him being cowed by anyone, even the Schutzstaffel.

Giselle stumbled breathlessly across the last couple of yards, and half fell through the unlocked door. The familiar scents of the house came at her instantly; polish and potpourri, with beneath it a faint drift of food, because Aunt Friede would have been overseeing the preparations of all the traditional dishes. Silke had written that the menu was going to be so lavish, she would probably put on at least five kilos and people would start nicknaming her Dumpling or Pudding Face.

The square hall with the black-and-white chequered floor was silent, but a small table had been overturned, and a vase of flowers lay in fragments, amidst spilled water. Through the open dining-room door a caterer's trestle table was partly laid with white damask and gleaming silver for the wedding breakfast.

Giselle opened the doors into all the other rooms, doing so tentatively, not knowing what she might find. But they were all empty, although there were traces of disturbance everywhere: overturned chairs, mirrors smashed, rugs ruckled.

In Uncle Avram's study there was a stench of burning, and the fireplace was crammed with a tumble of books, charred and burned beyond recognition. Giselle stared at this with anger and pain, then went back to the hall. If she walked out of the house now, she could retrieve her suitcase, and get a tram to the railway station. She could be back with Felix and the children by this evening.

But first she must find out what had happened to Silke and to her aunt and uncle. She climbed slowly up the wide sweep of stairs. Silke's bedroom was ahead, and Giselle went inside fearfully. The room was undisturbed, and she sat on the edge of the bed, trying to think what to do. Who did you go to if you wanted to find out whether your cousin had been taken away to a labour camp? Could she get a telephone call through to Felix? No, she could not do that, because he would be worried to death to think of her in this situation. Had Silke been worried about Giselle arriving and finding this desolate emptiness?

With this thought, something brushed the surface of her mind. She and Silke had always been close, closer than some sisters, even. They had shared all their secrets – not even Felix knew of some of those secrets. 'Better not,' Silke had said.

And now, Giselle had a picture of Silke coming up here to get away from the flurry of the wedding preparations. Lying on the bed with a book for an hour, perhaps? Whatever she had been doing, she would have heard the jeeps roar across the drive, and looked through the window to see what was happening.

There would have been no time for her to run away, and in any case she would not have abandoned her parents. But she had known Giselle would shortly arrive – was it possible she had had time to leave a clue? Giselle had a sudden strong sense of Silke wanting to let her know what had happened and where they were being taken. But what kind of clue could she have left in those last frantic moments? She stared round the room. There was a big wardrobe against the wall with Silke's clothes inside, all on hangers. Nothing in there. The dressing table had only its usual slight untidiness – boxes of face powder, scent bottles, hairbrushes. The drawers contained a froth of under-things and silk stockings.

But on the bedside table was a small reading lamp, a little clock, and the book Silke had been reading with the bookmark still in it . . .

Giselle snatched the book up, and opened it at the marked place. The bookmark was an embroidered one, silk tasselled, and scribbled across the top was a single word.

Sachsenhausen.

Sachsenhausen. Something hard and cold closed around Giselle's throat. Sachsenhausen was the labour camp that lay almost in the shadow of Wewelsburg Castle. It was the place about which it was whispered that torture was practised, and where brutal executions of political prisoners took place. But before she could think any more, downstairs in the main hall a door opened, and footsteps crossed the hall. As she thrust the bookmark with its telltale writing back on the table, the footsteps came up the stairs. They were sharp steps, like steel claws on the ground, and Giselle shrank back on the bed, staring with panic at the door.

Dust motes whirled in and out of the light spilling into the room from the big landing, and then a tall, black-clad figure stood in the doorway looking at her. One hand rested on the door handle, and even through the sick panic, Giselle saw the dull glint of the death's head ring.

The voice she remembered from the train said, 'I've been waiting for you.'

It was infuriating to be so powerless and so feeble that he could twist her hands behind her back, and tie them together with cold efficiency. His fingers felt as if the bones were steel.

Giselle swore and kicked out, feeling a savage satisfaction when he winced. But already there were sounds of other SS men downstairs, and she wanted to weep with frustration and fear. She did not, though. She clung to the anger because she would not let these men see how terrified she was.

There was a blurred time after that; she hoped, much later, that she had not actually fainted, which would have been spineless of her. Through the blur she was dimly aware of being half carried, half dragged outside, and of two jeeps roaring up to the house. Where had they come from? Had they been parked somewhere out of sight, waiting until this last captive could be taken? And why had they come back for Giselle – for one lone female who surely could not pose any kind of threat to the Third Reich?

The man from the train sat next to her in the jeep. He did not look at her, but after they had travelled several kilometres, Giselle said, 'Why have I been taken prisoner?'

It was a stupid question. The SS did not need reasons for anything, even for imprisoning people.

But the man surprised her. He turned to meet her eyes, studying her as if he might find her of some slight interest. With an un-expected note of politeness, he said, 'I am SS-Obersturmbannführer Reinhardt. Your cousin and her family were taken by the Schutzstaffel because they infringed laws passed in Nuremberg in 1935.'

'You always quote Nuremberg as your excuse,' said Giselle, angrily. 'The truth is that you incarcerate Jewish men and women in labour camps because Herr Hitler is frightened of them. I heard he's even becoming frightened of people who are half- or only a quarter-Jewish.'

She could hardly believe she had said this, but furious defiance was driving her. She would not have been surprised if the man struck her, but he only said, 'The Führer is striving for a pure race. But in this case, the man who I think is your uncle has involved himself in forbidden financial dealings and been part of secret negotiations that could damage the Third Reich.'

Giselle thought: but you don't know that there's another secret within that family – a secret that has nothing to do with shady financial deals. If you knew that secret, you'd already be taking them to the death trenches to be shot.

She looked out of the window, and said, 'I haven't arranged secret loans or anything. I haven't a clue about money or banking. Except for never having any money.'

Reinhardt – Giselle refused to think of him by his rank – said, 'You've been taken for a very different reason.'

Cold fear clenched Giselle's stomach. He doesn't know about Silke – about what she did – but perhaps he suspects. Perhaps that's why he's taken me – so he can torture me to find out.

But Reinhardt said, 'We have watched you – and your own family in Lindschoen – for some while.'

This did not sound as if it had anything to do with Silke, but it brought a different fear. Giselle was aware of sick repulsion at the thought that she and Felix could have been watched – that Christa and Stefan might have been followed to and from their small innocent activities.

'Today we followed you from your husband's music shop, and we boarded your train at a later station,' he said. 'During the journey I checked your identity papers to make sure we had the right person. You know that, though.' His eyes swept over her. 'And now here you are, Giselle,' he said, softly.

The situation was starting to feel as if it had been spun from nightmares, but there was an unreal element to it, because when Reinhardt said her name, Giselle felt a bolt of sexual interest from him. For several seconds she could not look away, but when finally she did so, her thoughts were in chaos. He's finding me attractive, she thought. He's even wondering if he might take me to bed. Am I imagining that? But she did not think she was. It might be purely because she was his prisoner – that he had power over her. But with the conviction that a spark had been lit, she knew that if Reinhardt were to beckon, and if it might mean escaping, she would acquiesce without hesitation. I wouldn't care who or what he is, thought Giselle; I'd get into bed with Hitler and the entire Third Reich if it meant I could get back to Felix and the children.

But he turned away from her, watching the passing scenery through the jeep's window, clearly regarding the discussion as at an end.

Keep that spark alive, thought Giselle. Don't let go of it. Keep him talking; move your leg slightly along the seat so that your thigh touches his. Good. He's reacted, I know he has. Forgive me, Felix.

In a gentler voice, she said, 'Would you at least tell me where I'm being taken?' It would almost certainly be Sachsenhausen. The place with the death trenches and the experiments. The humpbacked surgeons and the scissor man . . . Stefan, you odd, precious little scrap, where did you get those images? Because I have a terrible fear that I'm being taken to the black core of them.

Reinhardt said, 'You are being taken to Wewelsburg Castle.'

As he spoke, the driver engaged a lower gear, and the jeep began a steady ascent. Above them, grey and grim, exactly as Giselle had described it in her letter to Felix, (the letter that would never, now, be sent), the dark outline of Wewelsburg Castle came into view.

EIGHT

The journey to Greymarsh House was enlivened by Toby's enthusiastic plans for the compilation of an anthology of bawdy ballads, together with their origins. Phin vaguely remembered this possibility having been broached during the party.

Toby thought it was a splendid idea. They could do it together in their spare time, he said, and Phin became so swept along by Toby's enthusiasm that he scrabbled in his case for a notebook and pen.

'We'd have to go back as far as we could,' he said, trying to ignore Toby's erratic method of driving. 'Medieval at least. And divide the sections into the centuries, I should think. The Elizabethans would take up a big section.'

'Some very good Elizabethan drinking songs,' agreed Toby. 'And what about twentieth-century war songs? All those rude choruses about Hitler and Goebbels. Or would that be regarded as racist nowadays?'

'Well, it might.'

'Fair enough. Did the Germans have rude propaganda songs about us, do you think?'

'They certainly had propaganda, but I think it was a bit different. Postcards showing scantily clad German ladies tempting English soldiers who were supposed to be fighting the war. The Luftwaffe used to drop them over the Kent coast. I remember my grandfather telling me. He was in the Battle of Britain – he was shot down and taken as a prisoner-of-war.'

'Maybe we'd better leave war stuff alone,' said Toby. 'How about French boudoir ballads? Oh, and Bavarian drinking songs – we'd want to include those.'

It was at this point that Phin suddenly saw the proposed anthology as a genuine possibility. He wondered how his agent would view the prospect of trying to sell to publishers a book on the history of bawdy ballads, given that the name of Phineas Fox was more usually associated with the lives of serious composers and musicians. Most likely his agent would say, cheerfully, 'Sex sells,' and start firing off emails to publishers there and then.

They had lunch in Maidstone, where Toby consumed two platefuls of roast beef and assorted vegetables, followed by treacle pudding and custard. Phin fared more modestly on ham salad. He suggested he take the wheel for the rest of journey, although he did so hesitantly, having by now realized that the driving of Toby's car was an art form of its own. And in fact the car, when they went back to it, was grumpily reluctant to start at all, and had to be persuaded to fire by Toby bouncing up and down on the bonnet, which was, he explained, usually helpful in dislodging the recalcitrant starter motor.

'Don't worry, it'll catch in a minute, it always does . . . No, don't press the accelerator yet, it'll only flood the engine . . . Good thing I had that treacle pudding, isn't it, it adds a bit of weight to the bouncing . . . There it goes, what did I tell you? I'd better drive after all, if you don't mind – the clutch has a habit of slipping.'

As they drove off, Phin remembered he still had no idea what Toby actually did for a living.

'Eternal student,' said Toby, airily. 'No – that's not absolutely accurate. More what they call a mature student. The only difference is that it takes twice as long to get a degree.'

The student thing probably explained a good deal of Toby's current lifestyle, but Phin said, carefully, 'What exactly are you—'

'Medicine, old chap. Blood and bones and muscles and identifying a measle. Wasn't it obvious from the mad companions – everyone letting off steam after a solemn day on the wards or at the dissecting tables. It's a bit of a family thing, medicine, so after I'd racketed around, doing sod all, it was put to me that it was time I got down to some real work.' He frowned at a set of traffic lights. 'Three years along now, and the fourth looming. It's a lot of hard work, but I rather like it. I'll never be one of those high-flyers, finding a cure for something obscure, or performing complicated surgical procedures. Although I might trot over to one of those Third World places sometime and lend a bit of a hand there.' He shot Phin a half-embarrassed glance. 'Actually, I'll probably end up sewing cuts in A&E or changing catheters and dishing out antibiotics. Although I don't think I'd mind that.'

'I don't know whether to be astonished or full of admiration.
A bit of both, I think.'

'Oh, it's no big deal. All you do is memorize everything, and
quote the Latin, which impresses people, and not get mixed up
between hypo and hyper.'

Phin said, 'No lady in the picture? There were one or two very
attractive ones at your party.'

'Haven't met one I'd fancy as a permanency,' said Toby. 'I like
to love them all a little bit. Safety in numbers. Also, more fun.'
By way of illustration of this, he launched into a verse of, 'If I
Were the Marrying Kind,' which was abruptly terminated when
he spotted the sign for Thornchurch and swung the car across the
road.

As they went deeper into the marshland county, the landscape
began to flatten and the roads were intersected by drainage
ditches. There were glimpses of river walls within the rolling
marshlands, and here and there, old Martello towers jutted up
– most of them were derelict or completely ruined, although one
or two appeared to have been restored, and looked as if they
were even inhabited.

On the outskirts of Thornchurch itself, Toby pointed out an
old corn exchange. 'The godfather used to give language lessons
there. Adult learning classes – German language, obviously, but
with a sprinkling of German literature alongside, and a dash of
Jewish stuff here and there. Unusual mixture, isn't it? He was a
very good teacher, though, I think. Very patient and imaginative.
Arabella's picked up a fair amount of German from him over
the years.'

Phin liked Thornchurch, with its skewed buildings, and the
nice old shops in the main street. There was an air of contentment
about it, although he could not decide if this would be restful, or
if it was something that might start to seem slightly complacent
and a bit annoying after a while. But he could certainly sympathize
with Arabella, who apparently regarded the place as somewhere
to commune with nature and reach an inner gothic soul.

As they drove through the main street, his mind was racing
ahead to Stefan Cain's house. Would there be clues there about
Christa – about Giselle? Would there be dusty attics or cellars
with fragments of diaries or old music? This, however, seemed

to be straying so far into romantic novel territory that Phin abandoned the images. Even so, as Toby turned into a hedge-lined road just beyond the little town, he thought it would be a bit of a let-down if Greymarsh turned out to be a square modern box with symmetric walls and windows, and false cladding glued on to its front.

But Greymarsh was not square or modern at all. It was a nice old greystone house in modest gardens, with fields stretching all around it, and it had the air of having stood up to buffeting east coast winds for a good many years, and of being prepared to do so for a good many more. Twisty chimneys adorned the roof – in colder weather the mist would rise from the marshes and cling to those chimneys. Two tiny windows immediately under the eaves proclaimed the existence of attics, and old trees had grown up around the house. One was so close to the house that on windy nights its branches must tap eerily against the panes. Stefan Cain would know the sounds for what they were, though, and they would not spook him. Had they ever spooked Arabella? But Phin thought Arabella probably wove gleeful and improbable tales around any night-time window-tappings.

It was growing dark, and shadows had crept over the garden. Phin found the place so satisfyingly close to the secretive marsh-lands house he had been visualizing that he sat in the car absorbing its appearance for several minutes, until Toby's voice broke in, saying would he mind moving his arse and helping to get the suitcases from the boot, and not to forget Christa as well.

'We don't have to grub around under flowerpots for concealed keys or scale the walls to get in through the bathroom window, because I got the spare key from Arabella's flat yesterday,' said Toby, leading the way to the front door, which was set in a shallow porch. Once inside, he stooped down to pick up a couple of letters that lay in the hall, and Phin carried the painting in, propping it against a wall. He looked around the hall, which was larger than he had expected, and looked as if it might occasionally be used as a living area, because there was a deep button-back sofa against an open stairway, and two soft chairs. A large oak box-shaped piece of furniture stood at the centre – Phin thought it might be an old dower chest, pressed into service as an occasional table. Light filtered in from the narrow windows on each side of the main door and from a landing halfway up the stairs; it was a thick, blue-tinged light, and shadows lay everywhere. But they were gentle, comfortable shadows, and Phin had the feeling that over the years they had probably shaped themselves to fit round the furniture. Then Toby reached for a light switch, and the shadows jumped back and the hall came into friendly, well-lit focus.

'I'll go through all the rooms and check windows and things in case the intruder did rampage through the house,' said Toby. 'We can go along to The Woolpack for supper later if you want, but I daresay Stefan won't mind if we plunder the pantry.'

'Let's not bother trekking out again,' said Phin, conscious that Toby had done all the driving that day. 'If there's food in the house, we can put together a meal. Can I make a cup of tea while you look round, or d'you want me to come with you?'

'Cup of tea'd be just the ticket. The kitchen's through there.'

As Phin went into the big kitchen, Toby clattered around the house, calling out comments to Phin at intervals, none of which Phin could properly hear.

'All fine as far as I can see,' said Toby, coming into the kitchen. 'I haven't checked the attics, but you have to climb up through one of those hatches in a ceiling, and I shouldn't think anyone could get in that way. So for the moment I can't see how the burglar did get in. I suppose Stefan might have left a door unlocked, although that's not very likely.'

'He might have known whoever it was, and simply let him in,' said Phin, putting the mugs of tea on the kitchen table.

'Yes, although the police said it was very early in the morning. He heard someone and went downstairs to investigate.'

'There's plenty of bread and milk,' said Phin. 'And eggs and cheese in the fridge, and tins in the cupboards. Oh, and a few pizzas and things in the freezer. So we'd be all right for a meal here tonight – and tomorrow as well, from the look of it. And I checked the kitchen door – it leads to the garden, doesn't it? It's locked and the lock's fine.' He drank his tea. 'Where did the portrait live?' he said.

'Stefan's study. Sort of extra sitting room. I'll show you. Bring your tea.'

His sister's portrait must have faced Stefan Cain every night. Clearly he had sat in the deep wingchair with Christa in direct sightline. The portrait had left its ghost outline against the wallpaper.

It was a comfortable room. Books filled shelves set into the alcoves on each side of the fireplace, and there was a television and a stereo. Had Stefan Cain listened to music or watched television or read his books, with Christa looking down? Had he felt at home like that? If so, why had he so abruptly got rid of the painting?

Toby broke into Phin's thoughts, by remembering the letters he had picked up from the hall floor.

'When the medics told Stefan I was coming down, he asked if I'd check any post for him, and any phone messages. There were only these two letters – they both look like bills or circulars, and—'

'What's wrong?' said Phin, as Toby broke off, and stared at the top envelope.

'This one's from Arabella.'

'Are you sure?'

'Yes, she's put her address on the back. Stefan hasn't got an internet connection – Arabella usually phones him, but sometimes she writes. I'll have to open this.'

'But it's addressed to your godfather. You'll see him tomorrow – you can let him have it then.'

'Yes, but . . . Arabella hasn't been at her flat for forty-eight hours, if not longer, and somebody broke in here and bashed poor old Stefan on the head, and this might tell us something about what's been going on. Even the few hours between now and tomorrow's visiting time might matter.'

He looked at Phin like a hopeful spaniel, and Phin said, a bit reluctantly, 'Yes, I do see that. All right.'

Toby tore at the envelope and drew out the single sheet inside. It was printed, but the signature at the foot was a generous scrawl. At the top was the address of the Pimlico flat. Arabella had written:

> Dearest godfather,
>
> Didn't we have a terrific supper party for your birthday? And I've managed to match up that Sèvres bowl that so unaccountably broke – you were absolutely right when you said it wouldn't be ovenproof. But I found the *exact* same bowl in the Portobello Road. It'll be a copy, but it's a very good copy, and no one will ever know.

'That'll be Stefan's birthday dinner,' said Toby. 'She was going to cook a meal for him and a few neighbours. She can cook quite well, but you can't guarantee the results. You either get a five-course *cordon bleu* banquet, or it goes disastrously wrong and she has to phone for pizza delivery or send somebody out for fish and chips.' He returned to the letter.

> I'm going to Toby's party later this week on account of wanting to meet the fascinating Phineas Fox – Toby's new neighbour – I told you about him, didn't I? So far, I've only seen him from the window of Toby's flat, but what I saw was very intriguing indeed! I'm hoping he isn't indissolubly welded to some knock-out intellectual female who discourses academically on late-night BBC2 programmes about things nobody has heard of. I'm going to make a grand entrance at the party, then, like the old song, 'After the Ball is Over . . .' Well, you never know what might happen after the ball is over.
>
> Isn't it remarkable that I can say things like that to you? I can't to Toby – he's astonishingly strait-laced when it comes to me. I didn't dare tell him about that utter *rat* last Christmas, may he succumb to the Ten Plagues of Egypt. The one you said you'd horsewhip, do you remember? – which was gorgeously Victorian and protective of you.
>
> Now listen, when the roofing men come, in the name of the goddess Hestia will you *please* leave them to do all the work, and not caper around trying to help? [Scholarly footnote: Hestia is the virgin goddess of the hearth, architecture and the 'right ordering of domesticity'. I know this because I looked it up so as to impress you.]
>
> I know the work'll be disruptive and they'll have to clear stuff out of the attics, but that might be quite interesting, because you never know what might be found. Forgotten Old Masters, and ancestors' old mistresses.
>
> Lots of very high-quality love, Arabella.

Toby folded the letter and put it back in the envelope. 'She sounds as if she was all right when she wrote that, doesn't she?' he said.

'Very much all right.'

'I knew all about the rat last Christmas, of course, although I didn't know Stefan threatened to horsewhip him.' He sent Phin a grin. 'She sounds quite smitten with you, doesn't she? If it came to pistols at dawn between Arabella and your redhead, which one would you put money on?'

'You're sinking into fantasy,' said Phin, repressively, but he was suddenly reminded that the lady with copper hair had the habit of taking command in almost any situation, and that – faced with Toby's improbable duel – she might turn out to be rather unattractively aggressive. To quench this he said, 'Do you feel reassured about Arabella?'

'Well, I think I do. It's still odd that she isn't answering her phone, but she might be somewhere where the signal's poor.'

'What's the other letter? Is it anything you should check?'

'Looks like a circular,' said Toby 'Probably a local mailing. Oh wait, there's something enclosed . . .'

The second letter was not a circular and the enclosure was a door key. The letter was from a firm of roofing contracts in Thornchurch, dated the previous day, and it said:

Dear Mr Cain,

Enclosed is our estimate for the re-felting work to the south side of the roof of Greymarsh, as discussed.

We finished clearing out most of the attic in readiness for the work while you were out, and we put the majority of the stuff in your dining room, as you suggested. The roof hatch is back in place, and we cleared up the dust that got disturbed in the process. We will clean up more thoroughly after the work is completed, and we can take the attic things back up there at the same time. As you know, we hope to make a start early next week. Could you phone to confirm that this is all acceptable?

The door key you lent me is enclosed.

'That's the roofing work Arabella mentioned. And the clearing out of the attics.'

'Yes. Could it explain how a burglar might have got in?' asked Phin. 'If the men had a key . . . If a key was in circulation—'

'It raises the question, doesn't it? Especially if somebody in the roofing company's a – what's the expression? – "a snapper-up of unconsidered trifles". I don't know who said that, although I expect it was old Bill Shakespeare, because it usually was, and if it wasn't him it was the Bible.'

Phin said, 'Could we see what's been brought down from the attic?'

NINE

'I shouldn't think,' said Toby, leading the way across the hall, 'that there was anything in the attics except household junk.'

'It's worth taking a look, though.'

'In case there're mouldering diaries in Christa's fair hand?'

'You never know. Is this the dining room?' asked Phin as Toby opened the door, and switched on a light.

'Yes. I always think there's an atmosphere of old gravy and abandoned suet pudding in here. Stefan generally eats in the kitchen or off a tray if he's on his own. Arabella probably jazzed the room up for the birthday dinner, though. An ice sculpture or imported Nautch dancers between the main course and the pudding.'

From what Phin already knew of Arabella Tallis, either of these seemed perfectly likely.

Several battered-looking cardboard boxes stood on the table, together with a bundle of what looked like old curtains, and a tea chest containing discarded kitchen utensils.

'Did the roof people say they cleaned up after they'd stomped around in the attic?' said Toby. 'It doesn't look as if they cleaned these up; they're all thick with dust – oh, and a few spiders for good measure.'

'It looks as if Stefan – or someone – did take a look at them,' said Phin, swatting the spiders away. 'That flap's been prised up – quite recently by the look of it. And you can see marks where there might have been sticky tape or Sellotape across the top.'

'And fingerprints in the dust. Although that might be the workmen, of course. Is it worth looking inside?'

'We could make sure there isn't anything about Christa,' said Phin, sitting down at the table. 'Although at first sight – this one's mostly stuffed with old magazines and ancient gardening catalogues.'

'This one's got a stack of what look like the minutes from parish council meetings. 1960s, I think,' said Toby, pulling up a dining chair and reaching for one of the other boxes. 'And a handful of old postcards – the kind people used to send in the 1950s. Bognor and Bournemouth, and weather dreadful, wish you were here. None of this is the era we want, though, is it? Have you got anything more exciting?'

'I don't think so.' Phin had been investigating a bundle of old books packed into the third box. The pages were badly foxed and the covers were so rubbed it was almost impossible to make out the titles.

'These are nearly all in German,' he said, after several moments. 'They look like textbooks – from when your godfather taught those adult language classes, maybe.'

But alongside the books was a large manila envelope, creased and with the edges curling. Phin started to open it, then hesitated.

'Might this be private family stuff?'

'Shouldn't think so after it's been crumbling away in the attic for several decades. I'm near enough family, anyway. Let's see what it is.'

Trying not to hope there might be something about Christa or Giselle in the envelope, Phin reached inside. There was a faint dry rustle and the sensation of something old and forgotten stirring. He drew out the contents with care and laid them on the table, and the feeling vanished.

'Music,' said Toby, staring at the sheets Phin had spread out. 'That's unexpected. Or is it?'

'They're probably just discarded scores,' said Phin, although a pulse of anticipation was already tapping against his mind. 'There're only three – no, four pages. But . . .' He broke off, frowning.

'What is it?'

'The sheets are all handwritten. D'you see? Not printed. The music in Christa's portrait is handwritten as well.'

'The same music?'

'No idea.' Phin picked up the top sheet to see it more clearly. The inked notation had faded almost to sepia, but it was still readable. It was impossible to know if this was the hand that had written the portrait music, though, because music notation did not have characteristics in the way handwriting did. But at the top was a single word, as faded as the rest of the writing, but quite clear. And it did not proclaim this as *Giselle's Music*. It proclaimed it as something else – something so entirely unexpected that, as

Phin stared at it, a dizzying kaleidoscope began to whirl through his brain – a maelstrom of things half read, of fragmented stories half heard and imperfectly remembered, and of almost-forgotten rumours. He knew some of the stories and he had only ever quarter-believed them. He thought most people had only ever quarter-believed them. And yet there it was, written in sad, faded ink—

Toby's voice, asking what he had found, broke in, and it took a moment for Phin to realize where he was. He put the music carefully down on the table, and sat back, his eyes still on it.

'Phin, for pity's sake—'

'The title,' said Phin. 'My God, that title—'

'What about the title? Is it Giselle again, like the painting?' Toby came round the table to see.

'It's not Giselle,' said Phin. 'It's *Siegreich*.'

Siegreich. The word spiked deep into Phin's mind.

Toby said, 'What's a siegreich? Whatever it is, it's making you look bloody peculiar.'

Phin said, 'Music with that title is believed to have been composed sometime during the early 1940s, in Germany.'

'Yes?'

'It's a piece of music that's almost a legend,' said Phin. 'One of those curious stories that sometimes emerge from wartime. The kind where you don't know what's true, and what's embroidered truth, and what's outright fiction. The story is that the Nazis got hold of a composer who was living in Germany and persuaded him to write a piece of music for them. And when the Nazis used persuasion—'

'Point taken. For persuasion read force.'

'As far as I can remember, the details of the actual persuasion vary a good deal,' said Phin. 'Everything from awarding the Iron Cross and handing over the deeds of a small Bavarian *Schloss* – to the other end of the scale, with incarceration in Auschwitz.' A coldness trickled across his mind as he said this. 'Most sources agree the concentration camp was the likeliest scenario,' he said. 'But the gist is that a fanatical and very high-ranking SS officer wanted to present Hitler with a triumphal march – a specially written piece – to accompany the Führer's invasion of England. It was said to be a kind of affirmation of belief in Hitler's ability to succeed. And the music's title was *Siegreich* – which translates more or less as Victory or Triumph.'

'And that's the title of that music lying on the table,' said Toby.

'Yes.' Phin supposed he should be feeling excited at the possibility of having uncovered the *Siegreich* – of perhaps being the person who would prove the legend was true. But the childhood memory of his grandfather was too strongly with him – the memory of how his grandfather had lain in a POW hospital, unable to shut out the sound of the Führer's armies playing military marches in the square outside. It had been the day the doctors had told him his sight had been irretrievably lost – that the retinas had been destroyed in the burning plane. 'Since then I've always found military music so sad,' he had said to Phin.

And now it seemed that a legendary piece of German military music was lying on the table in front of Phin. He stared at it, and thought: if this really is the *Siegreich*, it was spun during a dark and terrible time, and whoever composed it was probably tortured into doing so.

'I didn't know Hitler intended to invade this country,' Toby was saying. 'I mean, not to the extent that somebody decided it should be done to music. Did Hitler intend his armies would blitzkrieg their way down Whitehall to the sound of bugles and military marching bands?'

Phin pulled his mind back to the present. 'I don't know about a military band,' he said, 'but the Third Reich certainly drew up actual invasion plans. Operation *Seelöwe* they called it. Operation Sea Lion. Churchill and the war cabinet knew about it. I think Hitler scheduled it for the spring of 1941, or thereabouts. Goering argued against it, but Hitler was insistent.'

'He would be insistent. I'm impressed with your knowledge, by the way.'

'I wouldn't have known it all offhand if I wasn't working on the commission about musicians who had to flee Hitlerite Germany,' said Phin. 'They call that kind of work deep background, these days. There's a lot of material to sift – primary-source stuff in the main, some of it very grim, as you can imagine. It isn't always easy to distinguish between fact and fiction, either.'

'Separate the genuine from the urban or internet myth,' said Toby, nodding.

'Yes.' Phin was grateful for Toby's understanding. 'But what does seem to be true is that there were SS officers who took a twisted pleasure in refining the punishments for musicians.' He made an abrupt descriptive gesture with his hand. 'They'd often focus on the musicians' hands,' he said. 'Damage them so they wouldn't be able to play again. In one of the camps – Sachsenhausen, I think – they had something called the *strappado*. Suspension from posts by the wrists, which were tied behind the prisoner's back. They'd leave the poor creatures like that for hours on end.'

Toby said, 'And for a pianist or a violinist or any musician at all . . . Even if the bones survived, over time there'd be damage to tendons and nerves. Without treatment – and it would need to be specialist treatment – the hands would be ruined, certainly for music.'

'That's the medic speaking,' said Phin, glancing at him

'I daresay some of the lectures get through,' said Toby, as if he had been caught out in something vaguely discreditable. 'What happened to the *Siegreich*?'

'It vanished, if it ever existed.' Phin reached into his memory for the scraps of knowledge he possessed about the music, trying to ignore the feeling that he was plunging his hands, wrist-deep, into something black and rancid, and something that was thick with old pain. Was it his grandfather's pain he was feeling, or was it the imagined pain of the people who might have suffered during the creating of the *Siegreich*? 'But whatever happened to it, it's believed it was never played – never heard by anyone except its composer.'

'Who was its composer?'

'No one knows. But it's generally agreed that he wouldn't have been very well known. I mean it wasn't anyone like Wagner or Richard Strauss. There were a few low-profile musicians and composers in Berlin and Munich at the time – it could have been any one of them, or none of them. There was one colourful character called Eisler who found his way on to a few concert platforms. I've come across a couple of mentions of him – I quite liked the sound of him. But probably,' said Phin, determinedly, 'the whole thing really is just a legend, and the title's pure coincidence. There's no copyright on titles, after all. There are several concertos called "Romance" for instance – well, several that are known just as

"Romance". Beethoven wrote one, and Mozart, and so did Chopin, and there's a beautiful classical guitar piece . . . Sorry, I'm getting carried away.'

'But,' said Toby, thoughtfully, 'looked at the other way round, this score is handwritten, and it's been stored in the attics of a man who was a child in Germany in the early years of World War Two.'

'Yes.' Phin reached for the music, and stood up with an air of decision. 'Where did we leave the portrait?'

'In the hall.' Toby looked at him. 'You're going to see if this is the music in the painting, aren't you? You're going to compare the two?'

'Yes,' said Phin. 'Yes, that's exactly what I'm going to do.'

Phin's stomach was churning with nervous anticipation as they carried Christa's portrait into the dining room, and propped it up on a big sideboard, so that it leaned against the wall. I don't want to do this, he thought. I don't want to find that Christa was involved in any of this – or that Stefan was. But he knew that if he did not investigate, he would always wonder if this really was the secret victory march of some long-ago Nazi.

'Is the painting clear enough to copy?' said Toby, who had found a torch, and was shining it on to the canvas.

'I think so. It's a pity that only one sheet is visible, though. You can see two or three more beneath, but the painter's only shown the edges of them. Did you find pen and paper – oh, good.' He drew the staves out on the paper, sketching in the treble clef, with the staves for the bass below each one. He covered two pages, which ought to be enough, then took the paper over to the sideboard immediately next to the portrait, and flattened it out.

As he began to copy the painted notes on to the paper, Toby, directing the torch, said, 'I should have known you'd be able to read music.'

'It's useful, but it'll never take me on to any concert platforms,' said Phin. 'And it doesn't rank anywhere near to being able to set a broken bone or whip out an appendix.'

'They haven't quite let me do that yet,' said Toby. 'I can wield a stethoscope with the best, though, and I can identify *Yersinia pestis* through a microscope at ten paces.'

'What on earth is *Yersinia pestis*?'

'Bubonic plague. I can't think why we were taught that in twenty-first-century England.'

'You never know what might come in useful.' Phin had got halfway down the painted score. 'I'll tell you another odd thing about this,' he said. 'The artist was very precise about painting this music – about painting the actual notation, I mean. Usually if you see a piece of music in a painting, the notes aren't very clearly defined – they're almost suggested. Often blurred. But this isn't like that. He's even put in the composer's time instruction – d'you see that? 4,2,2. That's fairly traditional marching time – Schubert's *Marche Militaire* is in 2,4 – so it does look as if *Giselle's Music* had a military flavour. Which you'd expect for the *Siegreich*.' He continued to write. 'B-flat, inverted chord,' he said, half to himself. 'Then a run of triads – that's a three-note chord. And then the tritone.'

'The chord of evil. Every time I say that,' said Toby, 'it sounds even more sinister.'

'It's not considered so very sinister nowadays. In fact you find it in modern music – Jimi Hendrix made use of it, and also Black Sabbath. It's like a sting within the melody. Film background music sometimes has it as a kind of warning to the audience that something bad's about to happen. That harsh discordance that tells you the killer's outside the door with an axe. Think shower curtains in *Psycho*. But it's surprising if a composer in Christa's time used it. And it's incredible if it's in the *Siegreich*. If this is the *Siegreich*.'

'Why would it have the devil's chord in it?'

'Well,' said Phin, thoughtfully, 'if it really was written under duress, it could have been a jibe at Hitler. Meant to imply, "Stuff you, Adolf." Or maybe a kind of a stage direction: "Enter the villain."'

'So it could be a message of sorts. Only the message is the musical equivalent of, "Balls to the Führer." Phin, you do realize,' said Toby, 'that you're moving into da Vinci code territory with this?'

'I am a bit, aren't I?' Phin grinned at Toby and set down his pen. 'OK, I think I've got it all copied now – at least as much as is visible.'

'So this is when we make the comparison? Moment of truth?'

'Moment of truth,' confirmed Phin.

They took the notes over to the dining table, where the *Siegreich* music still lay. As Phin flattened them out next to it, he had the feeling that Christa Cain's painted eyes flickered with life. Might she even have composed this? Surely she would have been too young. It was Giselle's music, anyway. But Christa might have played it. She might have been the one person, other than the composer, who had actually heard the *Siegreich*.

'Well?' said Toby, after Phin had pored over the two sets of music for some minutes.

Phin straightened up from the table. His neck muscles were aching with tension, and he felt as if something had looped a steel wire around his chest. In a voice from which he had determinedly smoothed all emotion, he said, 'They're exactly the same. Note for note, semi-quaver for semi-quaver, breve for breve, rests and fermata and the whole damn lot.'

'And the devil's chord?'

'Oh, yes.' Phin looked at Toby. 'The music we found in that box is the same as the music painted in Christa Cain's portrait. It's the *Siegreich* – Hitler's vanished invasion march. It's the music the Nazis tortured out of an unknown composer seventy-odd years ago.'

TEN

I mprisonment in a medieval castle was something you expected to read about in an old fairy story or a gothic romance. It was not something you expected to happen to you in your own life, in twentieth-century Germany.

As the jeep rattled into a courtyard and Wewelsburg's shadows closed around them, Giselle began to wonder if any of this was actually happening. Might it be a nightmare – her own or even someone else's? With this last thought, came the memory of Silke, who had scribbled that last frantic clue – *Sachsenhausen.*

Reinhardt and the jeep's driver pulled Giselle out of the jeep. All around the courtyard were soaring flat-fronted walls, with small, mean windows in them. Giselle stared up and shivered, but when they forced her towards an archway, she kicked at them with all her strength, and Reinhardt swore and called her a hellcat.

'Yes, and if my hands weren't still tied I would claw out your eyes,' said Giselle, viciously.

'Bitch.' He gestured impatiently to the driver, who picked her up and carried her through the archway, to where a deep-set, oak-studded door stood partly open.

The minute they were inside the castle, Giselle felt as if a thick choking darkness had closed down on her. This really was the sinister old castle of those teenage fantasies. This was the place where people suffered and died and were forgotten. As the driver carried her across a massive, echoing, stone-flagged hall, she tried to quench the panic, and take note of everything. It looked as if the rumours that Herr Himmler was renovating the place to use as an SS centre might be true, because workmen's tools and work-benches were strewn around, and in one corner were crumpled ground sheets and large tubs of paint or plaster mix.

She was carried up a flight of wide, shallow stairs and into a room at the top. At least they had not thrown her into the dungeons.

And in a general way she could fix the location of the room. It was at the top of a flight of stairs that led off the big stone hall. One flight of stairs meant it would not be too far from the ground. In stories, beleaguered heroines often climbed courageously out of windows – there was sometimes a friendly tree with thick branches usefully close to window ledges. But this was Wewelsburg – fortress, bastion, prison house and even torture chamber in the past – so it was not very likely to have any accommodating trees or conveniently flimsy locks on doors. Still, the room was better than it might have been. It was unexpectedly large, and by no means spartan. The floor was stone, but there were rugs on it, and a bed stood against one wall, made up with sheets and blankets. There was a deep chair with cushions, and a small table, with a narrow wooden chair drawn up to it.

Two windows were set into the thick old wall, and a plywood desk stood between them, where it would catch whatever light came in. The glass of both windows was thick and slightly blurred from age, and metal strips criss-crossed each one. This was a pity, because even if there had been that helpful tree outside, nothing short of Thor's hammer, with Thor himself wielding it, would have broken those windows. Surprisingly, there was electricity in here; a thin cable was fastened to the wall, and went all the way up to a light fitting high above. So it was not to be the classic candlelit prison, then.

The driver saluted Reinhardt, and went out.

Reinhardt turned to look at Giselle very intently. 'And now,' he said, 'we shall talk about why you are here.'

'Music,' said Giselle staring at Reinhardt in astonishment. 'You want me to compose music for you.'

'Yes.' Reinhardt was standing in front of one of the windows, silhouetted against the darkening sky. It gave him an aura of authority but also of menace.

'But I can't compose,' said Giselle. 'I can play the piano – the violin a bit, as well – but composing is a whole world away from reading music and playing an instrument. Why on earth d'you think I can compose?'

'Because in your house are several music scores with your name on them. We found them.'

The thought of Reinhardt or one of his jackals creeping secretly into the house was sickening. Giselle said, 'Yes, but I didn't— It wasn't—' Then she stopped, because the denial must not be made. The music Reinhardt had found had been written by Felix, of course; he had composed it as a kind of technical exercise, and even though it had not been very good, he had put her name on it because he had said she was his inspiration, no matter how poor the end result.

If Giselle told Reinhardt this, it was possible he would believe her. But that might mean Felix would be taken prisoner and forced to compose their music – which meant Christa and Stefan would be alone, because Giselle was not so naïve as to believe they would let her go.

'Giselle,' said Reinhardt, softly, and his voice licked across her name in a way that made Giselle feel as if her skin had been scraped, 'your family doesn't yet know where you are or what's happening to you. They know you were to be away for four, perhaps five, days, so they won't yet be worried at not hearing from you. And in four or five days—'

'But I couldn't compose a piece of music in five days,' said Giselle quickly. 'It isn't like scribbling a quick note to the grocer, or writing a laundry list.' Did that sound authentic? She thought so.

'It would be a pity if we have to exert pressure on you,' said Reinhardt.

'What d'you mean by pressure?' But shards of ice were already jabbing into Giselle's spine.

He came over to her, took her hand, and pulled her to the windows. 'Do you see that cluster of buildings across to the west? From here, and in this light, you'll only see a general outline. It's clearer in daylight. But if you look carefully, you can see black gates, rearing up.'

'I see all that.'

'Do you know what that place is?'

His eyes were on her, and after a moment, Giselle said, very softly, 'Yes. It's Sachsenhausen.'

Sachsenhausen, Silke had written, in that last desperate scrawl. 'Yes.'

'It's where my cousin and her parents are, isn't it?'

'Yes. If you look towards the western side, you'll see two massive brick chimneys.'

'I can see them.' A cold dread clutched Giselle.

'While you're here, there will be times when you see flames coming from them,' said Reinhardt. 'Never at night – that would attract attention. But during the day they will sometimes burn.'

'Crematoria,' said Giselle, in a voice of horror, then, half to herself, '"those who begin by burning books, end by burning men".'

'A romanticized line of poetry,' said Reinhardt, after a moment. 'Wasn't it Heinrich Heine who wrote that?'

'I can't remember.' But incredibly Giselle was aware that something had passed between them – that they had both recognized a fragment of long-ago poetry. That they had shared that recognition.

Then Reinhardt said, 'Possibly the words were prophetic.' Giselle shivered, and, as if her fear had aroused him, his hand came out to her, touching her face lightly, tracing a line across her cheekbones. 'Do what we're asking, Giselle,' he said. 'Give us the music we want.'

Because if you do not . . . The words were not spoken, but Giselle felt as if he had splashed them against her mind, like acid. Felix and the children would suffer if she did not do what was wanted. That was what Reinhardt meant. Perhaps Silke and her parents, also would suffer. *There will be times when you see flames coming from them,* Reinhardt had said, looking towards the monstrous brick chimneys.

His hand was still caressing her neck, and it moved lower, curving over her breasts. Giselle forced herself not to flinch. If he could be made to believe she would accept him in her bed, would he let her go? She turned her head to look at him through half-closed eyes, as if his touch was arousing her. But please, don't let him actually do anything to me now. If I have to, I'll do it, I really will, only, please, not yet.

In a soft voice, Reinhardt said, 'Well, spitfire?' His eyes were dark with strong emotion. Sexual desire? A treacherous wisp of curiosity slid through Giselle's mind. What would he be like as a lover?

It was a thought to push away at once, but the pretence must be maintained. With the feeling that she was standing on the edge of a yawning chasm, Giselle said slowly, 'There are many kinds of music to be made, Reinhardt.'

He smiled and removed his hand. It was all right. He believed she was attracted to him, and he also apparently believed that she could compose music – that she would agree to his demand. For the moment she was safe, and Felix and the children were safe.

A rush of relief went through her, but unexpectedly there was also a spike of curiosity. What was the music they wanted that must be created in such secrecy? And why did they want a Jewish composer when they were systematically herding Jews into labour camps?

And then Reinhardt said, 'You are to compose music that is to be presented to the Führer. To Herr Hitler himself.'

Giselle stared at him. 'What kind of music?'

'Music that will show our absolute belief and confidence in his ability to achieve his aim.' He studied her, then said, 'There's no reason why you can't know this next part—'

After all, said his tone, imprisoned in here, there's no one you can tell.

'—which is that plans are in place for the annexing of Belgium and then of France. After that—'

'Yes?'

Reinhardt smiled, and this time the flame that showed in his eyes was not that of sexual desire, it was plain, outright madness. Giselle repressed a shiver.

'The music I shall give to the Führer,' said Reinhardt, 'will be his march of victory to accompany our armies when they conquer – and when they occupy – England.

'And I shall call it the *Siegreich*.'

After Reinhardt had gone, locking the door, Giselle huddled on the bed, hugging a cushion for warmth and comfort, listening to the castle sinking into brooding silence.

Hitler would never be so mad as to march into more countries. Or would he? Giselle tried to think about this, because it was better than thinking about being imprisoned in this dreadful place. She knew a little about what had been going on in the world, and she knew that Hitler had already sent his armies into Czechoslovakia. When that became known, Felix had said it was only the start; Hitler would not stop with Czechoslovakia. He would want Belgium next, because Belgium was the only thing that stood between him and France. Nobody had given this much credence, but Felix had stuck to his point. And now Reinhardt had confirmed that Felix had been right.

The next morning two guards carried a piano into the room, and set it against one wall. One of them placed a sheaf of blank music scores on the top, together with several newly sharpened pencils.

The piano appeared so soon after Reinhardt's demand, Giselle realized angrily that he had assumed her acquiescence, and had had everything ready. She supposed they had brought her to this room because manoeuvring even the smallest piano up twisty turret stairs or down dungeon steps would have been virtually impossible.

The piano was very similar to one Giselle's grandmother had owned. There was a walnut veneer with the same ornate, polished figuring, and a candleholder so that light could be trained to fall on the music stand. Giselle found the sight of all this unexpectedly strengthening; it brought back memories of her grandmother telling her how she had escaped from the slaughter of Jews in Kiev in 1919. Giselle smiled for the first time since being brought here. Her grandmother, that doughty old lady, would not have been cowed by Reinhardt or Hitler's brutal SS men today, and Giselle would not be cowed by them, either.

Being manhandled through the castle had jangled the piano hopelessly out of tune, of course, but a real composer would not have cared overmuch about that. The great composers had often not needed instruments at all, because they could hear the music in their heads. Hands hitting a table-top, fingernails tapping against glass, the scratching of a blunt pencil on any surface . . . All those things were sufficient for them to spin music from nothing, like the miller in the old story spinning gold from straw. This was the kind of analogy Silke would have seized on with delight. If Silke were here now, she would weave the darkness of Wewelsburg into one of her wild stories, conjuring up its past, summoning ghosts and spectres, making them dance to her bidding.

Giselle could not make anything dance to her bidding, and she did not believe in ghosts, but if ghosts could have helped her now she would have called up every shade that had stalked every gothic

novel written, or had drifted across every eerie legend known to
humanity. She would have traded her soul to the devil, like Faust,
for the ability to compose the music the Nazis wanted.

As captivity went, it could have been worse. The food they brought
her was plain, but perfectly adequate. Bread and porridge for
breakfast, generally with a small dish of jam or honey. An apple
or a few plums. There was always enough bread for a second
wedge at midday, together with the fruit. Supper was more substantial: often a bowl of thick soup, and perhaps a chicken dish with
rice and vegetables.

There was a curtained recess with a tiny cracked sink and a
wooden-framed commode. Giselle hated this contraption, which
was emptied each morning, and the water from the rickety tap was
cold. But at least she was able to wash and keep reasonably clean.
Her handbag and overnight case had been brought to her, and each
morning she dabbed a little powder on her face and combed her
hair in the small handbag mirror. This was probably the ultimate
in vanity, but Giselle did not care, because she refused to become
raggle-taggle and unkempt, even in a place like this.

But lying in bed each night, the desolation closed suffocatingly
around her, and her arms ached with the need to fold Christa and
Stefan to her, and to lie alongside Felix and hear his quiet, even
breathing and feel his familiar warmth close by. She tried to send
out her love and her reassurances to Christa and Stefan – to tell
them she was all right, that she would find a way to get back
to them. She knew this to be ridiculous, but she did it anyway.
I'm here, my dear loves, she said to them in her mind.

Strangely, she had the feeling that of the two children, Stefan
would be coping better. Christa would appear to be all right –
she would seem to be dealing with the pain and the bewilderment
more successfully, but the trouble was that those very emotions
might feed that darkness that Giselle had always feared lay deep
inside Christa's mind.

Three nights after the piano had appeared, Giselle ate her supper
and put the tray by the door for it to be collected, which was the
routine. She was trying to keep track of the days, trying to assess
when Felix would be told she was not with Silke's family. Four

or five days, Reinhardt had said. She had no idea what they would tell Felix, and she did not dare ask.

She tried over and over again to think of a means of escaping. She would have burned the entire castle down if she had had the means, but there were no candles or matches. If she had possessed any knowledge of electricity she might have found a way of fusing the light, hoping it would plunge other parts of the castle into darkness and create a diversion, or that the power would crackle up into a fire. But she had no knowledge whatsoever of how electricity operated.

Shadows were starting to form in the corners. It was not very late, though; there was still movement within the castle. Footsteps came and went on the stairs. It was remarkable how distinctive footsteps could be. But tonight they sounded different, and Giselle could almost believe she was hearing a death drum tattoo, or the marching feet of a procession to an execution chamber. If those footsteps could be set to music, it would be music with slow, measured cadences and it would convey the approach of something dreadful.

The *Macbeth* line came into her mind . . . *By the pricking of my thumbs, Something wicked this way comes* . . .

Or was it – By the beating of a drum, something deadly this way comes . . .?

Something deadly. Memory looped back to herself and Silke in the bedroom in Salzkotten, sharing secrets. Giselle's secrets had been innocent enough, although she had occasionally embroidered them a bit to keep up with Silke, because Silke's secrets had not always been innocent at all. 'Never tell, will you, darling?' Silke had said, not once, but many times. 'It'd be deadly if anyone found out . . .'

Deadly. Giselle came out of the memory to hear footsteps approaching the door – footsteps that were not those of the guard coming to collect the supper dishes. It was Reinhardt – his footsteps were unmistakable. Her heart jumped nervously, and she got off the bed, and stood by the window, watching the door, clenching and unclenching her hands.

He came into the room, and his eyes went at once to the piano, taking in the blank music score, still in a neat stack on the top. 'It doesn't look as if you've done much work.'

'I haven't done any,' said Giselle. 'I can't. I've told you that composing isn't like scribbling a grocery list.'

'This is a great pity.' He looked at her for a moment, his expression unreadable, then went out.

Giselle sank back on the bed, her legs trembling. Something had changed. It was almost as if, seeing the blank music sheets, a decision had been taken. She curled up on the bed, wrapping her arms around her for warmth, watching the shadows deepen.

And then she heard Reinhardt coming back.

ELEVEN

Wewelsburg Castle, cont'd

Two officers followed Reinhardt in, and they seized Giselle's arms, roughly twisting them behind her back before she could speak or protest. There was the painful snap of steel around her wrists. Gyves? Handcuffs? She looked at Reinhardt, wanting him to tell her what was happening, but he only nodded to the two officers, and they took her out of the room and down the wide stone stairs. Were they going to throw her into some wretched underground cell, and leave her to die? If they did that, no one would know what had happened to her, and Felix and the children would wonder for the rest of their lives. This was so unbearable a thought that Giselle tried to thrust it away.

The big hall was lit by flaring lights from iron wall brackets, and Giselle tried to notice where they were going. But she was sick and dizzy with fear, and she started to wonder if she might have died – been murdered by Reinhardt – and was being taken to some ancient hell. She was not especially well versed in the teachings and the beliefs of her people – 'You're too frivolous, my love,' Felix used to say – but even the most cursory knowledge of it allowed her mind to present her with a few dark images from the Koran. Sheol, the underground abyss, the place where you worked out the sins of your life after death. And Gehinnom, the place of torture and punishment, fire and brimstone . . .

The cold night air when they took her outside was a shock, but after the days of being incarcerated, it felt good, and it snapped her out of the sick, phantom-haunted unreality. She drew in several grateful breaths, then they were pushing her into the back of a jeep that waited, the headlights glowering, and exhaust fumes creating misty vapour on the night air. One of the guards sat next to her, and Reinhardt got into the front.

As the jeep roared away, no one spoke. Giselle could not see where they were going, but the headlights picked out rutted road surfaces and hedges and trees. Occasionally something scuttled across the road and into the dark fields, and once a small winged creature dashed itself against the windscreen. The driver turned off the road, and black iron gates, like the waiting teeth of a shark, came into view. The headlights fell across the iron-scrolled words at the top – words that struck a chill into Giselle's whole body, because they were words that had become dreadfully familiar. *Arbeit Macht Frei.* Work makes you free.

The Nazi legend for the concentration camps.

Reinhardt had brought her to Sachsenhausen.

As the jeep stopped, Reinhardt turned to look at Giselle.

'We have information about a planned escape from that place tonight.' He nodded towards Sachsenhausen. 'That's why we're here. You're with us because you should see how we deal with people who defy us.'

Giselle managed a shrug, and sat back as if the whole thing was of supreme indifference.

'Look there,' said Reinhardt, and Giselle saw that two people – two men – were walking very cautiously and furtively along the edges of Sachsenhausen's boundaries. They were weaving in and out of the lights that shone down from parts of the higher sections of the wires, and although they were staying close to the thick barbed wire enclosing the camp, they seemed to be taking great care not to get too near to it. It was obvious, even at this distance, that they were trying to find a break in the wire through which they might scramble. Giselle could scarcely believe they would take such a chance. Or would you take any chance, however slender, to get away from such a brutal place?

The lights appeared to be on some kind of swivel mechanism, because every few moments they turned themselves from left to right, the cold beam sweeping across the enclosure. They were like huge, staring spotlights; they were ogres' eyes, swivelling back and forth. Each time the lights swung towards the two men they threw themselves flat on the ground to avoid the white glare. Then they carried on tiptoeing along the strip of ground, almost like children playing a game involving forbidden ground. Giselle could almost feel them hoping and praying they would get out, and she could hardly bear knowing their attempt was already doomed.

'They call that the death strip,' said Reinhardt, his eyes on the men. 'There's only one reason for a prisoner to walk on that band of ground, and that's to try to break out. If they're caught on that strip, they're shot. Executed on the spot. And they always are caught, Giselle.'

As Giselle stared at the furtive outlines, Reinhardt said, 'Sometimes the guards don't even need to shoot them. Sections of the wire are electrified, so that if anyone touches it the electricity does the execution very thoroughly. The prisoners all know about it – you can see how those two men are trying not to get too close. It's very dangerous indeed, but sometimes there's a couple like tonight who believe they can avoid the live sections.'

One of the men was pointing to the ground just below a section of the wire, and they both paused and looked about them. Then they dropped to their knees and began to crawl towards the wire.

At once, the massive spotlights blazed out, and both men flinched, putting up their hands to shield their eyes. Half a dozen guards sprang out of the shadows, surrounding the two men, their rifles aimed, and the two prisoners fell to their knees, and one held up clasped hands in the classic gesture of pleading for mercy.

Reinhardt turned to say something to the driver, and the man nodded, and drove the jeep closer. Its lights mingled with the ogre-eyed spotlights inside the compound, lighting the scene to even starker clarity.

The younger of the two was being held by the guards, but the other was being forced closer to the wire fence. He was struggling furiously, occasionally holding out his hands in that piteous, useless gesture of pleading, but the guards had already raised their rifles. A sharp command rang out, and the rifles were fired, in shocking rat-a-tat precision. Blood exploded from the man's body like huge blossoming scarlet flowers, and spattered across the barbed wire behind him, running down on to the ground. He fell back, thrown against the wire by the force of the shots, and a furious sizzling crackle of blue erupted from the fence. The man screamed, jerked again, then fell to the ground and lay there, not moving.

Reinhardt reached over to winch down the window of the jeep, and cold night air – dreadfully mingled with the stench of blood and burned flesh – flooded into the jeep. One of the guards was bending over the shot man, then he straightened up and nodded, as if to confirm death.

'He was a trouble-maker,' said Reinhardt. 'He would have known the risk he took. The other one . . .' He paused, and then, almost on a note of reluctance, he said, 'He is a German.'

'A German?' Giselle was so surprised that she forgot about maintaining a show of defiance. 'One of your own people?' This was remarkable because, as far as she knew – as far as anyone knew – the camps were solely used for incarcerating Jews.

'Until two or three years ago he was a member of the Hitler Youth,' said Reinhardt. 'He was loyal and hard-working, and he had just joined the Nazi Party itself. It was believed he could rise to high office in the Third Reich. But he deceived us all. Last year we discovered him to be a traitor – a defiler of everything the Führer holds dear. He was brought here, to Sachsenhausen, and several days ago he was told he would be executed. That's probably why he made this naïve attempt to escape tonight.'

The second prisoner was pulled back into the circle of the light, and there was a moment when his face was turned upwards and held in the glare. The features were lit to sharp clarity, and as he turned to look beyond the searchlights, as if seeing the jeep, Giselle felt horror wash over her. She swallowed hard, and bit her lip furiously to give herself a different pain to focus on. She would not be sick in front of these evil creatures, she would *not* . . .

In a voice she scarcely recognized as her own, she said, 'He is very young. Is it really necessary to – to execute him?' Please not that, she thought. Not this one.

Reinhardt said, 'Until lately he was a musician. Talented, or so he would have people believe.'

Giselle, still fighting the sick horror, thought: oh yes, he was talented. He was so talented you would never believe it . . . You can't shoot him, you musn't . . .

'Shooting is too good for him – especially after tonight,' said Reinhardt. 'He will die soon, but there is to be a punishment first. He betrayed us and everything we're striving for.'

I know he did . . . And I know exactly what his betrayal of you was . . . But I promised I would never speak of it – not if hell froze, not if the fires of Gehinnom came down to consume the earth . . .

*　*　*

'You must promise you'll never speak of it,' Silke had said, pouring out her heart and her secrets to Giselle on a rare two-day visit to Lindschoen.

Giselle had listened, fascinated as always by Silke's exploits and romantic tangles, at first intrigued by this latest one, then increasingly apprehensive.

'My parents would never approve of him,' Silke said. 'I know I'm of age and all the rest of it, but they'd be appalled and deeply hurt, and my father would do everything he could to put an end to the whole thing. And you know my father when he wants something.'

Giselle nodded.

'I don't think they'd mind about Andreas being a musician,' Silke said, hopefully, 'although my father would say there's precious little money in music—'

Silke's father had said precisely this about Felix, but Giselle had not minded because she had not needed Uncle Avram's approval to marry Felix, who in any case had had this shop, and his pupils, as well as his small orchestra. There had not been a huge amount of money, and there was not much more now, but there was enough.

'It's not the music aspect that would worry them or make my father stomp around issuing prohibitions and things,' said Silke, earnestly. 'And as for Andreas being – um—'

'Not being Jewish,' said Giselle, helpfully.

'Yes.' Silke seized on this gentle designation gratefully. 'They'd probably come round to that,' she said. 'The problem is that—'

'The problem is that Andreas was one of the Hitler Youth and earlier in the year he joined the Nazi Party.' Giselle instinctively lowered her voice, and even then she glanced at the door, to where Felix was deep in an earnest discussion with two men over their attempts to sell him a violin which they were maintaining was a Guarneri, but which Felix was saying was no more a Guarneri than the kitchen mangle.

'Yes, that's the real problem.' Silke dissolved into tears at that point, sobbing heart-rendingly. Giselle was horrified to suddenly think that this was exactly how Silke had cried over a pet rabbit who had died.

'I know I'm always having emotional storms,' said Silke, as if sensing Giselle's thoughts. 'I can't help it. I love things so very much, you see.'

'Including Andreas,' Giselle could not help saying.

'I've never loved anyone as much as Andreas,' said Silke. 'When he plays his music to me, it's as if he's drawing music from my whole body. I know that sounds like something from a romantic novel,' said Silke, 'but truly, Giselle . . . And he's so sensitive, so *sympathique*. He composes music as well as playing it. I've heard some of it – it's beautiful, inspirational, stirring. Some of it is heartbreaking. He would like to dedicate some of it to me, only he daren't, of course. He daren't let his name be linked to anyone who's Jewish. Not while Herr Hitler is striving for his pure race and setting up those frightful labour camps.'

She started crying again, and Giselle fetched dry handkerchiefs, which was usually what she had to do for Silke on these occasions. It was to be hoped Felix did not terminate the Guarneri discussion and come in until Silke had stopped crying.

But Silke was already feeling better, and, typically Silke, was reaching for a powder compact to repair the damage to her complexion. 'He's performing in a concert in Paderborn in a couple of weeks,' she said, having applied the powder. 'He wants me to go – I've never seen him play in public, and I'd love to. Only I can't go on my own – Paderborn isn't all that far from Saltzkotten, not as the crow flies, not that I'm a crow . . . But you know what my parents are. They always want to know where I'm going and who I'm with . . .' She looked at Giselle pleadingly.

Giselle said slowly, 'If I came with you, it would be all right, though. That's what you mean, isn't it?'

'It always was all right if you were with me,' said Silke, eagerly. 'They never believed I'd get into a scrape if you were with me. Or, if I did, they thought you would always get me out of it.'

There was a moment of amused acknowledgement between them, because there had been many a time when one of them had dragged the other out of an awkward situation. There had also been a few times when one of them had dragged the other into the awkward situation to begin with, of course.

It would be the height of madness to get involved in this latest tangle, but Giselle had never been able to ignore Silke's appeals. And Felix would understand if she wanted to spend a day – perhaps

a day and a night – away with Silke to attend a concert. A friend
of Silke's was performing, she could say. It hurt to think of tailoring
the truth in this way, when it was Felix. Was it possible he could
leave the shop – Velda would happily have the children for a night
– and come with them? But it was probably better not to involve
dear, scrupulously honest Felix in this.

So Giselle said, 'I might manage it.'

'You could, couldn't you? You're marvellous. I knew you'd
understand.' Silke instantly began to plan it all. How they could
tell her parents they were visiting an old schoolfriend who was
involved in the orchestra – it was as well to keep as closely to the
truth as possible. Giselle would come to Salzkotten and they would
travel to Paderborn together. There were good trains . . . And, of
course, they would spend a night in Paderborn, and it would all
be Silke's treat; Giselle would not have to pay a single pfennig.

'Just one night,' said Giselle, looking at Silke.

'Oh yes.' It was said guilelessly, with the most wide and innocent of eyes, but they had both known that Silke would spend
more than one night in Paderborn with the sensitive, sympathetic
Andreas.

Giselle enjoyed the Paderborn concert, which included a Brahms
piano concerto and a Bruckner sonata. She enjoyed the supper
afterwards with Silke and Andreas. He was courteous and intelligent, and Giselle liked his faint air of questioning his life, as if
he was starting to realize that youthful illusions and ideals were
not always good or safe. Felix would have liked him, except that
Giselle did not think she would ever dare tell Felix about Andreas's
existence. And she had promised Silke not to tell anyone, anyway.

Once home, she tried, and failed, to think how Silke and Andreas
might one day be able to be together openly and permanently. It
seemed to Giselle that there was only heartache ahead for them.

And, seven months later, it looked as if she had been right. A
tearful, barely legible letter arrived, saying Andreas had been taken
away by his Nazi masters because they had discovered he was
consorting with a girl who was Jewish.

'Absolutely forbidden by them, of course, and completely
against all of the Führer's tenets,' wrote Silke, splattering the page
with tear stains. 'They've thrown Andreas into some wretched

prison somewhere and they're treating him as if he's a traitor. I have no idea what's happened to him, or where he is, but I don't believe I shall ever see him again.'

Giselle had not dared telephone, mostly because Velda had said, only the other day, that telephone conversations were now being listened to by spies. There was no knowing if this was true or if it was one of Velda's exaggerations, but Giselle did not want to take the chance. She wrote a careful letter, thanking Silke for all her news, and saying she hoped she was well and safe. She emphasized the word *safe* slightly. Silke, intuitive and sharp, would know what Giselle was asking.

She did, of course. She wrote back at once, saying all that had been known was that Andreas had been involved with a Jewish girl of what they sneeringly termed, 'so-called good family', and that a marriage had been intended. Giselle had no idea if the marriage part was true, but it would have been unkind to question it. She had no idea how dangerous it was for Silke to have written the letter at all, but it did not seem to have been tampered with.

Later, Silke wrote that she had received a scrawled note from Andreas, although she had no idea how he had been able to get it to her or where he had been when he wrote it. It said he loved her, that he would always love her, and she was to remember all the good things they had shared. She had copied his closing words in her letter to Giselle.

'I made wrong judgements when I was very young and very impressionable,' Andreas had written. 'I was awed and dazzled by people whose motives and beliefs were deeply wrong, by the beckoning dream of a new Germany. And I was swept along by the charisma of a greed-crazed and bigoted leader. I see all that now – now that it's too late.'

Giselle thought greed-crazed and bigoted were apt words for Adolf Hitler, but she felt cold and sick thinking what would have happened to Silke if anyone had seen those words.

'They are certainly going to keep me a prisoner for a very long time,' Andreas wrote. 'And I think they will probably end in executing me. It's unlikely I shall find a way to escape, but you can be sure I'll take any chance I can, and that I'll try to get to you. But I can't see how it can happen. I think I will eventually be shot. So, will you do one thing for me, Silke? Will you somehow

ensure my music lives after me – that it's played for people? I
believe if death comes, I can face it quite bravely if I know even
one piece will survive.'

By this time, tears were pouring down Giselle's cheeks. This
was all the kind of impossibly romantic thing Silke would have
wanted, but it was still heartbreaking and tragic, and the waste of
it all was hardly bearable.

It was not until over a year after that had happened that Silke met
Dietfried, and their engagement was announced. Giselle dared to
breathe a sigh of relief. Andreas was probably dead by now, and
although Silke might not be wildly in love with the reliable-
sounding Dietfried, she would probably be safe.

But sitting in the dark jeep outside the gates of Sachsenhausen
concentration camp, her hands bound by steel gyves, Giselle saw
with a tumble of confused emotions that Andreas was not dead.
He was standing a few yards from here. He was held in a circle
of pitiless light, and surrounding him were upwards of a dozen
guards, rifles aimed at his head and his heart.

TWELVE

A s the Sachsenhausen officers moved around the helpless Andreas, Giselle felt the tension and the anticipation inside the jeep build. Reinhardt's expression was unreadable, but once he half turned his head, and she saw his eyes held a dark intensity.

She was trying not to think of the prisoner as Andreas, Silke's beloved Andreas, because she dared not let Reinhardt realize that she knew him – not only for her own safety, but for Silke's. Silke was somewhere inside that terrible place as well, and it would be dreadfully easy for the officers to think that if Giselle Klein knew – or even knew of – this traitorous musician, then so might her cousin. Forgive me, Andreas, thought Giselle. I have to behave as if you're a complete stranger. If I could help you, I would, but I can't see anything I can do.

The guards were motionless, waiting for the command, but as an officer walked towards Andreas, they came sharply to attention. The officer was carrying something, and as he came into the full glare of the lights, Giselle saw that it was a length of fibrous-looking rope, along with leather straps, and a thick black hook. The hook caught the light, glinting evilly.

Reinhardt said, 'You understand what's about to be done?'

'No.'

'You will soon see.'

Andreas's hands were tied behind his back with the leather straps, and the hook was fastened between them – Giselle could not see exactly how it was done, but the rope seemed to now be looped around the hook, and then pulled out to its fullest extent. There was some delay at this point, as if the guards might be making sure the ropes were secure, and then they seemed to be measuring it, and two of them walked to a section of the nearby buildings, as if calculating something. Giselle wanted to shout to them to get on with it, to get it over with, then she wondered if this slowness was deliberate, part of the punishment.

Finally, Andreas was taken across the compound to a gap between two of the buildings. One end of the rope around his wrists was thrown upwards, a little in the manner of a man casting a fishing line, and Giselle, at first puzzled, now saw there was a cross-beam linking the two buildings – a thick section of steel, some eight or nine feet from the ground. It took several attempts for the rope to loop over the beam and hang down on the other side of it, but it was finally managed.

Reinhardt said, 'They're about to administer what was once called the *strappado*. A very old method. I believe it dates to the Spanish Inquisition.'

Giselle had never heard of the *strappado*, but it was becoming dreadfully clear what was going to happen. Andreas's hands were still clamped behind his back by the gyves, but the rope attached to the gyves was now being wound firmly around the cross-beam. The guards pulled it until it was taut, then, on a terse command from the officer, they began to haul on it, gradually raising Andreas's shackled wrists above his head, then continuing until his whole body was lifted from the ground, his arms and shoulders taking the entire weight.

The searchlights fell pitilessly on to him, and he struggled and writhed, kicking out helplessly and uselessly. Several times he cried out, and twice at least Giselle thought he begged them to cut him down. But the minutes stretched out and out and no one in the compound moved or spoke. The only movement was the squirming of the tortured man, and the only sounds were his sobs of agony and his pleas to be freed. He was writhing into impossible, distorted shapes in an attempt to get free or to reduce the dreadful strain on his arms and shoulders. The hard spotlights made of him a grotesque silhouette – a nightmare figure dancing an ugly, misshapen dance on air.

It might have been no more than a few moments – although for Giselle time had become stretched and unreal, so that it could have been hours – that the outline of the figure suddenly seemed to distort, almost as if huge invisible hands had reached down and wrenched the bones out of true. A dreadful cry rent the air, and Giselle shuddered, and looked away.

Reinhardt said, 'There is almost always dislocation of arms and shoulders. That is what has happened now.' He paused, then said, very softly, 'It will put an end to his piano playing – to all his involvement in music of any kind.'

Giselle, still staring resolutely at the jeep's floor, said, 'How long—?'

'Will they leave him there?' Again there was the disconcerting perception of her thoughts. 'It depends whether he dies from shock and pain – from the strain on his heart. He's young and strong, so it could be some while. A day, perhaps longer. But if he's still alive by dawn they'll cut him down then.' He made a curious gesture, as if to repudiate what was happening, and said, tersely, 'There's no need for us to stay any longer. The point has been made. Drive.'

The driver nodded an acceptance of the order, and as the jeep was reversed, then driven forward, Giselle thought, in panic, I can't let them take me back to Wewelsburg yet. I can't leave Andreas here like this – Silke's Andreas.

But there was nothing to be done. The jeep was already driving away.

'And so,' said Reinhardt, facing Giselle in the stone room, 'you see what is done to people who defy us.'

Giselle was seated on the bed, rubbing her newly released hands, which were sore and slightly numb. Andreas's struggling, pain-wracked figure was burned into her mind, but she would not let Reinhardt see how deeply affected she was.

Instead, she said, 'I'm not defying you. I'm doing my best to do what you want.' She looked at him very steadily, and saw the light flicker in his eyes. He would like to make love to me now, thought Giselle. Now, here, this very minute, on this bed.

The thought of such intimacy with Reinhardt, while the memory of Andreas's pain was still so strongly with her was sickening, but she moved to the bed and sat down, curling her legs under her, deliberately allowing her skirt to fall to one side so her upper legs were uncovered. In a softer voice, she said, 'There's one aspect of all this that I don't understand. Would you explain it to me . . .? Perhaps if I knew a little more . . .'

His eyes were still on her body. 'You are owed no explanation. But ask what you want to know.'

'I don't understand why I was chosen for this task,' said Giselle. 'Not only a female, but a Jewish female – that's almost unbeliev- able. The Führer hates Jews – I suspect he actually fears us. He certainly wants to . . . to purge the country of all Jewish people, doesn't he? Three years ago you took all rights from us with your accursed Nuremberg Race Law. So why did you pick a Jew to write this music, this *Siegreich*?' Be careful, said a voice in her mind. Let him keep believing you can do it. 'If I do manage it,' said Giselle, 'you'd keep my name out of it, I know that – in fact you'd probably write someone else's name on the actual music – but you'd still be taking a massive risk. Supposing it came out that a Jewish female had created a gift for the Führer and that you had instigated it? You'd be facing a firing squad.'

'The choice of a Jewish composer was deliberate,' said Reinhardt.

'Deliberate?'

'After the work is done,' he said, 'after the music is completed – a Jew, any Jew, is expendable.'

Expendable. Horror closed down on Giselle and she stared at him. 'You mean – if I do what you want, once you have the music, you'll kill me?'

'We would have to. The truth could never be known.'

After what felt like a long time, Giselle managed to stop shaking and to get into bed and pull the clothes around her.

She had no idea if she would be able to blot out any of what had happened tonight, and although she had not expected to sleep, finally she slipped into an uneasy half-slumber. But Andreas was waiting for her in that sleep; he struggled at the end of the ropes around his wrists, and stared imploringly at her. The lips, bitten through with agony, whispered reproaches. '*You should have stayed with me . . . You should have tried to help me . . . For Silke's sake, you should have tried . . .*'

Giselle got out of bed, wrapped a blanket round her shoulders, and stood at the window, peering through the night towards Sachsenhausen. Was Andreas still out there? Was it worse to think he was dead than to wonder if he might still be alive, dying in that compound in lonely agony?

The piano mocked her silently from its place against the wall, and she tried not to look at it. She tried not to think about Reinhardt or about Andreas. She tried not to think about anything. It was impossible. Seeing Andreas had taken her mind back to another memory – a recent one of those frantic moments in Silke's bedroom, when she had realized that the whole family had been taken away by the SS. Almost immediately, she had also realized that the SS were coming back into the house. That was when she had made that panic-stricken search of the bedroom. The topmost layer of her mind had been urging her to find something – anything – that might tell her where Silke had been taken. And so she had; she had found that single scribbled word. Sachsenhausen.

But there had been another layer that was remembering Silke's liaison with Andreas. She did not think the SS had found out that it was Silke who had been the disgraced musician's lover, but they had armies of spies, and it was possible that they suspected. If so, they might be about to search the now-empty house for evidence.

It could not be allowed. Andreas was under sentence of death – he was probably already dead – but Silke must not fall into the same fate.

So Giselle had frenziedly torn open cupboards and drawers, aware that the men were already in the gardens, and commands were being shouted.

Please don't let there be anything here that might lead them to Silke's love affair, but if there is, please let me find it and get rid of it . . .

The seconds ticked crazily away, and the SS men were inside the house; they were going through the rooms. In another moment they would come up here . . .

And then, in the bottom of a small cabinet drawer, there it was. Three or four pages of handwritten music, inside a large envelope. Andreas's music? What else would it be? But was there anything that could identify him and therefore incriminate Silke?

And there it was, on the very last sheet. At the foot of the page, a slanting hand had written, *Silke's Music, From A.* It was as clear as a curse, and it would not take a blazing genius to make the link between this and a German pianist who had betrayed the Nazi cause by falling in love with – by planning to marry – a Jewish girl 'of so-called good family'.

There was no time to find a better hiding place for the music, and certainly no time to burn, or even tear up, the damning pages.

The SS were on the stairs, they were coming along the landing, and in about five seconds they would be in this room. Giselle crammed the pages into her handbag, snapped it shut, and turned as the bedroom door was flung open.

The music was still in her bag now, here in Wewelsburg. She had managed to fold it into the little side compartment alongside a couple of photos of her family and one of Felix's shop. There had been a cursory search of the bag, but Giselle thought it had only been to make sure she did not have anything that might be used as a weapon. The guards had not found the music, or, if they had, it had not conveyed anything to them. But there was still the possibility that more thorough searches might be made, and if that happened – if the music with that damning dedication, *Silke's Music, From A,* was found – it was likely that Silke and probably all her family would die. So the music had better be destroyed. It would not be difficult to do that. Or would it?

Giselle thought about this carefully. There was no conventional lavatory down which she could flush the music – there was only the loathsome commode and the ewer of water. Was there any means of burning the score sheets? She got onto the table to see if she could reach the light bulb in case its heat would scorch the paper, but even standing on tiptoe she was a good two feet short of the bulb. Could she tear the music up and throw the shreds from the windows? But the windows would not open, and the glass was so thick and so laced with lead it was impossible even to crack it. The bizarre thought that if she did tear it into tiny shreds she could eat it, page by page, occurred to her.

She sat down on the bed, her mind churning. If she did not destroy the music and if it were to be found, it would place Silke and her parents in appalling danger. But the image of that struggling, pain-wracked figure at Sachsenhausen earlier tonight was still agonizingly with Giselle, and alongside it were Andreas's words in his last letter to Silke. 'If death comes, I can face it quite bravely if I know even one piece will survive,' he had written. He had wanted Silke to keep his music, and somehow ensure that it lived on. That man who might still be enduring that cruel torment in Sachsenhausen's grounds, had wanted a fragment of his music to live on. With the thought, Giselle knew she wanted that for him, as well.

The thoughts ran to and fro in her mind, making her head ache. And then, from the confusion and fear, the cobweb thread of an idea began to shape itself. What if the music could be destroyed, but also preserved – but preserved in a form that would ensure no one would realize who its composer really was? What if Andreas's music could be disguised?

Reinhardt wanted music from Giselle – music for the Nazis. Could she somehow present Andreas's music to him as just that – as her own composition? It was a terrifying idea, a massive, risky concept to grapple with. And it would mean that if the Führer succeeded in his power-crazed march towards England, Andreas's music might form the background to a dark and terrible victory. That was a bad thought.

But there was another, far worse thought. If Reinhardt could be believed, by giving the Nazis the music they wanted, Giselle would be signing her own death warrant.

THIRTEEN

Rain swept across Romney Marshes, and small huffs of wind found their way beneath the eaves of Greymarsh House.

Phin and Toby had stacked the attic boxes in a corner of the dining room, and had carried Christa's portrait, the music and Phin's notes, into Stefan's study. Toby managed to coax the wood-burning stove into life, and regarded the glowing heat with satisfaction, remarking that it reminded him of a lively ballad called 'The Fire Ship'. He would make a note of it for their anthology before he forgot it.

'Splendid old song. Fire ship's an old naval term for a battered old vessel they would set alight and let loose among enemy ships to cause havoc, did you know that? But in the song, it's a what-do-you-call it? – a euphemism for a lady who turns out to be a fire ship on her own account, and causes havoc in sailors' beds. Well, when I say havoc, the poor chaps actually end up having to be treated for syphilis.' He reached for Phin's notebook and scribbled the song's title on a back page. Then, without warning, he said, 'You hate that music we found, don't you? You're hoping it won't turn out to be the *Siegreich*.'

Phin thought about saying that if he had been on his own when the attic boxes were investigated, he would have burned every scrap of the music there and then. But he said, 'If it's the real *Siegreich,* that could open up all kinds of unpleasant sections of the past.'

'About Christa?'

'About Christa's family.'

'Her family?' said Toby. 'You think the *Siegreich* might have come from Stefan's family?'

'We found the music in this house. That could argue—'

'That Stefan was involved with the Nazis? That's something I'll never believe. In any case, he'd have been far too young – he was only five or six when the war started. Christa wasn't very much older – maybe about fifteen.' He frowned, and said, 'But—'

'But how does Stefan come to actually have the music in this house?' said Phin, as Toby paused. 'Where did he get it? And why would he bother to bring it to England with him?'

'I don't know where he would have got it, but émigrés bring whatever they can carry. Whatever they've salvaged. You've only got to look at some of today's people fleeing from Syria and Aleppo and all those other bombed-out places. They carry their belongings on handcarts and in wheelbarrows, poor sods. It's heartbreaking to see the news clips. I can see Stefan – or whoever brought him to England – tumbling stuff into boxes, gathering up everything that had belonged to his family without necessarily looking at any of it.'

'Yes, that's true. He might not have known the music was even there.'

Toby looked across at the music, then said, 'If it's the real thing, how much d'you think it's worth?'

'Difficult to say. But a handwritten score of Mahler's *Resurrection Symphony* recently sold at auction for about four million pounds.'

'Four million?' said Toby, his cherubic face shocked. 'You did say four million?'

'Yes. It was an all-time high for any musical manuscript, I think, and the *Siegreich*'s not in that kind of category. But, if it's genuine, Stefan would be in line for a very large pay-out.'

'He'd live out the rest of his life in utter luxury,' said Toby. Then: 'Phin, is all this really taking you back to Stefan's family?'

'I'm certainly curious about his parents,' said Phin. 'But I was thinking of Giselle. I'd like to know who she was, and why her name's in the painting.'

'She might just have been the painter's *chère amie*. It might even have been a name he conjured out of nowhere because he thought it looked good on the canvas. She doesn't have to exist and, even if she does, she doesn't have to be the villainess of the piece.'

'If there's a villainess at all, I'd rather cast Giselle than Christa in the role.'

'Oh, you're obviously heading for a fateful end,' said Toby, promptly. 'Never fall for a villainess. Yes, you may well laugh, but it's good advice. Give any villainess you meet a very wide berth, Phineas Fox, because at best she'll strangle you with her

cloak or stab you with her jewelled dagger, and at worst . . .' He
paused for dramatic effect, and Phin waited.

'At worst,' said Toby, lowering his voice thrillingly, 'you'll die
the death of the Black Widow Spider's mate, and trust me, that's
a *shrivelling* fate in the worst possible way. If you take my point.'

'It's taken,' said Phin, grinning.

'Well, good.' With an air of changing tack, Toby said, 'Look
here, you said the music looked as if it had a military flavour to
it. Except for that chord?'

'Yes. That's massively out of pattern.'

'So the finished article would have been intended to include
– um – trumpets and drums and things?'

'Yes. It would have been the kind of music the Führer's military
bands played.' He frowned, and heard himself say, 'They sometimes marched past infirmaries that held captured British airmen,
deliberately playing German marches to emphasize their ascend-
ancy over the wounded men.'

'But,' said Toby, 'is that music we found – and the music that's
in the painting – is it written for those instruments? Should I say
scored for them? I wouldn't know a quaver from a quintet and,
as far as I'm concerned, to score means something quite different.'

Phin grinned again, then said, 'It could have been intended to
be transposed. Some instruments do need transposition. The
clarinet, for instance. But it isn't necessary to transpose for every
instrument, although different ones give different sounds from the
same note – a double bass, for instance, sounds an octave lower
than music written in concert pitch. What we've found could be
the core composition.'

'Written for the piano? Written *on* the piano?'

'Well, a lot of the greats worked without any musical instrument
at all. Bach, Beethoven, Mahler – most of them – could think in
music notation. But I'd guess this was written with pen, paper and,
yes, with a piano.' He discovered he was looking at the portrait,
visualizing the painted hands moving across a keyboard.

Toby stood up. 'How about finding something to eat?' he said,
firmly. 'I don't know about you, but all this delving into the past
is making me extraordinarily hungry. Let's forage in Stefan's fridge
and freezer.'

*   *   *

The foraging produced frozen pizza, cheese, bread, and ham, and was accompanied by a spirited, albeit erratic, rendition from Toby of 'The Fire Ship'. But over the meal at the kitchen table, he suddenly said, 'You know, villainesses and Black Widows aside, we still haven't found a reason for Christa's banishment.'

'Not yet. Is there any mustard for this ham? Thanks.'

'Supposing he saw the music when the boxes were brought down?' said Toby. 'Would he have made a connection to Christa, d'you think? I mean a Nazi connection.'

'And thrown the portrait out because of it? I shouldn't think so,' said Phin. 'He'd have been too young to know about the *Siegreich* at the time – it sounds as if Christa would, as well. And I'm fairly sure that the details of Hitler's invasion plan weren't generally known until years later. I only know because I was researching the exiled musicians. In fact, I only know about the *Siegreich* because my work takes me into musical places. And even there, the *Siegreich*'s more of a legend than anything else. I wouldn't have thought Stefan would know about it.'

'Nor would I. Ah well. I wonder if there's a bottle of vino anywhere to go with this banquet.' Toby got up to investigate the cupboards again. 'Stefan's quite partial to a glass or two of wine. Yes, here we are. Now then, corkscrew . . . Oh, and I think I'd better check phone messages as well as post. I've only just thought about that. Look for a corkscrew while I do it, would you – the answerphone's only just out in the hall.'

The answerphone was on the carved oak chest, and Phin, uncorking the wine, saw through the open kitchen door that Toby's hand hesitated over the Play button. Speaking as lightly as he could, he said, 'Are you afraid of hearing a ransom demand for Arabella?'

'It sounds mad, doesn't it? But you do hear weird stories, and Arabella does get into such complicated situations,' said Toby, and pressed the Play button with decision.

But the phone's messages held nothing more than a polite voice reminding Mr Cain of an optician's appointment, and then a man's voice announcing itself as Marcus Mander, thanking Mr Cain for the excellent supper party the previous week, and expressing a hope that his goddaughter had managed to successfully clean the kitchen floor where the *crème brûlée* had bubbled out of the grill pan.

'At least they got as far as *crème brûlée*,' observed Toby, re-setting the machine and coming back to the kitchen. 'I've known Arabella's dinners to plunge into disaster over the starter.'

Toby had suggested Phin should have the bedroom that was usually Arabella's. It overlooked the gardens behind the house, and there were rather endearing traces of Arabella herself in the room. When Phin hung up his jacket, a faint drift of perfume came from the wardrobe, and a silk scarf, vividly crimson and purple, lay on the edge of the dressing table, with a crimson-tinted lipstick on it, as if the owner had been trying to match the colours. A pair of shoes, purple and black patent leather with impossibly impractical high heels, stood under the dressing table, one lying on its side, suggesting the wearer had kicked them off with a sigh of relief and abandoned them as unwearable.

The bed was comfortable, but Phin was wide awake. He could not stop thinking about the music they had found. Was it really the *Siegreich*? Even the word conjured up the sounds of marching feet and that sharp straight Nazi salute, and cheering crowds, shouting the infamous cry. *Sieg Heil*. Hail victory.

Inevitably, with those images, came the memories of his grandfather. Phin smiled. He would never cease to be grateful to his grandfather for drawing him into the world of music – the music his grandfather had reached for in an attempt to make blindness bearable. He had taken the young Phineas to concerts with him, encouraging him to listen and understand the music. 'You'll enjoy this one,' he would say. 'It's Beethoven – splendidly dramatic.' Or, 'It's Mozart – listen to the patterns he makes.' Always, before the concerts, he would say, 'And you'll keep hold of my hand, Phin, so I don't make a spectacle of us by tripping over the stairs.'

Phin would never forget his grandfather's absorption and pleasure in those concerts, and the way the blindness had almost ceased to matter at those times. It had been as if the old man could see the music in his mind – as if it made patterns for him against the perpetual darkness.

He sat up, punched the pillow, and lay down again. It was a little after midnight. Greymarsh House was not entirely silent, in the way that most houses – especially old ones – never were entirely silent after dark. There were small rustlings from overhead, and the occasional gentle creak of roof timbers contracting in the cool night air. He found these sounds unexpectedly friendly. Arabella must often have lain in this bed listening to them.

He got out of bed and went to the window, drawing the curtain slightly back. A thin mist had risen from the marshlands beyond the house; wisps of it clung to the trees, lending a fantastical quality to the scene. It was exactly how any self-respecting garden in a remote marshland house should look at such an hour.

Had it been chance that had caused the composer of that music – *Giselle's Music* – to place that ugly discordance – the chord of evil, the *diabolus in musica* – at its core? Or had it been a last act of defiance – a sly, snook-cocking gesture to the people who had been torturing the music out of him? And had any of those torturers realized what had been threaded into the music's heart?

Moving quietly so as not to wake Toby, Phin pulled a sweater over his pyjamas, slid his feet into shoes, and went out of the bedroom and down the stairs into the sitting room. The *Siegreich* lay where he had left it. It had probably been a bit careless to leave something so potentially valuable strewn around; although Phin did not much care if the entire burglar population of Romney Marsh levered up a window and reached in to pilfer the thing, it could be worth a great deal of money to Stefan Cain. He picked it up, and carried it with him into the dining room, thinking he would stow it in his suitcase later.

The boxes from the attics were where he and Toby had left them, and Phin lifted them on to the table. Was there anything in here that he had missed earlier, or to which he had not paid sufficient attention? He did not really think so. And yet . . .

The warmth from the stove had permeated in here, and when he switched on the old-fashioned standard lamp it felt as if he had stepped into that fragment of the past more completely than before. As he began to sort through the boxes' contents, he again had the sensation that he was thrusting his hands, wrist-deep, into that lost era. Christa's era. And Giselle's, also?

But the boxes still appeared to contain only trivia, which once somebody must have thought worth keeping. Here were the old parish council notes found earlier – a thick bundle, tied up with string, the typeface blurred with age and slight damp. Phin leafed through them to see if anything lay between the pages, but there was nothing.

The magazines, which were mostly gardening publications, did not yield anything, either. The second box held the German textbooks, which he and Toby had thought would be from Stefan's adult language teaching classes. Phin shook each one, but nothing fluttered from the pages. In novels, people often came upon an overlooked train ticket between a book's pages, which gave away the criminal's journey to the murder scene. Or a left-luggage ticket, leading to the discovery of a dismembered body in a trunk. Phin did not think left-luggage departments actually existed any longer, and in real life when you went through old papers, all you got were tiny shreds of old, flaked paper, and dust that got grittily on to your skin, and empty envelopes.

Envelopes . . . An empty envelope lay on top of the magazines. Would anyone bother to put an empty envelope in a box? It was not significant of anything – other, perhaps, than somebody not bothering to throw it away.

Or might it be indicative of somebody finding the contents so astonishing that the envelope had ceased to matter, and had dropped, unnoticed, back into the box? There was no stamp on it and no name or address – only a smear of ink on one corner. Phin frowned and bent over the envelope. It was ink, certainly, but it looked like a mark from a modern blue biro. He considered this, and an image began to form in his mind of somebody casually looking through these boxes when they were carried downstairs. Of that somebody – he would assume it had been Stefan – rummaging through the magazines and the parish minutes, perhaps smiling reminiscently at the sight of the German textbooks. And picking up an envelope that looked as if it might contain a letter . . .? Absent-mindedly using the point of a biro to unseal the flap . . .? Then what would he do? He might read whatever was inside the envelope here in the dining room, or he might take it into his study.

Phin got up and went through to Stefan's study, switching on the desk lamp. The pale oblong where the portrait had hung above it was clear. Was this what Stefan would have done? Had he come to sit at his desk – the place where he was used to working – to read a letter from his past life, a letter he had only just found? Phin thought he might well have done that. But what would he do after he had read it? Depending on the letter's contents, mightn't he put it in the desk drawer, until he decided what to do with it or what to do about it?

He took a deep breath and slid open the drawer. It came open easily, as if often used. Inside was a miscellany of odds and ends: several biros, a couple of books of stamps, a small Filofax, a pocket calculator.

And a half-folded sheet of old, slightly discoloured paper. Only the first few words were visible, and they were in German. Phin had a smattering of German, because it was a language that was often useful in his work. But it did not need any particular knowledge of the language to see that this was a letter. A letter that halfway down referred to Christa.

Phin spent several minutes reminding himself all over again that this was Stefan Cain's property, and that it might be part of something very private indeed. If he could not translate the whole letter himself, there were online translation websites, and any one of them would be enough for such a short piece of text. But could he go that far without Stefan Cain's permission? Or even Toby's? Then he reminded himself that this house had been broken into, that Stefan himself had been attacked and was in hospital, and he gave in, put the box back in the corner of the room, switched off the light, and took the letter up to his bedroom. Halfway up the stairs he remembered the *Siegreich* and went back for it.

Closing his bedroom door so that Toby would not hear him moving around, he put the *Siegreich* in the zipped compartment of his case, then set the laptop on Arabella Tallis's dressing table, and called up an online translation website. He could probably have taken a reasonable swing at the translation, but by this time he did not trust himself to do so with sufficient accuracy.

Letter by letter, he typed the note into the site. He checked twice to make sure he had done this accurately, then waited for the translation. For such a short piece, it came up quickly. There was no date on it, and the translation was literal, of course, making no allowance for the difference in phrasing between German and

English. But it was easy to juggle the words into an English pattern, and in effect, the note said:

My dear Velda,

It was good to hear from you. After so much sadness and loss – in both our lives – it is important to stay close to the family we have left.

I have thought for a long time as to how – and even if – I should answer your question about Giselle. I could wish you had not asked it, but you have asked it twice now, and so I think that you are owed the truth. Half-understood facts can fester for years – speculation can be dangerous and damaging to those who come afterwards.

Even after so long, I cannot write the word that should be used for Christa, although I fear it is a word that may be used about her in the future.

I was still a prisoner in Sachsenhausen when it happened, and even though we were all closely and cruelly guarded, some of us heard what happened, and so we knew the truth. That truth is something I do not think I can ever forget – and certainly I can never forgive.

The truth is that Christa was responsible for Giselle's death inside Sachsenhausen.

That is as much as I can bear to write, but you will understand the word I cannot and will not use about Christa.

Forgive me for being the one to tell you this shocking information. I know it will be deeply hurtful, but I also know you will ensure Stefan never knows about it.

I often think of you and I am glad you are still living in Lindschoen. I have such good memories of my visits to you and Giselle there – in the days when we had no idea of the tragedies that were ahead. I remember so well how we would spend evenings in that house in that square with its beautiful and appropriate name. Are those old lamps still there? They used to cast such a radiance over the old stones, and I loved that. It all seemed magical and special. In my memory, it all still is.

I hope to hear that all is well with you.

Very much love to you,

Silke.

Phin stared at the screen for so long that the screen-saver kicked in, and the room darkened. So, here it was at last. Proof that Christa Cain had indeed been a villainess.

Christa Cain had been painted smiling and holding the music of her victim. Giselle. And the word that the unknown Silke could not and would not use was 'murderess'.

FOURTEEN

P hin, drinking coffee with a thin dawn streaking the skies, had spent most of the night trying to consider Silke's letter objectively.

Clearly it had been written after World War II – the reference to Sachsenhausen indicated that – although it was impossible to know how long afterwards Silke had sent it. As for its content . . .

It was a shock, but shocking things – dramatic things – were part of wars. Christa, despite her youth, might have been part of some kind of spying activity that had gone wrong. People spied and infiltrated and lived strange, secret lives for their country during wars, and age did not necessarily matter. And if Giselle had been working for the Nazis, Christa could have had justifiable reasons for killing her. Phin did not really like the idea of the mysterious Giselle having been a Nazi, although he quite liked the idea of Christa as a spy. This was probably because it made her a heroine rather than a villainess, though. As Toby said, you had to beware of villainesses.

But whatever the truth, Silke's letter must be the reason for Stefan's repudiation of Christa's portrait. Toby had said Stefan had adored Christa, and that the painting was the only likeness of her that he had. How must he have felt finding that letter, and reading that Christa had been a murderess? Might he even have known Giselle? He could hardly have lived with the portrait without being aware of Giselle's name on the music in Christa's hands. But whatever the truth, Phin thought it was small wonder that Stefan Cain could not bear to see his sister's portrait any longer.

And yet . . . Would Stefan, who sounded to be nobody's fool, automatically accept that letter at face value? Would anyone meekly accept that kind of slur against a sister he had known and loved? Especially when it related to the war years and a concentration camp. In those circumstances, wouldn't most people look for other explanations, as Phin, who had not even known Christa, was doing?

There's something more, he thought. This isn't the reason. There's more to find.

With the idea of attacking the problem from another angle, he wrote down the sequence of events to see if they dovetailed. The workmen had brought the boxes down from the attics three – no, four – days before Toby's party. Phin would check the date on the contractor's note, but he thought he had it right. Two days after that, Christa's portrait had been delivered to Arabella's flat, with Stefan's note saying he never wanted to see it again. Yes, it fitted.

And then two separate things – neither of which he had fully registered until now – struck him.

The first was the reference in Silke's letter to Sachsenhausen. Sachsenhausen.

Phin bounded upstairs, and seized the laptop from the dressing table, slithering back downstairs with it.

Sachsenhausen.

Researching into the exiled 1930s and 1940s musicians, he had come across mentions of a small orchestra based just outside Berlin. There had been several well-documented records of the orchestra's performances – they had not set the music world alight, but they had attracted quiet acclaim. The musicians themselves had seemed to be semi-professional performers – possibly they were mostly music teachers for the better part of their time – who came together for concerts and recitals at various halls. They had struck Phin as being dedicated and hard-working, and he had rather liked the sound of them. But one of the facts he had uncovered was that a member of the orchestra had apparently been seized after a concert given in 1940, and imprisoned in Sachsenhausen concentration camp.

'The concert's programme included a work by Mendelssohn – a composer whose work is specifically banned by the Third Reich,' one account said. 'It was an act of open defiance.'

Phin had tried to trace the imprisoned musician's identity, in case he could be included in the proposed book, but whoever it was had been recorded, with soulless anonymity, simply as *Jew No. 8643291ZI*. Such nameless entries were customary, of course – the SS had been rounding up Jews from all over Germany, and the Jews themselves had been of no account at that time. Phin knew all that, but it had still distressed him to see it written down.

The other thing to strike him about Silke's letter was her reference to having 'such good memories' of her visits to Lindschoen.

Lindschoen. The orchestra who had given that defiant performance of Mendelssohn had been known as the Lindschoen Orchestra. The only individual name attached to it that Phin had been able to find was in the German magazine, *Das Theater*, which had fulsomely praised the ebullient-sounding pianist, Herr Erich Eisler. Herr Eisler, it seemed, had frequently performed with the Lindschoen, and had been the soloist on the fateful night of the Mendelssohn performance.

Phin had translated the review with some help from the online service and saved it to the hard disc. He opened the document and re-read it. It described Herr Eisler as a maestro, referred affectionately to his always untidy appearance and untamed hair, and described how, under the quiet authority of his conductor, he had given a moving interpretation of the *Leibesträume*.

'However, in the second half, the orchestra played Mendelssohn's *Italian Symphony*. Music aficionados will know, of course, that Mendelssohn is one of the composers whose work is banned. This magazine understands that Schutzstaffel officers were in the audience, and we have been informed that shortly after the concert one of the musicians was taken to Sachsenhausen labour camp.'

Phin had tried, without success, to track down the relevant edition of *Das Theater* and also the name of the quiet conductor. It had not been Eisler himself who had been imprisoned in Sachsenhausen, though, because he had found a review of a much later date, when Eisler had entertained an appreciative audience in Paderborn.

Had it been the quiet conductor who had urged his orchestra on to that act of defiance? It would be a leap of faith to wonder if that conductor, the imprisoned Lindschoen musician and *Jew No. 8643291ZI* could be one and the same person, but Phin did wonder it. It was an even greater leap to wonder whether, if so, he had been the *Siegreich*'s composer, which would certainly fit with the legend. The arrest could have been not so much because of the Mendelssohn defiance as because the Nazis believed he could give them the *Siegreich*.

But hundreds and probably thousands of musicians had been imprisoned during that war, and the *Siegreich* could have been composed anywhere by any one of them. Phin would have to keep remembering that.

The sound of the shower whooshing upstairs, and Toby's cheerful voice raised in song, brought him out of the past. He closed the laptop and went to call up to Toby that he was making breakfast. As he scrambled eggs, he was thinking that unless he had severely mistranslated, or wildly misunderstood, Silke's letter, it seemed likely that the murdered Giselle had lived in Lindschoen.

Over breakfast, having brought Toby up to date with his findings, he said, 'Do you by any chance have a current passport?'

Toby, who had been spooning scrambled eggs on to a plate, looked up. 'Aha. You're going to Lindschoen, aren't you? And you'd like me to come with you.'

'I think I am going. I want to see if I can track down the conductor of that orchestra. I don't suppose you can actually spare the time to come with me, though—'

'I might manage it,' said Toby, thoughtfully. 'I can probably fudge things so that I'm not at lectures for about a week. And I sort of feel I owe it to Stefan to find out the truth about Christa. It'll be difficult to find the Lindschoen gang, though, won't it? It's a very long time ago, and they don't sound as if they were the Berlin Philharmonic.'

'I know. But,' said Phin, reaching for toast, 'I want to know the truth about the *Siegreich*.'

'I hope you aren't chasing phantoms,' said Toby. 'Do I mean phantoms or mirages? Or am I thinking about those capering hobgoblin things that beckon to the unwary, and promise a crock of gold at the end of the rainbow?'

'You said earlier that I was straying into da Vinci territory,' said Phin. 'Now you're going into Irish fantasy.'

Toby grinned, then said there were bound to be a good many really bawdy Irish songs they might add to their anthology. 'Storytellers of the world, the Irish.'

'I know,' said Phin, dryly, having recently spent some time on the west coast in pursuit of a chimera of a very different kind. 'But this is all linking together, and I've got to follow the links and see where they end.'

'Let's hope it's a crock of gold and not a crock of shit,' said Toby.

FIFTEEN

Margot Mander would never forget the night near the end of Marcus's final university term, because she knew it was the night she had nearly lost him for good.

He had come home for the weekend; mostly, it seemed, because he wanted to tell Margot and Mother that he had been offered a job with a firm of translators in south London.

'I've been for one or two interviews with other companies, but this is the one I wanted. They do a lot of conference work – interpreting for businessmen at conventions – which would be brilliant. There'll be a good deal of grunt work as well, of course – translating textbooks and manuals. I'll probably be on that at first, until I prove my worth.'

'How lovely,' said Margot.

'And I've found a flat, quite near to the office,' said Marcus. 'Well, it's a few tube stops along and you have to change lines midway, but it's not so bad.'

'It all sounds very exciting.' Margot was daring to hope that this might be what she had waited for; that he might tell her they could be together at last. Would she dare to actually live in London? But she would be with Marcus. She would do it if he asked her. And something could be worked out about Mother, surely.

But after Mother had gone up to bed, Marcus said, 'The flat I've got is pretty basic. Not much more than a couple of cupboards, but London prices are terrifying, and it'll do for the time being.'

Clearly Margot was not going to be part of this new scenario, and disappointment rose up, but then Marcus said, 'I haven't forgotten what we talked about that night, Margot. When we found the letter to Lina about that house, you remember. It was in a German town called Lindschoen'

'I remember.'

'Have you still got the letter?'

'Yes. Oh, yes.'

'We got a bit carried away that night, didn't we – well, I was pretty potted, I remember. But I said that all we needed . . .'

He stopped, but the sentence finished itself in Margot's mind. *All we need is for Mother not to be here any longer* . . .

'I remember everything,' she said, a bit breathlessly.

'Good girl. It can be our goal, that house.'

'When do you start work?'

'As soon as term ends. I'm moving into the flat as soon as I can.'

'That's nice. I'm really pleased for you. I'm glad about the flat, too.'

She waited for him to say she must come to see it, even spend a weekend there, but he did not. A vicious disappointment sliced through her. Again, thought Margot. He always does this; he always lets me down when I'm expecting something. She was aware of a stab of anger, because he should have sensed her feelings.

But he did want them to be together. He had said so. Margot reached for that memory and held it hard. *All we need is for Mother not to be here any longer,* he had said.

'I've got a cold starting,' said Margot's mother, a couple of weeks later. 'Actually, I think it might be flu.'

'Go to bed early. I'll bring you some paracetamol and some hot milk with whisky.'

'I might need the doctor in the morning. You'd better phone the office and tell them you can't go in. Flu shouldn't be neglected. Not at my age.'

Margot's mother was nowhere near an age where you had to worry about neglecting flu, but Margot helped her into bed, then went downstairs to heat the milk. Pouring it into a mug, she had the oddest feeling that it was not her hands that were doing this. Here were the paracetamol; the box said two tablets every four hours. How many would knock you out? Six? Eight? How many would tip you beyond being just knocked out?

She carried the tray upstairs. 'Drink the milk while it's hot. And I'll leave the box of paracetamol on the bedside table for you.'

'Could I make an appointment for my mother to see a doctor, please? Mrs Mander, Forest Avenue.'

'Next Tuesday at ten?'

'Couldn't it be sooner? It's Thursday today, so—'

'Is it an emergency?'

'Not exactly. She's had a touch of flu, I think. A bit of a high temperature. It's been a couple of days now.' And then, because it was important to keep as close to the truth as possible, she said, 'She was sick yesterday, as well.'

The receptionist said there were a lot of those kinds of viral infections around at the moment. Stomach bugs, if you wanted a layman's term for it. They generally cleared up within four or five days.

'It's left her very low, though. Very depressed,' said Margot.

'I expect it will. But unless you're telling me it's an emergency, next Tuesday's the earliest date I can give you.'

'Yes, all right. What should I do in the meantime?'

'Make sure she has plenty of fluids for the vomiting. And paracetamol for the fever. Only six paracetamol in any twenty-four hours, though – at the absolute maximum, eight. It's important to remember that.'

'Yes, I understand. I'll be careful,' said Margot.

'If the condition deteriorates severely, phone back, and if it's out of surgery hours, the out-of-hours number is on our voicemail. Or, in a real emergency, 999, of course.'

'Yes, of course. Thank you.'

Margot rang off, and went into the kitchen to make a hot lemon drink for her mother.

It rained for the whole of Thursday, and for all of Thursday night. When Margot got up on Friday morning, it was still raining – a ceaseless, despairing drizzle that turned the rooms into dim underwater caverns, and seeped through badly fitting window-frames, dripping on to the floors directly beneath. The house was in a shockingly run-down state. Margot mopped up the rainwater, and put down a couple of old bathroom mats to catch any more drips.

She took her mother breakfast on a tray, which her mother said she could not eat because she still felt sick. When, later, she complained of stomach pains, Margot brought hot milk with brandy, then fetched a hot-water bottle, because her mother said she was cold. No, she did not want the electric blanket on. She might be sick all over it, and electrocute herself, had Margot thought of that? Margot left a bowl by the bed, in case of sickness, then suggested bringing the small radio in – it could go on the bedside table and it would be cheerful and company. Or something to read, perhaps? But her mother could not be doing with raucous voices telling her about the dreary events in the world, and her head ached too much to read.

'Close the curtains, would you? The light hurts my eyes.'

Margot closed the curtains. In the dim light, her mother looked shrunken and her skin was sallow.

'I'll fetch Lina's walking stick, shall I? You can use that to knock on the floor if you need anything. I'll come up later, though.'

She found the walking stick, which Lina had used when her rheumatism was troubling her, and took in a jug of lemon barley water and the paracetamol. Six only every twenty-four hours.

She was doing everything a devoted daughter should do. It was important to keep that in mind.

Later, when she went upstairs again, her mother was asleep. That would be the paracetamol; they could build up, everyone knew that. Margot counted the pills left in the box.

She tiptoed in again at midday, but her mother was lying in the same position, so Margot closed the door and went out.

It was nearly nine o'clock that evening when she heard a tapping from overhead. It was startlingly loud in the quiet house, and Margot's heart lurched. It could not be her mother, it could *not*. Not after three days of so carefully administering the paracetamol. Of counting the pills so diligently. Staggered dosage, it was called. It built up in the body.

Margot pressed her hands over her ears, so she would not hear the sounds, but she knew they were still going on. And if you were a dutiful daughter, you would not ignore such a sound. You would go up to see what was wanted, or whether anything was wrong. It was the kind of thing you would tell people afterwards. 'I heard her knocking on the floor,' you would say, 'so I went up to her room.'

But you might not immediately hear the knocking. You might be in the kitchen clattering crockery around, or you might be watching television with the sound high. You might be washing your hair, water splashing around your ears. In any one of those situations, it might be quite a long time before you heard the tapping. Could it be as long as an hour? It was now quarter past nine. At quarter past ten Margot would go upstairs.

At ten o'clock the tapping came again, but Margot waited doggedly for the clock to crawl round to quarter past, then took a deep breath, and went out to the hall.

And once there, she almost laughed with relief, because she could hear the sound more clearly now, and she knew what it was. Something called water hammer. It had been a nuisance earlier this year, and a plumber had eventually come to the house. He had sucked his teeth and shaken his head, and said, short of ripping out floorboards and relaying the old pipes, there was not really a cure. The pipes were out of true with one another, that was the problem; they juddered when water was forced through them.

A dutiful daughter would go up to her mother's room about now, though. To make sure her mother was comfortable for the night, to see if anything was wanted. Margot made her way up the stairs, moving slowly.

The bedroom was almost exactly as she had left it. Well, not exactly, but near enough. She made sure the curtains were still closed against the rainy night, and she collected the used cup and saucer from the bedside table. She took away the jug that had contained the lemon barley drink so it could be thoroughly washed along with the cup and saucer, but she left the box of tissues, because they were things people wanted to hand when they had flu. After thought, she fetched a book from her own room and put that by the tissue box.

Then she said goodnight to her mother. There was no response, of course.

Margot went back downstairs, knowing that she had done absolutely everything right, everything a devoted daughter could have been expected to do.

At eleven o'clock she reached for the phone and dialled the number of Marcus's flat. There were several anxious seconds when she thought he was not going to answer – that he was not there, or perhaps he was too busy to pick up the phone. But then she heard his voice, and she said, a bit breathlessly, 'Marcus, I'm really sorry to phone so late, but I think you ought to come home. Right away, I mean. This weekend. Mother's quite ill and I'm not coping very well.'

'I can't possibly come this weekend,' said Marcus. 'A deadline's been brought forward for a client, and I've said I'll go in to the office tomorrow morning to finish things, so the printers can have the final cut first thing on Monday.'

'But—'

'Marg, I can't. I've been given sole control of this project, and I've only worked here five minutes, so I've got to prove my worth. You can understand that, surely?'

He sounded impatient, so Margot said, 'Oh, yes.'

'In any case, Ma's always being not well. What's wrong with her this time?'

'She's had a cold. She thinks it might be flu.'

'She always thinks a cold's flu,' said Marcus.

'No, I think it really is. And she's been sick and she's got stomach pains. The surgery said it would be a stomach bug.'

'If it gets worse you can call the doctor, can't you? No, all right, not at this time of night, but aren't there emergency paramedics or something? There's no need to panic.'

I am panicking, thought Margot. For pity's sake, just for once, can't you understand what I'm feeling! But aloud, she said, 'Marcus, I really don't know what I should do. Couldn't you manage to come? Could you bring the work with you?'

'I suppose I could bring the laptop,' said Marcus, a bit reluctantly. 'Ma's a sodding nuisance, though. She'll be as right as rain in a couple of days – she always is. But OK, I'll collect everything from the office early tomorrow, and drive straight down. Reach you around lunchtime, if the weekend traffic isn't too snarled-up.'

Tomorrow. Only twelve hours away. Say fourteen. But the entire night to get through, knowing what lay upstairs . . .

But Margot said, 'Thanks. I'll have some lunch ready for you.' She would not dare leave the house to get extra shopping, but there was food in the fridge and the freezer.

'How about if I speak to the old girl now? I can usually cheer her up. Take the phone in to her.'

'No, I won't do that. She's fast asleep at the moment, and I don't want to wake her.'

After she put the phone down, Margot discovered she was afraid to go to bed. Around half past eleven she switched off all the lights, though, because neighbours might notice if lights were shining into the night. People noticed each other's routines when they lived in the same road. They might notice the lights, and say afterwards that it had seemed a bit unusual, because Mrs Mander and her daughter usually went to bed around eleven each night. So the lights all had to be switched off, and ordinary things like putting out the empty milk bottles had to be remembered.

Margot did all this, trying to be systematic, trying not to forget anything. She was still quite frightened, but it helped to focus on these details. It helped even more to remember the exact conversation with Marcus, and how she had said her mother was asleep. And that phone call to the GP's surgery – she had asked that anxious question about what best to do for flu, and she had confirmed she understood about not exceeding the dose of paracetamol.

The house was dark and creaky all around her, and she huddled into a corner of the sofa in the living room. Around midnight she went into the kitchen to make a cup of tea, trying not to creak the doors, moving as quietly as she could. Turning on the tap sent the water hammer juddering and knocking again. It was important not to wonder if it might be frenzied knocking on the floor from the bedroom above.

The water hammer had a horrid macabre rhythm, and the cold tap started dripping as well, and Margot could not turn it fully off. The hammer would die away, but the dripping tap would go on maddeningly all night. Drip-drip. Like the drip of all those poisoning memories throughout her entire life. Christa Cain. A murderess . . .

Rain was still lashing against the windows, like frozen finger bones, tapping to get in, and the dripping tap was like a horrid sly voice saying, We-know-what-you're-doing. You-can't-run-away. We'll-find-you . . .

Marcus arrived shortly after lunch next day, bringing the cold wet morning in with him, setting down the laptop case and a small bag with his overnight things. He threw his jacket over the banister, and said, 'I suppose you're going to tell me she's recovering by now, aren't you?'

'She's asleep,' said Margot. 'So I haven't disturbed her. It's good to sleep when you've got flu, isn't it? She didn't even want the curtains opened, so I didn't.'

'I'll go up.'

He went up the stairs, two at a time, as he always had done. Margot stayed downstairs, clenching her fists. What if—

It felt as if centuries passed – as if worlds were born and died – before he came back downstairs. Margot found she was offering up a silent prayer. Please let it be all right. Please . . .

When Marcus appeared, his face was white, and there was a look of shock in his eyes, but when he spoke, his voice sounded normal.

He said, 'Phone the ambulance, will you? Now – this minute. Didn't you bloody realize?'

'What's happened? She was asleep—'

'She isn't asleep,' said Marcus 'She's unconscious. I think she's in a coma.'

SIXTEEN

'But she only had flu,' said Margot, after three nightmare days spent in A&E and then in ICU. She had said this several times to the doctors and the nurses, and to anyone who would listen. 'It was just flu. You don't die from flu.'

'We're so very sorry. Please be assured that we did everything we could, but there was renal failure – liver failure.'

Two men from the coroner's office came to the house next day, to talk to Margot and Marcus. Margot repeated that her mother had only had flu. She told them how she had made an appointment at the surgery, how she had phoned her brother for advice.

'It wasn't flu,' said the older of the two men. He had a rather severe look; Margot started to feel a bit frightened. 'We'll have to wait for the post mortem, but the medics say it's paracetamol overdose. Almost certainly taken over two, or probably three, days. Staggered dose, it's called.'

'But I was so careful,' said Margot. Her voice was shrill, and after a moment she began to cry. 'I was giving her the pills, and I knew not to give more than six in twenty-four hours – eight at the absolute most. I was really careful about it.'

The younger man came downstairs then, Marcus at his side. He held out two paracetamol boxes.

'Two boxes of sixteen,' he said. 'Both empty.'

Margot stared at him, then at the boxes. 'Those aren't the pills I got,' she said. 'The ones I got are on the bedside table.'

'Yes, we found those. But these boxes were in the bedside cabinet,' he said.

'Thirty-two 500-milligram pills add up to sixteen grams,' said the older man. 'That's well over the dose usually considered potentially fatal.'

'I didn't know she had them,' said Margot, crying even harder. 'And – oh God – I was giving her two anyway, every four hours. I never thought – I should have checked . . . But there was no reason to open that cabinet.'

The younger man, who had been in Mother's room, glanced at Marcus then said, 'We found this, as well.' He held it out.

'What . . .?'

'It had probably been under the pillow, but it had slipped down on to the floor,' he said. 'Mr Mander, will you read it to your sister?'

'You read it,' said Marcus. His voice was cold and distant. Margot glanced at him uneasily.

The letter said,

'My dears. Forgive me, but since Lina went and since Marcus left home, I have been so very alone. There seems nothing left for me in my life any longer. I go from one illness to another, and now there is this latest bout of sickness . . . My life is so empty, so dreary. Forgive me.'

Their mother's signature was at the foot.

Margot stared at it for a long time, her mind tumbling. What should she say? What should she feel? She twisted her damp handkerchief in her hands, then cried out, 'But she wasn't alone. I was here. I looked after her.'

'I know you did. And I'm sorry we have to put you both through this. But I have to ask you if this is your mother's writing?'

'Oh yes,' said Marcus, quickly. Too quickly?

'Yes, it is,' said Margot. 'I can show you other things she's written – cards, shopping lists.' A pause. 'This means – it means it was suicide? Does it?'

The men in the room glanced at one another, then the older one said, 'It'll be for the inquest to decide. But the note's fairly clear. I'd say it was almost certainly suicide.'

'Is it my fault?' said Margot. 'She said she was depressed, but you get depressed with flu, don't you? And the sickness exhausted her. It's horrid being sick anyway. Should I have done something more? I'd booked an appointment at the surgery, but it wasn't for a few days— Please say I'm not to blame. Please. I couldn't bear it.'

She looked across the room to where Marcus was standing by the door. He was staring at her, and there was a look on his face she had never seen before – a look that, if it were not Marcus who stood there, Margot would have thought was hatred. Or was it fear?

*   *   *

The inquest was bewildering, full of medical technicalities about hepatic necrosis and liver failure and renal failure, but, at the end of it, the verdict was definite and clear. Suicide while the balance of the mind was disturbed. Sympathy was extended to Mr Mander and Miss Mander – especially to Miss Mander who had nursed her mother so devotedly.

The funeral, the following day, was attended by several neighbours.

'They're here out of morbid curiosity,' said Marcus, as they got into the funeral car to go home. 'Same principle as the Victorians going to view lunatics and watch bear-baiting.'

'Will you help me to go through Mother's papers?' said Margot abruptly. 'Before you go back to London, I mean?'

He hesitated, then said, 'Yes, all right. We need to find the deeds to the house, and there's an insurance policy, as well, isn't there?'

They spent the evening sorting through the papers in their mother's bedroom cupboard. There were a few surprises, and the first was the bank statements. The savings account held only two hundred pounds, and the current account held no more than a few pounds. There was a rather puzzling standing order each month to a company neither of them had ever heard of.

'I don't know what that is, but I'm not liking the look of it,' Marcus said, his brows drawn down.

But the first real blow came when they found the insurance policy, and when Marcus read the terms and conditions. It stated, unequivocally, that the money would not be paid out in the event of suicide.

'It doesn't matter, though,' said Margot, a bit desperately. 'It wasn't much anyway. There's still the house.'

But there was not still the house. That was the second blow. There was a rental agreement for the house, made between Lina Mander and the company who were the subject of the mysterious standing order. They were a property company. Clipped to the agreement was a letter confirming an amendment to the original document, transferring the tenancy from Lina to their mother. It was dated shortly after Lina's death.

'Oh, God,' said Marcus, 'they bloody rented this house. They never owned it.'

Margot said in bewilderment, 'Mother said Lina had passed the house over to her. But I thought that meant the ownership.'

'So did I.' Marcus threw the tenancy agreement and the insurance policy down in angry disgust. 'No money,' he said. 'Not from anywhere. All those sodding years of hoping and waiting, and at the end of it, fuck-all.'

Margot thought: And all the things I did as well, if only you knew.

The following morning, he came into the kitchen where Margot was cooking his breakfast, and said with an air of decision, 'I've been thinking about this all night, and there's one card left that we might try to play. You know what I'm talking about, don't you?'

'The Lindschoen house,' said Margot, who had been thinking about it all night as well. 'That's what you mean, isn't it? The property that was held in trust for Lina.'

'Yes. I don't know much about the law, but surely when Lina died, if she owned the house by then it would have passed to Mother. And now Mother's gone, we're next in line. At worst we ought to have some kind of a claim on it.'

'We've never found out anything about it, though. There was nothing in Lina's papers or in Mother's. And you couldn't trace those German solicitors who wrote to Lina.'

'I think they'd long since gone out of business,' said Marcus. 'And we can't just go batting off to Lindschoen without knowing exactly where the house is. It might not even be still there.'

'How could we find out more?' None of this sounded very promising, so Margot went back to grilling bacon.

'I think,' said Marcus, slowly, 'that we start with Christa.'

Always Christa . . .

'Why her?' Margot lifted the bacon off the grill pan and put it on plates.

'Because Lina's childhood – her whole past – is tied up with Christa Klein. God, we had it drummed into us enough times when we were kids.' He got up to pour coffee.

'Yes.'

'And somewhere in that childhood,' said Marcus, 'is Lina's father. The man Christa murdered. He was the one who was given that house, so he's the one we need to trace – or at least, we need to find out as much about him as we can.'

'And you think Christa's past could take us to him?'

'I think it could take us to Lina's past, and then to her father. We've scoured this house to find out more about him, and there's nothing except that one photograph.'

The photo of a man with eyes that gave nothing away, and a mouth that might have been sensitive or brutal . . .

Marcus said, 'All Lina ever told us was that her father was murdered, and it's supposed to have happened in Wewelsburg Castle. But that's all we've got. We don't know where Lina lived as a child, we don't know who her mother was, nothing. But if we could find Christa – at least find anyone left from her family who might be around – we might find out more. And that,' said Marcus, 'could lead us to the Lindschoen house.'

Marcus did not go back to London. He said the company were happy for him to work from this house for the time being. They understood about the bereavement, and anyway, a great many people worked from home these days, with modern technology being so good. You could translate documents and books pretty much anywhere, and most people emailed material these days anyway.

It was lovely having him in the house, and Margot could not believe how protective he had become of her. He seemed not to want her to go out on her own; he often drove her to the office and collected her. On Saturdays he came with her to the supermarket to collect the shopping.

Margot thought she ought to be completely happy now; after all these years she had what she had always wanted – she had Marcus completely to herself. She almost was happy. If only she did not occasionally find him looking at her, with that expression that might have been fear but that might just have been hatred.

The property company who managed the house said they were extremely sorry, but they were not prepared to transfer the tenancy a second time. They wanted to modernize the house and sell it outright, which would be more profitable for them. They gave Margot and Marcus three months to find another place, which they said was being generous. Margot began scouring the local paper for rented properties they could afford, and phoning estate agents. Marcus said there was no need to panic; he was going to find

Christa Klein's family and from there they would find the Lindschoen house and prove they were entitled to it. He was already searching various sites online for archive material, he said. He had only struck dead ends so far, but he would stay with it.

After a month, he took her to London with him for three days, because he had to go into his office, and there were some promising leads to follow up about the Lindschoen house, and about Christa's family, as well. Margot did not really want to go, but Marcus said he did not want to leave her on her own in the house – not with all those memories that were there.

The noise and the crowds and the sheer speed of everything in London bewildered Margot, but she tried not to let Marcus see this, because she did not want him to think she was some frightened little provincial who could not share properly in his life. She stayed in the flat while he went out. It was very small indeed. Margot spent the time cleaning everywhere, and she managed to make a meal each evening from the sparse provisions in the cupboards. But on the second night they went out to a bistro. Over coffee, Marcus told her the meal was a bit of a celebration, because he thought he had found Christa's brother. Margot's heart leapt with delight, and she said, 'That's marvellous. Tell me all about it.'

'It is good, isn't it? I didn't want to tell you until I was sure – well, as sure as it's possible to be. I recently discovered a set-up called the World Jewish Congress archives. It's a remarkable organization. They did masses of work helping what they used to call displaced persons – survivors of the concentration camps – and they gave me fairly free rein in their archives. That's where I found Christa's brother. He's living in a place called Thornchurch in Kent – Romney Marshes, in fact – in a house called Greymarsh House. He's calling himself Cain – Stefan Cain. Lina always said the family anglicized its name, so that would fit. Klein to Cain. He came to England in the late 1940s – he was about thirteen at the time. That fits, as well. I'm almost positive that he's Christa's younger brother.'

Christa's brother. That anxious-eyed little boy in the photograph in the newspaper article about vanished killers. It gave Margot an odd feeling to think someone from Christa's family was still alive; it brought the past sharply into contact with the present.

She said, 'It's the first pathway back, isn't it? The first road we've found that might take us back to Lina's childhood.'

'Yes. And now we've found him, we need to get to know him. To make sure he really is Stefan Klein.' He paused, then said, 'So how would you feel about going to live in Romney Marshes?'

'It's a small place,' said Marcus, the following weekend as they set off for Kent. 'But it's within commuting distance of the office – just about. That's important, because they aren't very happy about me working from home as a permanency. So I'll have to be in the office for part of each week now.' He sent her an odd look. 'But you'd be all right, wouldn't you? You'd only be on your own for the daytime. I'd be home each evening.'

'Yes, of course.'

'It'll be cheaper than living in London, anyway,' said Marcus. 'We'd have to find somewhere larger for the two of us.'

'I could probably get somewhere back at home to rent. And keep working at the office.'

'Oh, no, you can't be on your own,' said Marcus, at once. 'This will be fine. And as far as I'm concerned, the journey from Thornchurch to London looks manageable – it's a straightforward drive along the M20 and turn off.'

None of this meant much to Margot, but she said, 'Oh, I see.'

'Thornchurch is on the edge of Romney Marshes, but it's quite an urban part, so don't go visualizing lonely fens and misty marshlands, or Holmes and Watson prowling through the boggy moor, looking for the spectral Hound.'

'That was Dartmoor, wasn't it?' said Margot, who had never actually read any Sherlock Holmes books, but had seen the films, which was surely nearly as good.

There were not many houses to rent in the Thornchurch area and they had to make a second trip the following weekend. But this time they found a small, two-bedroomed property which Marcus said they could afford.

'It's very small though,' he said, looking round the rooms.

'It's not so bad. I'll make it lovely and really cosy, you'll see.' Margot was already visualizing frilled pelmets to soften the rather small windows, and new covers for the chairs. Sanderson did lovely

prints and you could get remnants in sales. She would make sure
to salvage Mother's old sewing machine.

'Let's take it,' said Marcus decisively. 'They'll do something
called a short-term lease, or short-hold tenancy or something. Six
months. That should give us long enough to get to know Cain,
and find out if he really is Stefan Klein.'

'If it's not him, what do we do?'

'Go on looking. I hope we don't have to move again, though,
because it's bloody expensive, so for God's sake go easy on what
you spend.'

He sounded angry, so Margot stopped thinking about new curtains
and chair covers, and said she would try to get a job so she could
contribute to their income. It might be a bit difficult, what with it
being such a small place and probably not having many opportun-
ities for work, but she would do her best.

She had looked forward to being in Thornchurch, because it would
be their real home together – a place they had furnished and made
their own. But it was not quite as marvellous as she had expected.

It was understandable that Marcus should sometimes be a bit
snappy in the evenings, because he was tired from the commute.
He said it was a real bitch, that journey, more exhausting than he
had bargained for, what with the traffic, which could be unbeliev-
able, and having to park so far from the office itself – and pay
monstrous parking charges! – and then walk the rest of the way.

But he managed to meet Stefan Cain in the little town – a chance
meeting, he said, but a carefully engineered one.

'Engineered?' Margot did not understand.

'Well, of course it was engineered. Why d'you think I've been
going into Thornchurch every weekend, pretending to wander
around libraries, and take an interest in the corn exchange.'

'Why the corn—?'

'Because,' said Marcus, sounding impatient, 'Cain used to give
adult language classes there. German, obviously. I pretended I
might be interested in helping out if they were continuing the
courses. God forbid, but it meant I finally ran into Cain. And I'll
make bloody sure I run into him again, now I know he still goes
along to meet a few of his old colleagues.'

He still sounded impatient, in fact he sounded almost angry, but a week or so later he came home smiling. He had had an invitation for them to go along to a small supper party at Cain's house, he said. A birthday evening.

'There'll be a few local people there, but it's the very thing I've been hoping for.'

'Do I have to come with you?'

'Of course you do. It'd look peculiar if you don't.'

'I'd honestly rather not. I'm not very good with strangers. And you'll do it all so much better – talking to people, getting to know Mr Cain properly.' It was impossible to explain that if she said the wrong things, or made stupid remarks from nervousness, Marcus would be angry with her.

'We're both invited,' said Marcus. 'You'll be fine. Oh, and wear something smart, will you?' He looked a bit disparagingly at the old sweater and jeans which Margot had put on that day to clean the windows. 'Look your very best. I want us to create a good impression.'

The next day Margot withdrew what was left of her savings to buy a new outfit for the party. Marcus's salary had to be kept for household bills, and she was scrupulous about not using it for anything else. She spent quite a lot of money so she would look her very best for Marcus.

SEVENTEEN

Greymarsh House was quite large but, close to, Margot thought parts of it could have done with some attention. There were lights glowing in the narrow windows on each side of the front door, though, which was welcoming.

It was silly to be surprised because Mr Cain was elderly. If he was Christa's brother, he would have to be old. But he was rather distinguished-looking, and he had a nice smile. He said how good it was to be meeting new neighbours. It was difficult to connect him with the young boy with anxious eyes in the old newspaper cutting – to remember that he would have lived through that violent era in Germany.

There were a few other people already there, and before the meal they all had drinks in the hall – actually in the hall! Margot thought this peculiar. Halls were places where you left your coat or your umbrella or your wellingtons if it had been raining. You did not expect to have your jacket cast carelessly into a cupboard, then to be waved to a seat in the hall itself, with your glass of sherry placed on what looked like a large wooden blanket box with carving on its lid.

Margot hoped that she looked all right. The new outfit had looked nice in the shop; the assistant had said beige was always smart, so versatile, because you could wear brown with it, or black.

But the beige two-piece, however versatile it might be, looked drab next to Mr Cain's goddaughter, who – it appeared – had arranged the evening for his birthday. Margot took an instant dislike to Arabella Tallis, who was wearing bronze velvet and amber beads. It was annoying that Arabella did not even trail the amber beads in the food.

The dining room, when they went through for the meal, had dark red walls which closed in suffocatingly. Arabella said it was an absolute mausoleum and her godfather hardly ever came in here, but she had left the curtains open so they could see the gardens while they ate.

'Beautifully night-garden and fantastical-forest in this light. If anyone sees a dryad or a *rusalka* capering about, please say so immediately, because I'll get the camera.'

'What on earth is a *rusalka*?' asked somebody.

'Sort of Russian water spirit, but they like trees, as well. If I got one on film, I'd post it on Facebook, and it'd go viral inside ten minutes.'

There were little menu cards on the table, to tell people what they were about to eat. Margot thought this very ostentatious, and she thought the food pretentious. She ate what she was given, though, and made polite comments, and joined in with the sympathy when it seemed that one of the dishes, used to serve some outlandish vegetable concoction, had cracked in the oven's heat. Everyone seemed to think this was terrible, and Margot offered what she thought was a very useful suggestion about a stall she had found in Thornchurch Market that could repair crockery so you could hardly see a join. But it seemed the bowl was French from somewhere important, and could not really be made whole again. Margot thought, but did not say, that it served Arabella Tallis right for using it to cook the concoction of tomatoes and goodness-knew what else, which all the guests praised. Marcus even asked for a second helping.

It was during the meal that things began to take a faintly worrying turn, and it was Arabella – of course it was – who sent the conversation in that direction.

She began telling everyone about her new project – whether they were interested or not, thought Margot, resentfully. It seemed Arabella was always embarking on new projects, some of which she seemed to get paid for, and some not. Her latest one was the past – well, to be specific, said Arabella, it was the 1930s. She had discovered the era; well, not discovered it exactly, because it had always been there, but she had not taken much notice of it until now. Now that she had found it, though, she found it utterly fascinating. The Golden Age of Hollywood and Edward VIII abdicating, and Schiaperelli clothes, all padded shoulders and shocking pink. Then she looked solemn, and said she knew you had to remember those years had had a dark side, as well – that gathering menace brewing deep within Germany, like a black bruise starting to bleed outwards into the rest of Europe.

Margot shivered, and half glanced over her shoulder, because she had had the sudden ridiculous feeling that something had crept unseen into the room. She pulled her mind back to the conversation. Marcus was asking, very politely, where Mr Cain originally came from.

Mr Cain seemed to hesitate, but then he said his family had been very ordinary; in fact his father had been a lowly music teacher.

'He had a music shop in Germany,' he said. 'He bought and sold musical instruments, and also gave lessons – piano and violin. It was quite a small place called Lindschoen.'

Margot felt as if she had received an electric shock. Lindschoen. She looked across the table at Marcus, and saw him acknowledge the look.

'Have you ever been back?' asked one of the men.

'No, never. I occasionally hear from one or two people there. Not often, though.'

'Arabella, you should get Stefan to record all his memories,' put in one of the women. 'I bet there'd be some interesting stuff.'

'There's an idea, Stefan. What about it?' said the first man.

'Oh, never meet your heroes, and never revisit the scenes of your childhood,' said Arabella, cheerfully. 'Is anyone having any more ratatouille, or were you all put off by the cracked dish?'

'We're not put off in the least,' said the woman who had made the suggestion about recording Mr Cain's memories. 'In fact I'd love to have the recipe for it sometime.'

'We're saving space for the pudding,' said Stefan Cain. 'You did say there was pudding, didn't you, Arabella?'

'Pudding . . . Oh, my ears and whiskers, the crème brûlée,' shrieked Arabella, and dashed out of the room, wailing something about setting the grill pan on fire. Marcus went out to help her, which was very courteous of him, although not something he ever did at home.

After they had eaten the crème brûlée, which was extremely rich and which Margot thought would probably give everyone indigestion, they went into a room at the back of the house – it seemed to be Mr Cain's study, where he sat most evenings – to have coffee. It was a warm, quite comfortable room, although Margot would have wanted to re-cover the old leather chair with a nice chintz, and she would certainly have thrown out the hearth rug, which was as thin as a piece of old silk and looked as if the colours had faded.

'It's Egyptian,' said Arabella, seeing Margot looking at it. 'Beautiful, isn't it? So finely woven, and those colours are like an aquatint. I found it in one of those street bazaars when I was wandering around the souks, and I haggled fiendishly with the man to get it, because it's what you're expected to do in those places, isn't it, and then I sort of smuggled it through Customs – well, when I say *smuggled*—'

'We'd better not know any more,' put in the man who asked if Mr Cain had ever been back to Lindschoen, and everyone laughed.

'It's very nice,' said Margot politely, and thought she would not have wanted a hearth rug from a street market in her house, and that it was a pity someone had not taken a solution of soapy water and scrubbed the rug thoroughly.

And then she saw the painting.

It was hanging on a wall on one side of the fire, and it was of a young woman, standing against a partly curtained window, holding some sheets of music in her hands. As Margot stared at the painting, the earlier feelings of an approaching threat tugged at her mind a little more insistently, although there was surely nothing especially alarming about a lady with some music. Or was there? She went across to look at the painting more closely. There was a wall light immediately above it – its glow fell directly on to the canvas, lighting the details. Disbelief started to flood Margot's mind, because at the top of the music, painted in soft brown, presumably to emphasize the fact that it was handwritten, were the words '*Giselle's Music*'. *Giselle*. The warm room and the sound of the guests' voices faded, and Margot was back in the stuffy little music room, watching and hearing her grandmother play music with that name on it. How many pieces of music were there in the world with the name 'Giselle' written across them?

She realized that Arabella had come to join her; that she was standing next to Margot, looking at the painting with her.

'It's a stunning portrait, isn't it, Margot. I always think she's so unusual-looking. Her eyes have secrets in them, somehow.'

Margot managed to say, 'It's lovely. Who—?'

Arabella said, 'My godfather's older sister.' She glanced back to where Stefan Cain was talking to the two neighbours about recording machines. 'I never knew her, of course, and Stefan never says much about her, but I do know he adored her,' said Arabella, in a lower voice. A pause, then, 'Her name was Christa.'

Christa. It was as if the name exploded silently inside Margot's brain, and she had the sensation of invisible hands squeezing all the breath from her lungs. The room tilted slightly, and she reached out to grasp the back of a chair to stop herself from toppling forward, hoping Arabella did not notice that anything was wrong.

But it's Christa, said her mind. That's how she looked. Dark hair, dark eyes, not large, but narrow and watchful. But was there a hardness about the mouth as well? No, it was just the shaping of the jaw, surely.

She said, 'She was at Lindschoen as well?'

'I think so. Yes, she must have been. But she was a good deal older than my godfather.'

'She's dead now, presumably?'

'Oh yes.' Arabella glanced back to where her godfather was pouring brandy for the guests, and said, softly, 'I hardly know anything about her, but I've always had the impression of some deep tragedy surrounding her.' She sent Margot a quick glance. 'Don't tell the godfather I said that, will you? It's only my idea, and I'd hate to upset him.'

'No, I won't say anything.'

Arabella moved away and Margot finally managed to look across at Marcus, and she saw that he, too, was staring at the portrait, and that he had heard Arabella's identification of it as Stefan's sister. His eyes were glowing with triumph.

The woman who had wanted the recipe was asking about the music in Christa's hands.

'"Giselle's Music", it says. That's rather intriguing. Who was Giselle? Was she a relative or an ancestress? Or even the composer of the music? It's not printed – it's handwritten, so it might be something original.'

Margot thought Stefan Cain was about to speak, then appeared to change his mind, and it was Arabella who said, blithely, 'No idea in the world. Probably no connection.'

'It's a French name anyway, isn't it?'

'French or maybe German. I only know it from the ballet, though,' said Arabella, and Margot thought it was like the creature to show how cultured she was. She glanced at her godfather again, then said, 'But I always like to think of "Giselle" as someone mysterious and intriguing. I think I'd have liked her. Now, would anyone like more coffee? No, it's no trouble at all. I've only got to top up the percolator. And I'll bring the liqueur bottle from the dining room in case anyone would like a tot.'

'Let me help you,' said Marcus, following her out. 'I'll get the liqueur, shall I?'

Driving home, Margot could sense Marcus's delight. As they went into their own house, he flung himself down in a chair and said, exultantly, 'I was right, wasn't I?'

'You were.'

'All that proof – all those leads we've got. Christa's portrait – God, wasn't seeing that the most incredible thing? And the fact that Cain lived in Lindschoen,' said Marcus. 'And that his father had a music shop there.'

'And *Giselle's Music* is in the painting,' said Margot.

'Yes, that piece in the old music stool was called that, wasn't it? I'd almost forgotten.'

'What do we do now?'

'I'd like to find out if there're any more documents in that house,' said Marcus. 'Legal stuff. Cain's birth certificate, even – that would give his parents' names. Even address books. Cain mentioned occasionally hearing from people living in Lindschoen. And it's not out of the question that his family knew Lina's father.'

'The murdered martyr,' said Margot.

'Not everyone who gets murdered is a martyr.'

'How could we do all that, though? You can't walk into some-body's house and start searching.'

'Don't be stupid, I shan't do it openly. And the "how" is already in place.'

'What d'you mean?'

'When Arabella went to get more coffee, I went into the dining room for the liqueur bottle, you remember. I was thinking ahead by that time,' said Marcus. 'We'd seen the portrait – we'd heard that mention of a music shop and of Cain's father having a music shop in Lindschoen, and so on. So I thought there was very likely more to be found – certainly that it was worth looking around without anyone knowing. So I wedged that narrow side dining-room window very slightly open – only a couple of centimetres. I used one of those menu cards, folded up.'

'They'll realize. They'll see,' said Margot, in panic.

'I don't think they will. Arabella Tallis is more organized than you'd think. While everyone was drinking coffee, she had whipped all the dishes and the glasses out of the dining room and dunked them in hot soapy water. She had even tidied away the tablemats and wiped the crumbs off the table. And the curtains were halfway open, if you remember—'

'Dryads and *rusalkas*,' said Margot, dryly.

'Yes. I think it's a safe bet that the curtains will be left like that. And even if Arabella goes in there tomorrow to finish tidying up, she probably won't touch the curtains. As for Cain himself, I doubt he'll go in there for days.'

'Arabella did say the dining room's hardly ever used,' Margot admitted.

'Exactly. And even if it's noticed, a bit of card stuck in a side window wouldn't mean anything.'

'When would you do it?' asked Margot, after a moment. 'Tonight?'

'No. Arabella's not going home until later tomorrow, and it'd be better to wait until Cain's on his own. I'd prefer him to be out of the house altogether, but I can't lurk outside Greymarsh for days on the off-chance. So it will have to be the middle of the night when he's asleep. It looked as if the main bedrooms were at the front, so he wouldn't hear someone sneaking in through a room at the back. He's probably a bit deaf, as well.'

'He didn't seem deaf.'

'You're determined to find flaws, aren't you?' said Marcus, impatiently. 'I'm telling you, I've got it all worked out. The study's at the back of the house, if you remember, and I'll bet anything worth finding would be in there. I'll wait until Friday, to be sure Arabella's gone.'

'And then break in?'

'And then break in.'

Margot thought that Friday night would never come, and then, when it did, she thought it would never end. Marcus left at two a.m.

and Margot sat huddled in a chair, watching the clock tick round. He would not be more than an hour, surely. If he had not returned by three o'clock, she would start to worry.

She had offered to go with him – she could keep watch, she said, but Marcus said it would be better if only one of them was creeping around Greymarsh House.

'You don't trust me.'

'Not always.'

'Why not?'

'We both know,' he said, and when he turned to look at her, the disquieting glint was in his eyes again. Then he started to talk about finding an old black jacket with a hood so he could blend into the darkness, and the moment passed, and it was the familiar Marcus once more.

When three a.m. came and there was no sign of him, Margot began to get nervous. Supposing Mr Cain had caught him and called the police? She began to listen for police sirens.

Half past three. What would she do if the phone suddenly rang and it was the police saying they had taken her brother into custody? She began to wonder how long it would take her to walk to Greymarsh House to see what was happening. Marcus had been going to park his car in a layby a little way from the house. It would be well off the road, he said, with overhanging trees, and he would smear mud over the number plate as well. Anyone seeing it would think it was a couple who had parked up to have a bonking session on the back seat.

It was after four a.m. when Margot finally heard his car, and she ran to the door at once, prepared for a tale of disaster and failure.

But it was all right. He was smiling and patting his jacket pocket. He had found something.

'But not,' he said, throwing the dark jacket on to a chair, 'without a blip. Cain must have heard me as I was about to leave – that was a bad moment. I was about to climb out of the dining-room window when a light went on, and he was standing in the doorway.'

'Did he see you? Oh God, did he recognize you?'

'No,' said Marcus, very positively. 'I had the hood pulled well up and the room was in shadow. He would only have seen a dark outline.'

'What did you do?'

'A defensive reflex action,' said Marcus. 'I grabbed the brandy decanter and threw it at him.' He frowned, then said, 'It caught the side of his head, and it knocked him out. But it's all right,' he said, before Margot could speak. 'He was only stunned – I checked his heart and his pulse and everything was fine. And just as I was about to go I heard the milk cart trundling along the drive – you know that distinctive whirring sound those things make. So I opened the front door to make sure the milkman would see Cain lying on the floor, and then I beat it like a bat escaping hell.'

'It sounds all right,' said Margot, slowly.

'It is all right. And now listen to what I've found.'

It was a letter, and it was in German.

'It was in a box file over the desk,' said Marcus. 'I almost missed it, but there were three or four files, labelled with things like, "Insurance" and "Bank statements". One had what was obviously private correspondence – that was the one I grabbed, of course. It was mostly letters from friends, and they weren't of any interest, except for this one. I'm translating it for you, and I know I've got it correctly.'

Dear Stefan,

It was good to hear from you and have your news. Please accept the enclosed as a birthday offering – no doubt you'll use it to replenish either your bookshelves or your wine cellar! I hope the birthday dinner is enjoyable – your goddaughter will make sure of that, though. I so much enjoy the anecdotes you send about her.

I was in Lindschoen last week – you'll like to hear that it's hardly changed. Driving back, I noticed that the old Torhaus is still empty. It's always been a bit of a mystery, hasn't it? I believe attempts were made years ago to trace its owner, but it looks as if the authorities have given up. It's probably an impossible task – so much was lost during the war – documents and deeds vanished – also, as we both know, so did many people. I'm always glad to think that Velda was able to take you to England.

I hope to visit England again soon. It's been far too long, and it's time we got together and reminisced.

Kindest regards

'It's signed "Nathaniel",' said Marcus. 'And there's an address in the Paderborn district. I think that's more or less in the Lindschoen area, although I'll check the map.' He looked at her, and his eyes were alight with excitement. 'But you got the reference to the Torhaus, didn't you? That translates as gatehouse, by the way.'

'The house whose rightful owner was never found,' said Margot, slowly. 'You think that could be Lina's house?'

'Don't you think it could? If it's in the Lindschoen area . . . And even if that's a dead end, there's that other lead about Cain's father having a music shop.'

'You're going there, aren't you?' said Margot. 'To Lindschoen. To find this Torhaus?'

'Yes . . . And,' said Marcus, 'you're coming with me.'

'But can we do it?' said Margot, next morning. 'Can you get the time off work? And can we afford it?'

'I've got annual leave left,' he said. 'And if I say there are family problems, I don't think there'll be any difficulty. It'd only be for about a week – that ought to be long enough. I'll take the laptop so they can email anything urgent. As for the money . . .' He thought for a moment, then said, 'We'll have to do it on the cheap. Stay in quite basic places. It might cost less to drive all the way, rather than fly and hire a car out there. Maybe the ferry from Harwich across to Holland, and then into Germany. Or the Shuttle from Folkestone. I'll find out.'

Margot said, 'I'll get the last bank statement and see exactly how much money we've got.'

They heard, that afternoon, that the milkman had seen Stefan Cain lying on the floor and called the paramedics. It was assumed that an intruder had got in, and that Mr Cain had heard him, and had gone downstairs to investigate.

A terrible thing, people in Thornchurch said, if a man of that age could not be safe in his own home. Such a nice man as well, so gentlemanly, and those adult classes for German and German literature had been very well attended and very interesting. Still, apparently he had suffered only mild concussion and bruises.

Marcus had phoned Greymarsh House later in the day.

'Sort of to make an alibi,' he said. 'Behaving as if I didn't know about the injury. I got the answerphone, of course, but I left an innocent message, thanking him for the dinner party.'

'I'm glad he's all right,' said Margot. 'I'm glad you didn't kill him.'

'I'd have let myself be arrested for house-breaking sooner than kill him,' said Marcus. He had been studying a map of Germany, finding Lindschoen, but he looked across at her. 'What would you have done if I had killed him?' he said, in a very quiet voice.

'I'd have found a way of making sure you weren't suspected,' said Margot, at once. 'Told the police you were here, probably.'

'You'd have lied for me? Even if I'd murdered someone?'

'It's what sisters do for brothers, isn't it?'

'Oh, yes,' said Marcus, softly. 'It's what brothers should do for sisters, as well. You protect your own – even if it means lying.' He paused, then said, very deliberately, 'Not if it were to be a case of murder, though. I don't think I could protect anyone who had committed a murder.'

He looked at her for a moment, not speaking, then went out of the room.

Margot sat very still, his words reverberating through her brain. What had he meant? Had he meant anything at all? Or was he trying to tell her he knew what she had done – Lina and then their mother . . .? He could not know, though, not for sure. Or did he suspect, and was he trying to tell her that he suspected? Margot remembered how he had looked at her the night their mother died – how there had been hatred in his eyes; no, it had been more than hatred, it had been *fear*. And immediately afterwards he had insisted she must not live on her own, and he had taken over her life and they had ended up in this out-of-the-way place where no one knew them. But that was because of Stefan Cain being here. Or was that all it had been? Couldn't they have investigated Stefan perfectly well from a distance? Had it really been necessary to move to this small place where no one knew them?

But of course Marcus had not meant anything by that remark. It was only that his mind was taken up with going to Lindschoen and finding the house.

EIGHTEEN

Wewelsburg Castle, 1939

G iselle missed the house in Lindschoen more than she could have believed possible. Even after all these weeks in the castle – was it four weeks now, or five? – she ached for the familiar cobbled square and the comfortable untidiness of the shop.

She had no idea what Felix would have been told about her, although it would not be the truth. What would the children have been told? Stefan was too small to understand anything except that his mother had vanished, but Christa . . . What would Christa think? With a fresh jab of pain, Giselle remembered that it would soon be Christa's sixteenth birthday, and that she and Felix had intended to give a special party.

Reinhardt came to her room most evenings – Giselle had no idea if it was to see if she was attempting to write the music that was to be called *Siegreich*, or to make sure she was still alive, or even whether it was simply to gloat. But, incredibly, these visits had become the centrepiece of her day. She knew that this was because it broke the tedium of her days inside Wewelsburg, but she still listened for his step on the stairs.

She had begun to transcribe Andreas's score, note by painstaking note, onto the blank sheets brought for her, and she had written *Siegreich* across the top of the first page. She was determined to work as slowly as she dared, so that Reinhardt would think she was struggling for inspiration. Also, the longer she took, the more chance there was of something in this grim situation changing – and changing in a way that might open up an escape possibility.

She finished transcribing the first page, and confronted the necessity for destroying it before starting on the next, remembering her bizarre idea of shredding up the pages and eating them, one by one. It did not seem so bizarre now, in fact Giselle thought it was the only thing to be done. But could she do it? She would have to try.

It took longer than she had thought; the feel of the dry paper in her mouth and her throat made her retch, and once she had to run to the curtained recess to be sick. But she forced herself to keep trying, and in the end she managed it. She drank plenty of water afterwards to wash the minute fragments down thoroughly, and tried not to think about the ink on the pages. The prospect of dealing with all the sheets in the same way was horrid, but it would have to be done, and at least there would be long intervals between the times.

But Reinhardt said she was working too slowly. Each time he said it, Giselle knew they were both aware that once the *Siegreich* was finished she would have served her purpose. Would Reinhardt really hand her over to Hitler's butchers to be executed?

That a spark had been ignited between them was undeniable. Giselle hated herself for knowing this – if Felix had been at her side, such a spark would never have been lit. But it had, and she would acknowledge it. What was more difficult to acknowledge was that the attraction was no longer only physical. Reinhardt frequently understood her thoughts – he could sometimes follow the process of her thinking and complete her sentences, as she could his. He recognized allusions she made – to books, to poetry. Giselle knew by now that the cold, composed façade hid something far warmer.

She thought seduction had been in Reinhardt's mind from the very first meeting. I hate you, she thought, studying him covertly. I hate you and I loathe everything you stand for and believe in, and I would claw your eyes out if it would mean I escaped. But if it would get me back to Felix and to Christa and Stefan, I would let you make love to me until we were both exhausted and spent.

The next time he asked how much longer she would need to finish the *Siegreich,* Giselle looked at him thoughtfully, then curled up on the bed, leaning back against the worn cushions.

'It could be some time.'

He frowned slightly, then after a moment he came to sit by her on the bed. He had never done this before, and Giselle felt her heart miss a beat. Was this to be the night?

In a softer voice than he had yet used, he said, 'You have arranged your hair differently.'

'I wouldn't have expected you to notice.' She had, in fact,

combed it in a different style that afternoon, more out of boredom than anything else.

'I notice everything about you.'

'I know.'

She let her hand fall on to the bed, palm uppermost. Would he see the slight gesture as an invitation? She let her hand remain there, and the moment lengthened. Then he reached for it, and his fingers closed around hers. Slowly, he raised her hand to his lips and pressed a kiss into her palm.

Giselle was horrified at her own response. She felt as if a hundred-volt electric shock had torn through her. She drew in her breath sharply, then she took his hand and repeated his gesture, kissing his own hand, then pressing it against her cheek. His hand remained against her face and his eyes darkened, then his arms came out to her, and he pulled her against him.

She had thought she would resist being kissed on the lips. Prostitutes were said to do that – any sexual act with their clients was acceptable and allowed, but kissing was too intimate; it was something to reserve for the real loved one.

But as soon as Reinhardt began to kiss her, Giselle responded. His hands were on her body, moving with a kind of helpless urgency that was almost endearing. When he reached down to unfasten the belt of his trousers, she glanced down, and he said, softly, 'Yes, Giselle, you see how I am so very ready for you.'

'I do see.'

But she caught her breath on a half-sob. I can't do this, she thought. I mustn't. It's violating everything that matters – Felix – my own people . . . It's the action of a wanton. But if it's a question of behaving like a wanton or dying . . .

When Reinhardt took her hand and guided it down for her fingers to enclose him, she did not resist, and excitement blazed up again at his cry of pleasure. He pushed her back on the bed – not violently or insistently, but as if he could no longer contain his need.

'This has been a long time in the making, Giselle.' He was thrusting his hands under her skirt, and his voice was so urgent he might almost have been pleading with her to agree with him.

'Yes. Oh, yes, it has.' It came out breathlessly.

'Afterwards, we will never speak of it. I should be taken out and shot if it were to be known that—'

'That you had taken a Jewish female to bed? And that female your own prisoner?'

'Yes.'

'I'll be taken out and shot eventually, though.'

He shook his head, not in denial of the words, but as if it was too painful a prospect to contemplate.

The moment hung on the air – Giselle thought: do I ask him now to let me escape? No, not yet, not yet . . .

He had torn his clothes and hers aside; but again, it was the impatience of overwhelming passion rather than an act of violation. Giselle remembered how she had believed that when this happened, as she had known it would, she would be able to pretend it was Felix who was with her. But it was impossible. Everything was too different – the shape of Reinhardt's head when she held it in her hands felt different, the scent of his skin was his own. His caresses were less practised, rougher than Felix's had ever been, but Giselle could have wept because they still drew a violent response from her.

Once he said, in a harsh voice, 'I am satisfying a need, nothing more – you must understand that is all this is. And I will stop before . . . You understand that, as well? There will be no consequences.'

'Yes,' said Giselle. 'Yes, I understand.' She came up out of the shameful, sinful passion for a moment, to make a frantic calculation. Two weeks since her last monthly bleed. She had coldly requested one of the guards to send a female officer to her at the time, merely saying she required some private attention. The necessary items had been brought, and Giselle, hating the need to ask, had tried to remember that they would be used to such a request from female prisoners.

But two weeks meant this was now mid-cycle, which was supposed to be a likely time to conceive. *Good.*

Reinhardt was moving faster now, but when he gasped out, 'I must stop – in a moment, I must . . .' Giselle thought, not if I can help it, you won't, and writhed against him. He cried out, and drove harder into her, and she felt his final jerking spasms. He cried out again, his voice a mixture of pain and pleasure, then slumped heavily on to her, his head against her neck.

Giselle did not dare move, but at last he raised himself on one elbow and looked down at her. She had no idea what he would say, but his words startled her.

'You have tears on your cheeks, Giselle. For your home? For your husband?'

It would be too easy, but also too dangerous to say yes. Giselle said, 'The French call it *la petite mort.*'

'The small death,' said Reinhardt, softly. 'The *tristesse*; the little melancholy following love-making.'

'Yes.' How many men would have known that and, more to the point, understood about it?

Reinhardt said, 'I promised you I would stop in time, and I didn't.' A brief impatient gesture. 'I lost all control. I'm sorry.'

'It doesn't matter.'

But Giselle was not sorry at all. It was a very long shot indeed – the chances of conceiving from a single encounter could not be very high. But it was not impossible. And surely pregnancy would make them change their minds about that eventual execution?

As for Reinhardt himself – mightn't he feel very differently towards his own child? Mightn't he want to set free the woman who had given birth to his son? Or his daughter?

It was ridiculous, after that frenzied intimacy, to feel shy with him the following night, but Giselle did feel shy. She found herself looking at him differently, thinking: I know how you look when you are in the grip of helpless passion. I know how your body feels inside mine, and how you cry out and grip my shoulders when you reach a climax.

If Reinhardt was thinking similar thoughts, it did not show, and the cold, courteous mask was more firmly in place than it had ever been. He asked, politely, if she had all she needed, and whether the *Siegreich* was progressing.

'I have most of what I need,' said Giselle. 'The *Siegreich* progresses.'

He glanced across at the piano, where only two sheets of music score were on the stand. 'But still very slowly,' he said. 'Or so it seems.'

Giselle shrugged, and Reinhardt looked at her for a moment, then went out without speaking. But on his next visit, his expression

impassive, he said, 'An order has come to move you out of
Wewelsburg tonight.'

Terror clutched at Giselle's throat, but she managed to say,
'Why?'

'Because you have only written a very small amount, and it's
thought that you are being uncooperative and defiant. We do not
want any more delay; the Führer is impatient to begin preparations for the invasion of England. So someone else will be found
to compose the *Siegreich*.'

Without realising she had been going to say it, Giselle said, 'I
could be pregnant. That night with you—'

A faint colour came into his face, but then he said, 'I am aware
of that. If it proves so, you will be allowed to have the child. But
I shall disclaim all responsibility. I shall let it be believed that one
of the guards violated you. The child would be taken from you
straight after the birth.'

Giselle thought: Well, at least I might have bought nine months
more of life. But she felt a sharp pang for the child who would
be summarily handed to strangers. Would they let her know what
happened to it, that little, lost creature, conceived in that strange,
desperate passion?

He said, 'You are not going to be executed.'

Relief washed over Giselle in huge waves, but she would not
let him see it, and she said, 'Is that because you and I made love?'
Hateful to call it that, it had been sex, farmyard rutting, a million
light years and worlds away from what she and Felix had had.

'Emotion is something that must be controlled,' said Reinhardt.
'I can't – I daren't –ignore the order I've been given. Nor can I
countermand it. But all the same—'

'Yes?'

His voice softened. 'I can't let you be shot, Giselle.'

'You could let me go.' It came out too eagerly. 'We could fake
an escape. And if I promised – swore on whatever you hold most
dear . . .' She would have sworn on the name of Adolf Hitler
himself; she would have sworn on the Nazi swastika. 'I would
swear never to divulge where I had been, or anything about the
Siegreich . . .' She hated herself for pleading with him, but
the words tumbled out.

'It's no use,' he said. 'All the vows in the world won't help.

The order has gone out, and the arrangements to move you out of Wewelsburg are already under way.' He frowned, then suddenly said, 'I would wish for a memory of you. A photograph—?'

Hardly believing it, Giselle said, 'There's one in my bag.'

'I would like that.' He sounded grateful. Almost humble.

It was a photo of Giselle standing outside the shop. The wind had been blowing her hair, and she was laughing. Reinhardt took it and said, 'Yes. Thank you.'

He put it into a pocket, then said, formally, 'You will be taken from here in the next hour. Your belongings will be brought out to you later.'

Giselle said, in a whisper, 'Where am I to be taken?' But Reinhardt only shook his head, and went out.

Through the churning fear, one thing was at the forefront of Giselle's mind. There were two sheets left of Andreas's music, and one was that damning last sheet, with Silke's name on it. They were still in her bag, those two pieces of paper, and they must not be found.

But the guards were already stamping around outside the door and there was the sound of sharp orders being barked out. The hour Reinhardt had referred to must almost be up. Giselle did not think there was enough time to shred and eat those two pages. She had managed it with the others, but each time she had had to force herself to it and it had made her retch. Once she had been actually sick. And the memory of Andreas, tortured and struggling against the vicious strappado that night – the memory of how he had wanted his music to survive – was still deep in her mind. She would not destroy those last two sheets, but she could remove and destroy the part that had Silke's name on it.

She folded the bottom two inches of the final page to make a sharp crease just above Silke's name, then tore the strip off, using the crease as a guide. It was not as crisp as if it was the real edge of the page, but it would pass. She tore the shreds twice more, and pushed the pieces into the pocket of her skirt. It ought to be possible to drop the torn fragments somewhere later on without anyone seeing, and leave it to the wind to blow them away.

But supposing this was not enough? Supposing Andreas wrote in some particularly individual way that could be recognized? She looked helplessly around the room, and her eyes lit on the piano.

Where did you hide a leaf except in a forest? And where did you hide music except in a musical instrument?

It was relatively easy to prise up the lid of the piano, and to see at once that it would be simple to thrust Andreas's music so far down inside that it would not be seen, except by the most rigorous of inspections. Giselle put all the sheets together – Andreas's and the ones she had transcribed – then hesitated. Hardly knowing why, she reached for the pencil and in the bottom corner drew the ghost note. Felix would never see it, of course, but it felt extraordinarily reassuring. It felt as if she was sending a message to him. She slid the music down inside the piano, and closed the lid. She did not think it would be noticed that those two pages she had seemed to be working on were no longer here. Everyone would assume that someone else had taken them.

The guards came in then. They did not clamp her wrists this time, but they held her so tightly there was certainly no chance of escape. They pushed her from the room, down the steps to the courtyard, and into the waiting jeep. Giselle, half falling into the back, fumbled in her pocket for the torn-off paper. It was easier than she had expected to clench the pieces in her hand, and to let them go before the door was slammed. She did not see the shreds blow away, but a wind was whipping through the courtyard, and it would carry the fragments far from Wewelsburg.

The jeep moved off, jolting across the uneven roads, and then down hedge-fringed lanes. At length, its dipped headlights swept across high iron gates.

The tall brick chimneys of Sachsenhausen came into view.

NINETEEN

Christa sometimes had nightmares about tall brick chimneys that jutted up into the sky. For most of the time, they were black and silent, but there were times when they glowed with a dreadful heat and belched out flames and bad-smelling smoke. When that happened, it meant something terrible had taken place. Sometimes she tried to see deeper into the dream, to see what the terrible thing might be, but she never could. After a while she stopped trying, because it might be better not to see. It was only a dream anyway – well, it was a nightmare, but it was not real.

Stefan had nightmares as well, but they were not about the chimneys; they came from a game he and his school friends sometimes played in the lunchtime break. You had to cross a piece of ground that was chalked out into squares and triangles, and if you accidentally stepped on a piece that was forbidden you were counted out of the game. Christa used to play it as well when she was at school.

But in Stefan's nightmares, the forbidden ground of the game was a frightening and very sinister place, and it was called the death strip. If you ventured on to it, you were murdered. You were shot with huge, powerful guns that splattered your blood and bones everywhere. Or you were tied up by your wrists and all your bones were pulled out of their places.

Mother had been able to bring Stefan out of his bad dreams, and Christa tried to do the same. She ran into his bedroom and hugged him to her, and she thought it calmed him down, although she did not think she managed it as successfully as Mother had always done. Sometimes Father came in, but his bedroom was at the very top of the house, so he did not always hear Stefan's sobs. Christa thought Father often took pills to help him sleep, as well.

But he would sit on the edge of Stefan's bed and say that although bad dreams were horrid, they went away when you woke up. Nobody was going to hurt either of them, not ever. There were

a lot of things going on in Germany at the moment, but they were
all safe here in The Music House. Life would go quietly and
peacefully on. But, even as he said it, something flickered in his
eyes, and Christa knew that no one was really safe any longer.
She found a lot of what was happening difficult to understand, but
she tried to listen to what was said in the streets, and they had a
wireless, which broadcast news reports. Father hardly ever listened
to it, because he said it was too depressing.

Since Mother had left them, Father had seemed to step back
from the world and everything it held. He had not shut himself
away in the sense of going into a room and locking the door, but
Christa knew he had shut the door of his mind against most of
the world. She knew he did not want to be in a world that no
longer had Mum in it, and she understood this, because she did
not want to be in that world, either. The trouble was that it was
the only world there was. She wanted to ask exactly what had
happened, because Father had only ever said there had been an
accident on the way to the wedding of Mother's cousin, Silke, so
Christa supposed it had been a train crash. But she never found
the courage to ask, because she could not bear the pain in his eyes.
Telling him she was having nightmares would only make that pain
worse.

Their cousin, Velda, who lived on the other side of the square,
told Christa her father was starting to come out of his shut-away
state. He was not exactly recovering from losing Giselle – nobody
could really ever recover from losing somebody like Giselle – but
he was coming to terms with it. Just a very little. They must all
help him back into the world, said Velda.

Velda's idea of helping Father back into the world was to bake
cakes and savoury stews and walk across the square to the music
shop with them. No good ever came from starving yourself, she
said. She was inclined to be disapproving of the fact that Father's
friends – the musicians and the teachers and the people who simply
liked listening to music – still came to the shop on Friday evenings.
It was not showing respect, said Velda. But Christa knew they all
came because they wanted to help Father; they wanted to offer
their companionship and their friendship, and anything else they
could think of that might ease the loss.

Shortly after Christa's sixteenth birthday, Father said she could stay up for some of these Friday evenings, which was very good indeed. It meant Christa was grown-up, and that she could be part of grown-up things. She looked forward to Fridays all week, partly because they were lively and interesting, but also because of one of the men who had appeared a few weeks earlier. He did not come to The Music House every week, but when he did, he usually sat quietly in the corner by the bookshelves, his face half in shadow. Christa did not know his name, and he did not speak very often, but if he did say anything, everyone listened. His voice was nice; it made Christa think of stroking a cat's thick fur or putting on a soft silk scarf.

Sometimes she caught him looking back at her, and when that happened he always smiled, not with a stupid grin or with the kind of forced smile that grown-ups sometimes wore for people who were much younger, but as if he might really want to talk to her. Christa hoped she did not blush when this happened, but she had a worrying suspicion that she did.

On some nights, if there had been more wine than usual, the talk among the musicians would become very animated, with some of them saying be damned to Herr Hitler's disapprovals and bans: they would play whatever music they liked at their concerts.

'And didn't you say you were going to include a Mendelssohn piece next time, Felix?'

'You're not, are you?' said somebody, sounding worried.

'Well, I say we show the Führer what we think of his bans,' said someone else. 'Silly little man with all that posturing and ranting.'

'If we do the Mendelssohn we'd have to keep Eisler sober beforehand, of course.'

'I drink to celebrate the joy of life and the joy of music,' announced Eisler, grandly, positioning his chubby fingers on the keys again.

The unknown man leaned forward to pick up his wine glass, and smiled at Christa, as if he might be inviting her to share the affectionate amusement at Herr Eisler. Christa supposed she ought to ask somebody who he was, but she liked to keep him as the mysterious man of firelight shadows.

Then came an evening when several bottles of wine had been drunk, and Christa was curled up on the chimney seat, enjoying listening to a friendly argument that had sprung up about the interpretation of some nocturne or other. Herr Eisler was preparing to demonstrate the nocturne, providing somebody would find the music and refill his glass.

The stranger was sitting near the door, and firelight washed the walls, making the room warm and safe. The shutters were partly open, because Father liked seeing the lamplight on the old square outside. Soon, they might have to not only close all the shutters, but also cover the windows with black material because the Royal Air Force might send over planes to drop bombs on Germany, and no lights must show anywhere that might help them pick out targets. But tonight the lamps were lit and Lindschoen had its look of belonging to some distant age.

And then, without warning, came the sounds of footsteps marching across the cobblestones – sharp, rhythmic footsteps that rang out harshly on the ground. Marching. Christa's heart bumped with fear, and she huddled back against the wall. Everyone was listening to Eisler and no one else seemed to have heard the marching steps. Or had the stranger heard them? It seemed to her that he turned his head towards the door.

Eisler played a final cascade of chords, then swept his hair back in a deliberately over-dramatic imitation of a famous soloist. There was a shout of appreciative laughter, but as it died away, they all heard the sound they had grown to dread over the last few years: a loud, imperative knocking on the street door. A leather-gloved fist hammering for admittance.

No one moved or spoke, but Christa's father got up and said something about it being a latecomer, and he would open the door. But fear was pouring into the room, and Christa knew it was not one of Father's friends at all.

It was the Schutzstaffel.

One of the men said, very softly, 'Don't open the door, Felix.'

'Of course he'll have to open it. It's worse if you ignore them. If it's the Schutzstaffel they might just break in anyway.'

'And they've probably seen the lights.'

Christa wondered if she was the only one to believe the Schutzstaffel didn't always need lights, because they could see into all the hiding places with their skewer eyes . . . No, that was only in Stefan's nightmare.

People were looking round the room, as if trying to see if there might be a back door they could get through before the Schutzstaffel got inside.

'Of course I'm going to open the door,' said Christa's father. 'I've done nothing wrong, and no one here has done anything wrong, either.' But his eyes flickered with something that could have been fear.

The unknown man suddenly said, 'Herr Klein, should your daughter perhaps leave us for a little while? While we deal with this.'

'Yes, of course. Christa, go up and stay with Stefan, will you? Don't wake him if you can help it. And don't worry – you're quite safe.'

Christa went out obediently, but instead of going up to Stefan's bedroom, she sat on the bottom stair, leaning forward, her arms hugging her knees. It was dark on the stairway and it was a bit uncomfortable to sit there, but she could see most of the room through the narrow gap in the door, and she could hear what was being said. If the Schutzstaffel really did come storming into the house she would run upstairs and barricade herself into Stefan's room. Perhaps it would not be the Schutzstaffel, though.

But it was, of course. When Father opened it, they were there. Four men. Tall, grim-faced, authoritative in their sharp dark uniforms, the black breeches folded neatly into the tops of the leather boots and the black swastika emblem vivid on the red armbands. The cold night air swirled around them like indigo-coloured smoke.

Whatever Father felt, he did not appear to be afraid. He said, in an ordinary voice, 'Yes?'

'You are Felix Klein?'

'Yes.' Although Father's back was turned on the room, Christa saw the rigidity of his shoulders.

'You have a concert planned, we understand, for next February. It has come to our attention that you intend to play the music of a composer whose work is banned.'

Father did not speak, but one of the musicians said, almost involuntarily, 'Mendelssohn,' and the Schutzstaffel man seemed almost to snatch the name.

'Yes, Mendelssohn,' he said. 'A forbidden composer.'

Father said, 'The concert is on the anniversary of Mendelssohn's birth. The third of February. We're honouring him, and playing his music in his memory.'

The man stepped forward, and the light from the streetlamp fell across his face. There was a curious moment – a moment when Father's whole manner changed. It was as if he had suddenly been faced with something he had never expected to see.

The officer said, 'The Third Reich does not permit that composer's works to be played at all. This is an order not to include that piece in the programme, Herr Klein. You are to play something else.'

'And if I refuse?'

Herr Eisler and one or two others caught their breath in dismay and also in surprise, because Felix Klein was the mildest of men, and the very last person to defy the Third Reich like this. Christa dug her fingernails into the palms of her hands, because there was only so far you could push the Schutzstaffel.

Then the officer said, very softly, 'Herr Klein, you know the powers we have.'

'Oh, yes, I know,' said Father, but so softly Christa only just heard the words.

'You have a good memory,' said the officer. He stepped closer, and the light from the room fell across his face. Skewer eyes, thought Christa, shivering. Cold and hard, like bits of steel.

'People have been locked up for smaller transgressions,' said the man. 'But you know that also, of course, Herr Klein.'

He waited, but when Father did not speak, the man said, 'For your safety, you should heed this warning.' He clicked his heels slightly, and then he and the other men were marching back across the square.

Father came slowly back into the room. Inevitably, it was Herr Eisler who said, 'Well, Felix? It'd be monstrous to give in to that command, but—'

'But the SS are monstrous,' said somebody.

'That officer was wearing a death's head ring,' put in someone else, sounding a bit nervous. '*Totenkopfring*. Did you see it? Horrible thing. But Himmler only hands those out to his distinguished officers, so whoever he was, that officer, he was very high up.'

Father said, almost to himself. 'Yes, he is very high up.' He seemed about to say more, but then he frowned, and sat down.

'You could easily substitute something for the Mendelssohn, couldn't you?' That was the stranger. Christa leaned forward to hear better. 'What about Beethoven? You'd be perfectly safe there. Hitler likes Beethoven.'

'Hitler likes Wagner as well, but if you think we can stage the *Ride of the Valkyries* in that hall and with our small orchestra—'

'Beethoven's a good idea, though,' put in a man who was a violinist. 'We could do one of his violin concertos,' he added, hopefully. 'Well, we could do the Romances, at least. We all know them, and the length would fit.'

'Personally, I'd favour one of Haydn's cello concertos,' said a cellist.

'But why have they banned Mendelssohn?' demanded the violinist. 'There's no logic to that. Didn't Mendelssohn practise Christianity for most of his life?'

'It wouldn't matter if he practised satanism or tupped entire flocks of sheep,' said Herr Eisler. 'Mendelssohn's grandfather was a famous Jewish philosopher and scholar. And songs from his great oratorio, *Elijah*, are sung in Ashkenazi synagogues every Saturday. He's regarded by the Nazis as a thoroughbred Jew.'

'And Hitler is terrified of Jews,' murmured the cellist.

'They tore down Mendelssohn's statue from outside the Leipzig Gewandhaus,' put in the violinist. 'And used it for scrap metal. I heard about it from someone who watched it happen.'

From his seat at the piano, Eisler said, 'We're gradually being isolated. Everything we do or create – work, music, books – is being suppressed and destroyed. And let's not forget the ghettoes they've set up for people like us in Poland and in Czechoslovakia and Hungary.'

Christa knew that by 'people like us' Herr Eisler meant people who were Jewish. It was not often that any of Father's friends said it, but they all knew it was becoming dangerous to be Jewish.

There was an uncomfortable silence, then Father looked round the room. 'If I include Mendelssohn, will any of you abandon me?' he said.

'No, of course not—'

'How could you think it—'

The stranger leaned forward. 'I think we don't need to be especially worried, Herr Klein,' he said. 'You're a group of musicians, planning a concert. You're not a subversive organization plotting against the Führer's life, or a nest of assassins.' The stranger smiled as if the idea was absurd, and some of the tension went from the room. 'It was a show of authority, nothing more. They'll be going around the whole square – all the shops and houses. All the streets leading off. They do that quite often. They take a section of the town in turn, and make their presence known to all the residents. It's to make sure people toe the line.'

'How do you know that?'

'I listen. I take note. But it's all right,' he said, with a sudden smile. 'I'm on the side of the angels.'

Father nodded, but there was still a slight frown on his face. Then he said, 'I refuse to recognize any ban that outlaws music. Mendelssohn's *Italian Symphony* will be the centrepiece of our concert.'

Later, in the small flurry surrounding the leave-takings, the stranger took Christa's father aside. Christa, who had come back into the room to clear away the glasses and plates, heard him say, 'Herr Klein, you've made the right decision about the Mendelssohn symphony. I'm very glad.'

'Yes.'

'It was a brave decision, though.' He looked thoughtfully round the room, and his eyes met Christa's. Lowering his voice, he said, 'Will your daughter be at the concert?'

'Yes, certainly. She always helps me on concert nights. Her mother always did so, too,' said Father, and Christa heard the catch in his voice that was always there when he spoke of her mother. 'Why?'

'No particular reason,' said the stranger, but his voice was suddenly warm and pleased.

Taking the glasses out to the kitchen, Christa realized she was smiling. She almost forgot about the Schutzstaffel in wondering what she would wear for the concert.

TWENTY

Phin fell in love with Lindschoen at first sight. He thought it was the kind of place where, if you went along a particular street and took a particular turning, you might find you had fallen into its medieval past. He was entranced by the cobbled squares and stone buildings with their windows criss-crossed with lead, and the lime trees that threw their soft outlines across the old stones.

'*Linden*,' said Toby, when Phin pointed these out. 'Aren't there folk songs about the lime trees here?'

'Schubert,' said Phin. '*Der Lindenbaum.*'

'See?' said Toby, grinning. 'I don't only know rude rugby songs.'

Most of all, Phin liked the thought that the mysterious Giselle had lived here. Silke's letter had confirmed that, which meant Giselle must have walked along these streets, and looked into the shop windows, and stopped to talk to people in the little squares. How about Christa? Had his villainess or spy-heroine also walked these streets?

They had booked into a hotel a few miles from Lindschoen itself – Phin thought it was the German equivalent of a Travelodge, and, as Toby said, it was perfectly acceptable as their base. There was a coffee place on the ground floor and a fast-food shop, and there were tea- and coffee-making facilities in each room.

Before leaving London, Phin had wondered, a bit guiltily, whether he might find himself regretting having Toby with him, but he had not. Toby was so genuinely interested in everything; he clearly regarded the expedition as a kind of quest, midway between a Boys' Own adventure and a James Bond romp, and Phin thought he could not have had a better companion. The memory of the redhaired Canadian editor flipped rather annoyingly through his mind. She would certainly have jumped at the chance to join him on this trip – always providing her crowded schedule would have allowed it – and she would have been efficient and knowledgeable. It was disloyal to think she might have been just very slightly patronizing about a small set-up like the Lindschoen Orchestra, and also to think that she might have been a tad dominating, wanting Phin to explore avenues he instinctively knew were dead ends, and taking charge of the travel arrangements.

What was even more disloyal – in fact it was wildly absurd – was the thought that Arabella Tallis would have been exactly right as a companion; she would have bounced delightedly through the cobbled streets, eagerly discussing what they should do next, laughing if they got lost, wanting to celebrate if they found a useful clue. Phin dismissed these speculations, because Arabella would have been maddening and distracting, and he was not going to think about her again.

The day before they left for the airport, he looked at the *Siegreich* music for a very long time. He still felt its darkness strongly, and if the legend could be believed, this was music that had been created out of pain and fear – it had been forged in the grim darkness of World War Two at the command of the Nazis. But its composer – whoever that composer had been – did not deserve to have his work destroyed eighty-odd years later. Phin was by no means sure he wanted to actually hear the *Siegreich* played; what he did think was that he owed it to that long-ago composer as well as to Stefan Cain, who was the music's apparent owner, to make sure it was preserved.

Rather than risk damaging it in a photocopier or a scanner, he took several very careful photos of each page, which he uploaded on to his computer and printed. That dealt with, he swathed the original in several layers of bubble wrap, enclosed them in a large, padded envelope, and took it to his bank, with a request that it be stowed in a safety deposit box. He had never used this service, which he vaguely associated with jewel thieves stashing away filched diamonds, or espionage plots involving stolen government papers, or the plans for a new atomic warhead, but the procedure turned out to be simple and the bank's charge was modest.

'What about Christa?' demanded Toby, when Phin reported having done all this. 'I don't think we should leave her at Greymarsh, do you? Stefan's going to be transferred to that convalescent home for a week or so, which means the house will be empty. We're looking after the music for him – at least, your bank is – but there's still the portrait, and in view of the fact that some-body's already tried to break in to Greymarsh—'

'We can't leave Christa at Greymarsh,' said Phin. 'Could we leave her at my flat?'

'That ought to be safe enough. There's the security keypad on the street door. Oh, and you could ask The Pringle to look in every morning. Say it's to check your post. She isn't very likely to do it for me, but I bet she'd do it for you like a shot. She thinks you're a very nice gentleman – she told me so – and she can't imagine why you haven't been snapped up by some attractive girl years ago.' He sent Phin the mischievous grin. 'I didn't tell her about your redhead,' he said. 'Or about Arabella.'

'I wish you'd remember that I've never met Arabella, and that Arabella's only met me by looking through the window of your flat,' said Phin.

'It's the stuff of romance,' said Toby, promptly. 'Instant love through a glass darkly.'

'It's the stuff of nonsense,' said Phin, but he agreed that enlisting Miss Pringle was a good idea.

Miss Pringle expressed herself as delighted to help Mr Fox in any way she could, and was charmed to think her services were required for checking his post.

'And I'll nip up in the evening as well, shall I, and switch on a few lights and draw the curtains. You can't be too careful, and if you're both going to be away at the same time . . . You must take some photographs of your jaunt and let me see them when you get back.'

As Toby said later, it was clear that Miss Pringle was visual-izing, with fascination, the two of them yomping across Europe in a kind of modern version of the Grand Tour that Regency bucks had once taken.

'You'll have to take some photos for her; in fact you could even keep a diary like those colourful Victorian travellers did, and let her read it when we get back. By the way, I'm bringing my notes about our bawdy songs collection. I'll bet there're a few good ballads to be found in Germany.'

Christa's safety ensured, the *Siegreich*'s security dealt with, and Toby's travelling entertainment provided for, Phin booked flights to Berlin and arranged for the hire of the smallest and most inexpensive car that could be found at the other end. He did not dare check his bank balance to see how well it was standing up to this unexpected fiscal strain.

Phin had said, and Toby had agreed, that the first thing to find in Lindschoen had to be the place mentioned in Silke's letter. 'The house in the square that had a beautiful and appropriate name, and old lamps on the door.'

'It's probably a Lidl supermarket now.'

'It's a starting point, though.'

They spent the first day wandering around the various streets, but they did not find any buildings that seemed to fit Silke's description.

'Never say die, we're only at the start,' said Toby, as they stopped for lunch at a *Konditorei* smelling deliciously of fresh coffee and pastries. Over a wedge of plum cake, he said, 'Supposing we're approaching this from the wrong angle. Is there a library or something where we could find out about local concert halls? Because we want to find the orchestra as well, don't we?'

Phin managed to ask their waitress if there was a local library where they could get lists of old buildings, and was pleased that she understood him sufficiently to direct them not to a library exactly, for Lindschoen had no *Bibliothek*, sad to say. But there was a *Buchgeschäft* – a shop that dealt in reference books and also music, and had many papers of the past. That would be helpful, perhaps?

'Very helpful. Thank you very much,' said Phin, writing down the waitress's directions. '*Vielen dank.*'

The waitress indicated that she would be interested to hear how their research progressed. They offered coffee and very nice pastries in the afternoon, and there would shortly be a delivery of *Spritzkuchen*. They would come back for those and tell her how their search was progressing?

'Perhaps,' said Phin, who could not remember the German word for this.

In that case, the waitress would make sure to keep some of the *Spritzkuchen*. It would be very good if they returned. It was difficult to know if this suggestion was directed at Phin or at Toby, or at them both equally.

'It was directed at you,' said Toby. 'I think you've clicked there.'

Phin said he was not in a mood to be clicking with anyone at the moment, not with the *Siegreich* and the orchestra taking up all his time and mental energy.

'We might go back for *Spritzkuchen*, anyway; in fact it would be rude not to,' said Toby, hopefully. 'What is *Spritzkuchen*?'

'Deep-fried doughnuts, I think. Is that glint in your eye for the waitress or the doughnuts?'

'The doughnuts sound good,' said Toby, 'but the waitress was very nice, too. And we ought to have at least one romantic anecdote to take back to Miss Pringle.'

'We could go back after we've been to the bookshop,' said Phin.

'We could couldn't we? We'll probably need reviving, anyway.'

'We'll probably need more than doughnuts,' said Phin. 'I shouldn't think the *Buchgeschäft* will provide any leads.'

But it did. And it stood in an old square with traces of old cobblestones, and old-fashioned lamps.

'And look at the sign,' said Phin, pointing. 'Kerzenlicht Square. Candlelight Square. If that doesn't square with what Silke said in her letter about old-fashioned lamps, and a beautiful and appropriate name— I'll bet those streetlamps are pre-electricity, and maybe even pre-gaslight.'

'Let's go in.'

Phin was aware of a curious mix of anticipation and apprehension. Was this really the house Silke remembered as the magical, lamplit place of her childhood? Giselle's house, he thought. And if Silke's letter can be trusted, Giselle was murdered by Christa.

But if Giselle's murdered ghost – or anyone else's – lingered anywhere, it did not seem to do so in the nice old shop. It was a delightful old place, with a gentle feeling of welcome and a gentlemanly implication that it was not overmuch bothered about selling its wares. Phin, drawn irresistibly to the racks of CDs, found a recording of Mahler's *Symphony No. 6*, which had been a particular favourite of his grandfather's. His grandfather had been a great admirer of Mahler – Phin had never been able to decide if this was an act of defiance against the Nazis who had banned Mahler on the grounds that he and his music were degenerate, or whether it was a genuine love of Mahler's music. He bought the CD as a small nod to his grandfather's memory; the hire car had a CD player, and Phin thought he would listen to it while driving back to the airport in two days' time.

Toby, meanwhile, had discovered, with glee, a small volume of old local folk songs. He promptly bought this, along with the clearest German/English dictionary he could find on the shelves, and sat down to study it, informing Phin that, among other treasures, the book contained a refrain that appeared to be in praise of an eighth-century Bavarian duke who had gone by the name of Henry the Quarrelsome, and whose life had apparently been turbulent.

This all opened up a friendly conversation with the shop's owner, who appeared to have a fair knowledge of English.

'We have English people who come in here, so it is useful for me,' he explained. 'We are not a library in the usual sense, but I have some reference books – people sometimes come in for research, and I enjoy helping.'

Phin thought this would be the right moment to produce his business card, and explain that he was interested in tracing any members of the Lindschoen Orchestra.

'It's for background research relating to a forthcoming book about musicians in the 1930s and 1940s,' he said. 'And it's been suggested that you might have some old documents or local reference books we could look at.'

He had not expected any very positive response, but the man beamed. 'I know of the Lindschoen Orchestra, very well,' he said. 'Its leader was Felix Klein, and once he owned – and lived in – this very shop.'

Phin stared at the man and thought there were times in the research processes when something totally unexpected but entirely satisfactory came scudding up to greet you.

'He lived here? The Lindschoen Orchestra's leader lived here?'

'Certainly. My father acquired the shop many years since – I am not sure from whom exactly – but I know that in Felix Klein's day it was known as The Music House, and he bought and sold musical instruments, and also gave music lessons. The orchestra was his great love – he led it for many years, and there were often concerts in a small theatre just outside Lindschoen. Sadly it is no longer there, that theatre. But it was well known for theatrical performances. Also, children's plays at Christmas and at Hanukkah

– there was once a large Jewish community in these parts, you understand.'

'And Herr Klein himself? Do you know anything about him – I'm sorry I don't know your name—?'

'I am Herr Volk, but please call me Ottomar.' There was an exchange of hands. 'I think Felix Klein was known as very gifted, and also very well respected,' said Ottomar Volk. 'Not so much is known of his life, but the little that is known does not seem a happy story. I am sorry to tell you that. It was the 1940s, you understand – a difficult time. There were dangers, people were lost, and their fates never known.'

'And one night Felix Klein gave a concert that included one of the banned composers,' said Phin. 'Yes?'

'Ah, you know of that. Yes, it is so. I think he must have been a man not to bow down – submit? – to a ban he thought wrong. He was courageous enough to stand up for his beliefs. So, one night, early in 1940, he played Mendelssohn's *Italian Symphony*.'

'And,' said Phin, 'Mendelssohn's works were banned by the Nazis, yes?'

'Yes. It was open defiance by Felix Klein, but he could not have known that SS men were in the audience that night. And so he paid the price.'

'Herr Volk – Ottomar – my understanding is that Herr Klein was taken to Sachsenhausen concentration camp. Is that right? Did he die there?'

'One story says he was taken to Sachsenhausen, but no one ever knew for sure. He was what some people call one of the "lost ones". There were many of them. All that is known is that he never came back to Lindschoen or to this house. Sachsenhausen,' said Herr Volk, softly, 'was a terrible place. The stories told of it are shocking – perhaps the stories not told may be even worse. There are things people never spoke of – memories they did not wish to preserve in their minds. But there is also a story that says Herr Klein was taken to the Torhaus. You knew that?'

'No.'

'It was another of the mysteries handed down about Felix Klein, because people who defied the SS as he did were always taken straight to one of the concentration camps. Not so for him, though – at least, not at first.'

'What exactly was – or is – the Torhaus?'

'It is difficult to answer that. I think it was once one of the guardhouses – gatehouses? – to Wewelsburg Castle. For one part of the war it was the residence of commandants at Sachsenhausen. It has been empty for a great many years now, and it has a bad reputation.'

'Who owns it?'

'I don't think anyone knows. Ownership would be complicated, because the house stands so close to Wewelsburg Castle – perhaps even on the castle's land.' He paused, then said, 'But I know that it was whispered by local people that it was at the Torhaus that the infamous Wewelsburg murder took place.'

'We didn't expect that,' said Phin, as they walked away from the Kerzenlicht Hall.

'We did not,' said Toby. 'What was that about the infamous Wewelsburg murder and the Torhaus? Did I follow that right? Have we come across that reference before?'

'Don't think so. Volk didn't seem to know any more – just that there was a vague legend about a murder that had happened at the Torhaus.'

'Vague or not, we ought to see the place, oughtn't we?'

'Oh yes. Herr Volk admitted it was odd that Klein – who defied the SS by playing Mendelssohn at his last concert – wasn't taken straight to Sachsenhausen. And it is odd, you know. In fact, I can only think of one reason.'

'The *Siegreich*.'

'Yes. I think Felix Klein was the musician the Nazis tortured to compose their victory march.'

He paused to look back at the square, and Toby said, 'It's a marvellous place, isn't it? You can visualize candles in those lamps – and a lamplighter reaching up to light them with a wick on a long pole. And if you dare to tell me I'm an irreclaimable romantic—'

'Heaven forfend,' said Phin, deadpan. 'You did pay for that book with the rude song about Henry the Quarrelsome, did you?'

They reached the hotel and Toby promptly spread maps across Phin's bed to trace the route to Wewelsburg and the Torhaus.

'I know the car's got a sat-nav, but we'll take maps as back-up in case we can't understand the directions.'

'I'll see what I can find about Wewelsburg Castle,' said Phin, opening the laptop.

'OK, and I'll whizz down to that food-to-go place, and collect something for supper. We can work and plan while we eat.'

Toby returned fairly quickly, laden with braised beef rolls, crêpes with sauerkraut, and two tubs of what he said was German beer cheese soup, which he had not been able to resist. 'And some *Rumtopf*,' he said. 'I don't know what it is, but I liked the word. It looks like a squishy fruit preserve,' he said, having cautiously investigated. 'How's Wewelsburg and the gatehouse? Have you found anything?'

'Not very much. It's in Paderborn, so it'll be a reasonable journey from here. Mostly there's just details about its history, and how Heinrich Himmler acquired it and wanted to turn it into a kind of school for SS training and a high-flying meeting place for senior Gestapo. There seems to be a vague legend that Himmler might have wanted to create what he called a Grail castle – reproducing elements of Arthurian legends and images, presumably. He was supposed to be planning to have an eternal flame burning in the vaults.'

'You can't say he didn't aim high, that Himmler,' said Toby.

'There's nothing about any murders, though – oh, except that shortly before the outbreak of World War Two a group of Jews were imprisoned there – before being taken to Buchenwald. That doesn't sound relevant, though.'

'I've been thinking,' said Toby, who was setting out the foil and plastic dishes of food, 'that we've only got two days left before we fly back.'

'Yes.'

'And this Torhaus/Wewelsburg lead is sounding a bit – um—'

'Tenuous? Vague?'

'Yes. So, rather than both of us waste the better part of a day on what might be a dead end, how about dividing our strengths? One of us to drive to this Torhaus place – probably that should be you, because if there are any clues about the orchestra and whatnot, you'd recognize them better than I would. I'll go back to the shop in Kerzenlicht Square – oh, doesn't that sound

Dickensian! – and see if I can ferret into some of those old documents that Ottomar Volk's got stashed away.'

Phin saw the sense of this idea. He said, 'You're right that the Torhaus might be a wild-goose chase. Volk said not much was known about Klein, didn't he? Just bits of stories handed down. I don't want to ignore it altogether, though.'

'And,' said Toby, 'if either of us finds anything halfway interesting, we can join forces the following day.'

'Good thinking. Would you mind not putting the *Rumtopf* on my bed, in case it spills out,' said Phin.

Phin found it difficult to sleep that night. His mind was full of Felix Klein – of how they had found the house where Klein had lived, and heard the story about him having been taken to the Torhaus.

Then he began thinking about the Lindschoen Orchestra's last performance. Mendelssohn's *Italian Symphony*. It was a joyful, lively, piece – 'Jolly,' Mendelssohn had called it. But how had they felt, those musicians, when they performed it? Had they been defiant, or nervous, or fearful? Had Felix Klein rallied them? Had he – this was a bad thought – had he even bullied them? Phin did not want Felix, who might have been the *Siegreich*'s composer, to have been a bully.

TWENTY-ONE

Berlin, February 1941

Stefan was not coming to Father's concert. It was a long evening for him, and he would stay with Velda for the night. He liked Velda, and the two of them would probably make toffee together in the kitchen, burning saucepans and leaving a litter of caramel blobs on the floor which had to be scraped off when they had cooled.

Christa and Father went to the concert in Herr Eisler's car, which he drove bouncily to the hall, about ten kilometres away. She liked the concert hall. Father put on a lot of his concerts here, and there were sometimes plays that Christa and Stefan came to see. Just before Christmas there had been a stage version of the old fairy story, *The Tinder Box.*

They did not exactly celebrate Christmas – 'Although we respect it,' Father often said – but Hanukkah, the marvellous Jewish Festival of Lights, had fallen right at the end of December, and going to see a Christmas-type play had felt like part of the Hanukkah celebrations.

Christa had enjoyed *The Tinder Box*, with the soldier trying to get at the gold and having to tiptoe past the sleeping trolls, which Father had said were in the original Danish folk tale and were characters that were often left out nowadays. But Stefan had not liked the dogs with huge eyes that guarded the treasure – he had put his hands over his eyes, and refused to look at the stage until the dogs had gone away. People in the audience said some of the costumes – those trolls and the dogs' heads! – had been a bit frightening for smaller children.

There was a big audience for tonight's concert. Christa found a seat near the back, and looked along the rows, hoping to see the stranger. She still had no idea who he was and she had not liked to ask his name, but in case she did see him tonight she had put on her birthday-present frock for the evening. It was topaz-coloured with a velvet collar and she had little black velvet shoes.

If the stranger turned up, he would probably have some beautiful lady on his arm – somebody who would be wearing a proper evening frock. She would have perfectly arranged hair and be wearing lipstick and powder, and Christa's topaz velvet would look a bit dull in comparison. She surreptitiously pinched her cheeks to make them pink, which she dimly remembered her mother telling her people used to do in the past, in the days when wearing make-up branded you as a loose woman.

It was good to see the hall so full. Christa's heart suddenly bumped, because the stranger was here after all. She did not think he had seen her, because he was studying the programme, and seeming interested in it.

People were murmuring to one another, and Christa began to understand that some of them were here to see if Felix Klein was going to defy the SS ban and, if so, what would happen.

There was a short Brahms piece first, then a Berlioz *March*, which was splendidly stirring, and then there was Lizst's *Liebestraum*, which was played by Herr Eisler. He was applauded loudly, because everyone loved him, and there were even a few cheers. Any Schutzstaffel spies who might be around would certainly approve of this part of the programme; somebody inside the Third Reich had recently begun to use Liszt's music to open the weekly army broadcasts – most of which told listeners how victorious Germany was going to be in the war. All the broadcasts started with the first few bars of *Les Préludes*, which had thoroughly disgusted Father. 'They've filched Liszt's music like sly pickpockets and chopped it up like butchers,' he had said.

After the interval there were a lot of empty seats, as if some people had decided it was too dangerous to stay for the final piece, after all. It was dreadful that people could be so frightened of listening to music, but there was still time for Father to announce a change to the programme. Even at a few moments' notice, the musicians would be able to pull together, and play something other than the Mendelssohn.

It seemed that it was not only the audience who were frightened of the music, because the orchestra had shrunk noticeably since the interval. It was not a massive orchestra, of course – it was a bit of a ragbag of music teachers or dedicated amateurs who came and went, according to whether they could be free for a recital.

Tonight there had been about eighteen of them. Now Christa counted just twelve. Two of the violinists had certainly left, and Christa thought one of the flutes and a clarinet and a bassoon had gone, as well.

Father appeared perfectly calm. He raised the baton, gave the count, and the music began.

Played by the depleted orchestra, it sounded a bit lightweight. It even sounded tinny, although Christa would not say that to Father. Between the first and second movements, several more people went out, and by the time the music reached the last bars, the hall was less than a third full. She began to be thankful that as symphonies went it was fairly short – no more than half an hour – so it would soon be over.

At the end the applause was ragged and hasty, and as Father gestured to the musicians to rise in the traditional acknowledgement, people were already grabbing coats and scarves and making for the exits, their eyes nervously looking about them. But it's all right, thought Christa, relaxing slightly. Nothing bad's happened. She tried to think that she should be proud that Father had stuck to his beliefs.

Felix Klein turned to face the audience then, and scanned the rows. He's looking for the SS officer, thought Christa, with sudden fear. The man who came to the shop that night, and who he seemed to know. He's thinking the man might be here, to see if Father's defied the order.

And then, with slow horror, she saw that the SS man was here – that he must have been here all along. He was seated at the very end of a row quite near the platform, and he was wearing a dark overcoat with squared shoulders and a hem that almost reached the floor. The collar was turned up, and his uniform, if he was wearing it, was hidden. But Christa did not need the uniform to recognize him. He was watching Father very intently, and Father stared straight back, then he inclined his head slightly in the man's direction. Was it a half-nod of recognition? No, it was not recognition, it was *challenge*.

It was as if Father had deliberately and publicly disobeyed the Schutzstaffel's order, knowing the man would be here to see him do so.

*   *   *

After the audience had left, Christa stayed in her seat. Somebody had switched off the auditorium lights, and it was dim and shadowy. From beyond the stage were the sounds of the musicians packing up, somebody calling out to know who had taken a clarinet case, somebody else asking if the music had been gathered up. The violinist who had stayed to brave out the Mendelssohn shouted that he was going across the square to the wine bar, in case anyone wanted to join him, and there was a chorus of assent to this, with Herr Eisler's cheerful rumble the loudest. Then came the sounds of a general exodus, and Christa heard Herr Eisler calling out, 'Hello – didn't know you were here, friend. You'll be most welcome to join us.'

With another bump of pleasure, Christa heard the stranger's voice, saying something about being very happy to go with them. If she went up to the backstage area now, she would catch up with them – the man might speak to her.

She was about to do so, when she realized that the SS man was still in his seat. He was sitting quite still, blending with the shadows. But if Christa walked up to the stage, he would see her, and if he turned round he would see her, so she remained very still.

The man waited until the musicians had clattered their way out, and the exit door leading to the alleyway had clanged shut. Then he got up and walked towards the stage, going up the steps at the side, and through to the backstage area.

There was still no sign of Father, who was most likely talking to the manager of the hall, or the caretaker, arranging about locking up. When he came in, they would probably not wait for Herr Eisler, but go home on a late-night tram. It sounded as if the SS man had gone, but you could not be sure – people said Schutzstaffel officers were as sly as a whole skulk of foxes when they wanted to be.

The dark auditorium began to feel vaguely eerie, and at last Christa got up and walked quietly down the hall to the stage and up the steps, pushing her way through the thick, bunched-up curtains. The side of the stage was very dark, but she picked a careful way between discarded stage props and bits of scenery and lengths of rope. There was a smell of dust and glue and of paint and old timber.

There did not seem to be anyone around, and everywhere was quiet. Or was it? Christa paused, listening intently, hearing something coming from beyond the stage. A knocking sound, as if somebody was knocking on a wall. Could someone be shut in somewhere? The sounds came again, and Christa began to feel nervous. She moved forward again, and as she did so something stirred in the gloom and reached out to touch her face with thick, rough-feeling fingers. Christa gasped and clawed wildly at the air, then realized it was one of the ropes that dangled from overhead. She pushed it out of the way, and went towards the door that led to the long room behind the stage. This was where performers and actors assembled before a performance. It was large and untidy and friendly, and she had often been there to help with running errands and finding things people had forgotten or had lost. The sounds seemed to have come from here; perhaps someone was repairing a bit of scenery, although it was a bit late for that. And it had sounded more as if someone was hammering on a door.

'Dad? Are you in here?'

Her voice echoed a bit spookily in the empty room, but there was no response, although her father's jacket lay across the back of a chair, so he could not be far away.

There did not seem to be any places where anyone could be shut in – the room had no cupboards or anything . . .

Except that it did. It had the inner door in the far corner – the door that led to a costume store. It was always locked, because costumes and stage props had to be kept safe, and Christa had never been in there.

The sounds had stopped, but she thought she should make sure no one was shut into the costume place. If the door was locked, the keys were probably in Father's jacket, because he was always loaned keys to the hall for his concerts. Might he even be the person shut into the costume store? It would be easy for the care-taker to lock the door not realizing anyone was in there.

Christa reached for Father's jacket, and the keys were in a pocket, just as she had thought – a heavy bunch on a clanking metal ring. Good. She had to try several of them before she got the right one, but it slid home and the lock turned. She was starting to wish somebody would come into the room, or even that the knocking would start again, because this was starting to feel a bit scary. But then rooms that were always kept locked were bound to feel spooky. You had the feeling that they might hold macabre secrets, like in the story of *Bluebeard*, where the heroine was warned never to enter a particular room. 'You can have the keys to all these rooms in the castle, my dear, except this one, and that you must never enter . . .'

But she was only going to take a quick look in this room, which was hardly Bluebeard's castle with its sinister seventh chamber, or the Arabian Nights' copper castle with its forbidden and fateful Golden Door. Christa dropped the bunch of keys in her own jacket pocket, pushed the door wide open, and stepped inside.

TWENTY-TWO

The store was bigger than she had expected, but it was quite narrow. A faint bluish light trickled in through a tiny window high up in one wall.

Christa fully expected to be greeted by Father or one of the musicians – certainly by someone laughing with relief at being rescued from a ridiculous predicament – but there was no sign of anyone at all.

Or was there? She stood in the doorway, and as her eyes adjusted to the dimness, she began to have the uncanny impression that the room was full of people – no, not people, *creatures*. Beings with massive, distorted heads and faces, and monstrous ears and evil, gap-toothed grins beneath thick thatches of hair. Grotesque things with misshapen heads, and eyes like saucers, like mill wheels . . .

But the impression lasted no longer than a few seconds, because of course these were the costumes from *The Tinder Box* that she and Stefan had seen a few weeks ago. All the costumes had been flung in here and they lay in untidy floppy heaps on the floor and against the wall.

Pieces of scenery were stacked against the walls, as well. They were painted with fragments of caves and forests and leering trees, so that it looked as if somebody's nightmare had been chopped up and the pieces thrown down. There was a scent of paint and sawdust, and of clothes that might not be very clean because they had been worn under hot lights by people with sweat on their bodies and greasepaint on their faces. But there was a smell of something else, as well. It was not something Christa recognized, but it lay on the air like copper and it made her feel slightly sick. It was clear that Father was not here, though, and that nobody else was here either.

But she could not stop looking at the distorted heads and the staring faces. There were the heads of the giant dogs that guarded the treasure from the soldier-hero – those were the dogs that had frightened Stefan so much. Seen like this it was obvious that they were only canvas and pretend-fur and glass eyes. In another corner were the costumes of the trolls who had slept while the soldier had tiptoed through the hall of a hundred lamps. Christa had quite enjoyed the trolls in the play, but seen like this, shadowy and close to, they were quite scary. The costumes were made from sack-like material, thickly padded to make their bodies look heavy, and there were massive deep-soled boots at the bottoms of the trousers. The heads had been left in place, propped into the necks of the jackets. The nearest three had lopsided faces with garishly painted mouths that hung open, and huge hollow eyes. The fourth—

The fourth did not have a lopsided face or thick lumpen features, and it was not lying down. Somebody had hung it from a large black hook on the wall, but had not done so very neatly, because it flopped down in a jumble, the head lolling forward on to the chest. The hook was smeared with paint, and the curved tip had burst all the way through the costume so that the jacket's padding was spilling out.

Something cold and frightening began to stir within Christa's mind. There was something dreadfully wrong, but she could not work out what it was . . . Was it because the fourth troll did not look like the other three? Because it had been hung on the black hook, rather than folded up? She took a step nearer, and the thing she had been trying to pin down in her mind fell into place.

There had only been three trolls in the play.

The room suddenly seemed very still, as if something might be waiting and watching to see what she was going to do. Christa's heart was thudding uncomfortably, and the palms of her hands were suddenly wet with sweat. The figure was not wearing sack-type clothes like the others – it was wearing a long black overcoat, but the overcoat had fallen off the shoulders, and beneath was a uniform. Around one of the arms was an emblem that even in the dim light was clear, and it was an emblem that everyone Christa knew dreaded. The Nazi swastika. The badge of the Schutzstaffel, the skewer-eyed men who came to your house without warning, who hammered on doors and came into bedrooms, and stole people away from their beds, and sometimes murdered them.

The iron hook was not glistening with paint, but with something far worse, and what she had thought was the torn costume padding

spilling out of the front of the jacket, was something that was
sloppily and messily wet . . .

It was Bluebeard's forbidden room after all. It was the room
with the mutilated, clotted bodies of previous brides hanging from
butchers' hooks . . .

Sickness rose in Christa's throat, but she forced it back and
took a shaky step closer, to reassure herself she was mistaken. She
was not mistaken, of course. It was the Schutzstaffel officer, and
he had been pushed back against the wall, then lifted and impaled
on a huge iron hook, so violently that the hook had burst all the
way through his body to the front.

Christa thrust her fist into her mouth, praying not to be sick.
In a moment she would be able to move, and she would run
somewhere to get help, and something would be done. Even though
the man was dead, things would have to be done for him.

And then something far worse happened. The feet in their smart
leather boots moved. They did not quite reach the floor, but the
heels began to drum against the wall behind, and Christa realized
this was the sound she had heard earlier. Because he was not dead
– he was writhing on the iron hook like a fish writhed on the end
of a line when it was caught, struggling to twist itself free . . .

Almost as if these frantic thoughts had reached the man's brain,
the dreadful head lifted, moving inch by tortuous inch, until the
eyes – cold, steel-splinter eyes – stared straight at Christa. The
features were distorted with pain and fear and blood dribbled out
of the mouth. One hand came out to her, as if reaching for help.
The fingers were bloodstained, and the death's head ring glinted
faintly in the thin light.

'Help me . . .'

The words were barely audible, but the thin cobweb string of
sound seemed somehow to have tugged at Christa's own hands,
because she discovered she had taken the man's hand in hers.
Blood from the fingertips smeared her skin. Dreadful. Sickening.
But beneath the panic and the repulsion, a dark layer of thought
was forming.

Because this man whose guts had been half ripped from his
body was one of the hated, hateful Schutzstaffel. He was one of
the men who burned the homes of Jewish people and shut them
inside the grim labour camps, and forced them to work until they

dropped from exhaustion . . . Who stole children away and pulled out their bones, then threw them into the ovens . . .

I could lock the door and just go, thought Christa, staring at the man's distorted features. No one would know and no one would find him for ages – months, even, because hardly anyone ever comes in here. And murderers deserve to die, don't they?

She could not do it. When the man's hand clutched at her again, she clasped it in both her own hands, trying not to mind that his fingers were wet with blood, and his skin was clammy and heavy, like a piece of dead meat. It was then she realized he was holding a small oblong of card. Trying to give it to her? Trying to tell her something? Or was it something he was trying to see in his dying moments?

It slithered from his grasp, and lay, face upwards, on the ground. The faint light fell across it, and Christa looked down and felt as if something had dealt a blow across her eyes. The small room, smelling of blood and fear, tilted and spun around her.

The piece of card was a photograph. It was creased and worn, and one edge had become dabbled with blood, but the image was clear. A woman, standing in a cobbled square, immediately beneath a lettered sign that said, *Felix Klein, Music lessons by appointment, musical instruments and sheet music sold and bought* . . . The sign was the old sign that Father had had there for years and that he was always going to have replaced, and never did.

Christa had no idea how long she crouched there, staring at the photo of her mother, seeing the dark eyes that could smile and light up, feeling the ache of loss all over again. But then she became aware that the SS man had stopped struggling, and that a deep silence had descended on the small room. He's dead, she thought, raising her head to look at him. He really is.

She had no idea what to do. She felt as if she had been shut into a frozen nightmare, and that if she ever managed to fight her way out of it, it might be to find other terrors lying in wait for her. Who killed him? said her mind. Because supposing the killer is still here?

With the thought came the sound of footsteps crossing the stage, coming towards her. Christa's heart jumped with new fear, but then Father's voice was calling her name, wanting to know where she was, because it was high time they thought about getting home.

This was so normal, so reassuring, that Christa was able to call out a reply. Her voice sounded dry and cracked, but Father heard it, because he walked across the big room outside, and then he was in the doorway.

As he took in the scene before him, Christa waited for him to say something that would make it all right, that would make the world come back to normality. But he did not. Then she saw that immediately behind him was the stranger.

Christa did not remember how they got back to The Music House, but somehow she was in the familiar room by the fire, with the various instruments scattered around, and the stacks of music score everywhere.

Father and the stranger were drinking whisky from Father's small secret stock. Christa had a mug of hot milk.

The stranger said, 'You have an appallingly difficult situation to handle, Herr Klein, but it's possible that I can help.'

'I don't need anyone's help—'

'You do. The man who died tonight was a high-ranking officer of the Schutzstaffel. I locked the door of that storeroom, but he'll be found. And however careful we are to cover things up, the trail could lead back to this house. If so, we both know you'll be suspected, Herr Klein.' He paused, then said, very deliberately, 'And we know why.'

'The Mendelssohn ban?'

'We both know it's not because of the Mendelssohn ban,' said the man, impatiently. 'The man who died tonight was SS-Obersturmbannführer Reinhardt. The man who . . .' He broke off, and something seemed to pass between him and Father.

Then Father suddenly said, 'Christa, it's very cold in here. Would you be a dear girl, and make a pot of coffee?'

It was impossible to refuse, but as she went out Christa left the door slightly open so she could hear what else was said.

'Herr Klein, what exactly were you told about your wife? About her disappearance?'

'That man – Reinhardt – was her lover. There was a letter from her— I was shown it.' There was a break in Father's voice, then he said, 'If I hadn't read it, I wouldn't have believed it. I still try not to.'

'Life can deal some unexpected blows. But we should focus on what happened tonight. Because when the Gestapo find Reinhardt's body – which they will – you know what your punishment will be.'

'Execution,' said Felix, whispering the word.

'Yes. But this is the death of one of their own, and the Gestapo would inflict their own punishment before you even reached the death chamber. We can delay the discovery a little, but only a little. You locked the door of that room – I saw you do so. You brought the keys back here?'

'Yes.'

'How many sets of keys are there? Who has them?'

'Two sets. One is kept at the hall – there's a caretaker. The set I have is kept for people who use the hall for concerts and plays. I was given them a week ago for rehearsals and for tonight's performance. It's a usual arrangement. It's understood that I'll return them tomorrow or the day after.'

'That can be dealt with. Keys can be altered and they can be switched for keys that don't fit the locks. But it will have been known that Reinhardt was at that concert, and that hall will be searched. If I could get rid of the body I would do it, but it's too risky. I'll cover your tracks as much as I can, but bodies aren't so easy to dispose of. But I'll help you to evade the Gestapo.' In a voice that was somehow strong and gentle both at the same time, he said, 'Felix, I could get you away from here. Into hiding.'

'I won't leave this house—'

'You must. You may be prepared to risk your own life, but you can't risk the lives of Christa and Stefan.' There was a movement, as if the man had leaned forward. 'Felix,' he said, 'this is not just you who will be suspected; it is also Christa.'

'No one would suspect a sixteen-year-old girl of—'

'Of murder? But girls of that age have murdered,' he said. 'They are emotional – intense. Their feelings run deep. And Christa was in that concert hall tonight. Also, she would have hated her mother's lover almost as much as you do.'

'She didn't know about him. I never told her.'

'Oh, Felix,' said the man, almost indulgently, 'of course she would have known. She would have listened – heard gossip. If she's suspected – and she would be – her youth won't save her.'

Pain was blurring Father's voice, but he said, 'Where would we go?'

'Have you ever heard of Wewelsburg Castle?'

The name dropped into Christa's mind like a black, icy lump of rock, and instant and dreadful recognition scudded into her mind. Wewelsburg Castle. The place that's old – that's always been old.

'Wewelsburg,' said Father, very quietly.

'It would not be the castle itself. There's a house nearby – it stands on its own piece of ground, and it's called the Torhaus. You would be safe there.'

'I don't quite understand—'

'At times,' said the man, 'the Torhaus is used to hide people of your kind—'

'My kind?'

'Jewish people.' It came out quite courteously. 'There have been painters there and writers – sometimes as many as eight or a dozen. At the moment there is also a very gifted silversmith. And now there can be a musician.'

'Why would you do this for me?'

Christa could almost hear the man thinking how to answer, then he said, 'The Nazis are salting away a great many treasures. Paintings, statues, silver and gold objects. Probably they won't be seen again until the war is over. I deplore what they're doing, you understand, but their principle can be applied in a different way – a benign way. So I'm salting away not inanimate objects, but the people who create them – the people currently in danger from the Third Reich. And as a Jew, you must understand and even embrace the principle of a commune.'

'A kibbutz,' said Father, his voice thoughtful. 'It's not something that's always worked. And what you're saying sounds a bit idealistic. A bit too romantic.'

'Castles in Spain? Striving for Utopia?'

'Yes.'

'Many of the great philosophers have believed in the concept, though. Schelling, Schopenhauer, Immanuel Kant. And in Germany at this very moment there are others working in secrecy to get your people away from danger. To keep them safe from incarceration in the camps. And from worse than incarceration,' he said, in a voice so soft that Christa had to lean forward to hear. 'What I'm doing is saving – trying to save – on a different level. I have good connections with the Torhaus – a distant cousin of mine is its housekeeper. Fräulein Elsa Frank. A taciturn soul, but reliable and trustworthy. Also . . .' A deprecatory note was in his voice, 'Also, she is almost embarrassingly devoted to me. She would do whatever I asked her.'

'If I'm to even consider this, I need to know more about you,' said Father. 'I don't even know your name.'

'I could give you several names. I could show you papers that appear to confirm those names. But most of the papers are forged, and all of the names are false. Please believe, though, that I'm on your side.'

In a voice Christa had never heard Father use, he said, 'If I were to agree to go to this place, this Torhaus – you would expect me to work? To work on music? How, exactly?'

'To compose.'

'Compose?' said Father, startled. 'I haven't any gift for composing. I've written a few scraps of stuff, but they're very lightweight. Technical exercises, that's all.'

'Not so. You have skill and depth, Felix, I would have tried to save you from the Gestapo for your own sake anyway. And I would wish to save Christa as well, because of her youth and her intelligence.'

'And the price is that I compose music.'

'Yes.'

The coffee was ready now, and Christa had to move away from the door to set the jug and cups on a tray. She missed the next part of the conversation, but by the time she went back to the room, the matter seemed to have been decided. The stranger said, 'Christa, I'm afraid we have to leave Lindschoen as quickly as possible.' He looked at Father. 'Stefan will be better staying here with your cousin.'

'No,' said Father at once. 'I couldn't leave Stefan.'

'It would be safer. But Christa,' said the man, turning to look at her, giving her the swift, secret smile, 'you are coming with us.'

'But where will people think we are?'

'That's easily dealt with. We'll let it be known that your health has been a cause for concern – or perhaps that it's Christa's health, and that you have taken her to friends – or family – in a different area. And when you return, your neighbours will welcome you back without the smallest suspicion.'

'We would return here?' Father almost sounded as if he was pleading; Christa hated hearing him speak in such a way.

'Of course.' The response came quickly – too quickly?

'Back to Stefan? Back to this house?'

'Most assuredly.'

'I don't know your name,' said Father, again.

'To people with whom I work – people who trust me and whom I can trust – I'm known as Brax.'

'Brax.' Father appeared to try the name out in his mind. 'Just that? Nothing more?'

'And nothing less.'

Brax. It was a name that might belong to any nationality or any religion or any profession, or any era. You might see it inside a synagogue or a church, or above an ordinary shop doorway. You might as easily see it on an old manuscript, or in a book of ancient legends.

Christa moved around the house, trying to think what they should take, folding things into the battered suitcases. The thought of leaving Stefan was almost unbearable.

'We can't,' Christa had cried. 'He's too little. He won't understand—'

'You must. You can write to him to explain tonight,' said Brax, very gently. 'I'll take the note to Velda's house. And you will write to him from the Torhaus, of course.'

'Can I do that?'

'Of course. This won't be for very long, you know.'

'Promise?'

His hand came out to touch her face, tracing the line of her jaw very lightly. Christa stood very still. It was as if tiny electrical shocks had trickled across her skin. 'Christa, you have my word.'

So Christa packed her things and Father's, and wrote a careful note for Stefan, which Father and Brax took to Velda's house. She thought Father was on the verge of tears when he came back, but he gave her his familiar smile, and said Stefan was all right – he thought he was having a little holiday with Velda. They must look on this as an adventure, and they must trust Brax.

Throughout all this, two facts kept forcing themselves to the forefront of Christa's mind. The first was that her mother had not died – she had run away with a lover, and the second was that the lover had been the man who had died in messy agony tonight.

She knew it must be true, because Reinhardt had had her mother's photo. As he died, he had held it before him, looking at it with an expression that might have been love.

The Torhaus was larger than Christa had been expecting, and it stood at the end of a tree-lined track, which gave it an air of being apart from ordinary things. It was surrounded by a high stone wall, which must shut out a good deal of the light, and there were tall gates which had to be unlocked to let them in.

And there, in front of them, was the house. It was built of the same dark stone as the wall, and it was four-square with small, frowning windows. It stood in a small hollow, so that Wewelsburg Castle seemed to rear above it. The castle itself was further away than Christa had thought, which was good, but it was still visible. Surprisingly, she did not mind it as much as she had expected.

Her bedroom lay immediately under the eaves, and at some time in the recent past somebody had put up wallpaper with posies of cornflowers tied with pale lilac ribbon. Christa thought that it was incongruous to see such feminine wallpaper in such a dark old house.

On the first night she knelt on the window-seat of her room, staring across the darkening landscape towards a huddle of buildings. At first she was not sure what they were. They were too large to be farm buildings, and too neatly laid out to be a village. She thought the word for it might be regimented. Might it be a factory? But as she went on looking, her eyes began to adjust to the darkness – or perhaps the moon simply came out from behind clouds – and she could make out tall gates. She was seeing more details as well now, and sick horror was starting to sweep over her. Because on the eastern side of the buildings, almost exactly as she had seen them in her nightmares, were jutting brick chimneys.

It's a concentration camp, thought Christa. It's one of the places where people are shut away and where the skewer-eyed men and the humpback surgeons pull out their bones. Where the brick chimneys sometimes glow with heat, because people – dozens of people – are being burned. For the first time since leaving Lindschoen, she was grateful that Stefan was not with them.

TWENTY-THREE

Father had a room on the ground floor of the Torhaus – a kind of bedroom-cum-study. There was a small cottage piano with a walnut veneer with elaborate figuring and a candleholder alongside the music stand.

'Where did the piano come from?' he said.

Fräulein Frank, who was thin and cold-eyed, and had wide bony shoulders like a coat hanger, said, 'From a place where it's no longer needed.'

'Brax caused it to be brought here?'

'He gave the order.' Something approaching reverence showed in the cold eyes at the mention of Brax.

'It needs tuning,' said Father, disapprovingly, having tried a few bars of Chopin. 'Particularly if it's been moved—'

'You must do your best with it as it is,' said Elsa Frank, and Father frowned, then shrugged as if in acceptance.

'Brax wants me to write music while we're here,' he said to Christa after they had been given supper. 'I think he sees himself as a kind of patron of the arts. He says he's saving the artists from the Nazis.'

'Do you believe him?'

'I don't have much choice He wants a particular piece of music – something military as far as I can make out. He's quite – insistent about it. I shall have to make the attempt, I think. And he did get us out of Lindschoen – I mustn't lose sight of that.'

Christa's mind went back to the night in The Music House, to the overheard conversation. It had sounded as if composing music for Brax was to be a kind of payment for him getting them out of Lindschoen after Reinhardt's death. It was a curious way to settle a debt, but these were strange times.

Father was saying, 'The trouble is, Christa, that I'm not much of a composer – I haven't the originality.'

Christa thought they both knew this was true, although she would not have said it for worlds. Father was a very good musician indeed, but the few pieces he had written were a bit boring. It was disloyal to think this, but it was still true.

It was slightly alarming to find that Fräulein Frank locked all the doors that night, and that they were not able to go outside.

'There will be no need,' she said when Father questioned her. 'You have everything here you need. There will be books and school things for the girl—'

Christa retorted coldly, 'I'm not a child. My schooldays are behind me. I'll be helping my father with his music, and perhaps sketch and explore the countryside—'

'You will not explore the countryside,' said Fräulein Frank. 'You won't go beyond the gardens of the house. The gates will be locked, and you will find the wall is too high to climb.'

Father said, very politely, 'I don't think we realized this would be a prison.'

'It isn't a prison. It isn't to keep you in, it's to keep the world out – to hide you from it.'

'For the time being,' said Father.

'Yes. And my cousin has gone to considerable trouble to bring you both here. His work is vital and he is inspirational.' Again there was the change of tone. 'You must not disappoint him.'

It was not exactly captivity, but Christa thought it nearly was. However, as Father said, it would not be for very long, and he would have the musical project to absorb him. It might be that Christa could help with that. As for Stefan, Brax had promised to bring regular news of him, and Elsa Frank said Brax came regularly to the house. In any case, they would soon be back in Lindschoen and life would resume its normal course. Christa knew life would probably never resume its normal course, but this could not be said.

Mother's faithlessness could not be mentioned either, of course, but Christa would never forgive her for putting the bleak despair into Father's eyes for ever, and for leaving Stefan bewildered and uncomprehending. I hate you, said Christa to the memory of the woman she no longer thought of as Mother, only as Giselle. I hate you and I'm glad your lover died in agony. She did not dare frame the thought that it could only have been Father who had killed Obersturmbannführer Reinhardt. She was horrified to realize she did not care that he had.

There were three other people at the Torhaus; Christa supposed they, too, had been brought here for safety by Brax, although she did not like to ask them, or at least not until she had got to know them better. One was a painter who smiled vaguely and had paint stains all over his hands, and one was a writer who spent his time shut away in a small room at the house's rear and who was very secretive about whatever he was writing, and seemed very angry about everything. The other was a silversmith, who had a kind of workroom adjoining the house.

Unexpectedly, life inside the Torhaus had its own routine. Meals were taken with the writer and the painter, and with Jacob the silversmith. There was a girl who came and went, and who scrubbed floors and helped with the cooking, but it seemed to be expected that Christa would help with that as well. She did not mind, because she had usually cooked for Father and Stefan at home after Mother went. She tried to talk to Elsa Frank, but met only a cold response.

Sometimes Christa heard piano music coming from her father's room. It was not anything she recognized, so it seemed that he had begun work on the composition for Brax. Father had said Brax wanted something military, but this did not sound particularly military. It sounded flat and dull, as if Father had simply cobbled together bits of other people's music. Christa did not think it was in the least what Brax wanted.

Jacob turned out to be a nephew of Herr Eisler. 'So I know your father's work,' he said to Christa. 'All my family admire him very much and I'm very pleased indeed to meet him. He will compose something fine while he's here.'

'Yes, but I don't think I can,' said Father, when Christa reported this. 'And apart from anything else, that piano is so out of tune that anything I play sounds like nails rattling, and even if it sounded like a Bechstein, I'm no composer.'

'How bad is the piano?'

'Come and try it for yourself.'

The piano was fully as bad as he had said. Christa tried a scale and then the opening of *Humoresque*. The keys twanged with painful discordance. 'It's as if the hammers aren't striking properly,' she said. 'I suppose the wires are all intact? Could we look inside?'

'Could we? How could we?'

'I don't know, but – oh, wait, the lid's hinged,' said Christa. 'Can we lift it? It might be stuck though, because it's probably been closed up for years.'

But the piano's lid lifted smoothly and easily, and they folded it back against the wall. Father reached up to the wall sconce to tilt it slightly so that the light shone straight into the piano's innards.

'The wires look all right,' he said. 'At least – they look more or less as the one at home looks when the tuner comes in.'

Then Christa, peering into the depths with him, said, 'There's something in there. Papers . . . They're wedged against the wires – that's what's stopping the hammers striking properly.'

'For heaven's sake be careful.'

But Christa had already reached into the piano, and pulled the thin sheaf of papers free.

'Music,' she said, spreading it out on the small side table. 'Handwritten.'

Across the top of the first sheet, handwritten, was a single word. *Siegreich.*

'Victory,' said Father, softly, then he drew in his breath sharply. 'Look,' he said, pointing, but Christa had already seen the tiny sketched outline at the foot of the page. The musical symbol called the ghost note. The small private signature her mother had always left on letters and note. 'Because I'll always be around like a ghost,' she used to say. 'Even though you mightn't hear me, I'll be there.'

It seemed to Christa as if the two of them talked for most of the night. Several times she thought someone walked across the hall outside the room, and each time she tensed, expecting Brax or Elsa Frank to come in, but they did not.

'Only your mother would have added that note,' said Father, hope shining in his eyes. 'And that means she must have been here or somewhere nearby. It might mean she didn't leave us voluntarily.'

'It's all right,' said Christa, as he looked up suddenly, clearly realizing what he had said. 'I heard what Brax said about – um – about her having run away with that man. The one who was killed.'

'Reinhardt,' said Father. 'I never wholly believed that letter, but it was her writing, so I didn't dare hope too much that it wasn't true. But seeing this, I do hope it. I think she was forced to write that letter telling me she had run away with a lover. What I don't know is why she was forced to do such a thing.'

'Do you really think the letter was a lie?' said Christa, eagerly.

Father smiled. He said, 'At the foot of that letter she had drawn the ghost note. That's what gave me that tiny strand of hope. And now there's this.' He tapped the music, his fingers lingering on it, as if even by touching it he felt a link to Christa's mother.

Christa felt tears well up, but she fought them down. 'Is it possible Mother could have actually written this music?' I'm thinking of her as 'Mother' again, she thought with relief.

Father was studying the music again. 'I never knew her to compose anything,' he said. 'That doesn't mean she never did, though. But as to where she is now . . .'

He broke off, and Christa glanced towards the window, to the rearing iron gates and the brick chimneys of Sachsenhausen in the distance. A shiver of apprehension scudded across her.

Then Father said, in a determinedly optimistic voice, 'You know, Brax can't have known this music was in here. Tomorrow, I'll try it out, and if it's any good— Christa, supposing I copied it onto clean score sheets? That I let Brax believe I've written it as the music he wants from me?'

'Dare you do that?'

'Yes, I do dare,' he said.

After their first week at the Torhaus, Jacob gave Christa the most beautiful silver bracelet, made up of smooth links of thin, satiny discs and loops.

'It's lovely.' Christa was delighted. 'Thank you very much,' she said, clasping the bracelet around her wrist with pleasure.

'I enjoyed making it for you. A beautiful object for a beautiful lady.'

'Oh, God, what a cliché,' said the writer from his corner, and banged out of the room to go back to his room and write his angry prose.

'It's not so much a cliché as all that,' said the painter, who was lounging on a window-seat, sketching the view beyond the window.

His eyes flickered with something Christa could not understand, then he said, 'Christa, can I paint you sometime? Or even just sketch you? Quite soon, I mean.'

'I didn't think I was particularly paintable,' said Christa, trying not to sound pleased. 'I'm not very pretty.'

'You're better than pretty,' said the painter. 'It's something about your bones. Jacob, I'm right, aren't I?'

'Oh yes,' said Jacob, smiling.

Christa hoped she was not blushing. She said, 'Um, well, all right, if you really want to.'

If it had not been for the gnawing anxiety about Stefan, and the perpetually locked gates in the high old wall, life inside the Torhaus might almost have been friendly.

Occasionally, late at night, Christa stole downstairs to curl up on the small chair immediately outside Father's room, and listen to him playing the music by the unknown composer. It felt like a link to Mother because of the ghost note. The music itself was lovely, it was strong and stirring and rich, even played on the tinny old piano in this sad, dark house. It was music to keep in your mind to give you strength if bad things happened to you.

Jacob sometimes brought pieces of jewellery for Christa to see, or asked her to help him with some small process in his little workshop. This she found very interesting. Christa wanted to ask Jacob why he was here – whether he had been in danger from the Nazis – but she did not want to appear to be prying, particularly when he was so friendly and nice. They talked about his uncle, dear flamboyant Herr Eisler, who had played at so many of Father's concerts. Jacob said his uncle had been a marvellous influence in his life.

The writer was not friendly towards anyone. He did not always appear at meals, and he was abrupt with everyone and sometimes called Elsa Frank shocking names. The painter told Christa writers were often bad-tempered, and not to take any notice. He arranged for Christa to go up to his studio at the top of the house for an hour each morning. Christa was pleased, because it filled up some of the day, although she sometimes got cramp from keeping still in one position for so long.

But then came the day when everything changed.

*   *   *

Christa had gone up to the painter's studio at their usual time. As she went up the stairs, he came into the hall below and called up to her to go along to his room; he would be there in a minute, and they would continue with the sketch he had started yesterday.

Climbing the stairs to the studio, Christa was feeling almost happy. Yesterday Brax had come to the Torhaus – Elsa Frank had flown into a flurry of cooking and house-cleaning because of it. Ben, the writer, said it was revolting to see such slavish adoration; the woman might as well put down a prayer mat and make obeisance and he would not come in to the communal supper that evening.

Brax had brought Father and Christa a letter from Velda, which included a carefully written note from Stefan, telling about things at school, and sending lots of love. He sounded happy and normal, and it had been a huge relief to read it. Velda's letter contained no news about the SS finding Reinhardt's body or of any enquiry being made in the town about his murder, and, as Father said, Velda was the most gossipy person you could meet, and she would certainly have written about that. We're going to be safe, thought Christa. Father's transcribing that music for Brax, and Brax will think it's Father's own work and be pleased, and everything will be all right. And soon we'll be able to go home.

The painter's room was littered with easels and canvases, and painting things were strewn around, but Christa liked the feeling of stepping into a slightly bohemian world. Here was the makeshift dais he had set up, with the draped velvet curtain which was the backdrop he was using for her portrait. The velvet was rubbed and old, but the painter would make it look good. It had slipped down, though, and it would save time if Christa could get it back in place. She reached for the edges and lifted it to pin it back on to the wall. There was a small cabinet pushed into the corner, which the velvet had hidden, and which she had not realized was there. Probably it held brushes and palette knives and things.

Christa had certainly not intended to look at the drawer's contents, but the top drawer was open, and in reaching up with the velvet, she could not help seeing the scatter of what looked like postcards in the drawer. It seemed vaguely odd that the painter should have postcards sent to him here.

There were six altogether, and they were larger than normal

postcards. The colours were vivid – almost crude – and the images were dreadfully clear.

The first was obviously meant to portray a British soldier – the khaki uniform was unmistakable. He was lying on a bed with a female who was as near naked as made no difference, apart from a fold of the sheet here and there.

The caption across the top, said: 'Is this what your husband is doing while you think he is fighting a war . . .?'

The next postcard showed a semi-nude, fair-haired female, lying seductively on a bed. She was wearing a British Army helmet, and looking into a full-length mirror. But the image that looked out of the mirror was different – it was of a dark-haired female, with the yellow Star of David across her front. And again, a besotted-looking British officer – this time in an RAF uniform – was kneeling at the foot of the bed. The caption was much the same as the first: 'Your husband, your sweetheart, your brother, tell you they are fighting for your country – but this is what they are really doing . . .'

They were sickening in a number of ways, but the terrible thing was that in every single one, the face of the female posing so alluringly was Christa herself.

Christa gave a deep sob, and ran blindly out of the room and down the stairs. Arms grabbed her and held her, and Jacob Eisler said, 'Christa, my poor love, what on earth's happened?'

TWENTY-FOUR

'I thought you knew,' said Jacob, facing Christa and her father in his small cluttered workshop. 'I thought you both understood.' Father's face was white and he was holding Christa's hand very tightly, as if he feared she might slip from him if he did not cling to her.

He said, 'We were told – we were promised – that we were being saved from the Nazis. Hidden from them. I was suspected of – a particular crime against the SS. Brax wanted to get me away from them.'

Jacob said, in a voice of extreme reluctance, 'Felix, you're not being kept *from* the Nazis. You're being kept *for* them. Everyone here is. We're all working for them.' He made a gesture with his hands that reminded Christa painfully of his uncle, who used to make almost exactly that same gesture when audiences applauded him.

'I'm here because they found that I was still making Jewish jewellery, despite all the bans,' said Jacob. 'Menorah candleholders for Hanukkah. Silver rings with Jewish emblems – lockets and pendants with the chai.'

Father nodded, understanding.

'They told me I could either work for them, or be thrown into somewhere like Sachsenhausen or Auschwitz. And it wouldn't just be me they'd imprison – they said they'd take my uncle and that when they had finished with him, he would never be able to play a piano again.' Again the characteristic gesture. 'Some people would say I'm a coward,' said Jacob, 'a traitor. But I will admit to you both that I would rather do this and try to find a way to outwit Brax and his people, than be half starved and probably eventually gassed and burned. And,' he said, in a voice that was suddenly blurred with pain, 'told they have cut off my uncle's fingers, one by one.'

'Yes. Oh, my poor boy, yes of course, I understand,' said Father, reaching out to pat Jacob's shoulder a bit awkwardly. 'You couldn't do it,' he said. 'I couldn't have done it, either. So you work for them here?'

'Mostly making death's head rings for Reichsführer Himmler,' said Jacob, and the earlier pain in his voice had given way to such bitter hatred that Christa was startled, because Jacob had been so gentle and even shy until now.

'And a silver bracelet for me,' put in Christa, and he smiled at her.

'And the others?' said Father. 'Daniel and Ben?'

Jacob hesitated, then got up and went to the door, opening it slightly to listen.

'It's all right,' he said. 'I thought I heard a footstep, and Brax is here today, and he prowls around like a cat. There's no one out there, though.' But when he spoke again, he lowered his voice. 'The others have similar tales. Ben is writing news items for the British and their allies, telling how victorious the German armies are. Quite a lot of the stuff he writes is used for wireless broadcasts – they're broadcast into England. They call the programmes *Germany Calling*, and they're sneering and dreadful. The English absolutely hate them. And what they say is all lies, of course, but Brax's people have got Ben's wife in Sachsenhausen, and if he doesn't write what they want and make it sound authentic, they promise they'll kill her. That's why Ben's so furious with everyone all the time. He daren't disobey Brax, though. And it's agony for him to see Sachsenhausen from his window and know his wife's so near.'

'And the postcards of Christa?' said Father. 'How would they be used?'

'They'll be meant for propaganda of a different kind. The Luftwaffe drop batches of them over England – or their spies over there leave them in public places. There are several kinds – not just the ones Christa found. They're meant to demoralize the English. To dent their fighting spirit.'

'That's absurd,' said Father, furiously. 'That kind of thing wouldn't dent anyone's fighting spirit.'

'If it's any consolation, I believe the English make jokes of them – they use them as dartboards in pubs. There's even one story of how a British air marshal – Sir Arthur Harris, I think is his name – said the only thing the propaganda leaflets achieved was helping the supplies of lavatory paper for the troops.' He gave his sudden shy smile. 'Forgive me for such a coarse reference.'

'You can be as coarse as you want,' said Father, with force. 'It's all those things are fit for. They're sick and twisted.'

'Of course they are. But Daniel is a widower – his wife died when their son was born. If Dan doesn't create the posters and the leaflets they want, the Gestapo will take his son to one of the camps.'

'That's dreadful.' Christa's mind went at once to Stefan.

'Yes, it is. Dan's a very fine artist, though, and they want him to start making copies of some famous art treasures as well. He'll try to resist, but he won't resist very hard because of his little boy,' said Jacob. 'As for you two, I suspect you were a double prize for Brax. He wanted a model for the propaganda illustrations and Christa was exactly right. Also, he wants music for the Führer's armies – something that can accompany the occupation of the next country, I think. And most likely Britain.'

'Is that what I'm meant to be composing?' said Father, horror in his voice. 'Music to celebrate the vanquishing of Britain?'

'Yes. You didn't know?'

'No, I did not,' said Father, angrily.

'Brax could get the music from any one of a dozen approved German musicians, but the thought of forcing it from a Jew pleases him,' said Jacob. 'I think the concept was originally someone else's idea, but Brax has picked it up, and he'll take any credit for it that he can. Felix, can I ask – does Brax have some sort of hold over you? Don't answer if you'd rather not, but you mentioned a crime against the SS . . .'

Christa looked at Father, and there was a moment when she thought they both wondered how far to trust Jacob. But at once came the instinctive knowledge that they could trust him completely.

Father said, slowly, 'He does have a hold over me – and over Christa. There was a brutal killing – the death of a senior SS man. It looked as if I could have done it – or even as if Christa could. I would certainly have had a motive.'

'Did you kill him?' said Jacob. 'I'm sorry, I shouldn't ask. Don't answer. I don't care if you did kill him, whoever he was. I'm glad if you did, in fact.'

'I didn't kill him,' said Father. 'Neither did Christa. But it was made to look as if either of us could have done so.'

'Brax would almost certainly have killed him,' said Jacob. 'Or had him killed. But he would have set the stage so that you were – what do they call it? – the prime suspect. Then he'd offer his help, and you'd be so grateful you wouldn't question things too closely.'

'Jacob – my own small son is still in Lindschoen. You don't think—'

'No.' It came out swiftly and with such reassurance that Father relaxed. 'Your boy will be safe,' said Jacob. 'That murder is Brax's hold on you. He likes to employ different tactics – he's used that one once with Daniel, and he's holding Ben's wife. With you he wanted a different method. It's part of his subtle brutality that he likes variation with his cruelty.'

'It's a vicious kind of cruelty,' said Father.

'He's a maestro at cruelty.'

It was two nights later that Christa heard the music change. Most of it was still the same, but something had been added. Something that was like a jagged piece of glass tearing through the cadences. Ugly and harsh.

'You've added something to the music,' she said to him, the following day.

'You heard it?' Father sounded startled.

'Sometimes I come downstairs when everyone's asleep. I like listening. I'm right, aren't I? There is something different?'

For a moment something mischievous – something very nearly malicious – showed in Father's eyes. Then he said, 'It's a small touch of my own. Didn't you recognize it? It's a tritone.'

A tritone. Christa thought: yes, of *course* that's what it is. It's the *diabolus in musica*. The chord once regarded by the Church as the sound of the devil. She said, 'But why would you add something like that?'

'So that no matter how the music is used, anyone hearing it – anyone who understands about music – will know what its composer really thought about the Nazis,' he said. 'Which is that they're devils, one and all. Harsh and cruel and warped.' He frowned. 'The music is wonderful,' he said in a gentler voice. 'Whoever composed it, was very gifted indeed. It's a bad thing I'm doing in distorting it like this. But it's something I believe has to be done.' He smiled at her. 'I doubt the Nazis will know what I've done. I doubt they'll recognize the chord for what it is, and even if they do, I'm not sure I care any longer.'

Sleep was impossible. Christa lay awake, worrying that even though Brax might never have heard of the chord of evil, he would certainly know that something ugly and jarring was at the music's core. Tomorrow I'll beg Father to remove the devil's chord, she thought.

She was just slipping into an uneasy sleep at last, when she heard footsteps downstairs, and the sound of a door opening. It sounded as if it was at the back of the house. Father's room? Christa sat up, listening, then slid out of bed, and stole down the stairs to the big hall at the house's centre, and along the narrow passage that led to the back of the house.

Light showed around the door, and she heard her father say: 'The truth is, you're a vicious, cold-blooded killer, and a manipulator of everyone you meet. You've used me, and you've used my daughter, and in the most repulsive, disgusting way. I've only just found out.'

'Ah. That,' said Brax, 'is unfortunate.'

'I won't write another note for you. I won't write a victory march for Hitler's armies.'

'A great pity,' said Brax, and his voice rapped out an order. Two men, both in the dark sharp uniform of the Gestapo, crossed the hall. Christa heard her father cry out, and then the sound of steel snapping. Restraints? Please don't let it be the sound of rifles being primed. She dug her fingernails into her palms.

Then Father's voice came again, still defiant. 'Where are you taking me?'

'To Sachsenhausen. It was where you were destined to end, anyway. Once we had the *Siegreich* you would have become expendable. You had started to write something – you told me it was evolving well. Where is it?'

'Destroyed. Burned in that very hearth. You can sift through the ashes if you like, but you won't find more than a few charred fragments,' said Father.

'Burned,' said Brax, half to himself, then let out an oath. 'I had such hopes – we all had such hopes – of presenting victory music to the Führer. Well, you will have time to reflect on that in Sachsenhausen.'

'What will happen to Christa?' There was a note of sudden fear in Father's voice.

'I haven't finished with Christa yet,' said Brax, and then, with a harsh authority that Christa had not heard him use before, he said to the two officers, 'The girl's in the top bedroom. Lock the door. I shan't have time to deal with her until tomorrow. But the waiting will put an edge on my appetite.' Then, as if in an afterthought, he said, 'Post several of the guards outside in case any of the others tries to escape.'

If Christa could have got down the stairs and out into the garden and somehow hidden there, she would have done so, but there was no chance. The Gestapo man was already on the stairs, and before she could do anything, there was the sound of the lock turning. She darted to the door, and banged on it, yelling to be let out, but there was only the sound of his steps going away again.

She sat down on the bed, feeling more helpless and more alone than she had ever felt in her entire life, then went to the window to kneel on the window-seat, in case she could get one last glance of Father. She could not, of course; the window overlooked the back of the house. She could see the smudge that was Sachsenhausen, though. Within the next hour, Father would be in there. He had told Brax that he had burned the *Siegreich*, but Christa knew he had not. She knew he would never have done that, because he believed Mother was somehow linked to the music.

There was a small fragment of comfort in knowing that Jacob and the other two were in the house. Between them, couldn't they make some escape effort? But when Christa leaned right over the window, she saw the Gestapo below, and she remembered that Brax had told them to mount guard.

There was nothing to be done but wait until tomorrow when Brax came to do what he had called 'deal with her'.

The hours of that day were impossibly long. Elsa Frank brought Christa a mug of coffee and *Brötchen*, and she and the scullery girl took Christa along to the bathroom.

This was repeated at midday, this time with a small bowl of

fruit and a jug of water. Christa tried to ask Fräulein Frank what was happening, but received no reply.

It was late afternoon when she heard the sounds of arrival downstairs, and then footsteps on the stairs. He was here. He was coming to her room to 'deal with her'. Was he going to kill her here in this room? His own private execution? Would they bury her body in the grounds of the Torhaus, so that no one would ever know what had happened to her? Her mind went to Stefan, innocent and unaware in Lindschoen. Please don't let Stefan be told she had been murdered. But she knew, of course, that Brax intended something other than murder.

The strange thing – the very worrying thing – was that when he opened the door and stood looking at her, it was no longer the cruel sly villain who had talked to Father last night. It was the velvet-voiced, gentle-eyed man who had come to The Music House – the man who knew and loved good music, and the man who had helped them to get away from Lindschoen. The man who had smiled at Christa in a way that had made her think he wanted to take her into some marvellous intimate world where there would only be the two of them.

He said, 'Christa,' and there was the same sensation that he was caressing her name, 'you must have wondered what was happening. I've come to reassure you.'

'Where's my father?'

'He's going to spend a bit of time somewhere else. He'll be quite near this house, though.'

'What will happen to him?'

'I don't know. It could depend on several things.' Brax sat on the bed, and his hand came out to her, touching her hair. Christa sat very still.

'What kind of things?' It was even possible, she discovered, to put a softness into her own voice. Would it fool him? Was he so incredibly vain, so arrogant, that he would believe she could still be under his spell? It was the darkest spell imaginable, but even so . . .

He smiled, and it was a smile that sent shivers of fear over Christa.

'I think we both know what kind of things, don't we? And, in any case, I think we knew almost as soon as we met how it

would one day be for us. You and me, Christa. Together. Here
– tonight . . .'

Somehow he had unfastened the buttons of her blouse, and his
hands were inside, caressing her breasts, and it was dreadful; he
was a cold, cruel murderer, a Nazi, and she had never hated anyone
as much as she hated him.

But if she let him do what he wanted to her, it might mean her
father would come back. That was what he meant, wasn't it?

Christa said, 'You're saying that if I – if I let you do what you
want to me, my father would come back here?'

'Of course. You're such a beautiful little innocent, and I won't
hurt you, Christa . . .'

He was pushing her back on the bed, and he was lying alongside
her. I can't let this happen, thought Christa. But is there a choice?
If I fight, won't he force me anyway?

'Oh, God, you're so soft and young and sweet,' he said, and
now his voice was thick with emotion, and he was breathing as
if he had been running. Christa could feel him thrusting against
her – there was a hardness pushing against her thighs, and then her
lower stomach. 'I promise I won't hurt you,' he said, again. 'It will
be marvellous.'

But it was not marvellous at all. It was painful and embarrassing.
He thrust his hand between her legs, and jabbed at her with his
fingers, making her cry out, because one of his fingernails was
jagged, and it tore into her.

Then suddenly and shockingly, the insistent masculine hardness
was inside her, dreadful, agonizingly painful, and Brax was moving
quickly and then even more quickly, clutching her shoulders,
gasping and moving frenziedly in a horrid rhythm. This could not
be the thing that people raved over and wrote poetry about, and
died for. It was undignified and painful, and all of a sudden it was
messy, with a wet stickiness that seemed to flood into her in jerky
spasms.

Brax half fell on her, his weight heavy and crushing, and then
rolled off. Christa slowly turned her head to look at him. His eyes
were half closed and there was a faint sheen of sweat on his face.
If ever there was a moment when he was defenceless . . .

She did not stop to think and she certainly did not stop to
plan. She sat up, seized the jug that had held the water, and brought

it crunching down on Brax's head. He gave a surprised cry, flailed at the air with one hand, then fell back on the bed. His eyes were half closed, but he was still breathing. Sobbing with fear and panic, but still in the grip of the same resolve, Christa grabbed the belt he had flung off. It went around his neck easily, and she pulled hard, making it tighter, tighter . . . He was partly conscious now, sufficiently so for him to realize what was happening, and he clawed at the belt, trying to get it off, thrashing with his legs. Christa could hear herself sobbing, and she thought she might be sick in a moment, but she pulled the belt even tighter, seeing it bite into his flesh, seeing blood start to bubble out of the skin.

Brax's face was turning deep red, and veins were showing in his cheeks. His eyes were beginning to bulge – they were threaded with tiny crimson veins – and his tongue was protruding. Spittle ran down his chin, and he was making dreadful choking sounds.

I don't care, thought Christa. You're evil and cruel and I hope you're dying really slowly and really painfully. This is for my father, and it's for what you've just done to me. It's for what you've done to all those other people, as well – all the people you've deceived and brought here . . . Daniel and Ben and Jacob – yes, dear, gentle Jacob. She gave one final vicious tug, and there was the feeling of something snapping. A terrible wet sound came from Brax's throat, and then he was still. His head flopped to one side, the eyes wide and staring.

The sickness overwhelmed Christa then, and she retched and vomited over the dead face. Dreadful. Appalling. I've killed him, I'm a murderer.

She finally managed to clamber off the bed, and she was trying in a bewildered way to think what she should do, when the door was flung open, and two guards, their rifles pointing at her, stood in the doorway.

Before she could do anything, they dragged her from the room that stank of Brax's blood and her own vomit. They gave her no time to collect anything – not her bag with her comb and purse, or any clothes, not even the silver bracelet Jacob had given her. Absurdly, it hurt to leave that in the room. It felt as if she had repudiated Jacob's gift.

As they took her down the stairs, there was a swift glimpse of Jacob, and also of Daniel and Ben, standing together in the hall.

Jacob put out a hand as if he wanted to clasp hers, but the guard knocked it away.

Daniel did not try to touch her, but he said, 'Christa – remember that one day I'm going to paint you properly. I promise it.'

Pushed into the back of a jeep, Christa managed to say to the guards, 'What's going to happen to me?'

'You will be executed as the murderess you are,' said the harsh voice of one of the guards who had brought her. 'You killed Count von Braxen.'

'He raped me,' cried Christa.

'You lie. Senior members of the Gestapo do not commit rape. You seduced him, then regretted it, so you killed him. You will face the firing squad. You will not escape.'

TWENTY-FIVE

Margot had thought that the prospect of seeing the Torhaus – of actually starting to track down whether it might be Lina's house and therefore, possibly, hers and Marcus's – would drive away the stupid suspicion that Marcus had realized the truth about the deaths of Lina and their mother. But it did not. As they drove across the country, she was still remembering that soft insinuation he had made on the night of Stefan Cain's dinner party; of how brothers and sisters protected one another – except if it came to murder. She kept remembering, as well, how he had looked at her with shocked fear the night their mother died. He looked at her in the same way several times during the journey to Lindschoen – but if their eyes, met, Marcus at once looked away.

But once they had found this gatehouse place, and established it was theirs, all those feelings would go. Margot was sure it was the right house; she said so, several times.

'I wish I'd been able to find out a bit more,' said Marcus.

'You found out an awful lot.'

'I found out a bit about German land registration,' he said. 'It's a similar system to our own, but it isn't as easy to get information from it. You have to explain why you want to see a particular entry, and you have to apply to the correct district court. They check whether you've got a legitimate claim, and I'm not sure how good our claim would be. There's only that letter sent to Lina, and it's half a century ago, and the firm that sent it hasn't existed for decades.'

'Let's find the house and go from there,' said Margot. 'That letter you found in Greymarsh House said it was empty – it sounded as if it had been empty for years – so there must be keys somewhere. Somebody must have responsibility for it – even if it's only to make sure squatters don't get in or the garden's kept tidy.'

She did not much care for Lindschoen, although Marcus said it was charming and full of interesting little pockets. If Margot had not known better, she would almost have thought he was putting off finding the Torhaus and tracing its ownership. Perhaps he did not want to admit that he did not know where to start.

But on their second day, he suddenly said they would try the civic office. He was a bit abrupt about it, but they found the office, which was on the outskirts of Lindschoen and which was a bit like a council office at home

Marcus talked to several people while Margot waited. She heard the words Torhaus several times, and then she thought Marcus asked about a key – *Schlüssel*? he said, several times. The man at the desk laughed, and said something to a colleague, who laughed as well.

'What did they say?' asked Margot once they were outside.

'That there haven't been any keys to the place for years,' said Marcus. 'They were lost decades ago, apparently, and nobody's ever bothered to have new ones cut, because nobody ever goes there. It's been empty ever since anyone can remember.'

'Did you ask who's supposed to own it? Or if anyone looks after it? Are there neighbours for instance?'

'Yes, I did, but they just shrugged. They said no one knew who had any responsibility, and that they don't think there are any neighbours. It probably stands in the middle of a field or halfway up a mountain or in the centre of an aerodrome or something,' said Marcus. 'Still, they found a map – bit like our Ordnance Survey map – and they've marked the route out.'

'Good. Shall we have some lunch and drive out there?'

And again there was the curious hesitancy, almost as if he might be trying to make up his mind. He darted that strange, almost-furtive look towards her again. Then he said, 'Yes, all right.'

'We might be able to get in,' said Margot. 'Even without keys, I mean. It sounds as if it's pretty ramshackle. And it's what we've come to see.'

They had their lunch, and Marcus followed the directions on the map. There was only one occasion when he swore at her, stopped the car, and snatched the map from her to see the route for himself. Then he apologized. He was tired from the driving, he said, and it was a bit of a strain, still, to keep on the right.

The journey took longer than they had thought, and by the time they came in sight of the gatehouse, it was starting to grow dark.

And as soon as she saw it, Margot knew it would have been better to have stayed away.

They had to drive up a winding, deeply rutted track to reach the house and Marcus swore because if the suspension went or a tyre punctured or the exhaust was wrenched off out here, he had no idea what they would do.

Thick, overgrown hedges thrust against the car, and once Margot had to get out to push some aside before they could drive on. Halfway up the track was a rickety gate which, when she got out to open it, fell off one of its hinges, so they had to carry it to the side of the path and prop it up. Marcus swore again because he had stepped in a patch of thick mud.

'If it is mud,' he said. 'It smells as if it might be from a cow. God, this is frightful. I don't want to stay here.'

The Torhaus was almost entirely enclosed by a stone wall, which Margot had not expected.

'And gates as well,' said Marcus. 'Can you see them? They're quite high. I bet they're locked. Even if they aren't, they'll be rusted up and we'll never get them open. They're too high to climb over, as well.'

He almost sounded relieved, and Margot looked at him in surprise. 'Let's try, though,' she said. 'And there's a bit of wall over there where the stones have fallen away. Can you see? We could climb through.'

'I suppose we could. Yes, all right. Having come this far . . .'

The odd thing – the vaguely worrying thing – was that when he said this, Margot had the impression he was not talking about the house. But he reached in the glove compartment for the torch, and they went across the uneven ground to the fallen-away part of the wall. It was easy enough to dislodge a few more bits and squeeze through the crumbling stonework. And there, in front of them, was the Torhaus.

It was ugly and bleak and lonely, and it looked as if it had been quietly decaying for the last fifty years. Margot's heart sank, and she said, 'If this really is the place, it would cost a fortune to prove it. And it would cost another fortune to put it right. Because we'd never sell it as it is.'

'No one would come within a mile of it.' Marcus had not taken his eyes from the house, and there was an expression in his face that Margot could not interpret.

'What a disappointment,' she said. 'What now? Shall we go back? It'll start getting dark soon.'

'No, let's at least try to get in.'

He walked towards the house, shining the torch to see the way, Margot, hardly believing this was happening, stumbled along at his side. The house loomed over them, as if staring down at the two intruders, and she looked up at the upper windows. Had something moved behind one of them? No, it had just been the reflection of the scudding clouds across the sky. But just for a second or two it had seemed as if a figure walked to a window just under the eaves, and as if a pallid face pressed against the glass.

Marcus did not seem aware of it. He was peering into the ground-floor windows, shining the torch. 'There's still furniture in there,' he said, turning to call back to where Margot was waiting. 'It looks as if someone simply walked out of it one day and didn't come back. You'd have thought it would have been long since plundered, wouldn't you? Although, it's so far off the road, maybe no one realizes it's even here. It's a lonely place, isn't it? It's a place where anything could happen and no one would know about it for a very long time.'

Again there was the strangeness in his voice and the almost-frightening look had come into his eyes again. Margot shivered, hating the house more with every minute. But if this really was Lina's house, they should find out as much as they could about it. And perhaps it could be renovated after all – made into a small guesthouse, even.

Marcus was reaching for the iron ring-handle of the house's main door. It would be locked, of course, even with the house in this battered state, because no one, not even a madman, would leave a house unlocked, unsecured, out here.

But the door was not locked, or, if it had been, the lock had rotted away. Marcus pushed it inwards, shone the torch.

'Stay here while I look,' he said, and there was a moment when he was silhouetted in the doorway, then he went inside and the darkness closed down again.

Margot stayed where she was for what felt like a long time. It was getting very dark now, and once she saw the flicker of his torch behind one of the ground-floor windows. She thought the movement from the upstairs room came again.

The old trees surrounding the Torhaus were whispering and dipping their branches. It was uncomfortably easy to imagine they were watching her, and murmuring to one another. The wind stirring the branches and the leaves could almost be voices. Margot thought she would step through the partly open door and call out to Marcus to hurry up. When she did so, he was there, as if he had been waiting for her, standing at the foot of a wide staircase.

'Come inside and take a look,' he said.

It was not pitch dark inside the Torhaus because there was some overspill from the fading daylight outside, and there was also the light from Marcus's torch. But the house felt horrid; there was a smell of damp and age and old vegetation. Margot repressed a shudder.

Marcus's face was lit from below by the torch; it created hollows and pits where his eyes were. It was unnerving; it was almost as if it was no longer Marcus who was standing there.

'In here,' he said, taking her hand.

It was a small room, thick with dust, and with a lingering sadness, and there was a piano, set against the wall. It was small and old, the elaborate wood figuring on the front dull and slightly rotting on one side.

Margot said, 'How odd—'

'Isn't it? And a piano can be a murder weapon, can't it, Margot?'

A murder weapon. Margot shivered, and her head began to feel as if something was wrenching it apart.

'Look,' said Marcus, shining the torch onto the stand. 'You recognize it, do you?' he said.

Margot would have recognized it after a hundred years. A handwritten score, with *Giselle's Music* written across the top. It had been there when she had whispered through the shadows to Lina – when Lina had clutched at her heart in fear, then fallen.

She said, 'Did you bring it with you, that music?'

'Yes. And a few other things from Lina's desk. Things I didn't want to leave for anyone else to find.' Again the smile that made him look like a different person. 'You thought we found everything

there was to find, didn't you? But I found other things, Margot
– things you didn't know about. Things that told me a great deal
about Lina. And about Christa.'

'What kind of things? And why on earth would you bring them
out here?'

He reached to the music stand, and from behind *Giselle's Music*
took a sheet of creased paper. 'Read it. *Read* it.'

Margot took the papers unwillingly, and looked at the top one.
At first the words did not seem to make sense, but gradually she
sorted them out.

The paper was a birth certificate. It was in German, but the
layout was simple to understand. But what she was seeing sent
the room spinning into a whirling confusion. In the section for the
name of the newborn child it said, Lina Mander.

Father: Count Karol von Braxen (deceased).

But alongside that, next to the section for the mother, was a
name that seemed to rear up from the page.

Mother: Christa Klein.

Margot felt as if she had been pulled into a dark echoing tunnel.
She waited for her mind to steady, then in a thread of a voice, she
said, 'Lina was . . . she was Christa's daughter.'

'Yes. But she gave her away. Had her adopted. She must have
done. You see the place of birth?'

Margot had not looked beyond the name of Lina's mother, but
now she did look. In a voice she hardly recognized as her own,
she said, 'Sachsenhausen. Christa had a child – born inside a
concentration camp?'

'Yes. And the child was Lina.'

'And Christa killed the child's father.' It squared with the story
Lina had always told about Christa killing Lina's father. Butchered
by that harlot, Christa Klein, Lina used to say. What she had never
said, was that Christa had been her mother, or that Lina herself
had been born in a concentration camp. Only the hatred and the
bitterness had come through. Margot, looking again at the names
on the birth certificate thought, for the first time, that she could
almost understand Lina's feelings over those years. To know your
mother had killed your father . . . That you had been given away
. . . I'm sorry, Lina, she whispered in her mind. If you had told
the whole story, perhaps it might have been different for us all.

Marcus remained silent, and when Margot handed the certificate back, he slotted it behind the music again.

'Why did you bring those things with you?' said Margot again. 'The birth certificate and the music?'

'I didn't dare leave them behind. I didn't want anyone to find them and make assumptions.'

'Not to prove we've got a claim on Lina's house?'

'Lina's house probably doesn't exist,' he said, impatiently. 'That was a pipe dream, a castle in the air. Something hopeful to hold on to in those dreary years.' He put out a hand to her. 'And now, Margot, come upstairs with me.'

Come upstairs with me . . . His hand closed around hers. There was a time when his touch and those words would have sent shivers of fearful delight through Margot, but now they terrified her. She said, 'Can't we just go back – Marcus, I really don't like this house. Even if it is Lina's—'

'Of course it isn't Lina's house,' he said, at once. 'If Lina's house exists anywhere, it'll long since have belonged to someone else quite legally. I realized that ages ago. You'd have realized it too, if you'd had any sense.'

'But that letter you found in Mr Cain's house . . . It talked about the Torhaus and how no one could find out who owned it, and you said it all fitted.'

'That letter gave me the idea, that's all,' he said. 'A lonely old house, empty for so many years – a place where no one ever goes, and that no one knows who it belongs to . . . It was the ideal lure to get you out here. To get you to a place where you could vanish.'

He studied her, then said, 'I did tell you that I'd draw the line at protecting you if you'd committed a murder, didn't I? I drew that line a long time ago, Margot. And there's the question of self-preservation, as well. I don't trust you, you see. I can't risk you letting out what you did – or being found out. And if that were to happen . . . Well, I don't want to be seen – to be known – as the brother of a murderess.'

Margot tried to pull her hand free, but he was holding it too tightly.

'Don't you know, Margot, that I've hardly dared let you out of my sight since that night – since I realized what you'd done? I've watched you and I've guarded you, but I can't do it for ever. Also,' he said, very deliberately, 'I don't trust you not to mark me down as your next victim if you suddenly thought it would be to your advantage. So that makes it a case of kill or be killed.' He was pulling her along the hall. 'I looked all over the house while you waited outside. I was still making the decision, even then. It hasn't been an easy decision, I'd like you to know that.'

Those furtive glances, thought Margot. Those sideways looks. All the time he was making this decision. Oh God, what is he going to do to me?

They were at the wide stairway, and he was dragging her up. Margot struggled and fought to get free, but she could not.

'Marcus, let me go – where are we going—?'

'At the top of this house is a room with a lock and a key,' he said. 'The minute I saw that room, I knew it was the answer. I hadn't dared hope that I'd find somewhere like it, but there it was. Exactly right.' As they reached a small landing he twisted her arms behind her back, wrenching painfully at her shoulders as he did so, then forced her up a second, smaller flight. At the end of a small passage a door was open, and Marcus pushed Margot through it, then stood in the doorway, barring her way out.

'This is where you'll stay,' he said. 'You can't get out – the window's too small, and you'd break your neck if you tried to climb out anyway. There's a lock on the door – if there hadn't been, I'd have had to use physical violence or some kind of restraint. I didn't want any real physical contact, if I could avoid it. You always did, though, didn't you? All those times – did you think I didn't know what you would have liked from me? And didn't you realize I was repelled?'

'You're going to lock me in?' Margot focused on what was happening, because she could not bear to hear that Marcus had been repelled by her.

'That's exactly what I'm going to do. I'll stay downstairs for a while, though,' he said. 'Partly to make sure I'm not going to change my mind. I know I won't, though. I know I'm going to leave you here. No one will know where you are, Margot, and if anyone at home asks, I'll just say you've travelled to stay with friends. But you don't know many people, do you? No one in Thornchurch, and no one anywhere else. So no one's very likely to ask.'

Before Margot could get to the door, he had slipped through it, slammed it, and turned the key.

It would be useless to try the door, but Margot tried it anyway. It was locked of course. How about the window? But, as Marcus had said, it would be impossible to get through it, and in any case there was a sheer drop to the ground below.

The room smelled of damp and dirt. There were patches of mould on the ceiling where rain must have got in, and around the window, discolouring the plaster. Once there had been wallpaper on the walls – in places it was still possible to see the pattern very faintly: small bunches of cornflowers tied with lavender ribbon.

Beneath the smell of damp and mould there was somehow another smell – something deeper and older – something that might almost have printed itself on this room a long, long time ago . . .

There was nothing in the room except a chair and a small dressing table. When Margot opened one of the drawers there was a comb that somebody must have forgotten about, and a silver bracelet, made up of thin, glossy links.

She sat down on the narrow window-seat, and tried not to give way to fear. Marcus would not do this to her. It would be some sick joke – or she might have fallen asleep and be having a nightmare . . . Or she might have been given a drug and be hallucinating.

He had said he would not go away immediately. Probably he would come back soon. But the minutes went along, and there was no sound of his step on the stairs.

He had left her here in the dark old house. He had left her here to die and there was no way to escape.

TWENTY-SIX

Sachsenhausen, 1940

Giselle had never lost sight of the possibility of escape. Even inside Sachsenhausen she had clung to that hope. She had clung, as well, to the thought that she might find Silke or Silke's family. But it soon became apparent that there were several thousand prisoners in the camp – she might be here for months or even years without seeing Silke or knowing what was happening to her.

She had not been able to forget how they had forced her to write the letter to Felix, telling him she loved Reinhardt – that she was going to be with Reinhardt. She had written it, because Reinhardt's masters would have executed her if she had not done so, but she had dared to add the ghost note, hoping Felix would understand that it signalled the letter's contents were not true. Lying in the hut every night, she tried to reach out to Felix. Please don't believe what I wrote, my love, she thought. Please don't think I ran away from you or that I ever ceased loving you.

There was a kind of grapevine network in Sachsenhausen. Whispers were passed to and fro, usually at the Appellplatz, where prisoners had to line up for morning and evening roll calls. Sometimes fragments of news could be exchanged during work. The rigorous work regime had come as a shock to Giselle, and the work itself had surprised her very much. Forged British and American currency was produced here, so that Nazi spies could introduce it into those countries as part of a plan to undermine the economies. Aircraft parts were made here, as well, although it was believed that some of the people put to work there had dared to deliberately sabotage the parts, so that the German planes would crash.

The work was gruelling and long, but it was infinitely better, the others told Giselle, than being taken to one of the laboratories for medical experiments. When she heard this, Giselle's mind went instantly to Stefan's nightmares. The scissor man, he had sobbed. The people who pulled bones from bodies.

Each morning, when the inmates of her hut were marched to their work, they went past a section of the infamous death strip. Was it the section where Andreas had been tortured? Andreas, whom dear, irresponsible Silke had loved, and who had written music to her. Was that music still inside Wewelsburg Castle? Would anyone ever find it? Would Felix ever see it?

She waited for signs that the night with Reinhardt had resulted in pregnancy, but within the first three weeks it became apparent it had not. Curiously, it was a blow; Sachsenhausen would be a terrible place in which to bring new life into the world, but Giselle thought she might have got slightly better treatment if she had been pregnant. But it was not to be.

She lost real track of the time; the women she was with said this happened very quickly. Days blurred into one another. There were no landmarks – no weekends, no ordinary family things such as birthdays.

Throughout, Giselle ached to see Felix and to hear his dear voice again. Just one last time. Half an hour would be enough. About Christa and Stefan she did not dare think.

And then one night, as she was being marched back to her hut after the day's work, the gates were opened, the security lights came on, and a jeep came screeching through the gates and pulled up.

Two Gestapo dragged a young girl out of the jeep, and half carried her to one of the isolation cells.

Giselle felt as if the entire world had been wrenched apart and torn up, and the pieces flung down. Because the girl was Christa.

Somehow Giselle got back to her hut – she thought some of the women had to almost carry her – and she lay on the narrow pallet, trying to make sense of what she had seen.

At first she questioned whether it had really been Christa she had seen – whether it had just been a similarity of features and colouring. Because, watching the girl as she was taken across the courtyard, Giselle had felt as if the past had snatched at her, and as if she might be watching her own seventeen-year-old self.

Then she wondered whether her own constant longing for both her children had conjured up a chimera. But she knew it was not that. There was more to a person than just a set of features; recognition – acceptance of an identity – happened at a deeper level. And at that level, Giselle knew it was her daughter she had seen.

And the isolation cells of Sachsenhausen were only ever used for one purpose.

Execution.

There did not seem to be any definite reasons for executions in Sachsenhausen, although often they were people who had tried to escape or had been found plotting against the Gestapo. There were a number of what were called political prisoners here, and there were also criminals, as well. Murderers, rapists. Whatever the story might be, the condemned were marched out, made to stand in a trench, and shot. Occasionally they were hanged and the hanging was usually public. But, as the prisoners said, if the Gestapo wanted to be rid of someone, they did not need a reason. They just shot you.

And now Christa was facing that. Giselle knew she would not be able to bear seeing her bright, lovely girl led out to the firing squad or the hangman's rope. But the memory of the darkness she had sometimes sensed deep within her daughter was strongly with her. Was it the menace of Sachsenhausen that she had sensed? Had it always been ordained that Christa would die in this way?

Images from her daughter's childhood danced agonizingly across her mind, and with them came the memory of Felix saying, with such love in his voice, that Christa was the image of what Giselle had been as a very young girl. An exact copy, he had said. A duplicate.

A *duplicate*. The idea slid into Giselle's mind with the word.

She could not organize an escape for Christa – in any case, there were hardly ever successful escapes from Sachsenhausen. The picture of Silke's Andreas writhing in agony on the night he had attempted to break out was still sickeningly with her.

She could not help Christa to escape, not without risking both their lives. But there might be a way in which she could save her from the firing squad or the hangman's noose.

The more she thought about it, the more possible it began to seem. The more she listened to the whispers among the other inmates about the planned execution, the stronger her resolve grew. It could be done. If ever an execution in Sachsenhausen could be manipulated, this was that one.

But the longer she thought about it, the more it horrified and terrified her.

The days had blurred for Christa. She thought this might be because there was so little light inside the small room where they had put her that it was difficult to know when it was day and when it was night. Guards came and went. There was food of a kind – just about enough to keep her alive. Once they brought water so she could wash. After that she was left alone. She hated the smell of the airless room, and she hated the smell of her own body. Several times she was sick, which was disgusting, but after the first time she managed to reach the tin bucket in the corner, crouching over it, retching miserably.

She had thought, in a frightened, distant way that there would be a trial because she had certainly committed murder. She would speak out for herself, though; she would describe how Brax had raped her, how he had forced himself on her, hitting her across the face when she struggled against him. She had killed him in her own defence, she would say. But even as this thought formed, she was remembering how she had knocked him out, and then had strangled him while he was virtually unconscious. I could have escaped while he was stunned, thought Christa. I could have tried to get free – found Jacob and the others, and somehow we might have got out and got away. I didn't have to kill Brax.

The next time one of the guards brought the food, she asked what was going to happen. Was she to be tried for murder? She was pleased that the question came out firmly and without wavering.

'Tried?' he said, scornfully. He had a coarse skin, like porridge that had not been properly stirred. 'You won't be tried, Madam Bitch. They're saving you for the next firing squad.'

'When—?'

'One week from now,' he said, and went out, turning the lock.

And now night really did leach into day, and time became something that distorted and mocked. One week. Seven days. At first Christa tried to keep count of the days, but she lost track, and each morning when the guards came in, she expected it to be the day they would take her out to be shot.

She could not find the courage to ask about her father, who must also be in this grim place, because she was afraid of the answer. She thought about her mother every day, and when she remembered how her father had found that familiar ghost note on the music inside the piano – when she thought her mother might still be alive – she was aware of a faint, far-off comfort.

Giselle knew it was absurd to try to send out love and reassurance to Christa lying in that cell, but she could not help it.

She had to leave her plan until the day before the firing squad was to assemble. This was leaving it dreadfully, dangerously close, but she could not see any other way.

It was general knowledge, now, that the forthcoming execution was to be on a more ceremonious scale than the customary squalid trench deaths, or the casual hangings of escaping prisoners.

This was the execution of a woman who had murdered a very high-ranking officer of the Third Reich – a man who was not only a confidante of and advisor to the Führer himself, but who was also the scion of a noble house. The Weimar Constitution of 1919 declared all Germans to be equal, of course, but the man that Christa Klein had brutally killed was a member of an ancient house of the Prussian nobility. A Freiherr. A baron. And for such a one there must be a public display of the punishment of his killer.

Gradually, it became known that Christa Klein was insisting the baron had raped her. She was pleading self-defence for her crime. None of the prisoners dared comment on this, even among themselves, but Giselle saw that most of them believed Christa was speaking the truth.

It also became known that on the day before her execution, Christa would be brought out to the Appellplatz, where she would stand before a carefully chosen group of prisoners and the commandant and all the officers. A description of her crime would be read out. She would then be returned to her cell to await her execution the following morning.

Giselle, listening to the whispers, understood it meant that for that short time – perhaps no more than an hour – Christa would be outside. But would the women from Giselle's own hut be taken out to the Appellplatz? She waited and listened, and it began to be whispered that they would. It was good for the women to see how their own kind were dealt with when they committed a crime.

Giselle immediately began to put her plan into action. In the guards' hearing, she started to talk about von Braxen, making it sound as if she had known him very intimately indeed. It was unlikely that anyone would believe von Braxen had actually had a liaison with a Jewish female – it sounded as if he was far too deeply committed to Hitler's anti-Jewish pogrom. It did not matter. They would regard Giselle as a fantasist, but that would make her actions believable.

As the day of the execution approached, she stepped up her talk, making it wilder and louder. Several times she railed against the creature who had killed the man she had loved.

'It was two years ago – perhaps even longer,' she said, several times. 'But I have never ceased to think of him. If it had been a hundred years, I would still remember him.'

She was sure the guards heard her, and she thought there was a good chance that they would report what she had said to senior officers. Gossip was rife in Sachsenhausen, and every shred of information, no matter how mad or fantastic, was passed on. To make sure, she began to sketch in a few slightly more salacious details. Sex usually attracted people's attention. With that in mind, she made von Braxen sound like a mixture of Casanova and Rudolph Valentino, although if von Braxen had raped her beloved Christa, Giselle would prefer to think of him as the twelfth-century Peter Abelard, whose eventual fate had been castration.

Two nights before the execution, she told two of the women in her hut what she was going to do.

'You don't need to be involved if you'd rather not,' she said. 'And I know you won't betray me to the guards. But if I do what I'm hoping, will you keep Christa here?'

There was a bad moment when she thought they would refuse, because punishments for any kind of secret plotting were harsh and usually fatal. But then one of them reached for her hand, and she saw the other was crying, and they both said, 'We'll do it. Of course we'll do it.'

'It's the maddest thing I've ever heard of,' said the older of the two. 'I don't know if it will work, but I understand why you have to try.'

'We'll be with you all along,' said the woman who was crying. 'And if you succeed, we'll keep your girl safe.'

Giselle cried as well then.

It was raining when the prisoners were ordered to the Appellplatz. Giselle welcomed this, because rain blurred things. She had lain awake for the entire night, going over and over what she intended to do, praying to whatever powers might be listening that she would have the courage to go through with it.

Once in the Appellplatz, she sensed very strongly the anger against what was being done. There were about a hundred prisoners, and they were all too frightened and too cowed to do anything, but they saw this parading of the victim ahead of execution as cruelty taken to the extreme. It was a show of power, of course; the commandant was showing the inmates of the camp what was going to happen to the one who had killed Freiherr von Braxen. The might and the vengeance of the Third Reich were being demonstrated.

Giselle had managed to stand on the edge of the line, hunching her shoulders, not looking at anyone, but keeping her eyes on the guards who would bring Christa out at any minute. There was a large contingent of guards, of course, because so many of the inmates were assembled. She risked a glance towards them. Yes, they were all there. Curiously, a woman was standing with them – a thin, square-shouldered woman with stern, hard features. One of the female guards? – no, she was not in uniform. It did not matter.

Giselle's plan now hinged on whether Christa had been forced to wear the shapeless Sachsenhausen garb, which Giselle had had to wear since being brought here. If Christa were not wearing it, the plan would certainly not work. Her heart began to thump with fear and apprehension.

But when Christa was brought out, Giselle saw at once she was wearing it. She was pale and hollow-eyed, her hair was tousled and unkempt, and she had already acquired the dreadful hopeless anonymous look of most of the prisoners in there. Seeing this drove a fresh knife into Giselle, but she clung to the fact that – like this – Christa could have been any age.

Hideous doubts were flooding her mind now, because it was mad in the extreme to believe a woman of thirty-seven could pass for a girl who was barely seventeen – could switch places with her and get away with it. But this was not a normal situation. Giselle was thin after the sparse rations of Sachsenhausen, her face waiflike. Her hair was ragged and unkempt, and she thought that in a curious way it all made her look very much younger. She put up her hand as unobtrusively as she could to ruffle her own hair into the same outline as Christa's, and she clung to the knowledge that, although the guards knew her, hardly any of them would know Christa. Only two or three of them would have been guarding her and, in any case, she had only been here for a week. It will work, thought Giselle, clenching her fists. I'll make it work.

She waited for what would be the moment when the guards were looking at the prisoner, when their attention, however briefly, was not fully on the assembled prisoners. Now? No, wait another minute or two – let them start scanning the rows of prisoners to make sure everything was orderly; they always did that at any kind of mass gathering . . . They were doing so now – the thin, hard-faced woman was looking about her as well, as if wanting to claim a place alongside the guards. Was this the moment? Yes . . .

Giselle broke away from the line, and ran with all her power across the courtyard. With every step she expected to hear gunshot and feel bullets tear into her, but people were shouting and some of the prisoners had surged forward – was that her two good friends creating a diversion? – and she reached Christa unchecked. Christa turned, startled, and shocked recognition flared in her eyes. Giselle shouted, 'You're the one who killed my love!' and seized Christa, clutching her hard and pushing her to the ground.

'It's an escape,' she gasped, pulling Christa's face close to hers. 'When the guards grab us, I'm taking your place. You run back to the women behind us – they're waiting – they know. You take my place.'

She thought Christa said, 'No—'

'Yes!' They rolled over together on the ground, as if struggling. 'Fight me,' hissed Giselle. 'We need to change places. But, oh Christa, never forget I love you.'

She was aware that the guards were all round them by this time, their rifles were raised, waiting for the order to fire. Giselle expected to hear it at any second, but an authoritative voice was rapping out a command.

'Don't shoot. The bitch who murdered the Baron von Braxen is to be saved for full execution.'

Giselle broke free then, and cowered back. Christa stood over her, and she heard, unmistakably, Christa saying, 'I love you too . . . So much . . . Thank you . . .'

The child had understood. She was already turning to run back to the waiting women – Giselle saw her two friends dart forward, and she heard them shouting that she must come back – she must stop this madness. One yelled to the guards that it was only that mad creature Giselle again, and please let them get her back to the hut. They were dear, good friends, and Giselle knew she could trust them. Christa would be all right.

She was still on the ground, curled into a defensive ball, her hands covering her face, and she could sense the presence of the guards all round her. As they pulled her roughly to her feet, she saw a man detach himself from one of the lines of the prisoners, and run towards them.

The isolation cell was the grimmest place in the world, but it did not matter. The wild, impossible plan had succeeded, and even if Christa had to spend the rest of the war in Sachsenhausen, she was still alive.

And then the door was unlocked and two guards thrust into the cell the man Giselle had glimpsed running forward as she and Christa fought. He half fell against the wall, and they banged the door shut, turning the key in the lock. Giselle, huddled on the narrow pallet, stared at him, not believing, not wanting to believe, and yet if only it could be . . .

As the man sat up, she saw that it was Felix.

The isolation cell was still the grimmest place in the world, but to have Felix's arms around her was the sweetest thing Giselle had ever known.

'It's agony to know you're here,' she said. 'But even so—'

'It's agony to know you're here, as well,' he said, holding her against him in the never-forgotten way. 'I think it's the Gestapo's last cruel twist. I'm to face the firing squad in the morning, and they wanted to – I suppose to turn the screw a bit by putting me with the girl they believed to be my daughter.' He regarded her. 'That was the maddest thing you ever did,' he said.

'I know. But it worked. What you did was even madder.'

'I had no plan at all,' said Felix. 'I just wanted to snatch her away from them. Create a diversion, maybe. But I think you've saved her.'

'There's a good chance. Felix – where's Stefan? Is he all right?'

'He's perfectly all right,' said Felix at once. 'He's with Velda. She'll look after him.'

'One agony removed,' said Giselle, gratefully.

'Christa killed Brax – did you know that?'

'Everyone in Sachsenhausen knows it. But Felix, what I shouted across that yard – about von Braxen being my lover—'

'Was part of your plan,' he said. 'I know. You never even met him, did you? No, I thought you hadn't.'

'It was all I could think of.'

'Brax raped Christa,' said Felix. 'That's why she killed him. And I'm glad she did,' he said, with uncharacteristic anger. 'We had all trusted him. We believed he was going to take us to freedom . . .' He hesitated, then said, 'There was a Gestapo officer. They told me you had left me to go to him. There was a letter—'

'Reinhardt,' said Giselle. 'He imprisoned me at Wewelsburg. Later, they forced me to write that letter. But there was never anything between us.' As she said this, she knew it was not a lie, but she also knew it was not quite the truth. What did it matter now, though? She and Felix had only a few hours left.

Felix said, 'When I saw the ghost note on the letter, somewhere in my heart I was able to hope I hadn't really lost you.'

'You never did lose me. You never will. Tell me about Brax,' said Giselle.

'Brax – or one of his men – murdered Reinhardt, and set the scene so it looked as if only I or Christa could have killed him. Then Brax got us both away to the Torhaus. But once we were there, he forced me to write music for the Third Reich. As,' said Felix, 'I think someone did with you.'

'You knew about that?'

'I found the music. I kept feeling I was getting closer to you.'

'Felix, will Christa be safe?'

'As safe as anyone can be in this place. She might even get away,' said Felix. 'I know hardly anyone escapes from here, but there's a young man who was with us at the Torhaus – a nephew or a cousin or something of dear old Herr Eisler. Jacob's his name. He and Christa rather took to one another. He's a quiet boy, but very determined. I wouldn't put it past him to stage something.'

'I'd like to think she might have someone like that working for her in the real world,' said Giselle. 'But I'd just like to think she'll live.' She leaned against him. 'We won't, though, will we? Live, I mean?'

'No. But I'll be with you to the last moment,' said Felix. 'And it will be very quick indeed.'

'We might even be making history,' said Giselle. 'Through that music, I mean.'

'I'll never forget how I felt when I saw the ghost note on the music. I knew it meant you might be quite near – that you might even be still alive.'

Giselle took his face between her hands. 'Tonight I'm very much alive,' she said, and began to kiss him.

'My dear love, this is madness . . . And the guards could come in at any moment—'

'I don't care. And haven't there been other lovers who spent one last night together – one gaudy night, isn't that the line? – knowing they would die in the morning? They became little fragments of history, those lovers. Tonight, let's make our own fragment of history,' said Giselle, and pulled him down to her.

TWENTY-SEVEN

P hin had been slightly worried about driving to Paderborn and the Torhaus, but when it came to it he managed well enough. As he drove he listened to the Mahler symphony bought in the shop that had once been Felix Klein's. It seemed appropriate to play it here, in these surroundings, engaged on this astonishing search. His grandfather had said it was a symphony that seemed to be almost a precursor of the Great War that had exploded eight years after it was written; that it was full of driving, relentless, militarist rhythms and mechanistic percussion.

Like the *Siegreich*? thought Phin. Only I don't ever want to hear that music. He shivered slightly, and turned up the car's heating. Had Felix Klein been brought along these roads after that last concert? Had he been frightened – not knowing what might be ahead?

Rain was falling by the time he spotted the turning that led off the main road and along a complexity of secondary roads. There was an occasional break in the trees, through which he glimpsed Wewelsburg Castle, remote and majestic. At least I'm going in the right direction, thought Phin, and saw the small side road that Toby had marked as leading to the Torhaus. Good.

The road was very narrow and uneven. There was certainly not room for two cars to pass if they met, although Phin doubted many cars ever came out here.

Or did they? As he came out into a small clearing, he saw a car parked close against a wall which clearly enclosed a fairly large building. The Torhaus? It must be. High gates were set into the wall, but no house was visible.

Phin glanced towards the parked car, which probably belonged to a pair of lovers, out for a bit of illicit love-making. All the way out here, and in this weather, though? Still, if you were keen enough, and needing to avoid a jealous husband or wife . . .

But as he drove cautiously towards the gates, he saw that the other car was empty. Might it belong to someone checking the place out – a surveyor or a builder? Someone from a letting agency or a forestry organization? Or, thought Phin, a burglar or potential squatters assessing the possibilities? Squatters did not usually own cars, though. On the other hand, they probably did not jib at stealing one either. He began to wish Toby had come with him after all, and he thought he would take a very brief look at whatever building lay beyond these walls, but that he would keep a wary eye and ear out for burglars or squatters. Or, of course, for any ghosts that might be wandering about, mopping and mowing their way through the rain. This last thought cheered him up. He was, though, starting to think that there would not be anything here to be discovered about Felix Klein or any of the other players in this strange story, and that being so he would soon be bouncing the car back down the uneven track, to civilization.

He was just preparing to get out of the car and try the gates, when his phone buzzed. It was Toby.

'I've just got here,' said Phin. 'I think it is the Torhaus, but I haven't got in yet, although it's a grim old place from what I can see so far—'

'Grim away, old boy, there's great news here,' said Toby, sounding so enthusiastic that Phin almost expected him to explode through the phone and materialize in the car.

'What?'

'Arabella,' said Toby. 'She's in Lindschoen. Actually here and staying at the . . . Hold on, yes, at the Lindenbaum.'

'How on earth—?'

'I'm forwarding you an email she sent to Ottomar Volk here at the bookshop,' said Toby. 'That'll explain everything. What happened is that I got talking to Ottomar while he was looking for the old stuff about the shop. And he said that Tallis was an unusual name, and not one you'd expect to trip over twice in the space of a week. But only two days ago an English lady with that very name had been in his shop. He described her as a vivid lady,' said Toby, and Phin heard the smile in his voice. 'And then he said she had emailed him last night, and he would show me the email in case it was a relative. Well, by then I knew,' said Toby. 'Because vivid is exactly the word you'd use to describe Arabella, and it would be exactly like her to turn up in the last place you'd expect— Hold on, Ottomar's forwarded the email to my phone, so I'm forwarding it to you now. Read it, then call me straight back.'

The email came pinging in and Phin closed the connection to Toby, and opened the email.

Dear Ottomar.

Thank you very much for your help in my search for people from my family. It was all extremely useful and interesting.

I'm sorry I lost a contact lens halfway through our discussion, but it was very nice of you to help me find it. I'm also sorry it meant crawling around on the floor for so long – your shop is beautifully clean, by the way. It was unfortunate, as well, that I knocked over your nice arrangement of CDs of some of Beethoven's symphonies, and I do hope the cheque I posted last night has reached you by now, and that it will cover the replacement, and also the disruption. I think we managed to sweep everything up satisfactorily.

It was very kind of you to take me to lunch after the sweeping-up. I did enjoy that. What beautiful pastries that shop has. I've gained pounds and kilos in one day.

If you do turn up anything else about The Music House's past I would be eternally grateful if you could let me know. It really does look as if my godfather is Felix Klein's son.

Very best wishes,
Arabella Tallis

Phin stared at this extraordinary email for a very long time. Then he phoned Toby back.

'Remarkable, isn't it?' said Toby, answering on the first ring. 'Ottomar says Arabella was staying at the Lindenbaum, and that was only yesterday.'

'And Felix Klein was Stefan's father,' said Phin. 'Should we have made the connection? Maybe we should, although . . . But Toby, that's extraordinary about Arabella being here.'

'I'm not sure it is,' said Toby. 'I think Arabella was intrigued when Stefan threw out Christa's portrait, and I think she wanted to find out more about Christa's life. She'd want to do it in secrecy, as well – she'd see herself as a kind of female spy or something.'

'And if she found Silke's letter at Greymarsh House, which is quite likely . . .' said Phin.

'Exactly. I'm heading for the Lindenbaum now,' said Toby. 'I'll call you later. Or you call me if there's anything to report.'

'All right.'

The Torhaus, seen through its tall gates, was a daunting place. It was fairly large, and its walls were of harsh stone. There were darkened windows, behind which anything might lurk – or out of which anything might be peering. Phin glanced uneasily at the windows, but nothing stirred.

The gates were firmly locked, but there was a section of collapsed wall, and Phin, who was by this time starting to feel uneasy, made his way to it. He might as well at least try to get a bit nearer to this place that Ottomar Volk had said was the scene of the Wewelsburg murder.

As he went towards the house, his misgivings increased, because the door at the house's centre was open. Phin took a deep breath and went inside.

The house was dim and there was a smell of damp and age and desolation. At this point, Phin remembered that he might be tres-passing – that the owner of the parked car might even be the house's rightful owner – and he called out, at first automatically in English, and then in hesitant German. He did not really expect any response, but there was a sound from the rear of the house. Phin's heart jumped nervously, then a young man came out of one of the rooms.

'Hello?' he said, in English. 'My God, you made me jump about a mile – I didn't hear anyone drive up, and I certainly didn't hear you come in.'

'I did call out,' said Phin. 'And I'm sorry if I'm trespassing. I expect I am, but I was intrigued by the house.'

'Glad to meet a fellow countryman. I'm Marcus Mander.' He did not move; he stayed in the open doorway.

Marcus Mander, thought Phin. I know the name, don't I? Then he remembered Toby talking about phoning neighbours of Stefan – and saying their names were Marcus and Margot Mander. And there had been a voice-mail message at Greymarsh House from

Marcus Mander. This is all a bit coincidental, thought Phin, but he smiled, held out his hand, and said, 'Phineas Fox.'

He waited for Marcus Mander to ask what on earth he was doing out here, but he simply said, 'This is a gothic old place, isn't it? An old gatehouse to the castle, I believe. I've been trying to trace a property that might have belonged to a great-aunt of mine.'

'Is this it?'

''fraid not. Much too grand. I couldn't resist looking inside, though. The door wasn't locked.'

There's something very wrong about all this, thought Phin. Marcus Mander hasn't just come here because he thinks his great-aunt might have owned it. Who on earth owns a castle gatehouse these days, anyway?

Marcus Mander stepped out of the room, closing the door as he did so. Phin glimpsed a piano inside the room. Its lid was open and there was even music on the stand. It seemed incredible to find a piano in this desolate old house – or did it? Might it be anything to do with Felix Klein? Surely it could not hold a clue after so long, though. He was about to make some suitable farewell and go back to his car, when sounds cut through the silence. Someone in an upstairs room was screaming.

Phin was halfway up the stairway almost before he knew it, going instinctively towards whoever was shouting with such desperation. But Marcus was after him, dealing him a blow that knocked him against the wooden banister. There was a sharp crack of pain against his head, but Phin struggled to get to his feet, fighting against the spinning dizziness. Marcus seized his arms and dragged him up the remaining stairs.

'Let me go,' shouted Phin. 'There's someone shouting for help – someone's locked away—'

'You're perfectly correct,' said Mander. 'But it's a pity you heard it, isn't it?'

They were at the head of a narrow flight of stairs now. Phin was struggling to get free, but his senses were still confused from the blow. Marcus unlocked a door, and pushed him through it. The door was slammed, and a key turned in the lock.

This time Phin did manage to get to his feet, and he hammered furiously on the door.

From beyond it, Mander said, 'At least you've got company in there. That's my sister who's with you. She's a murderess. That's why I locked her away.'

Phin turned to look into the room, and saw a thin-faced young woman huddled on a window-seat, staring at him.

'I intended,' said Mander's voice from beyond the door, 'to leave her there to die. She deserves it, the bitch. And no one would come looking for her. But now there's you.'

'People will definitely come looking for me,' said Phin, at once. 'There's someone – the friend I was travelling with – who knows I was coming out here. In any case, I can phone . . .' He thrust a hand into his jacket pocket, then realized that the phone he had so carefully remembered to bring from the car was no longer there.

Marcus Mander was laughing. 'First rule of imprisonment,' he said. 'Disable your victim's means of communication. An old army rule, probably, not that I was ever in the army. I took your phone after I'd half knocked you out and I was dragging you up the stairs. It's a pity you've come blundering in, though, because I'll have to rethink my plan. I don't think I can just leave you here. My mad sister was one thing, but the two of you together might manage to break out. Let's see – if I start a fire in the hall, it should work its way up here reasonably quickly. What do you think?'

'It'll be seen,' said Phin, hating the note of desperation in his voice, wishing his head would stop throbbing. 'The fire services will be here at once.'

'Of course it won't be seen. This place is miles from anywhere. By the time anyone spots smoke rising, it'll be too late. Sorry and all that, but I really can't risk you talking.'

Phin stayed where he was, against the door. He heard Marcus go back down the stairs, and he heard him pause – that would be the turn on the half-landing, which was narrow. There was a sudden bump, and a cry, and then a series of bumps. And then silence.

Behind Phin, Margot said, 'What's happened?'

Phin turned to look at her. 'I think he's slipped on the half-landing,' he said. 'I think he's fallen down to the foot of the stairs. And,' he said, not moving from the door, 'it's a very steep flight of stairs.'

'He'll be unconscious?'

Phin said, 'Unconscious or dead.'

'Yes, I see. And,' she said, 'no one knows we're here, and there's no way of getting out of this room.'

It was then that Phin saw the half-open drawer and the silver bracelet.

TWENTY-EIGHT

'It's a very long shot indeed,' he said. 'But this looks like silver, so it ought to be tough enough to use on the door hinges. It's certainly worth a shot.'

'Can you do it?'

'If I can stand up long enough. That was a hell of a blow your brother gave me.'

'I'm sorry,' she said, in a rather colourless voice.

As Phin began to chisel at the hinges, he spared a thought for the owner of the bracelet who had left it here – when? why? – and who might unwittingly have provided the means for them to escape.

At first he thought it was not going to work, and he tore the skin of his fingers several times in the attempt to loosen the hinges, and had to wind Margot's handkerchief around them. As he did so, he was remembering Marcus's accusation. 'She's a murderess,' he had said. 'That's why I locked her away.' Phin did not dare wonder how much truth there was in what Marcus had said.

The metal of the hinges was still sound, but it was becoming apparent that the wood of the doorframe was not.

After about ten minutes, he said, 'I think the hinge is coming loose,' and he was so pleased that he turned to smile at his companion and forgot, for the moment, about her being a murderess. When, after a further ten minutes, the door suddenly sagged as the hinge broke free, he said, 'Grab the door – no, from that side – keep it as firm as you can so I can loosen the other hinge.'

'All right, I've got it.'

The second hinge, already loosened when the heavy door sagged, came free more easily, and the door fell sideways. Phin grabbed it, and pushed it to one side, and there was the shadowy landing and the stairs.

'We've done it!' he said, so relieved that he managed to ignore the pounding headache and lingering dizziness. 'I'll be forever grateful to whoever left that silver bracelet.' Almost without thinking, he dropped it in his pocket. 'Downstairs now, and I'll find my phone and call for help.'

Marcus was lying in a distorted sprawl at the foot. There was blood on one side of his head, and one leg stuck out at an unnatural angle. Margot went to him at once, and bent over, feeling for a pulse in his neck, and then thrusting a hand inside his jacket to find a heartbeat. Phin, seeing his phone nearby, snatched it up gratefully.

'I'll call the medics at once – do you know the number for emergency services out here?'

'No,' said Margot. 'I don't actually know any German. Actually, I don't know a lot of things. Driving a car, for instance. What to do in bed with someone. Sad, isn't it?'

It was as if her voice had changed key. Major to minor, thought Phin, unease stirring again. But he scrolled down for Toby's number, thinking Toby would still be with Ottomar Volk and Volk would know the numbers to ring for help. As he did so, Margot bent over her brother, and Phin saw her hands go around Marcus's neck, and press down hard.

His unease ratcheted up into real fear, but he managed to keep his voice normal. 'Is he all right?' he said. 'Is he dead?'

Margot straightened up. 'He's dead now,' she said, and Phin saw, for the first time, the madness staring out of her eyes. She began to walk towards him, and he backed away, then saw that – although the front door was still open – Margot was between Phin and the door. He felt for the phone, trying to find the last-number button to get Toby, but dreadfully aware that it might take some time for help to get here.

Margot began to walk towards him, and Phin hesitated, remembering the stories that people in the grip of genuine insanity could possess three times their own strength. He backed away, hoping he could get into one of the rooms that opened off the hall and barricade himself in. The room with the piano was the nearest – he took a deep breath, and sprinted into it. She was after him at once, but he was inside the room, and slamming the door. Did it have a lock? Yes, but there was no key. Of course there wouldn't be a key, thought Phin, with helpless fury and frustration. But if I can keep her out for long enough to phone for help . . . He was leaning against the door, but she was pushing against it, and Phin felt it give slightly. He groped for his phone, and this time he managed to tap Toby's number in. Please don't go to voicemail, he was praying. Please pick up.

Toby's voice said, 'Phin? How are you getting on? Listen, I've—'

Phin said without preamble, 'Toby, I'm in the Torhaus and I'm in dreadful danger. You must get police and medics out here at once. Yes, I am being serious. As quickly as possible.'

The door gave way again, and Phin dropped the phone into his jacket and threw all his strength into keeping Margot Mander out, thankful that at least the door of the room opened inwards. He had no idea how long she would keep up her attempts to get to him, but she would certainly want to stop him telling the police what she had done – and what Marcus had said about her. He had no idea how long it would take for the police to get here – it would depend on where the nearest police station was, and it could be ten minutes or the best part of an hour. Might she give up and make a run for it? Where to? She had said she didn't drive.

He would have to barricade the door. There was a small desk just about within his reach, and a table . . . And the piano. It stood against the wall, but it was only a few feet from the door. If I could get that across it, she'd never get it open, thought Phin.

By dint of stretching out his leg, he managed to hook his foot around one leg of the desk, and drag it across the door. Margot pushed against the door again, and although it opened by a good six inches, the desk impeded it considerable. But Phin had already dragged the table across, and wedged that in place as well. Better. Now for the piano.

At first it felt as if the piano had been bolted to the floor. Margot was hammering at the door, and the desk and the table were already being pushed aside. Phin gasped, and threw his entire weight into moving the piano, and felt it shift, and then slide across the floor. It came to rest against the already dislodged table, and he pushed it more firmly into place. Now then, murderess, get through that! He thought exultantly.

He was just getting his breath back, and trying not to count the time and wonder how long it would be before help arrived,

when he heard what were obviously German police sirens. Phin
thought he had never heard sweeter music.

Marcus Mander's body had been taken away by paramedics,
one of whom had checked Phin for concussion, and pronounced
there were no signs of it, but please to call for help if there was
any drowsiness or double-vision, that was understood?

'Completely understood,' said Phin.

The courteous German police officers had taken careful statements from him, and asked if he could perhaps call at their offices
tomorrow to sign them and make sure everything had been recorded
correctly. They would provide an interpreter for reassurance.

'Of course I'll come,' said Phin. 'I'm more grateful to you than
I can say.'

Was Herr Fox feeling able to drive himself back to his hotel?
If not, they would happily provide a driver?

'I'll be perfectly all right,' said Phin, who now wanted nothing
more than to get away from the Torhaus and return to some semblance
of normality. He explained that the friend he was travelling with
would be arriving soon anyway. While the officers went on with
their evidence-collecting and photographing of the scene, Phin
wandered back into the music room. The piano had been shunted
more or less back into its original place. Even the rough handling
it had received had not dislodged the music from the stand.

And then everything seemed to stop, because for the first time
Phin saw the words written across the music. *Giselle's Music*. It's
the music from the portrait, he thought. It's the copy of the
Siegreich. Or is this the original, and is what I found at Greymarsh
House the copy?

He glanced back to where the police were still working on their
evidence-gathering. Would the music be classed as evidence? It
did not seem to have any bearing on Marcus Mander's murder or
Margot's actions. With a deep breath, feeling almost as guilty as
if he were committing a murder himself, Phin lifted the sheets
from the music stand, and put them inside his jacket.

He went back into the hall, to hear a car drive up, hasty footsteps half running towards the house, and Toby's voice calling out
to know where the devil he was, and what in God's name had
been happening.

Toby himself appeared in the doorway, his hair dishevelled, looking like a worried puppy, and behind him was another figure.

A female voice said, 'It's a bit late to be rescuing the hero from deadly peril, and it's supposed to be the heroine who gets rescued, anyway. Phineas Fox, I hope you realize that this is the wrong way round.'

'Phin,' said Toby, 'this is my cousin, Arabella.'

Arabella Tallis was not in the least what Phin had expected, and as they sat in the shop that had once belonged to Felix Klein, the shutters just sufficiently open to glimpse the old square outside, he was aware of a faint disappointment. Arabella was small and fine-boned, with a tumble of fairly ordinary brown hair that was scooped up a bit untidily allowing curling tendrils to escape, large, dark-lashed eyes and a mouth that was a bit too wide. He thought he would have passed her in the street and certainly not given her a second look.

Ottomar Volk, delighted at the drama, had bustled around pouring drinks, eagerly anticipating hearing what had happened. When Herr Volk sat down, Phin said to Arabella, 'Toby thought you'd been kidnapped. I still haven't fathomed how you came to be in Lindschoen.'

She smiled at him, and Phin's opinion was instantly revised, because – after all – this was the vivid creature who had organized dinner parties that might have included extravagant entertainments; who had looked for *rusalkas* in the garden of Greymarsh House, and who sometimes considered wearing curtains to parties. In that moment he understood why people did not mind if Arabella ruined Sèvres dishes and burned puddings, or caused people to crawl around floors looking for contact lenses.

'What happened,' said Arabella, 'was that when the attics at Greymarsh were cleared, I found that letter from Giselle's cousin, Silke. You found it later, didn't you, Phin – well, Toby told me you did. And what a lot of fluff and speculation! All that rubbish about how Christa had been responsible for Giselle's death in a concentration camp, and how everybody had known, and Silke couldn't bring herself to use the word murderess. Personally, I think she sounds utterly feather-brained, that Silke,' said Arabella, 'and I don't think she had the merest inkling as to what really happened to Giselle. Anyway, when Stefan flung Christa's portrait out with that marvellously theatrical gesture . . . Actually, I must ask Stefan sometime if there's anyone in his family who ever took to the boards, because of all the grandiloquent melodrama—'

Phin wondered if there was anyone else in the modern world who would have used the word 'grandiloquent'.

'—I guessed he'd seen Silke's letter,' said Arabella, unexpectedly picking up the thread of her sentence. 'I daresay he brought boxes of stuff when he left Lindschoen and some of the things would have been Velda's, and I expect the letter was in one of the boxes. The boxes probably got shovelled into the attics without the contents being looked at.'

'And then,' said Phin, 'the roof at Greymarsh House had to be fixed.'

'Chaos theory,' said Toby, nodding wisely. 'A butterfly bats its wings in Hong Kong and there's a tornado in Texas.'

'I thought I'd make a bit of an investigation into Christa,' said Arabella. 'With the idea that I could tell Stefan the letter was all jabberwocking and fantasizing, and that Christa was pure as a saint. But I didn't want to tell anyone what I was doing, in case I didn't find anything out, or—'

'Or,' said Phin, 'in case you found out something that indicated Silke was right. That Christa really had been some kind of cold-blooded killer.'

'Well, yes.'

'And,' put in Toby, 'because you liked the idea of being a lone female sleuth.'

'It was the greatest fun,' said Arabella, mischievously. 'I bought masses of new clothes, so I could look the part. I had a cloak and a marvellous wide-brimmed hat that shadowed my eyes, and I thought about a cigarette holder as well, but since I don't smoke . . . Anyway, I was a mysterious foreign lady travelling alone, and you wouldn't believe how kind people were. I had so many offers of help with luggage and plane tickets and things.'

'You'd better leave out those parts,' said Toby, hastily.

'I behaved impeccably,' said Arabella, with guileless eyes.

'First time ever if so. Go on with the tale, and don't prevaricate with cigarette holders and hats.'

'First,' said Arabella, 'I went to Sachsenhausen itself. It didn't yield much, though – it's a kind of war museum and memorial place now, so anyone can go in. From there I came to Lindschoen and this very shop. And Ottomar's been so helpful – he even unearthed the old deeds from Felix Klein's day. Is deeds the right word, Ottomar? It's what we'd call them in England.'

Ottomar, pleased to be called on, said it was the right word, and he had the very deeds here for them to see, and if Herr Toby would not mind moving his glass of whisky . . .

'Ah, thank you. I spread the documents out for you to see.'

'You see that,' said Arabella, indicating a single sheet of paper clipped to the main deeds. 'It's a copy of a letter addressed to a Miss Lina Mander. Carbon copy, which is why it's so smudgy.'

'Lina Mander,' said Phin, staring at the letter. 'So Marcus Mander really was looking for some great-aunt's house.'

'And Lina could have been that very great-aunt,' said Arabella, eagerly.

'I have made for you a translation,' said Ottomar. 'A date finds itself at the top of the page, but it is not clear for reading. Very blurred.'

'I think the date's nineteen-sixty-something,' said Arabella.

'It looks like that,' said Phin, studying the letter carefully. 'It could be 1963 or 1965, couldn't it? Thank you for the translation, Ottomar. My German wouldn't be equal to legal phrases.'

The letter said:

Dear Miss Mander
Thank you for your letter and enquiry.

However, I regret that I must inform you that the Trust you believe was created to give you entitlement to the house acquired by your father, Count von Braxen, in or around 1940, is not legal. Indeed, it seems not to have existed.

Land and property were certainly bestowed on senior members of the Gestapo during World War II – frequently where the rightful owners had been taken prisoner. There were, though, a number of cases where Gestapo officers simply appropriated properties themselves. After the war many (although not all) of those illegally acquired properties were restored to the original owners – or, more often, to the descendants.

The house you believed to be held in Trust for you fell into this latter category, and it was later returned to the descendants of its former owner, Felix Klein, who was executed in Sachsenhausen concentration camp in the early 1940s. I believe the charge against him was that of conspiracy against the Nazis. The house passed to his children.

My enquiries indicate that the house is in Lindschoen and that it was a thriving music shop, known as The Music House. It continues with that use today, and recently was extended to provide a bookshop.

I am sorry not to have better news, but I am afraid that your claim to this property has no validity whatsoever.

I return the copy of your birth certificate which you sent as part of your claim.

I am yours very sincerely.

'So Felix died in Sachsenhausen,' said Phin, and found this so deeply sad he had to pretend to take a drink from his whisky.

Arabella silently passed him the soda syphon. 'Good for diluting the emotions,' she said, then, without missing a beat, 'I wonder if Marcus Mander knew the house he was trying to find was really this one, and if he was simply using the Torhaus because it was conveniently abandoned.'

'To get rid of his sister? Yes, that's possible,' said Phin, remembering some of the things Marcus Mander had said.

Ottomar said, 'I have the deed here showing how this house transferred itself to my great-uncle from Felix Klein—'

'From Felix Klein and from Giselle Klein,' said Phin, staring at the document. 'Joint ownership. That can only mean Giselle was Felix's wife.'

'Which would mean she was Christa's mother—' said Toby.

'And also Stefan's. No wonder it knocked the poor old love sideways to read Silke's letter saying Christa had killed Giselle,' said Arabella. 'His sister killing their mother. It's Greek tragedy, isn't it?'

'Yes, but did Christa kill Giselle?' demanded Phin. 'We've only got Silke's word for that.'

'Phin doesn't want Christa to be a villainess because he's conceived an irrational passion for her,' murmured Toby to Arabella.

'Have you really? I once conceived a passion for Lord Byron. Then I remembered he had monumental debts and was given to sulking, so I thought, well, that's not what you'd want to encounter over the breakfast table, is it?'

'It's a pity we don't know a bit more about that Mander gang,' said Toby. 'Phin, you didn't by any chance go through Marcus Mander's pockets, did you?'

'I didn't,' said Phin. 'The music was there though – *Giselle's Music*. I don't know if Mander brought it with him – I can't think why he'd have it in the first place, but I can't think how else it got there.' He said, a bit awkwardly, 'The police didn't seem interested in it—'

'So you lifted it?'

'Well, it was *Giselle's Music* and it didn't seem relevant to the murder—'

'Oh, who cares if you made off into the night with the whole of the Torhaus's contents,' said Arabella. 'I'd have taken that music without a second thought. Good for you, Phin. Let's face the music. I mean, let's look at it. There might be a clue we've overlooked.'

By this time Phin had taken the music from his jacket and flattened it out. 'Oh,' he said. 'Oh, my God.'

'What?'

'The back page isn't part of the music. I hadn't realized – I just picked up the sheaf of papers. But this is a separate thing . . .' He broke off, staring at the creased paper.

'It's a birth certificate,' said Toby, leaning forward to see. 'You do produce these things bang on cue, don't you?'

'It's Lina Mander's birth certificate,' said Phin, still staring at it. 'Or a copy of it. I suppose if Marcus Mander really was trying to track down his aunt's house, he'd bring it with him to substantiate any claim he was able to make.'

It was Arabella who leaned forward to read out the details. 'Father: Count Karol von Braxen. Mother: Christa Klein. Place of birth: Sachsenhausen. Well!' she said, sitting back. 'That's something we didn't expect.'

'No, we didn't, but it's the link between Marcus Mander and the Klein family,' said Phin. 'It would explain why Marcus had that music. His great-aunt – or cousin or whatever she was – was Lina Mander. Lina was Christa's daughter.'

'So Christa had a relationship of some kind with Count von Braxen,' said Arabella, thoughtfully, 'and there was a child. She flew high when it came to gentlemen friends, didn't she?'

Phin said, 'It's not much of a stretch to think Lina Mander had the music from her mother – from Christa. Maybe Lina was given Christa's possessions and this was among them.' He studied the music intently. 'This mightn't have *Siegreich* written across the top,' he said, suddenly, 'and without comparing the two I can't be sure. But I think essentially it's the same as the music we found at Greymarsh House.'

'A copy of it?' said Toby. 'Or was the Greymarsh one the copy and this is the original?'

'It could be either way round, couldn't it? Did Stefan know Christa had a daughter?' said Phin. 'Or about von Braxen?'

'I don't think so,' said Arabella. 'He would have said.'

'I'm sure he knew Christa was in Sachsenhausen for a while, though,' put in Toby. 'At least, he knew she'd been imprisoned by the Nazis.'

'Did Christa survive Sachsenhausen?' Phin had not realized this question had been in his mind, but as soon as he said it, he knew he had been wondering ever since he had read Silke's letter. 'I know there's the portrait, but it might have been done after she was dead.'

'I don't know,' said Arabella, after a moment. 'I've never asked Stefan when she died – or where. He's always been so reticent about her.'

Phin said, 'So now we know that Christa had a daughter – Lina – and it's a fair guess that Lina was taken from Christa very early – probably while she was just a baby.'

'Is it a fair guess?' asked Toby.

'Well, Lina was born in a concentration camp. Her father – or his family – could have removed her and put her with adoptive parents.'

'And when she grew up, she wrote to solicitors to find out about the house she thought she'd inherited,' said Arabella. 'That's the action of someone who doesn't have any family she can ask.'

'Yes. But,' said Phin, 'we still don't know what eventually happened to Christa.'

TWENTY-NINE

n Sachsenhausen no one noticed you very much. For most of the time you were faceless, anonymous.

But Christa was neither. She was noticed – it was realized who she really was, and there was a lash of fury that Giselle Klein had dared to cheat them. But she had not done so in the end, said the camp commandant, Oberführer Hans Loritz. The execution machinery would be re-assembled at once. The creature who had murdered Count von Braxen would still be shot and the entire camp would see it happen. The stupid females who had tried to hide Christa Klein would be shot, also.

Then a further discovery was made. Christa Klein was to have a child. Von Braxen's child.

'This does not mean you will escape execution,' said Loritz. 'It merely means that execution will be postponed. A child of the von Braxen line must not die before it is born.'

Christa supposed it did not matter what she said now, so she asked what would happen to the child.

'It will be taken to its father's family to be brought up by them. There is a distant cousin of the Count living very nearby.'

Elsa Frank, thought Christa, dismayed. She said, 'The child will be kindly treated, won't it, though? Can you assure me of that?'

'It will be brought up to revere its country. Also to know that its father was highly regarded and that his death at your hands was a great tragedy.'

'I see,' said Christa. 'And the women who tried to help me . . . They did so because of the child – you do understand that?'

This was a lie; the women had had no idea of the pregnancy, but Loritz appeared to accept it. He said, 'There will be punishment for them, but it will not be execution.'

'Thank you.' Christa was glad to know the good friends who had helped her would not die.

As she was taken back to the hut, Christa thought about Elsa Frank. At least the child would not have to endure Sachsenhausen, and although the thought of Fräulein Frank was dreadful, Elsa had always displayed that slavish emotion for Brax – to the point of adoration. Christa dared believe that Elsa would be kind to the child for Brax's sake.

After this, time began to blur. Normally, pregnancy and births were not especially of interest in the camp; prisoners were left to get on with such things. There might, if they were lucky, be minimal medical help, but most of them shied away from any kind of doctor in Sachsenhausen. There were whispers of atrocities in the medical block – terrible stories of brutal experiments.

But Christa Klein's case was different. Her unborn child was the son or daughter of von Braxen, never mind it would be illegitimate. Doctors sometimes came to see her, and prodded her, and nodded, as if satisfied, then went away.

Christa did not want to count up the weeks, because as soon as the child was born they would take her out to be shot. She did the work she was given, and she ate the food that was brought, understanding that she was not being treated as harshly as she might have been, because her captors believed they owed it to Count von Braxen's memory to ensure his son or daughter was safely born.

It began to feel as if a thick glass wall had formed around Christa, and as if real life was no longer completely visible or audible. Some memories were still with her, though. Glimpses of a warm house with lamplight on cobblestones outside. She could not bear to think of her parents, but she thought about Stefan with his dear, trusting face. Please let Stefan be all right.

There were more recent memories, as well. The Torhaus and the people she had known there. Jacob, with his gentle eyes and his kindness. Daniel, who had made that promise that one day he would paint her. That would not happen now, thought Christa. And then – or would it? A tiny spiral of defiance uncurled within her. It was said that hardly anyone ever escaped from Sachsenhausen. But a few did.

The child was born after a night of pain. Christa, swimming in and out of the pain, clung to the hand of the doctor who had been brought to her, wanting reassurance.

But he was cold and impersonal, although she thought he dealt with her efficiently. Presently, he said, 'We have the child.' A hesitation, then, 'A healthy girl,' he said. 'Fräulein Frank is waiting to take her at once.'

Christa did not dare ask to see the child; she would not have borne seeing it and knowing it would be the only time she would do so. She said, 'What will happen now?'

'A few days,' he said. 'Perhaps a week.' Christa understood he meant that in a few days she would be considered fit to walk to the big square and stand before the firing squad.

Then, three days after the birth, a note was thrust into her hand.

'Try to be near the death strip between the two western search-lights after the supper call. Keep between all the searchlights.' It was signed simply *J*.

J. Jacob. Christa's heart leapt, but she managed to tear the note into tiny pieces, and drop the pieces into the latrine bucket.

Jacob was trying to get her out. He had obviously found out about the camp's routines, and he would be waiting by the western searchlights. Or was it a trick, a trap? Christa considered this, but could not see any point in anyone trapping her. They were going to execute her in a few days – they had been perfectly open about that. Why bother to set a trap? And even if this went wrong – because very few people escaped from Sachsenhausen – what did she have to lose? Except for Jacob, said her mind. I might lose Jacob, because he might die with me.

The day was spent in a ferment of excitement and terror. Supposing she could not manage to walk to that part of the compound? She was still quite weak from the birth; she had only been out of bed twice, and each time she had only walked a short distance. The memory of her mother came to her then, and she knew her mother would not have flinched from this opportunity to get out. Somehow, I'll do it, thought Christa determinedly. And Jacob will be there. That was a very good thought indeed; she would focus on seeing him again, even if it were to be for the last time.

During the afternoon she went into the half-screened cubicle with the latrine, but she took with her the bedcover. She hid it in there, folded as small as she could manage. When she left, she would wrap it around her. It was dark grey, so it would cover the pale prison dress, and help her to blend into the darkness. She had no shoes, but that would not have to matter, and she would have walked barefoot over broken glass if it meant getting out.

Once supper had been called, the infirmary room was more or less deserted. Security was not quite as stringent here, because hardly anyone was ever brought to the infirmary. Illness was not recognized or acknowledged in Sachsenhausen. But Christa had no idea if the door would be locked, although if it was, she thought she might be able to climb through the narrow window.

The door was not locked. Her heart in her mouth, her throat dry with fear, Christa stepped outside. So far so good. Now she must make her way to the western searchlights. Jacob had chosen well – had he known they were fairly near the infirmary block? It was suddenly warm and reassuring to think he must have done. He's not far away, thought Christa. I'm going to reach him.

She scarcely felt the hard ground under her bare feet, although she was aware of a soft rain falling about her. Was that good? Yes, it might mean the guards would be huddling inside their boxes. She kept as close as possible to the walls of the huts, and went on until she could see the perimeter fences. There were the search-lights – or were they the right ones? She had a moment of hideous doubt. No, she had the right ones, she was sure. Between the two, Jacob's note had said. Near the death strip. Oh God, the death strip . . . Stefan's nightmares . . .

If you went on to the death strip, you were shot, he used to say, sobbing from out of the bad dreams. Your blood and bones were splattered everywhere.

Christa put this determinedly from her mind and concentrated on reaching the appointed spot. She was starting to feel dreadfully shaky; this was the furthest she had walked since the birth, but that must be ignored. She would collapse when she was outside and free.

She crept forward. Her legs were starting to feel like cotton threads, and with every minute she expected the lights to blaze up, and to hear shouted commands and feel bullets tear into her. How close did she dare get to the death strip? Panic rose again, in a thick, near-choking flood, because supposing she had got it all wrong – supposing she was in the wrong part of the compound?

She could see the wire clearly now. She could see the death strip. Once she stepped on that she would be dreadfully, dangerously close to the wire, and if she touched it at the wrong point it would send a fatal jolt of electricity through her. Would it be better to fry on a wire fence than be shot by a dozen gunmen?

And then something moved in the darkness just beyond the fence, and Christa's heart leapt again, but this time with hope. Was he there? It must be him. He would not let her down.

'*Christa . . .*' It was the faintest cobweb of sound, but it reached her, and she knew it was Jacob. She did not dare call back in case her voice was picked up by a nearby guard, but it gave her new strength and she went towards the sound.

The whisper came again. 'We've neutralized part of the wire – it's still a hell of a risk, but if we go we'll go together. All right?'

Christa nodded. There was someone with him, apparently. This was reassuring.

And now she was walking on the death strip itself. It felt exactly the same as the rest of the compound, which was unexpected; she had thought it would be different. Harsh, hard, painful.

'Kneel down as low as you can manage,' said Jacob's voice – it was much nearer now. 'Get flat if you can.'

Christa thought she would burrow into the ground itself if it would get her to safety. She lay flat, ignoring the slight cramping pain in her stomach.

'Good,' said Jacob's voice from the darkness. 'We've loosened the wire, and made a bit of a hollow under it. You have to get through.'

Even though Christa had thought she would happily have burrowed into the ground, she had not realized she might actually have to do so. The cramping pains were increasing, but they had to be ignored. She began to inch her way into the hollow, which she could just about see.

'Stay clear of the wires,' said a second voice. Daniel? Yes. 'They're probably all right, but don't take any chances.'

'Can you see the guards looking towards us?' That was Jacob again.

'No, but the quicker the better,' said Daniel. 'Christa, you're halfway there – are you all right?'

'Yes.' Christa resolutely bit her lip against the pain that was clenching at her more definitely. She thought she might be bleeding now, but that would have to be ignored, as well.

Sharp footsteps rang out on the compound, and Jacob's voice said, 'Freeze.' Christa put her head down, and stayed motionless. There was the sound of someone calling out – one of the guards saying something about it being almost time for the next ones to come on duty.

'We'll be in the village, having a few drinks, within the hour,' said the second man.

Then nothing.

'It's all right, he's gone,' said Jacob. 'And you're almost there.'

Almost there . . . Terrified and in pain, and probably bleeding all over the ground, but almost free . . . Christa gave a sob, and felt Jacob's hands close around hers, firm and warm and infinitely reassuring.

'I've got you,' he said, and pulled her the rest of the way through the fence. The ground scraped at her arms and her legs, but she no longer cared. Then Jacob's arms came around her. 'I've got you,' he said again. 'And I don't think I ever want to let you go.'

'Please never do,' said Christa and, to her everlasting annoyance, fainted.

She revived to discover she was in the Torhaus – she only found out a long time afterwards that Jacob and Daniel had carried her there, that they had taken her inside, and bathed her feet, and cleaned her up.

'There was blood,' she said, ashamed and embarrassed. 'I had a child—'

'We know,' said Daniel. 'We heard. That's why we waited all these months to reach you.'

Jacob said, a touch awkwardly, 'I think the blood's stopped. I don't think there's any more.'

'Not uncommon after a birth,' said Daniel, and Christa remembered gratefully that he had a son.

She said, 'What now? Aren't there guards here?'

'There were, but we neutralized them as well,' said Daniel.

'What do you mean?'

'Once Brax was no longer here,' said Daniel, 'the guards weren't nearly as watchful. And then Elsa left – that was two days ago. We don't know where she went or why.'

Christa thought: I know why. She's taken the child – my daughter. A pang sliced through her.

'And so it was surprisingly easy to catch the guards unawares and knock them out. At the moment,' said Daniel, 'they're lying in their own blood outside that window. No – don't look.'

'But we daren't stay here any longer than absolutely necessary,' said Jacob. 'We can't risk other guards turning up – or Elsa returning.'

Christa, who was starting to feel better, said, 'What are we going to do then?'

Jacob smiled. 'It's all arranged,' he said.

Christa thought that one of the most extraordinary things about this entire extraordinary experience was to find herself in the back of dear Herr Eisler's familiar rattletrap car, and to be bouncing over the roads, with Herr Eisler himself at the wheel, Jacob beside him, and Daniel and Ben wedged in the back with her.

'There is extra petrol in the boot,' explained Herr Eisler, confidently. 'It is against somebody's law to carry petrol in that way, but we say pshaw and pish to laws.'

They had packed as much as they could into the car. Christa had gone into her father's music room – there were not many of his things there, but there were a few. And there might be the music . . . As she opened the piano's lid, her heart had been racing. Probably he really had burned it, but . . .

But he had not burned it. Both sets of music were there – the copy he had made to fool Brax, and the original – the one with *Siegreich* written across it, and the familiar ghost note at the foot. Christa held this music to her for a moment. She would take it with her, and if possible, one day send it to Velda for Stefan. She would like him to have that memory of their parents, that small, affectionate ghost note.

'Is this the copy your father made?' said Jacob, picking up the other one. 'He's put your mother's name on it. Did you see? *Giselle's Music.*'

'Yes.'

'Shall I put that in the box, as well?'

'Let's leave that here,' said Christa.

'For Elsa Frank to find? She's bound to come back – her things are still in her room; Daniel checked.'

'Even so, I'd like to leave it,' said Christa. And thought: because it was written – or at least somehow compiled – by my mother. And one day Elsa might give it to my daughter.

'What if we're seen – stopped – questioned?' asked Christa, as the car careered forward.

Eisler made one of his extravagant gestures. 'I do not get stopped or questioned,' he said, grandly. 'I am known and loved, and I am famous. Today I am with my family, and we are going to a rehearsal of . . .' He paused to think, then said, 'A rehearsal of Wagner's *Tristan*.'

'Hitler's favourite composer,' said Christa, smiling for the first time for hours.

'Indeed. During the Great War, Hitler carried the music of *Tristan* in his knapsack. I shall be playing the overture at the rehearsal,' said Herr Eisler, firmly. 'I shall play it better than even Paderewski did.'

'But where are we really going?' asked Christa.

Herr Eisler half turned to look at her, and beamed.

'We are going south,' he said. 'To Switzerland.'

'And if the car gives up we'll walk,' put in Daniel.

'I don't care if we have to walk all the way,' said Christa.

'My car will not give up and we will not have to walk.'

THIRTY

P hin's flat was welcoming and blessedly familiar. Miss Pringle was delighted to see Mr Fox and Mr Tallis again and – oh, and Miss Tallis, as well, how very nice.

'I've kept an eye on both flats,' she said. 'And everything is perfectly fine.'

'Thank you very much,' said Phin, handing her the lavish box of German *Spritzkuchen* they had collected en route to the airport from the friendly *Konditorei*.

Toby contributed a large bottle of Kirsch, and Miss Pringle retired to the garden flat, overcome with gratitude.

Phin flung his case into the bedroom and set the kettle to boil. When he went into the study, Arabella was prowling along the bookshelves. She had donned a large pair of tortoiseshell glasses, which probably meant she had lost her contact lenses again.

'Marvellous collection,' she said. 'Scholarly and solemn, but here and there a glint of frivolity. They say a person's books reflect his or her personality, don't they?'

Phin could not think how best to reply, so he simply said, 'Tea?'

'Yes, please, and – oh, here's Toby. Is your flat all right?'

'Sound as a pound – not that that's saying much these days. Is that tea you're making, Phin? Good man. I've unpacked the plum cake we got at the *Konditorei*. It's travelled quite well.'

Phin, having handed round the cups of tea, propped up Christa's portrait and studied it.

'We still don't know what finally happened to her,' he said.

'And we can't ask Stefan, because we haven't found out whether she really did kill their mother,' said Toby, cutting into the plum cake.

'I suppose the portrait doesn't have any secrets to yield?' said Arabella. 'I mean the frame and the canvas—' She reached for the painting.

'Arabella, for God's sake, you can't start ripping the backing off!'

'I'm not,' said Arabella, with palpable untruth. 'I'm just easing a bit of it away from the frame. In all the best books there's often something secreted behind—'

'There won't be,' said Toby.

'There is,' said Arabella, peering through the opening she had made. 'Actually, it looks like a letter.'

It was a letter, and after a few moments, between them, Phin and Arabella managed to translate it.

> Dearest Christa,
>
> Here, finally, is the portrait I promised you that night the SS took you away after the death of the evil von Braxen.
>
> For me this painting captures what you really are. Beautiful and good and courageous. I've painted in the music, but, as you wanted, I've shown the title as *Giselle's Music*. I know your father died in Sachsenhausen because of the *Siegreich*, but I like your idea of remembering both your parents through this small secret memorial – especially since your mother made that extraordinary sacrifice. I shall never forget your story of how she took your place before the firing squad – of how she gave her life for you. Let's never forget her, Christa, and let's hope that somewhere in the future, someone might hear her story and that she'll be remembered.
>
> Daniel

'So you see, Godfather, Silke got it right, but she also got it very wrong indeed.'

Arabella was curled into one of the comfortably battered chairs in Stefan Cain's study, and Christa's portrait was back on the wall in Stefan's direct sight.

Phin said, 'Christa was responsible for Giselle's death, but not in the way Silke understood. Giselle died in her daughter's stead, and she did so voluntarily.'

'Silke was always light-minded,' said Stefan. He was pale and his eyes were very dark, but Phin thought he probably always looked like this, and that it was not due to the recent bang on the head or emotion.

He said, 'Do you know who von Braxen was?'

'Oh, yes. We knew him just as Brax in Lindschoen. I can't

remember much, but I think he was what would today be called charismatic. But he manipulated my father and Christa like an evil puppet-master. And when he violated Christa—'

'We thought it might have been that,' said Arabella.

'He terrified her and he assaulted her in the worst possible way,' said Stefan. 'That's why she killed him that same night, and that's why she was taken to Sachsenhausen. But all I ever knew was that she escaped – a musician friend of my father's, called Erich Eisler, was part of that. Somehow he and his nephew, Jacob, got her to Switzerland. Once there, she never dared leave. She never really felt safe in the world – she had committed murder, you see.'

'The murder of a man who had brutally raped her,' said Arabella, quickly.

'Yes, but the Nazis didn't see it like that. Brax was almost a godlike figure to them – he was close to Hitler, and they would have brought Christa to trial if they had found her. I don't think there was a hunt for her – too many of the Nazis were being hunted themselves in the years after the war – but if it had been known where she was . . . She believed she would have been hanged. I believed it, as well, and so did Jacob. Dear, kind Jacob. They married in Switzerland. They were very happy together.'

'I'm glad,' said Phin, fervently, and Stefan smiled at him.

'I'm glad as well,' he said. 'But Christa kept her distance from almost everyone. And she was always afraid that she could be traced through me. I feared it, as well. I changed my name after the war, and I arranged for the Lindschoen shop to be sold in case it might give someone a lead. But even so—'

'Even so,' said Arabella, gently, 'you weren't going to risk drawing any more attention to her than you could help. You destroyed anything that might lead to her.'

'Yes. There were whispers about her, of course. Murmurs of a vicious schoolgirl murderer. These things get out, and usually in a distorted version. But I always knew where she was and she knew where I was. When she died . . .' He broke off, and a shadow seemed to pass over his face. 'When she died,' he said, 'Jacob sent me the portrait. He said she had wanted that. He told me she said, "Tell Stefan to see it as the ghost note. He'll know what I mean. He'll know it means that even though he might not actually see me, I'll always be around."'

For a moment none of them spoke, then Arabella took Stefan's hand.

Phin said, 'Yes. She will always be around.'

It was as they were preparing to leave, that Stefan Cain said, 'Phin – there's one more thing, isn't there?'

'The music,' said Phin, at once. 'There's one copy of it here, and there's one in my flat in London.' He glanced at Stefan, then said, carefully, 'Christa wanted her parents remembered through the music, didn't she?'

'Yes. It's a fragment of history, nothing more, of course, but—'

Phin said, 'But it would be a small memorial to them all if we preserved it.' He hesitated, then said, 'Would you want it performed?'

'No.' The response was immediate and definite. 'It symbolizes the badness – the evil of the Nazis,' said Stefan.

'But you'd want it preserved?'

'Yes.'

'I would, too,' said Phin. 'Some long-ago musician was forced to write that music – maybe tortured to do so. I don't suppose we'll ever know who it was, but he – or she – is owed some sort of recognition, even if we don't have an actual name.'

'You think it was my father who wrote the *Siegreich*, don't you?'

'Isn't it possible?'

'It's very unlikely. He was a gifted and a dedicated musician, but he was no composer.'

Phin said, 'There are university libraries with music departments. They would value the *Siegreich* for what it is.' He paused, then said, carefully, 'But Sachsenhausen has its own museum nowadays. Arabella mentioned it.'

'Sachsenhausen,' said Stefan, thoughtfully. 'The place where they both died – my mother and father.'

'And perhaps also where the music's composer died.'

'I would like to think of the music being there,' said Stefan, after a moment.

Phin said, very gently, 'I would like it, too. I'll see what can be done.'

As he and Arabella drove off, Phin said, 'There's only one loose end left, isn't there?'

'Margot Mander.'

'Yes.'

'She's awaiting trial for her brother's murder, isn't she?'

'Yes, and I think she'll be found guilty. But I wonder what might be ahead for her after she's served her sentence.'

'More to the point,' said Arabella, 'I wonder what's ahead for us after we reach London this evening.'

Phin glanced at her. She was wearing the tortoiseshell glasses again. He thought it might be with the idea of looking scholarly and serious. It had not quite come off, however.

He concentrated on the road for a moment, then said, 'We could start with dinner tonight.'

Arabella considered this. 'Yes,' she said. 'Let's start with dinner tonight.'

MEMO FROM EDUCATION DEPARTMENT OF HM BRONZEFIELD PRISON, ASHFORD, SURREY.

I'm glad to report that the prisoner, Margot Mander, is adapting well, and has asked to join the recently-started language classes. She expressed a particular interest in learning German – apparently there was a great-aunt or an elderly cousin in her family who was German, and on her release Mander wants to trace the aunt's background and a house she believes belonged to her.

As you know, it can be therapeutic for prisoners to feel they have a goal somewhere beyond their sentence.

It has been pointed out to Mander that it will be some way in the future – her sentence is fifteen years, although with remission she will probably be out in twelve. However, Mander says she does not mind how long she has to wait.